Michael J. Luciano

# QUEEN ANNE BOLEYN

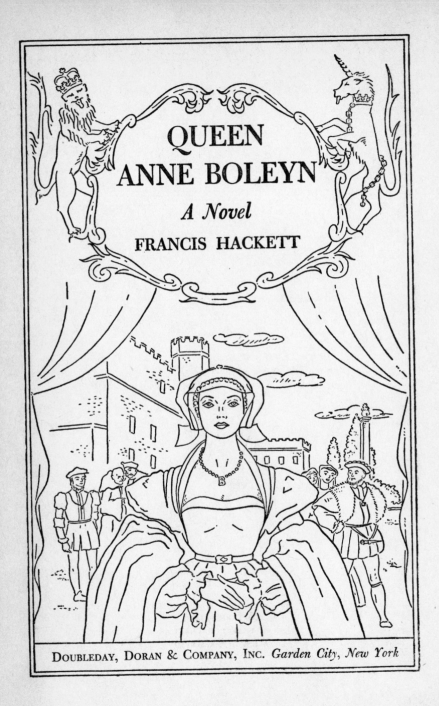

# QUEEN ANNE BOLEYN

*A Novel*

## FRANCIS HACKETT

DOUBLEDAY, DORAN & COMPANY, INC. *Garden City*, *New York*

PRINTED AT THE *Country Life Press*, GARDEN CITY, N. Y., U. S. A.

*To*

*The Memory Of*

OTTOLINE MORRELL

QUEEN ANNE BOLEYN

# Chapter 1

MASTER COWLEY was there, to help Lord James Butler to dismount, when they came to set foot in London. It was in the courtyard of the Queen's Head, and the innkeeper himself ran down from his gallery to greet the young lord with an effusion proportionate to his twelve followers, while the ostlers, one of them Irish, led away the weary, hang-head horses.

All was as it should be, the entry and the fuss, with Robert Cowley striding long-footed from one chamber to another, picking out the best, fluffing out his young master's importance.

But it was not this duty of the major-domo or the respect it worked up that touched Cowley's long face with its full importance. He shone with a bigger excitement. No entry, however appropriate, could quite account for his lifted look unless it was an entry to a greater munificence, and it was precisely this that gave him his turkey-like pomposity.

He was too recently from London, and from the English Court, not to enjoy the ampler meaning of this return in London. Lord James's bedstead had to correspond, he felt, to the matrimonial bedstead he was destined for. Bear-leader he might seem, even to his lordly charge, but he was leading his bear to a high altar. Cowley was too shrewd not to have judged his Irish Butler from the English one. It had been easy enough to talk of wedding him to Anne Boleyn in the large and loose negotiations of the Cardinal's chamber at Hampton Court. But now distance was actually wiped out, Lord James was here, Mistress Anne Boleyn was within reach, the marriage was no longer a surmise. Not until he should see Thomas Cromwell, of course, and land James Butler at Greenwich, could Cowley be entirely sure of Anne Boleyn for his master. Yet just to be in London, so near the Thames, was to be within grasp of the bride, and the very immensity of the town, with 80,000 dwelling in it, made the prospect all the more throbbing. Robert Cowley allowed himself that sharp anticipation that quivers in the later stages of a gamble. But there was still a way to go, and he burned to hasten the final move.

London itself, however, was the first rival to Anne Boleyn that Cowley had to encounter. He was dealing with a very manful, positive and high-handed young master. By the time James Butler had taken one good look at the great city—great, at any rate, in his experience— a jerk came on the silken leash by which Cowley was drawing him to Greenwich. It was soon clear that nothing could be done about either Court or courtship until James had first had a go at the Town.

At home, as a keen captain, under his gouty father's eye, he was the model of discipline, and unrest in Ireland kept him on the stretch. But London, this London of an indulgent inn and the swarming indifferent streets, was so novel and liberating that no sailor home from sea had a hungrier curiosity about it than Butler. He took his squire, Simon Langton, on eager foray. They began with the shops and markets and inns and taverns, but these led to mummeries and travesties, and the beauties of Holborn by night. At times they had their hands on their swords, ready to answer as need be, but London had another use for them and more often they had their hands in their wallets.

Something frisky in James Butler amused and astonished even his constant squire. He was lavish of time and spendthrift of money in this splash into the town, and none of the plunderers he met, male or female, could impair his buoyancy.

It had set him wild from the start, indeed, to reach England. Here was a settled land stretched round him. It was King Edward IV who had said of a Butler that he was the goodliest knight he ever beheld and the finest gentleman in Christendom, but that was an English Butler who had removed to Court. James was still on the frontier for his King. He had to brace himself against the headwind, he and his father. And the minute he landed at Bristol he could feel an amplitude of life, an air of peace, security and ease.

As they cantered across England his mind had roamed into the city ahead of him. He had built his London from the bricks of Robert Cowley, the dry mortar of his little learning, from rhymes in the nursery and a chance phrase of a sailor in New Ross. Born to a world of harsh fact, he still had a touch of imagination. This would be a city bright at night, a brilliant bird born from its evening death, glowing festive with its torches. Yet this picture, made from a simple phrase, was doubled by shadows. He saw a black river wide from the sea, and slapping with the tide. He saw a house-crowned Bridge, cold water washing under it, with wet steps down to it, and lights high in the houses to pierce the dark rampart of the Bridge. His London was crested by a Tower, not benign and familiar like the Castle at home, but frowning and dungeoned, where Richard had murdered his nephews, and where Buckingham had been beheaded. He thought of the lions housed in the Tower, and boyishly longed to see them. He had seen few beasts from foreign lands. His London had St. Paul's in it, groping into the city with a mighty hand and scooping up a multitude of worshippers, with its hucksters in the aisles, and St. Paul's Cross at its mouth, where the King came to hear a sermon, and where preachers burned the books of heretics. In London there were shops for everything, for books, for silks, for dainties. There would be jewels and plate at the goldsmiths', and new headpieces and swords at the armourers'. This would engage him. He saw strange faces in his dream of London, the Portuguese who was to come to Kilkenny as their gunner, Germans at the Steel-yard, rolling Dutchmen, Frenchmen who smirked, dark-eyed Italians, and Red Men from across the Ocean.

James Butler had his banal revery. He was already planning for himself at Court. Not this leathery warm self, whose smell rose pungent to his nostrils as he rode on the highway, but a James Butler in his noble gear. He had his father's letters to peers of the old school, men who honoured the name of Ormonde and wished a Butler to bear it. By marrying Anne Boleyn he could gain the title from Sir Thomas Boleyn, who deemed himself heir of the original Earls. He sighed at this duty, and promised himself a frolic before he met Anne Boleyn.

They had made such good time, under the spur of eagerness, that they neared London of a bright afternoon. And Butler's young fears, all his intimations of a London heavy with doom, were wafted away in the gentle April air. Springtime was early, and to his astonishment the city was not cut off from spring. Walled as it was, he found London nestling in the green countryside, overflowing here and there into clusters of houses, timbered villages and mansions behind hedgerows, but with clear streams chattering freely and lambs in the snug fields. The banner of spring waved to him as they neared the gate. He saw gaily painted wagons, heard whips cracking, saw windmills spanking in the breeze, and caught the clipped and saucy London speech.

There was so much life, such variety, such brimming spirits in so many of the wayfarers with colour in their costumes and brightness in their eyes, that at once his heart lightened. He looked at his squire, who had caught the same contagion. Sometimes separated in the press, they flashed a glance from time to time.

But these impressions dissolved in the actual clamorous town that opened its arms to him. He rollicked for days, or rather for days and nights, and the one dangerous thing, as Robert Cowley discovered, was to shorten his rest in the morning, so that weeks went by without a single serious word on the duty of approaching the Boleyns.

Cowley at last risked his master's displeasure. One morning he dared to open the bed curtains and peered in. "God bless us, my lord!"

"Yea," yawned the young fighting cock, "still a-bed, and my throat a kiln. A drink, Cowley."

Master Cowley picked up an empty silver pot. He was not baffled by the clothes that were strewn around, but stepping over the heavy fur night-gown which sprawled as if slain he went to his own room and returned with red wine. Lord James's outstretched hands took the pot into the benevolent gloom of the bed. There was a gulp, a pant for breath, more gulps. Then the voice gasped, "How now?"

"You found Holborn, again?" Cowley asked drily.

The youth laughed for a moment and then turned out of bed. "I must be up." His bare legs, quite shapely, swung to the floor. He sat laughing again, pensively scratching himself. "Wait till I say my prayers." He wheeled round and said his prayers while Cowley picked up his gown in readiness. Lord James then rose up. "You have more pieces for me?"

"This London!" Cowley grew solemn. "Black with our blood. Your father will rage."

"Come," Lord James decided, "those sovereigns!"

"Take these angels, my lord," Cowley pleaded. "I am nearing the end of our purse. We are here for a reason and I dare not go to Cromwell dry-fisted."

"Attend!" said Lord James cheerfully. After his wash in a quart of water, Cowley held a towel for him. "Angels, so be it!" James Butler mopped his face. "But I am not ready for Greenwich. Look at that Dublin cloak there. A mile too long! And my gold chain, is it yet mended? Without it I might as well go stark naked."

"You shall be meet for the King and Queen, my lord. Master Langton fetches tailor and goldsmith. And now I go to Cromwell."

"We'll dally no more," Lord James assented. "Hold Cromwell to the point."

Cowley held up a purse. "The golden spur!"

## II

Master cowley did not walk straight in to his friend Cromwell. He was let into the house at Fenchurch Street, not by the homelike old Susan who used to open the door but by a page who did his best to reduce a stranger to submission. The hall itself was brighter than before, and Cowley noted that it was dignified by hangings from Antwerp. But this did not impress him. He was primed for the good Cromwell.

At last that worthy came from within, brisk and hearty. "Your young master is with you?" He was so spruce in new broadcloth that Cowley hardly recognized him.

"Here we are in London, as we promised."

"Yea," jerked Cromwell, "and you did not break your necks. Here, page!" He pointed to his sword, and Cowley watched the two of them adjust it with great care. "I am in train for Blackfriars," said Cromwell, chin down. "We meet at parliament."

"The devil 'we' do. Are 'we' a member?"

"Even so! Come, my friend, we'll parley as we go." So the two black-clad figures moved riverwards.

Thomas Cromwell was plump beside the raw-boned Cowley, but plebeian as he was, hard-faced and cold-eyed, scanning every passer-by with a quick glitter, there was something daemonic in his knifing glance. He had escaped from the ranks. He was now in parliament, and though he could not stop his fellow members' babble when he stood up to speak, his head was already filled with positive schemes, privately scorning the French war, uniting Scotland to England, electing a Protestant policy before there were Protestants. Ireland, for example, he saw jiggling and jangling behind his visitor, and to weld Anne Boleyn to James Butler was as natural for him as to lay a plank across the mud. But he hurried along, with Cowley lunging along, and Cromwell could not help nudging his provincial friend with the importance he was achieving.

"Parliament!" he grimaced. "Was there ever such waste of breath! War and peace, riches and poverty, treason and murder, justice, equity, truth, falsehood—on and on we prate, with Thomas More as speaker."

"And to what conclusions?"

"The same as our predecessors—as well as we may, and leave where we began."

"But you furnish an army?"

"A great army, under Suffolk, God knows to what end, and a subsidy the like whereof was never granted before. The realm has not gold for it."

"Anent gold, good Cromwell. Mistress Anne Boleyn is she privy to our visit?"

Cromwell gave Cowley a look. "She is no more at Court."

"How now?"

"Ye may seek her at Hever."

"Nay! Was she sent hence? Is she in trouble?"

"In dudgeon." Cromwell's eyebrow ran up and he laughed. "She defied his Grace the Cardinal, so we packed her home. For you, in truth, we saw to this."

They were on the wharf. "Boat!" cried Cromwell. He took Cowley by the ear. "We have saved it for you. We have her for Master Butler." The wherry was below him. "Soon we meet! Commend me to your master."

With his friend's broad back to him, the angular Cowley watched the boat pull westward. Cromwell's arrogance made him boil. "The churl!" he muttered. His jowls sagged. "How happened this?"

## III

IT WAS NOT the Cardinal's fault that it had happened, but one of the last to know the danger of defying the Cardinal was Anne Boleyn herself. Hers was a family that irked under the Wolsey yoke and carped at him; hence Anne was young enough to despise him.

But it was not the Cardinal, in any event, that Anne feared because of young Percy. It was Percy's father she dreaded, the Earl of Northumberland, and even this did not darken her for a long time, until her feeling for Percy had deepened.

In the Queen's outer chamber, where gallantry was the habit, no one had thought of Percy as Anne's suitor. He was clearly marked as Anne's, but there was something so boyish and airy, so immature about him, that the experienced ladies and the clear-eyed damsels who sat embroidering as they listened to music could only smile at his rather distracted appearance. He lived in his wavering fancy, they thought, and Anne did not noticeably share it. Lady Boleyn watched him serenely, Beth Darrell looked at him benignly, and even Jane Parker was clement. Henry Percy was no Hotspur; he was a creature who floated about, proud and ethereal, while Queen Catherine sat with her maids, repairing shirts for Henry.

The Queen's eyes would acknowledge Percy's entrance, but only to say, "Good Vives, proceed."

Luis Vives, the Spanish humanist, read aloud to them in Latin. That was the giddy pastime for young ladies who sat under Queen Catherine. He was young enough, and had a good voice; he was a Spaniard straight out of that nation now opening to Erasmus with passionate eagerness, and he himself was an enthusiast, but single-minded and ascetic. The girls yawned. The sun shone outside.

"Master Vives," Catherine laid down the shirt and changed from her rugged English to her Aragonese. "You think war will ever end?"

The older ladies included several Spaniards. They pricked up their ears.

The sallow scholar became enlivened, grateful to discuss an idea with his beloved mistress. "For myself, Madame, as for my master Erasmus, war is a madness, but more than that—a stupidity. That is why we pass our frontiers, your Highness, and seek to think as Europeans."

"You are a Spaniard, Vives," Queen Catherine frowned, "a subject of the same Emperor as Erasmus."

"A Spaniard to the core, Altessa. Yet if Castile and Aragon could unite to give us Altessa, why cannot powers more sundered come together in like manner?"

"It is God's will that we maintain the right," Catherine shook her head. "Else we had not driven the Moors from Spain."

"Driven out the Moors—who knows the day they return! We may reap the whirlwind."

"Look after your vagabonds, Vives, and leave high politics to the princes."

"I cannot, Madame. The wars make vagabonds. Vagabonds swarm in every land. Germany seethes. Italy breeds war. Spain revolts. War is the scourge of a humankind that feels and thinks too narrowly. That is why we urge reason."

"Not in Spain."

"Erasmus conquers Spain."

"My confessor comes." Catherine rolled up her work and arose. They all stood up. "You are Utopian, Vives. And you are in danger of forgetting that you are a Spaniard."

Master Vives bowed profoundly. The Queen went out frowning, her beads in her hands.

Such talk fell on Anne's deaf ears. She was engrossed in Percy. In company he was sometimes high-handed, but with her he was so inexpressive, with eyes so haunted and forlorn. Before summer ended she had passed from the ache of his silences to the greater ache of his absences. He had succeeded, even with his longing for immolation and his perfect incapacity for words, in taking gradual possession of her imagination.

Ashen blond, with long black lashes, he was the most elegant of Wolsey's nobles, and Anne's slender litheness made them a couple. She dreamed of a future with him in Northumberland. They talked of little beyond themselves, their own preferences, their community of likes and dislikes, and in this delicate pursuit of intimacy they floated out of themselves, Anne scarcely knowing the little voice she spoke in, or the dreams he answered to. For him to be able to disclose himself gave him ecstasy, and Anne knew she could release him from his ancestral prison.

Yet, by a chance word, he might withdraw from her, close into his armour, and foil her by desolation. Strangely enough, this wrung her heart. It was not his fire that captured her, or his hard fineness. It was a helplessness in him that, like naked flesh under riveted mail, moved something primitive in her. Whatever his father laid down, he needed her. Sometimes it was a wraith she held, but whenever she began to lose faith he could, by a single smile, renew his magic. She then was not obliged to deny his vagueness or to remember his promises. She felt an agony of tenderness. Time and again she had to hurry him at the last moment to join the retinue of the departing Cardinal, and on more than one damp evening, shivering with exaltation and hooded like a nun, she climbed the hill to catch the last glimpse of the spangled barge moving up the dark river.

In those long weeks she heard Catherine and Vives droning in a mist, her will was wooed. She looked as if listening to lost music.

It was unlike Anne, yet never could she break through her fear of hurting him. He was a reed, so strict in its beauty that to lay hands on it might bruise it, and she could not endanger it. His frailty gave him power over her. Anne's hands folded round him, and she was alert against being surprised. Even Beth Darrell, who had eyes, did not see through her. Jane Parker teased her, and tried to catch her, but in vain. Her sister Mary, occupied with her new house, only rejoiced at Anne's amiability. So, by attentive steps, she moved toward union with Percy, and instinct made her wary.

Anne was too well used to the witty asperity of her own family and the unsparing tongues of her companions to offer herself to comment. To be a mere object of idle worship was something that this group would understand. Yet what they took for Percy's inexperience and Anne's coquetry was not so simple as it looked. He was a being of such distinction, so elegant and yet negligent, so wild and yet remote, so held and startled, all at once, that she was secretly wooed, but what stole most sweetly into her wary heart, and captivated it completely, was the perfect innocence of his adoration. No thought for himself alloyed him, and when she realized the elusive wing he came on, and then this helplessness, her young heart flowed to him. No one else saw this in him. He gave them his thin profile with its tart aloofness. Anne knew it was not himself. His worship was so constant that it asserted itself each time he appeared. It was the great solace of her first year after France, a relief from the loneliness of groping for England, a well in the desert. He became able to trust himself to her, and she had enough girlish experience of gallants at both Courts to be aware how freely, how ardently, Percy put himself at her mercy. This was new in her life, new in her circle, but in the restrictions that surrounded the maids in waiting she was tortured never to see Percy alone, never to reach him in the endless need for his company.

Yet difficult as it was to evade Anne discovered that by departing swiftly from the Queen's chamber Percy could make his way to her by a back flight of stairs. Near Lady Boleyn's rooms in the Palace there was an empty landing, lighted from a high grilled aperture in the thick walls. It led to these back stairs, and here, in this unprepossessing corner, Anne could meet him. Here, as they snatched an hour, no longer under amused glances in the Queen's chamber, Percy protested that only death could keep him from marrying her, and Anne swam in his intensity.

"They think me light-brained," he said without looking at her, his violet collar framing his fair hair. "Mayhap you may not trust me."

"I trust you, dear Percy."

"You are Surrey's niece, so what of rank! That cannot let us."

"Not if you love me," she said softly.

"Were it but that! Have you not looked in me? Have I a secret?" His ardent face, its lines grooved hollow, turned to Anne.

She touched his face. "Be not so sad."

"But I drag you hither. What if a scullion come?"

"These stairs are out of use, dear. Who can pass? There's a closet there for us, we'll hide if come a step. I cannot bear to see your pain. Be merry, sweet, till the trumpets sound."

"This shames me. You are my pride, Anne."

"My pride's in you, and you are here. Below we're slaves."

"Hark! There was a sound."

"A daw outside," smiled Anne. "Or 'tis your heart?" Its warmth was under her searching hand. "How it liveth!" She gazed on him, sombre and intense. "Can it be mine?" Her voice had perfect tenderness.

Percy's head bowed to her shoulder and his tears flowed from him. "That you could care!" he whispered, holding Anne. "They cannot part us."

## IV

Much as Percy dreaded the humble subterfuge by which he could see Anne, she thought no more of it than a painter of his paint-rag. She had ears so acute that a footfall at the end of the corridor, out of sight, could tell her whether or not to hide. Her heart raced with fear and joy when they had to slide into her little hiding-place. There they joined in tense listening. Her heavy robes were like an armour, but the light perfume she had brought from France floated from her low-cut gown and filled the little cell with such an evocation that Percy almost fainted to bend his head and kiss her. So divided, and timid, in the world outside, here he discovered her in the protective dark. His fears dissolved in her courage. His tenderness overcame her. Closing eyes that filled with tears, she gave herself to heaven. She knew that for all his fearfulness she had tamed him. She knew he loved her.

Yet, acutely as she listened, Anne did not know that twice her disappearance had been detected from the corridor. One of the Cardinal's ushers had followed Percy. No footsteps approached, but the usher was as sly in tracking them to their lair as if he snared a fowl. Unsuspecting, they stepped from their retreat as he slid down the stairs. They heard a creak, and waited. No one came. Percy went pale, though Anne smiled to hearten him.

Ned Lark took his piquant message to Thomas Cromwell, who passed it to the Cardinal.

Though Anne had reassured her lover, Percy spent a nerve-wracked night. Only toward morning did he fall asleep and then he dreamed he was in one of the new Tudor houses that were all windows. As he stole from room to room, anxious to quench the lights that revealed him, a man with a lantern circled outside, catching him mercilessly from one side or the other. This inimical man, bullet-headed and leering, filled Percy with nameless fear, and he awoke with his heart frantically beating.

It was no surprise to him, that afternoon, to be bidden to see the Cardinal.

## V

CHILL TWILIGHT was gathering in the pompous ante-chamber at Hampton, but no one had lit the candles. The room took the twilight into itself as if it were a fabric, wrapped itself in every dim fold of it, enriched itself with sombreness in its glinting recesses, in the golden lagoons of the ceiling and the ponderous velvets by the embrasures. On a long polished table the light blurred itself into a dark silver. A tapestry on the wall lived as a brooding magnificence with red in it. The chairs stood in obdurate stateliness, their carvings stiff, on each of them a cushion dull in the crushed light, gold-bound and heavily tasselled.

In this slowly dimming room Percy sat waiting. He sat rigid, twisting his hands as he bent his head and watching his hands without seeing them. The twilight fell on his cheek, showing its thinness. In the shadows of his long white face there was a tinge of violet, his eyes were violet rimmed, and his mouth a thin stain of pale violet. The twilight showed grey on his tight, dull-red hose.

The passing minutes twisted his nerves like a coil drawing tighter, and his hands twisted themselves in the endless straining of this coil. Inside him his heart was like a wild bird encaged. It thudded madly to escape, beating itself against the walls that held it, ceasing for a moment, allowing the coil to slacken, then beating itself madly again.

The image of Buckingham came to Percy's mind, the thoughts of the Tower. Tense in his stiff chair at last he shifted miserably, lifting his eyes to the heavy encrusted ceiling. To wait! His white face was fine, but meagre and bloodless. It had no hope in it, yet his body had the thin flexibility of youth.

The massive door at last opened.

Thomas Cromwell came out. "My lord, attend his Grace on the morrow. In the gallery at Westminster."

## VI

THOUGH Percy was early in the gallery it was a long time before the Lord Chancellor's court finished its hearing. At last there was a rustle of feet. Without a glance at the victim the good Cardinal, magnificent in red taffeta with his sables around his neck, took his place in his high chair. His jaws locked, the muscles knotted under his jowls, the priest brooded for a minute. Then he called to his tallest usher, "Summon the servants of my chamber," and motioned Percy to step forward.

"To your knees," muttered Cavendish, the gentleman usher.

Percy went to his knees at the Cardinal's feet. The servitors gathered swiftly, each bending a knee as he arrived, and so falling into place around the kneeling figure. Percy flushed, and then paled. His humiliation was complete, even if he could not see Thomas Cromwell in the background, or the useful Ned Lark, who hung behind a curtain.

The Cardinal suffered from a cold. He cleared his throat noisily, spitting in his handkerchief and examining his spittle. He began quite casually. "I marvel not a little," he said in an ironic voice, without looking at Percy, "of your peevish folly, that you would entangle yourself and engage yourself with a foolish girl yonder in the Court. I mean Anne Boleyn."

He spoke it out to the whole household. Percy winced. Wolsey's coarse powerful face and his contemptuous expression for Anne made the youth's blood turn to water.

The Cardinal looked down on him. "Do you not consider the estate that God hath called you unto, in this world?" he asked roughly. He glanced around the group to confirm his words. "You are most like to inherit one of the worthiest earldoms in the realm."

He coughed and spat again. "It had been most meet and convenient for you to have sued for the consent of your father, to have also made the King's Highness privy to it, seeking his princely favour, submitting all the whole proceeding to him; and, I assure you, he would advance you much more nobly, and matched you according to your estate and honour. But now!"

The Cardinal bellowed at Percy. "Now behold what you have done through your wilfulness!"

He paused, to gather force. "Ye have not only offended your natural father, but also your most Gracious Sovereign Lord, and matched yourself with one, such as neither the King, nor yet your father, will be agreeable with."

Stung by these words Percy opened his mouth to speak, but the Cardinal swept him down. "To put you out of all doubt, I will send for your father, and he shall either break this engagement or else disinherit thee forever. The King's Majesty himself will complain to your father on you, and require no less at his hand than I have said."

This tirade, with its heavy emphasis on the King, shook Percy to his core. But the Cardinal had another move to make. Ignoring the culprit he turned to the members of his household, gentlemen and nobles who had every reason to dread the King's disfavour, and every object not to thwart his will. "His Highness," he confided in a reasonable voice, "intended to have given Anne Boleyn to another person, with whom the King hath travailed already. Although she know it not, yet, upon the King's motion, I doubt not she will be right glad and agreeable to it."

Hearing words so suave and unexpected, with everyone gazing at him, Percy burst into tears.

"Sir," he cried out, "I know nothing of the King's pleasure herein."

The Cardinal let it stand. He motioned to Percy to continue.

"For the King's displeasure," the boy said, "I am very sorry. But I—I considered I was of good years to choose where my fancy served me best. I doubted not that my lord my father would have been right well persuaded. Though she be a simple maid, and having but a knight for a father, yet she is descended of right noble parentage. As by her mother, she is nigh to the Norfolk blood: and of her father's side lineally descended of the Earl of Ormonde." Percy ceased to weep. "Why should I then, Sir," he said more calmly, "be anything scrupulous to match with her, whose descent is equivalent with mine, when I shall be in most dignity?"

The argument told on the Cardinal's servants. They began to look at one another, and Percy took heart.

"So I humbly entreat your Grace of your favour, and also to entreat the King's Majesty most lowly on my behalf, for his princely benevolence in this engagement which," and he raised his voice earnestly, "I cannot deny or forsake!"

"So, Sirs!" thundered the Cardinal, who heard the crowd murmur. "Ye see what conformity and wisdom is in this wilful boy's head." He turned to Percy. "I thought when you heard me declare the King's intended pleasure you would have submitted——" Percy tried to answer—"submitted yourself," deftly added the Cardinal, "to the King's royal will and prudent pleasure, to be ordered as his Highness should seem good."

"Sir, so I would," Percy wavered, "but I have gone so far, before so many worthy witnesses, that I know not how to clear myself or discharge my conscience."

The Cardinal gleamed. "Think you," he said in a sober voice, "that the King and I know not what we have to do in as weighty a matter as this? Yea, I warrant thee." Then he frowned. "Howbeit," he said severely, "I can see in thee no submission to the purpose!"

"Forsooth, my Lord," Percy trembled, "if it please your Grace, I'll— I'll submit myself wholly unto the King's Majesty and your Grace in this matter, my conscience being cleared."

The Cardinal sat back. "Well, then!" he breathed contented, "I'll send for your father out of the North, and he and we shall take such order for correcting thy hasty folly as the King think most expedient. In the meantime, and in the King's name, I command thee, presume not once to resort into her company, as thou hopest to avoid the King's high indignation."

This said, he rose up and went into his own chamber.


## VII

Percy did not dare to see Anne Boleyn or even to scribble her a line. Yet he still feverishly hoped that all was not lost. His father was coming, and he believed his father might be persuaded to intervene for him.

But when Percy's father received a summons in the King's name to present himself to the Cardinal, the last thing that occurred to him was to intervene for anyone. When it rains pitchforks a man does not bare his head. In the King's name! So had the Duke of Buckingham been summoned, and the Earls of Northumberland were far too near the borders of rebellion to clear themselves from the taint of suspicion if the Cardinal chose to believe in it. The Earl did not lose an instant to speed from the North. In the King's name! He reached Westminster with his loyalty so brushed and ordered that he hardly dared to draw a breath lest he displace it.

Percy was in the gallery at Westminster to see his father go straight to the Cardinal. Everyone except the Earl knew what was a-foot, and for a long while the conversation went forward with the Cardinal haranguing and the Earl pondering and assenting. This dumb show was agony for Percy; his heart sank when a cup of wine was at last sent for, and the Earl and the Cardinal drank together.

Percy could not catch his father's eye as the Cardinal's gentlemen formed a dignified procession to lead the Earl from the gallery. But when they came to the gallery's end, the Earl stopped and sat him down on a form that stood against the wall, for callers to take their ease. He then allowed himself to see his heir, and called him up to him, with everyone standing by. His face was so closed and his manner so guarded that Percy was unable to penetrate it. He had not long to wait.

"Son," said the seated Earl, raising his head with a frown, "you have always been a proud, presumptuous, disdainful and very unthrift waster!"

This rebuke made Percy rigid. "And so you have now shown yourself," the father emphasized. "What joy, what comfort, what solace should I take in you, when, without discretion, with no regard for your natural father, with none for your Sovereign Lord to whom all bear humble obedience, nor yet to your own high estate, you have so rashly plighted yourself to her for whom you have earned the King's displeasure—intolerable for any subject to sustain!"

It was again the Cardinal's tirade. Percy had missed winning his father. He bowed his head. He bit his lip, so as not to break down.

Without losing his tone for a second the Earl continued, "But that his Grace is so wise as to consider how light-headed and wilful you are, his indignation were sufficient to wreck me and my posterity! But he is so good a lord, so singularly good and favourable a prince, that he clearly absolves me of your lewd act, and rather laments your lightness than maligns it. He has a plan for it for which you and I will be more indebted than we can well convey. I pray God that this will be a warning——"

Percy no longer heard his father's endless words. The sounds pulsated in his ears, now loud, now low, but all that he understood was his separation from Anne Boleyn. To her he had pledged his word, his sacred honour. His precontract with Anne, in the eyes of the Church, was as binding as marriage, and on this he had relied. It was this that had woven them together, with every touch of her hand, every look, every breath, with every tender and warm moment they had shared. Anne's breasts he had kissed. Anne's whisper of endearment he still could hear. The enormity of the disaster was so painful that he suffered it as if it were a blow, staggering him though he stood upright, quivering in the fibres of his heart and the cells of his brain. His bloodless face was so tragic that even his father stopped droning about the Earldom and the heir to it.

"Now, masters and good gentlemen," he turned to the household, "I desire you all to be his friend, and to tell him his fault when he doth amiss, wherein ye shall show yourselves to be much his friends."

He stood up from the bench. "Go your ways," he said lamely to Percy, "and attend upon my Lord's Grace, your Master, and see that you do your duty."

With this admonition, to which his blanched son bowed his head, the Earl went his way down through the hall into his barge.

## VIII

"Go!" urged Anne like a wounded creature that can stand no more. "Go! Go!" They were at the fountain.

For a second Percy held his ground. He must not continue to hurt her, he must go. But he dared not leave her now, or it might be forever. Afraid of hurting her, afraid of deserting her, he stood irresolute.

"Anne!" he half-sobbed.

She heard him through the daze of her pain, and the note in his voice, so like the sob in her own heart, brought home again the power that was opposing them. She was moved to turn to Percy and fall into his arms, aware that only by loving him, only by sustaining him, could she help him to come through. She turned round slowly, as if to yield, but, in the instant she did this, the hopelessness of sustaining her lover immediately undermined her impulse, and her face was so glazed that she looked at him as if she hardly knew him. To think that the upstart Cardinal could browbeat this son of Northumberland! She could see Percy's wounded gaze, the gates open for her love or for her hate, and that tender defenselessness was so complete that never could she doubt the love that possessed him, but in the very moment he entered her heart forever, she lost faith in him. He became her child, not her lover, and she recognized his dependence on her as the sign that the Cardinal could defeat him. This swept her like iced wind. The Cardinal was all-powerful, yet in her eyes he was a swollen, bloated upstart whose plots stirred her contempt. He could decree, but whatever he decreed she could defy it, and she needed to feel that Percy could defy it. That alone could bind them, and if Percy bent under the Cardinal's insolence she alone could not go on.

"Go!" Cruel to him, cruel to herself, Anne's voice was hard and unmistakable.

Percy had from the beginning been alive to Anne's contempt for Cardinal Wolsey, and her disappointment with his own hesitation had made him feel how weak he was, how incapable of being her hero. But she did not know the Cardinal as he did. Percy was walled round by his awareness of the Cardinal, who commanded the King, who dominated his father, who held him to ransom because of his recent extravagances. How oppose the Cardinal, the boy asked himself in dismay. Unless his father helped him he was a boat without oars. Where could they live, what could they do, where could they go? He knew that so long as Anne loved him, he could continue to live through the storm, though he must drift helpless and shaken, but at the first sign of her impatience, for which he had been waiting with the miserable acuteness of the feeble, he could only succumb. Without her faith in his love, he was lost. He had no more to give.

Her voice pierced him through. Without a syllable, his face quivering, he turned from the fountain and his feet guided him into the dark wood. He bent his head only when a low bough had first clouted him almost insensible. That pain he welcomed, with despair smothered in his heart, poisoning him with each surge of his frustration.

The girl stood by the fountain, her hands clenched, her elbows pressed close, as if to avert any other blow that might fall.

Percy was gone. She knew this, but she could not admit it to herself. Even though she had nerved herself to send him away, the impossibility of sending him away was too clear to her. Her mind raced round the circle that had closed in on them and, like a deer in the open, she took in each avenue of escape and each enemy that blocked it. Tense and sharp, with one bound she would have pursued Percy into the wood, if her brain had not closed the avenues one by one. To pursue him through the crisp leaves, under the boughs, into the secret depths where the loam exhaled its wet pungency, to close with him and bury herself in his sobbing love, to hold to him in that warm security—her body yearned for it. But of what use, when the Cardinal still encircled them and hovered sneeringly outside?

Anne Boleyn stood riveted by the fountain until a cold shiver ran through her. Slowly she took the path to the Palace, her arms crossed, her brows knitted.

# Chapter 2

SILENCE FOLLOWED THE Cardinal's rebuke to Lord Percy, but the entire Wolsey household had listened to it so that the news of it ran brightly through the Court. Percy's name and Anne's flew from mouth to mouth. Up till then they had been minor figures, but the world loves a little scandal, and when Anne appeared, whether in chapel or hall, eyes were glued on her and whispers fluttered. Even in the Queen's chamber, though Catherine was too correct a Spaniard to give a sign of curiosity, her gentlewomen were much too human not to watch the girl closely. Notoriety is usually good for a second explosion.

Anne said nothing and did nothing. She bent over her sampler with a grimness like hardened lava. Yet toneless as her responses were, noticeable as her sallowness became, she went about her duties and her pleasures with a stiff pretence that nothing was amiss. The draw-bridge was up. Not one of her friends, not even Madge Shelton with her warm abundance or comforting Beth Darrell, could break the tension that set her face so hard. They watched her with distress. Defeat was written on her. Unspoken though it was, she could not go into the Queen's chamber without betraying it, and in vain they yearned over her. But Anne's injury was beyond any kind or senti-

20

mental help. Percy had released a nature far from trusting, but the stream into which it had gently broadened in those months of expectation was now clenched in a mill-race, gripped by anger, and day by day, with a force that sprang with amazing vigour from her depths, she poured fury through this channel, grinding bitter sustenance for hate. She could not say to herself that her dream of being a Countess was shattered. It had been her dream. She had set herself against everyone to win Percy, and to marry him in spite of the elders. But it was Percy she had espoused in her dream more than the heir to Northumberland. Into that unwonted tenderness she had come to blossom, until a single rude storm had stripped it from her. The Cardinal did it. What consumed her, though she gave no hint of it, was her hatred of the Cardinal. The outrage was to her true heart as much as to her pride. This smouldered in her. In these rebellious days she grew from girl to woman.

Lady Boleyn saw it unsympathetically, but she could find no way to control Anne. At the merest word Anne became sulphurous, which sent her mother to perch on her dignity, out of reach. Quite soon, however, a sandalled friar, who spoke both for King and prelate, brought private word that Anne must leave the Court, and then Lady Boleyn could go to her daughter.

"George will be at Hever with you," the mother placated, "and Thomas Wyatt is back at Allington."

"And you hold with the Cardinal, mamma?" Anne's brows contracted.

Lady Boleyn folded her embroidery with precision. "My dear Anne," she replied, "to gain the day he hath used means we cannot counter. Let us waste no words."

"My place is in the Queen's chamber," Anne quivered. "Cannot the King save me?"

"This is but for a season," Lady Boleyn answered with pretended calm. "You may bend, or you must break. Have you no pliance in your nature?"

"Then you do not choose to help me, mamma?" Anne's face was dark.

"Help you?" said the mother drily. "You were not blind. You knew that Percy must marry as the Earl chose, just as I had to, just as your

father did. Did you give me or your father a single thought? Nay!
Nor did you think that Percy must face the Earl. Had you spoken,
mayhap I could have helped you. Now it is late!"

The mother and the daughter exchanged looks as if crossing swords.
Lady Boleyn was the first to look away. "No help for it now! Wait
till your father comes."

"Father!" Anne's lips curved scornfully.

"Or my brother, Surrey."

"Neither would lift a finger."

"Then make no care and go to Hever. It is but for a season."

In the meantime, Anne knew, Percy was to be forced to marry Mary
Talbot. She clenched her teeth and went her way.

## II

A WINTER IN KENT could drive a girl to religion. When the cold rain
lies stale on the clay and the sodden earth exhales misery up to the
inglenook, when the gravid sheep huddle against wet banks and the
sky blears at withered grass, it takes more than warm tankards to
revive the human spirit. Kent, in wintertime, a school for saints, but
Anne was a young sinner. Sent home to brood, she had nothing to
counsel her but hurt pride and starved feelings. As the vapours of Kent
rose listless about Hever, uncertain whether to wreathe it in oblivion
or plod on it in tears, Anne pursued anger through every phase of her
injury and punishment up to that final thirst for revenge which, in its
own way, is as sweet as love.

The impetuousness with which she had taken Percy's worship, the
simplicity with which she had given her pledge to him, showed little
of her mother's dry prudence. Had she been like Mary, she reflected
bitterly, she could still be at Court. The Court could be defied. The
Duke of Suffolk had defied it when he married the King's sister out
of hand. But feeble Percy was very different from the stout, thick-
skinned Charles Brandon. Poor Henry Algernon Percy, now chained
to Mary Talbot. Anne did not reproach him, though she could not
bear to think of it. Neither he nor she had been quick or bold enough
to forestall the Cardinal. She had lost Percy because they had had no

foresight. She had lost him through ignorance of the forces that ruled this world.

Anne obeyed the routine of a young lady's existence at Hever—prayers to say, meals to eat, friends to see, dogs to walk, music to play, clothes to wear, weather to talk about. But for all her occupation she kept liaison with an inner self that had been baulked of its alliance. Day after day she stole time in which to probe humiliation. She lay brooding on the connivance of the Cardinal with Percy's father, and it was the Cardinal she blamed, no one else. It was not malice, perhaps, that had induced him to break Percy's sacred contract with her. He had done it as a scornful master who, attaching no particular importance to foolish girls, dismissed her with the light contempt that power feels for weaklings.

No one had dared report to Anne the mysterious marriage that the King had proposed for her. All she conceived was the Cardinal's contempt. Her short days and long nights at Hever were given to pondering this lesson. For every ecstasy of which she had been cheated, every ardour deprived, every tenderness muted, she now pent up a fire that lay sombre in her eyes.

## III

THOMAS WYATT RETURNED from Calais. England was still at war with France, and great things were promised for the next campaign, provided money could be found, but meanwhile John Russell and Francis Bryan were Sir John Russell and Sir Francis Bryan, knighted by Surrey during the rape of Brittany, and home to display this little frond that had sprouted from their names.

Thomas made his way to Hever. Tall and lean, he looked less boyish. His brief excursion in the world had burnished his spirits. He came from contact with it in a glow, as if a breeze brightened him, and, in spite of sombre Anne, he had such comedy, with such little touches of good nature and shrewd irony that he compelled her to cease nursing her wounds, and laugh despite herself.

The "sudden glory" of laughter is relief to the humiliated. The forest folds away, they come into the open, amused, assuaged.

Thomas understood it. One glance at Anne had revealed how she was smitten. He could tell it in the droop of her shoulders, the withheld consent of her voice, the barb of her tongue. She was not a mime. She had not invented a mask that held a grimace or draped anger under pallor. Thomas was grateful for this nature in her. What she had suffered from the Cardinal he knew in every detail, and sometimes he could feel the Cardinal jutting out, like the teeth of a reef, under the passionate flood. But in these casual visits he kept to the surface. He said enough, as he clipped along, to flick contempt on Wolsey, and then he went another way. In this he was so nonchalant and audacious, so perceptive, that there seemed nothing for him to learn about Anne Boleyn.

Yet when it came to his own feelings for her he could do nothing. Honestly as he consoled her, though he had hated her entanglement with Percy, and fallible as he thought her impulse, she became impenetrable when he sought her for himself. Her cool decisiveness then took on a certainty which seemed to him infallible. Her moods then threatened him, as if salvation hung on them. She was not only sacred to him, as his imagination quailed, but she could exalt or dash him, as the whim possessed her. He trembled at the slightest transition from his honest friendship to anything fateful between themselves.

Anne knew this. She knew that he was courting her. And while her sense of loss grew no smaller, and her desire for revenge held fast, the sharpness of her injury took another contour, slowly yielding to this warmth that breathed from Thomas. Yet he never spoke out to her.

"Why so glum, Thomas?" one day Anne dared to ask him. "You are not yourself."

"Myself, alas, but not my master." And he would say no more.

"Why doth he come?" Anne asked herself that night, and this time the thought of Thomas's wife did not arise. She lay in bed, her little cap close on her black hair, her chin rounded as she pressed down her head. Her hand played with a ribbon, rolling it and unrolling it, while she mused with big eyes on these visits from Thomas. They were sweet. Their comfort dropped balm on a wound whose abruptness had spiked it with eternal anguish, yet in some rare way that anguish was beginning to blur.

As she reminded herself of it, of the conflict that held her, and the duty that held Thomas, a sense of his immeasurable devotion suddenly and completely overwhelmed her. The eyes that had been looking at the candle no longer could see it clearly. As if a drilling pain had ceased, Anne's nerves surrendered, and the flame swam in her tears.

The moment was undesigned. Hostility had become Anne's rule, the soreness of defeat feeding her anger. No change of mood could remove her injury, yet now that she seriously, slowly, apprehended the love that signalled to her from Thomas's presence, its infinite solace dawned on her injured spirit, and the pain that gnawed her made her all the more aware of its perfect benignity. This was outside her will. She gave a few short, quick breaths, stabbed with her emotion as the wind seems to shiver when the weather changes, and tears welled from her eyes as warm as the rains of spring.

## IV

ANNE'S TEARS, to a great degree, were natural self-pity. She had gone through a dark period at Hever. She had suffered the loss of Percy as a vital wound, and with this had come the change from a thronged existence to a bare one. She could not have endured Greenwich after her humiliation. It would have been intolerable, with the hard light it shed on her wound. But, for all this, Anne was born to Court. It was her metier. No actress, in the years to come, could love her life of fantasy more than Anne loved Greenwich. The Court was itself a fantasy for which she was trained, in which she was learning to excel. She had glinted there with perfect pleasure, banqueted in it, sung in it and danced. She had not hardened herself to practise there without falling in love with a member of the cast, and in this way hampering the performance. She was not an old hand like her mother who could accept one role or another. But she was enough her mother to feel dispossessed from darling sights and sounds, the trumpets of the banquet, the heralded barge, the surprise and glory and dismay that, to a young woman still eager, gave salty drama to existence. To be banished from all this, confined to Hever, was as melancholy as mourning. Under her grief she had her sharp appetite for life, and the life for which she hungered was this glorious one, her birthright, for which she was fitted, which sustained her soul. Hever was starvation.

So she ached to revive. When she woke on the April morning that followed her burst of tears she immediately thought that she had heard good news. On remembering Thomas Wyatt, she lazily and nonchalantly stretched herself, as though her body were her own, refreshed and sensuous. This recalled Percy. Shamefacedly she ceased to arch herself, with a prompt sense of tragedy; but in ten minutes she was humming, and later she could not help picking up her Murano mirror—of glass, an you please, and not silver—with a point of curiosity.

The next time Thomas came he happened to look across the room at her as she was glancing at him. Their eyes met. He gave a start, and immediately afterwards went out. Anne waited anxiously until he returned. She was not at peace until he entered. He took a place far away from her. She thought he avoided her.

As the hour approached for music she hovered near him, and when they were alone, with her hand on a book that she had the air of examining, she said, "Thomas, why hast been so long-suffering with me?"

Thomas turned his back on the others. In a thick voice he said, "You can ask me?"

"I could not have endured this without you," she said. Her head was still cast down.

Thomas looked at her without a word.

She glanced up and gave him her hand. "Now for music."

They seated themselves to hear the music. Thomas sat in a window, across from Anne. He could see her as the musicians played.

She was in grey, her coif nunlike, her eyes guarded. Thomas knew the fire that was screened. She did not so much as glance at him, yet every time she moved, to let her gaze wander to the window, or turn her profile to the music, his blood was uncontrollably stirred. And then, as she raised her hand, he had a shock. Quick as his eye, his brain confirmed it: it was the deformity of her finger, a small second tip growing from the side of it. Just as he was strangling this ugly perception, so involuntary and so ruthless, she caught his look. Unknown to himself a flood of tenderness had followed his perceiving this blemish. In the instant of recoiling he had identified himself with Anne, and this was so prompt, so intense, that she caught nothing of his horror, only gentleness. Her eyes were arrested by it because he was gazing at her directly. She did not understand it. But unconsciously she set her protecting hand to hide the unnatural one, hesitating over the benign enigma of his look. He quivered. She had caught him, and he feared she would connect his glance with the hand she had exposed. His tenderness, and her wonder at it, mingled for a space too short to be measured. Then by chance or by persuasion the danger passed; she had not seen his horror nor ascribed his look to its origin. She took it as a sign that Thomas was soon to return to Allington. For the first time since the morning she willingly met his eyes, with a kind of gay tenderness. He had not hurt her. His relief was immeasurable. Her hands, as he knew them, were as beautiful as anything about her—long, very slender, with each finger so refined in its modelling that their touch seemed curiously expressive. They were the essence of herself, not only the means by which her delicacy was made known, her tenacity and fire, but in themselves inexpressibly personal, with something in them which alone said yes or no to him. That one of them should be grotesque, malformed, dishonoured, was an affront from nature. Thomas was her partisan against it. Yet there it was, the flaw in the masterpiece, and had she seen him an instant too soon she would have trapped his recoil from her. Once again he saw how she hid the poor blemished hand. This little gesture, more than anything else, moved his young heart when he thought of Anne Boleyn.

He stood up when the music finished.

"Fare thee well," he murmured as she gave him her cheek to kiss.

"Remember what I said," she whispered.

## V

THOMAS'S RIDE HOME that night was slow and in a way inarticulate. There are countryfolk who remain inexpressive, except in a set style, and the Tudor courtier who strove to obey classic utterance was scarcely better able to give tongue to what was inside him or about him. He had a living self. He burned to find its rhythm. But not until sensual Shakespeare broke the shell of the inarticulate could those who groped inside it come to their senses. Thomas would later know what it was to be chained in prison; now he was fettered by the modes of feeling that were in vogue. But what distinguished him from nearly every soldier at the Court, nearly every lover in it, was the hard birth of the poet in him, the feeling man. He could not bend this feeling to a chivalry that had become rigid, or devote it to a religion whose mysteries were savagely debated. He was not nailed to scholarship or the exactness of science. Thomas was an uncharted adventurer in another realm, as much to be explored as the globe that Magellan's ships had just circumnavigated, their timbers stained with blood, bringing strange report of perpetual fires and the giants of Patagonia, but with their captain murdered. Thomas, with no better craft than Magellan's, was setting out to find those father Isles, the land that forever beckons the feeling man, and to reach it he would plunge through fire. There were no maps for him, only the compass of his instinct, and faith in a sharp star above him.

On this kind night he rode in a whirl of ecstasy. He could feel the pungency of the earth, wet from a shower, with the little bite of primroses in the air and the whiff of an early thorn tree. He could feel about him the mantle of the dark sky, spangled above him in a profundity on which a cloud was sailing white, and he could hear in the dark the whirr of nested birds, the click of moving sheep, and the whimper of a fox-cub. The beeches were waiting for May, as he could tell by the low cloud he saw through their branches. But it was not the smell of the earth, the renewed comfort of the spring, or the nearness of young beasts that opened his heart. It was something going through them in waves of such ardour that they were no more than a melting chorus against a voice rising to enchantment. He felt as though all the bonds had been loosened, all the barriers removed; as though a power had streamed into him so sweet he could only endure it by stretching to spaces out of reach, yielding ecstasy to the tranquil heavens. He pulled up his pony, leaning on his stirrups, while he gazed over the country. This was Anne's Kent, her country and his own. His heart gilded its low hills with her young beauty, while his memory dwelt on the few syllables she had spoken. To believe that he had helped her was the miracle. He had been wandering homeless since he met her, but at last he had this sign he had not lost the way. Now he could feel the universe benign. In this quiet and open night he was no longer outside the universe, and it was no longer outside himself. He caught a phrase of its music.

## VI

LUKE was at the gatehouse to let him in.

"There be word of the King at Hever, Master Tom?"

"Not that I heard of."

"Would not that confound a mortal!" Luke held up his lantern, gravely regarding Thomas. "Am I gone daffy?"

"Most likely, Luke. Where heard you this?"

"At eventide, as the bells rang, damn the lie. I had it from Master himself."

"And what said my father?"

"That our Lord the King be written down for Hever, no word to the contrary, that they are to make good cheer but no great case, that a barrel be broached at the inn for all and sundry, and that a young Irish kinsman comes in train, who rode in from yon Bristol."

Thomas shook his head. "No word of it at Hever."

"Sir Harry brought it fresh himself. The messenger must still be on the road."

"That could hap," said Thomas indifferently. "Good night, old Luke."

"He'd be cousin to the Boleyns, belike," mused Luke. "Maybe they make a match for Mistress Anne."

"Who knows! Good night!"

"I'd be proud to see her wooed and won."

"And so should I. Now, Luke, good night."

Luke turned the heavy key. "I'm an old chuff to caw like this. Sound rest, Master Tom."

Thomas yawned as he climbed the turret. He longed for rest. He had taken a dislike to this Irish kinsman.


## VII

BUT THOMAS WYATT FORGOT this pang of jealousy when his father sent for him.

Sir Henry was clad for a day's work, agile and powerful in spite of his years; nothing of the young trifler about him. He mumbled a greeting, burrowing Thomas with a look. "Perchance you return to Hever?"

"Not on the instant, father."

"Nay? Methinks you may hie to Cobham."

"Bess bade me not to come."

"That I knew not," muttered Sir Henry. "I called to have a look at the boy. She doth require to see you, Tom."

"She said so?"

"Even so. She hath somewhat to say to you."

It was a pearly morning, unveiling itself with the delicacy of a nuptial, but Thomas had no eyes for its gentleness nor for the tender shoots that spread a green mist on the broken earth. More than one of the workers gave him a wayside greeting. He responded always, but his heart was not present. The only thing present was the judgment he must fear from Bess. He could not guess why she had sent for him, but, incongruous as it was, his imagination began to torture him for his failure as a husband. Anne Boleyn was at the centre of his being and he did not disguise it. The love with which he had flamed, the vista which her few words had opened, took such hold on his spirit that it could never loosen—it melted the edges of life for him last night, mellowed the night sky, and gave him wings. But little as Thomas denied that he had surrendered, the completeness of it could not wipe out his feeling as a husband. Last night he had forgotten Bess. This morning he went to her with apprehension. She was going to say something to him. He feared it. He feared for the irreparable damage to her, and to the boy, that could come from the failure of their marriage. This was no empty sentiment. Pale and drawn, with his eyes liquidly dark, Thomas dwelt on this quandary into which marriage had brought him. He thought of his father, so like a rock, and of himself, who should be like him. He could not deny Anne. He could not be indifferent to Bess. He let his pony walk, his eyes bent to the ground, wondering how to solve it. On the edge of the grass he saw what looked like a stick: it was a deer's foot, the foreleg broken off above the joint. He winced. He could see the beast limping. The imagination that love had seized yesterday now grasped the horror of all crippled things, and that he himself could cripple anyone became revolting. It was not his sentiment that held him. His was a marriage to which religion had given gravity: it was sealed by an oath, and weakened though the religion became for him, Thomas could not escape his oath: he was in honour bound. Rather than betray the steadfastness which alone meant honesty to him he tortured himself to renounce his love for Anne and go back to his marriage. To be just and true, to flee from doubleness! "I mean no guile," burst from him with passionate simplicity. "I mean no guile." And then he saw Cobham before him, to remind him of the loyalty he endangered.

VIII

THOMAS WYATT'S WIFE was waiting for him. When old Sir Harry called, the day before, she had made up her mind to end uncertainty.

"Find Francis for me," she whispered to Beth Darrell, who had come to her with Francis Darrell, her brother.

Beth did as she was told. Much as she wished to hang on the visitor's words, she left the great hall and ran across the courtyard to a far turret. Just as she tripped up the steps the Angelus began. It was not an old devotion, the midday Angelus. King Louis XI had thought of it fifty years before. But now the bell smote and wafted through Cobham as if from immemorial time, and the girl stood patiently saying her Angelus until the last clang melted into peace.

Her brother was inside the tower. Under the slit of the loophole she caught the gleam of his sleeve and the fierce white of his eyes. He did not visibly pray; he was too intent on his hawk. What that captive made of the clamour could not be guessed; something had so startled her wild blood, sent such quivers through her hot body, that she whirred in frenzy. Francis Darrell stayed quiet. He loved to man a hawk. So shrewdly did he wait for the flurry to cease, so subtly resume his caresses, that very soon the proud head bent and she was rending her meat. A thin smile crossed his face but faded when his sister called his name and he saw her in the door.

"Where is Bess?" he demanded.

His sister knew he was irritated. "Sir Henry Wyatt hath called," she said.

"Oh! Wyatt." He dislodged the hawk and walked out to her, peeling his gauntlet.

Brother and sister had physically little in common. One branch of these Darrells had modelled the girl tall, giving her a fair tint and dusting her hair with gold. Her brow was touchingly serene. Francis Darrell was an edged human being of another strain; nervous, lean and sharp. He made something of a picture as he sauntered down the steps in his salmon surcoat and pale yellow hose.

"He may ask us to Allington," said Beth as they crossed the court, "and we should go to Hever?"

"Must we go to Hever!" he drawled. "I do abhor it."

"But why?"

"That prancing talk! George's poems! Nay, I am too slow for Hever."

"Not slow." Beth smiled at his covert insolence. "Out of conceit."

"So be it," he bowed. "Spare me the Boleyns. Now must I wash my hands."

He let her pass. She watched the arrogant profile, with the receding brow and the keen chin. This was his simple method of evading a promise. Instead of conducting him to Bess she had to go in alone.

The elders turned a kind look on her. They were standing in a deep window, privately chatting.

Bess Wyatt raised grey eyes to her emissary, and then she drooped them.

Nothing, not an ash nor a willow, could droop more beautifully than Bess Wyatt. Of a chalky white, she had the immobile face of a conscious heritage. It refined its way back through the de la Poles to King John, and for that matter back to Odo and Fulk in dim Anjou, where the Melisandes lamented. She was a grave creature, remote as a swan, with great grey eyes instead of red ones.

Her father, Lord Cobham, a rough-hewn baron, had the bow legs of a confirmed horseman. A flat hat was perched on his head, indoors and outdoors, not unlike a small pancake, and he had jutting cheekbones and stark eyes. Bess Wyatt brooded less on this recent progenitor.

Being beautiful, she would have averted herself from the elderly

men in the window, but the instinct that had made her send for
Francis Darrell kept her unhappily aware of their murmurs.

Henry Wyatt was rumbling to the lord of the castle, and Bess Wyatt
thought him very ugly. He was certainly not in his first youth, the
master of Allington—a rock of a man with a heavy head that lurched
a little forward, a big bulbous nose, and a mouth that fell in for lack
of teeth. He found it easier to talk out of the corner of it, but it was
a noble head, stained and seared by honest experience, welling up
with an occasional chuckle that was as good as bubbles in wine. Lord
Cobham hung on his words, partly because they were worth hearing and also because it was hard to hear them.

They muttered politics, to tell the truth; a dead theme when the
juice is out of it, but the moment leaping with dangerous life, the
fate of everyone in the room depending on it. It was the King, of
course, and the Cardinal, that they were talking about. And as they
talked Bess vanished to find Francis. Without a word she sped over
the moat and made her way down to the stream. Here was a sunken
field, a tangle of bushes, laced by dog roses that climbed to the
height of a tree.

"You look at our tree," Bess hailed Francis.

Up against the sky a rose thorn tossed into a curve and looped
down with a swerve of grace.

"It is so sheltered here," said Francis. "It will be massed with
flowers again."

She heard him and her heart melted. Here she had first brought
him when the blossoms poised on every spray. Some were freshly
pink, the leaves curled like shells from the centre. The older flowers
had turned paler, relaxing their leaves until their faint colour came
to white, but whether they were blooming in a first crisp pang or
unfolding to decay, they showered so profusely that Bess remembered not so much the single blossom as the plenitude that repeated
and exalted it. There had been bright roses, pale roses, a dust of
yellow and a flick of white, yet as they fluttered and alighted, a
cascade of little flames, they had exhalted ethereal scent. She had led
dark Darrell to see her secret rose bush. She still breathed its
fragrance, that had whispered bliss. She turned to Francis.

"Can they part us?"

"Never," he said quietly.

She looked at him with an ache of mournful surrender. "I am unable to think," she said. "I feel that some dreadful thing creeps towards us."

He smiled. "Oh!"

"Yea." She was grave. "I feel I must think, to save ourselves. I even try to pray, though I cannot. There are ill omens. Forgive me. I am but a little fool. Forgive me, Francis."

"Bess!"

"Am I a fool, Francis?"

"Oh, darling."

"Then why am I so fearful? I am afraid."

He kissed her. "They cannot touch us." He caressed her with his fine, nervous hands. "I'll kiss you for every rose that was on the rose bush."

The young wife, pale and remote, clung to him with intensity. "I am sending for Thomas. I mean to tell him. But I am afraid for you and me."

He took her into his arms. "Trust me," he said fiercely.

"I do trust you." She touched his face proudly. "I trust you."

Then she went back and gave her message to Thomas's father.

## IX

THOMAS was met by the friendly porter at Cobham.

"Your boy, Master Wyatt, hath gone in—he's playing on the back stairs."

Thomas went up the servants' stairs to overtake young Thomas, but stopped at the sound of voices.

"Oh ho!" said a loud gleeful voice, "you are a pretty rascal, you are. I'll catch you and eat you for supper."

Rough sounds of eating, with growls and grunts, came down the stairs.

A varlet, thought Thomas. And then his boy piped out, "What's your name?"

"My name's Higgs. So, now, what's yours?"

"My name is Thomas Wyatt."

"Thomas Wyatt, from old Allington. And where's your dad, Thomas?"

The child made no answer.

"See now," said Higgs; "lift up your pecker. I can do tricks."

"Can you lay an egg?"

"Only a goose's egg."

"Lay one now."

"Let's see. Is this a fish day? But George Higgs can do better than that. I can take a ring from your nose. Oh ho!"

Thomas heard a chirp of astonished delight.

"Do it again!"

"Nay, get thee hence, Thomas. I must to Master Darrell."

Then George Higgs clattered down the stone stairs, a chubby footman wreathed in a grin. His grin faded when he saw Thomas Wyatt.

## X

BESS WYATT TURNED to Thomas with a courtesy that chilled him. "You have seen the garden?"

She was his wife. She had borne him a child. And yet, as she bent her head to the gauntlet she was drawing on she was as aloof as the lily behind her. Of her loveliness, Thomas thought, there could never be a doubt. But his pride was wounded by the glance that averted him, by her colourless voice, by the passivity, the formality, that excluded him. She moved gently. Her face was serenely modelled. Oddly enough, Thomas thought her virginal.

When they were alone she turned to him.

"Your father said nothing?"

"Only that you would see me."

"I see." She looked at the ground. "I find it hard to open."

"Spare me not, Bess. Out with it."

"You have never loved me, Thomas." She looked at him fully.

"You can say this."

"Is it not truth?"

"I was set right firmly to love you."

"Nay." She smiled faintly.

"You despise my love, Bess?"

"I cannot despise what you have never given me."

"You seek to dismiss me?"

"Since you ask honestly, Thomas, I answer you. I entreat you to live honestly. Give me over."

With these words, to his own amazement, an extraordinary emotion flowed into Thomas as he looked at his beautiful wife. "As you list, Bess, you must order me. Yet my heart is yours, my mind is yours, my affection yours."

She gazed at him sharply. Then she slowly shook her head.

His eyes filled with tears. "You are resolved? There is no remedy?" She made no answer.

"How is it with you?" he gently insisted.

In a low voice she said, "I have made promise to another."

"You made promise to me."

"Take your liberty." Her voice was no longer alien. "Be honest."

So touching was her voice, and so gentle her glance, that Thomas could not bear it. He went to his knee and seized her gloved hand. Bess felt a tear on her wrist. She allowed him to hold her hand for a brief moment before drawing it away.

"Be kind," she said faintly.

He remained kneeling, and tears poured from him.

It was some time before they could control themselves and walk from the garden.

As he left her she said, "Tell Lady Wyatt that I am sending Thomas to her, for the present."

Thomas rode home with this message to his mother. Then he shot the bolt in his turret door.

# Chapter 3

THOMAS WYATT WAS not at dinner at Allington and his father was troubled. Sir Harry stood in the new long gallery after dinner, looking out the window, pensively plucking his lip, with his forehead wrinkled. At last he released his lip and turned to Lady Wyatt. "I have not seen Tom."

"I saw him but for a moment," the mother said.

The father looked up and down the gallery. He was disquieted by his son's absence, and Lady Wyatt watched him anxiously.

"I fear you have bad tidings," she said. "You were again at Cobham, dear? You saw his wife?"

Sir Harry nodded.

"And young Darrell?"

Sir Harry nodded abruptly. "Bess will fall in with Tom's wishes. The boy may live at Allington."

Lady Wyatt scarcely seemed to hear. "I no longer blame Thomas," she said earnestly. "Bess is very beautiful, but she would break a heart of stone, not to say a heart of gold. Yet it passeth me that he should rush to put himself in the power of another like to her. Do men never learn, husband?"

Sir Harry gave her a mournful look. "Then he has gone to Hever?"

"He cannot avoid Hever."

"Well, he may."

"How so, dear?"

"Anne Boleyn is to marry that Irishman, to remove to Ireland."

"No! James Butler?"

"So it seems, Jane. His Grace wills it, and the Cardinal gave it out not long since—to his full household."

"Glory to God!" exclaimed Lady Wyatt. "Can it be? Can Thomas be saved?"

"That's too strong, wife," Sir Harry smiled. "A man's not lost who pays a little court, even in the wrong quarter."

"Anne is so little kind!" Lady Wyatt did not smile. "I dream of it o' nights. I cannot see why good men are drawn to cruel women."

"Or mice to cats," sallied Sir Harry. "We cannot save a mouse. Have you no faith in our son Thomas?"

"Forgive me, husband, I should not wail. Yet I could wish him anywhere but Hever. God send she go to Ireland!"

## II

THOMAS had no thought of Hever when he mounted to solitude in his turret. The glorious mood in which he had ridden home to Allington, so sure of his love for Anne, was now completely overwhelmed by the blow his wife had dealt him. Had he been cool and mature he would have accepted the liberty his wife thrust on him, and welcomed it for the sake of Hever. But he was twenty years old, he was of a serious strain, his belief in his own honour was so essential to his love of Anne, so deep in his nature, that he could no longer enjoy the delight that she had awakened in him. He was a bad husband. This failure to be a good husband, to satisfy Bess, to fulfil his duty, arose accusatory before him. He could not deny that from the beginning he had been unable to forget Anne Boleyn. He admitted this. But now he understood how honestly, how zealously, he had desired to obey the pledges that marriage had exacted from him. Not only for his own sake, but for his father and for his mother, for Lord and Lady Cobham, and for his son's sake, he wished to believe that he had done everything in his power to be a faithful husband. His room became a prison cell as he beat around in its miserable

confines, so like the confines of his conscience. The smallness of his
room, so delicious when he possessed himself, became intolerable as
he twisted from one unhappy alternative to another. He wished to
escape, and the moment dawn bruised its first tinges into the sky
he found himself on the road. His instinct headed him for Hever,
but even as he rode there his misery grew in him. He had believed
that Anne could count on him, yet the hope on which he had soared
was now as wan as the sky itself. The phantom of Percy had not
vanished. He tortured himself with the image of Anne pining for
him, and, at the same time, from Luke's few idle words, he pictured
Hever as visited by the King, and built up a vision of Anne, cloaked
in beauty, surrounded by a mob of admirers. He saw the unknown
James Butler as so persuasive that he found himself conjuring Anne
with Percy on one side and Butler on the other. This folly swelled in
him until at last, in desperation, he wildly laughed at himself. He
could not believe himself jealous. Yet his jealousy, which no laughter
could refute, left him with a foreboding of catastrophe. Goaded by
his conscience, lashed by his imagination, he arrived at Hever as taut
as a crossbow.

## III

THE KING had not come to Hever. There was no word of him. Anne,
who smiled on Thomas, was free, untroubled and alone. His arrival,
unexpected as it was, made her sparkle and for a few moments, learning from her eyes that he was in favour, Thomas was on the point of
mastering himself. But something in his manner aroused Anne's
instinct as a woman. She looked at him sharply. "You are in travail,
Thomas?" It was this that unsettled him. He was unable to answer
Anne, his eyes cast down on the path before him.

"Speak. You are nigh distraught. What goads you?"

"My doubleness. We have said farewell."

"What!"

"Bess gives me my liberty. We are now parted."

"And you bemoan it?"

"I bemoan my doubleness, Anne. I was not stedfast."

Anne's eyes dwelt on him. He heard her voice, detached and
measured. "Your holy oath, Thomas. You intended it?"

"How else? I cannot deny it."

"And, because of me, you feel you failed her. So you think. You must do me this justice."

"Not so."

"It is in your mind."

"We took an oath, Anne, and now I see it cancelled."

"Wherefore?"

"Was I a husband?"

Anne gave a sharp sigh. "Bess must have wrenched your heart at the end. Confess, Thomas."

Thomas, his eyes sorrowful, said as much.

"She can be very lovely," mused Anne. "Yea, I can see her. I hear her voice. Spoke she of me?"

"Nay," Thomas replied, "we spoke of parting, nothing more."

Anne pondered. "I were a fool to belittle your marriage. Yours is too good a soul. But were you alone to take this holy oath? Bess, perchance, did share it?"

Thomas agreed.

"And holds she by it? Or speaks she of another?"

"Yea, she doth."

"And so leaves you for him?"

"But was I stedfast, Anne? Was I not unworth?"

"Then go hence, Thomas. Seek her again. She still may heed you."

Thomas shook his head.

"Now take me to the door. We cannot linger here."

They walked back in silence. Anne's face was clouded.

As they parted Thomas gazed hard on her. Anne's eyes shone brilliantly.

"Suffer not so much, Thomas. She still may heed you."

As they reached the gatehouse a messenger came forward and bent the knee. He was from Lady Boleyn, with a muddled story of delays. In a few moments of sharp questioning Anne learned that her father was on the way, to prepare for the King's visit and for Cousin James Butler.

Anne held out her hand to Thomas. "Mayhap," she said, "you'll help us with his Grace's visit. Your sister Margaret was to come, so return with her."

## IV

IT WAS LADY BOLEYN who had decided on this visit.

A week before, with her chin lifted rather like the proud figurehead of a ship, she had gone to her husband.

"Now, Thomas," she said to the returned ambassador, "James Butler has been to Greenwich to wait on Anne. I saw him and I like him well. Had you not better open the matter to her?"

Sir Thomas took an opiate pastille and munched it. "The toothache," he said forlornly.

"Yea," assented his strong-minded wife. "Send for the tooth-drawer. Have it out. Methinks you must to Hever."

"My dear, I cannot rush to Hever with my face swollen."

"But Butler is express from Ireland."

"So it may be, Elizabeth, but what haste! Mayhap Anne would hate Ireland."

The mother frowned. "Anne's hates! Butler is no farther afield than Percy, and more welcome at Court."

"Butler!" Sir Thomas jerked out. "How know we he was born in wedlock? Hath that occurred to you? He may be a bastard. Were his parents dispensed aright? Was it a clear dispensation?"

"Pah!" exclaimed Lady Boleyn. "That is for attorneys to sift. Let us stick to the point. His Grace speaks of a privy visit to Hever, with Butler in his train. Are you not of a mind to prepare Anne for it?"

"No!" retorted Boleyn. "I do not pretend it. Anne is still of an age——"

"Anne is a full twenty years," her mother cut in grimly. "And should she marry elsewhere, so lose you Ormonde."

"Then you have sounded his Grace?"

"There was no call to, Thomas."

Sir Thomas glared. "What does the King intend?"

It was a dangerous question, and Lady Boleyn narrowed her fine eyes.

"He is wont to speak for himself," she said acidly. "He goes with a little train to Hever, to have a night in peace. Do you deny him this?"

"That cannot be said, Elizabeth. But we talked of Ireland."

"Then think on Ireland." She compressed her lips. "His true
henchman yonder names himself Ormonde. You dispute it, but the
King must ponder it. The day your services outweigh this soldier's
you may require to be named Ormonde."

Sir Thomas pulled his fine moustache.

"You go on embassy," soothed Lady Boleyn, "and you write faithful despatches. But why not take this way his Grace opens? James
Butler is young and promising, he is true metal. I esteem him."

"High as you vaunt him," Sir Thomas said, "take my poor advice:
Anne is not one you serve like this."

Lady Boleyn was flint. "Anne has her duty." She looked at Sir
Thomas firmly. "And so, I hold, have you." She went forward to her
husband. "Come, which tooth is it?"

Sir Thomas opened his mouth. "There!" He prodded with his finger.

"I see," Lady Boleyn said. "How foul! Attend! I send the tooth-
drawer."

With a whirl of her robe Lady Boleyn swept round and departed
to find the useful man who plied the pincers.


# V

"By your leave, your Grace, my youngest daughter Anne."

Sir Thomas Boleyn bowed as he said this, and Anne made her
curtsey in the great hall at Hever.

For a moment King Henry bristled. "The devil take Boleyn," he
seemed to say, "I know Anne." His face clouded and his head went
back, so that he chided Boleyn by his manner. Then the irritation
passed. He was all smiles. He gave Anne his hand, and the person by
whose aid she arose looked as indulgent as he was certainly magnificent.

It was her nose, strangely enough, that was fully informed of his
kingship. He was exquisitely perfumed, and she breathed him as if
he were a garden. Not only had he the aroma of a rose bed but he
shone and glowed with the subtlety and translucency of roses,
jewelled on his fingers, around his turret of a neck, and in his cap.
She felt that his head could never bow down, so strong, so stubborn
was the shaft that supported it. But, while she had caught the merest

flicker of the look that had rebuffed her father, her chief impression was from his eyes. They were small and quick and they twinkled with intelligence. His eyelashes were so fair that they were white as against his golden-red eyebrows, and in some odd way these white eyelashes in his warm, ruddy face were like an insincerity.

Perhaps because he had made Mary his mistress, perhaps because he and Lady Boleyn were old friends, Anne was ready to find this in him. He must have read it in her face, though his quick eyes glanced off hers in an instant. He knew himself that he had evaded looking at the younger sister, and because he felt that he had condemned himself by doing this he tried to catch her eyes again and to win her.

It was strange, this magnificent prince, trying to catch the young girl's approving eyes.

He uncovered his bald head as he looked at her, giving her his undivided attention.

"You are entirely French, Mistress Anne, they tell us?" He said this in French, in his rather squeaky voice.

"Not an atom of me, your Grace," she replied in English.

"It is not there that you have left your heart?" he smiled again.

This slyness disarmed her. She showed her pretty white teeth as she tilted her head back and actually laughed.

He laughed in unison. Just as he had rhythm in singing and dancing he desired it in intimacy, and he felt he had broken down the stiffness he detected in her.

"One of these days," he turned to Sir Thomas, "her Grace must see Mistress Anne at Greenwich." He passed on, with a superb air, his eyes flitting from laden cupboard to tapestry.

It was the public Henry who had encountered Anne, with attendants nearby, and every word eagerly listened to. To fulfil his public role the King had made a buskin for himself, on which he stalked at the proper altitude, bestowing, rewarding, patronizing, charming. But these pedestals in which he trod so nimbly, almost forgetting he wore them, could not lift him above the need for human intimacy. Those few words with Mary's sister were like sweet water to the parched. He foresaw happy hours at Hever.

Anne Boleyn had carried off her first real encounter with the King far better than she had hoped. She had dreaded meeting the man, and yet it was the man, rather than the King, who left her pleasantly aware of herself—and of him, of course. He was included.

Until he spoke to her Anne had not found her tongue. Her mind could not escape from the approaching ordeal, and though her younger friends had flocked to her, bemoaning her exile, chirping with that bright hollowness which leaves so much unsaid, she could only give a vague word and a vapid smile. But the minute the King had opened her way to Court Anne's heart gave a great thump of joy. Her relief was so enormous that within an hour, once more in the centre of her companions, with Margaret Wyatt on her arm, she had made such clever sallies and bubbled with such humour that all the world was merry as a jig.

Jane Parker, George Boleyn's wife, and Nan Cobham, Thomas Wyatt's siser-in-law, were well able to resist Anne's mood. In spite of Anne's mounting spirits and her rising voice they stayed on a sober level, cross-cutting every general hilarity with a much more earnest and sincere conversation. But at last even these dear friends had to yield, with a bewildered inquiry: "What? We could not hear? What says Anne?" In spite of them, to everyone's delight, Anne was sparkling; her return to Court shone in her eyes and in the speed of her responses.

She was still lustrous with high spirits when her father took her apart. It was the moment when, in spite of himself, he came to fulfil Lady Boleyn's command.

As Sir Thomas solemnly told her why James Butler was at Hever, the young girl's eyes flashed with a harder light. Her bosom rose and fell with a storm's violence.

"Nay, father," she flared out, "you cannot mean it."

"How so, Nan? He is much to our liking. He is our good cousin."

"Were I to die for it," Anne exclaimed, "I refuse it. You never thought of it. It is still the Cardinal! Now I see! And you lend yourself to it!" Her brow darkened, and she turned on her father with such fury that he actually recoiled from her. "It is the butcher's cur. This is his doing."

"Butler is a gentle, comely——"

"He is nought to me, gentle or comely. I'll have no part in this, father."

"But he is here!"

"Without my seeking. Let him go his way."

"Your mother——"

"No, pappa. I am not to be passed from hand to hand. My brother George will understand it. I detest this."

"The King——"

"His Grace hails me to Court. It is the Cardinal who sets the trap. I know his cunning hand."

"You cannot entertain Butler?"

"Were my head to be struck from me, I decline him."    .

"Tut-tut! Enough! Enough! I told your mother, Anne, that you would baulk. I have no more to say."

As Anne curtseyed he shook his head. "Even so! No docility in you."

## VI

COUSIN JAMES BUTLER was gradually chilled by his reception at Hever. The place itself attracted him. After his father's great castle he found it an amiable small manor, and its graciousness won him, but he could not say the same for the young Boleyns. They nipped him with one neat incivility after another; and when they gathered at table, though they revelled among themselves in the small talk of the Court, prattle of yesterday and the day before it—have you heard? did you know? have you seen? "oh" and "ah" and "yea" and "nay"—they contrived to pass him over as if he were an unwelcome bumpkin, leaving him to dip lumps of bread in the dish and drain the wine-cup when it reached him.

James chafed. By the time he had drunk liberally, however, he began to be amused. He guffawed once or twice uproariously, so that George Boleyn was constrained to look him over.

"You are fresh from Ireland, cousin?" said George sweetly. "Mayhap you miss your usquebaugh?"

"Nay," said James; "I scarce touch it. A pint for my breakfast, and I have done with it."

"My uncle Surrey deemed it beastly, yet the wild Irish, he said, who neither drink water nor wash in it, love usquebaugh as their mother's milk."

"Yea," said James, "we are all baptized in it."

"But you do not wrop in a blanket, ride bareback and wear long hair?"

James looked at his cousin's scanty beard. "The Irish wear their beards hindwise, yet, for the rest, are we not all Irish by night?"

"You'll not find us very Irish in Kent, I trow," smiled George Cobham lazily.

"Wrap ye not in a blanket at night, fair cousin, and oft ride bareback?"

The gleam in James Butler's eyes did not invite further pleasantries. He was rough, his cousins thought, and they went back to small talk.

Thomas Wyatt saw them making it difficult for him. He was relieved when the supper ended and they took to playing mumchance.

As for James Butler, incapable of unravelling the animosity that stirred George Boleyn and the others, he drank all he could but not so much that he was unable to gamble. His nerve and his craft were hardened by long practice at playing cards, and he gave such an account of himself that he bulged with the crowns he gathered.

He sank into bed, childishly pleased with his cheap triumph. But he could not sleep. And after several hours he began to wax angry. His claim to the Ormonde title was, after all, the first article of his faith; the folly of relaxing this claim for the sake of a marriage with Anne Boleyn, suddenly broke through his brain. He sat up naked in bed, and folded his strong arms.

"Curse them!" he growled. "Bullen, a lord mayor's whelp! His poor cracked mother, how could she make him Ormonde? The devil take them; I'll have it, in the teeth of them, or die plain Butler. I'll have none of them!"

A warm, clear feeling breezed through James Butler as he framed his simple will. He turned round, gave his bolster a clout, and within ten minutes he was soundly sleeping.


## VII

THE NEXT DAY was wet; and nothing could disguise it—the King was yawning and fidgeting. He was bored.

Sir Thomas Boleyn became more than nervous. Had Mary been able to come, all might have been well, but Mary was nursing her young baby Catherine and unable to leave Greenwich. Sir Thomas whispered to his son George, who grimaced but went to Harry Norris; and the equerry, spying a cessation of the rain, made his way to his master with a suggestion.

"What is that?" snapped the King. He pursed his lips when he heard it, but finally nodded, stood up, stamped his feet, and was ready to sally into the moist, warm green of Kent.

They were led, with trumpets sounding, to a near field in which a shallow gravel-pit had been rounded into an arena and in this smooth arena, chained to a pole, there swayed a bear.

He was an unprepossessing bear, with a wicked pink eye and dirty matted fur.

When he saw the company above him, fretting the grey skyline, he gave them such a surly look that the King's funnybone was tickled, and he began laughing. The bear heard his laughter and, with a rattle of his chain, shambled away with that baggy, slightly comic gait which is so amusing to children.

But he was quick to stop and turn. Three mastiffs had leaped into the pit, and before they barked the bear knew of them. A wave of ferocious resentment ran through his powerful old body. He raised himself on his hind legs, turning his front to them.

The dogs bristled at the huge beast. Whether for his smell or because of his ungainly inimical posture, they snarled with a vibrancy so savage that every spectator—and all the males from the stables and the gardens had joined his Highness to see the sport—felt the wolfish threat rip into their marrow, the dogs tensed to spring, their fangs grinning.

The bear braced himself ominously. He held one paw ready to smite, while his growl gave grim answer to the clang that encircled him.

The first bandog that leaped the bear knocked silly, but the two others had rushed close on the instant, and there started a mêlée so murderous that no one could tell which animal was in agony. They whirled and howled in the pit, the chain rasping, the dogs first on top, and then the bear, sound and sight confused by rapid change, with yelps of pain and frothing gargles of fury.

Henry was no longer bored. His laughter had passed into a fixed smile. His little eyes quite brilliant, he leaned forward over the struggling, pouncing, panting, bleeding animals, and his own blood raced in excitement. He was quicker than anyone else to see that the bear was doomed. While the watchmen still feared for their bandogs, two fresh ones having come, Henry saw death in the bear's dismayed eyes. Even the wounded dog dragged himself to the slaughter, which was so bloody and prolonged that it ceased to be amusing.

They turned away from this shambles in the gravel-pit, brisk and diverted.

"Without reflecting on my good host," said the King in a low voice to Harry Norris, "that were a crass poor beast! Had he been prouder, methinks the mastiffs could cry pax. Yet 'twas a lusty battle, bravely won." He had fully recovered his spirits. "And now," he sought out Sir Thomas, speaking in his natural, glad, compelling voice, "wine and a song, Sir Thomas."

## VIII

WHEN WINE was served to King Henry by a kneeling squire, and a few comfits nibbled, no one thought any longer of the sodden bear's meat in the damp arena outside. That was a rudeness excluded. The ladies, with their jewels alight and their bosoms bare, had filed into the hall. A fire had been kindled, a few great candles lighted, and in the polished darkness there were glints and dazzling gleams. The company, on the whole, was young. Every eye was fixed on Henry as, with a flashing smile, he struck the clavichord. The sounds had no resonance; they tinkled; but in their twang there was a sweet and delicate refinement by which the company was charmed. Henry had written the song himself. They knew it. And they sunned themselves in the art with which he trilled it, his voice clear and blithe.

> *Pastime with good company*
> *I love and shall, until I die.*
> *Grudge who list, but none deny!*
> *So God be pleased, thus live will I.*

He nodded to them for the refrain:

> *For my pastance*
> *Hunt, sing and dance,*
> *My heart is set.*
> *All goodly sport*
> *For my comfort*
> *Who shall me let?*

This appetite for "pastance," for pastime, Henry chanted in his high, garlanding voice.

> *Youth must have some dalliance,*
> *Of good or ill some pastance.*
> *Company methinks the best,*
> *All thoughts and fancies to digest;*
> *For idleness*
> *Is chief mistress*
> *Of vices all.*
> *Then who can say*
> *But mirth and play*
> *Is best of all?*

They sang with him cheerily, "mirth and play" in every glance. Even James Butler's squire, Simon Langton, felt an abundance of life behind it, a secure confidence that flourished. Yet as he gave himself to their love of life the last verse shocked him:

> *Company with honesty*
> *Is virtue, vices to flee;*
> *Company is good and ill,*
> *But every man has his free will.*
> *The best ensue,*
> *The worst eschew!*
> *My mind shall be,*
> *Virtue to use,*
> *Vice to refuse;*
> *Thus shall I use me.*

"Oh, God!" groaned Simon Langton. He heard them still trilling, "Virtue to use, Vice to refuse" with the same glee as they had trilled "All goodly sport," and their blandness floored him. The little beads of sweat on Henry's bald brow suddenly appeared comic. "His Grease," he noted, with half-concealed contempt, seeing the King as an adept at self-deception.

## IX

ON THE MORROW, in the fresh sunshine, Thomas Wyatt was early afoot. He had shared in the festivities at Hever without encountering Anne herself, and he had just come from a word with Sarah in the pantry when Anne accosted him. She was pale in the early morning, with her dark eyes strangely open and tender. Thomas's heart bounded as she looked at him. They went into the wood.

"You are still out of heart?" asked Anne gravely, "you still deplore me?"

He walked silent by her side. The very accent in which she spoke revived his spirit. He felt as if the heavens were about to open.

"I never deplored you," he murmured.

"Nay, but your spirit is troubled."

"No longer."

"You have seen Bess?"

"No."

"How can you know yourself?"

"She is Francis Darrell's."

"Are you content?"

Thomas looked full at her. She quickly dropped her eyes. "Yea, now! But you were forlorn, Thomas, three days since."

"It is impossible, Anne. I cannot return to Bess."

"She has not besought you."

"Even so. But you said to me——"

"That you must know your true mind. So did I say."

"Yea. If I am not honest, you cannot regard me. Yet how to prove myself to you?"

Anne's eyes deepened. "Mayhap you crave her underneath."

"Crave!"

"Aye. You spoke wistfully. I could not see you divided thus."

"Great God! She was my wife." He made a gesture. "I must ask myself, have I hurt her?"

"And how answer yourself? What saith your heart?"

"Be stedfast—to my love."

"May you heed it!"

"Do you hold me fickle if I tell you what is in it?"

Anne paused. "We were not here, Thomas, did I hold you fickle."

As she spoke he stopped dead. He slipped his wedding ring from his finger. "I have ever worn this," he said. He balanced it in his palm and then looked at Anne. "Am I cruel?"

She shook her head.

With a quick, clean gesture he cast the ring into the depths of the greenwood.

Anne said nothing. They walked in quivering silence for several minutes. It was only when he dared to look at her that he lost himself in a maze of divine relief. The misery of doubt that had possessed him left him like an exhausted fever. He felt free at last, with Bess Brooke willingly relinquished to her lover; and at this inner acquiescence there came that miraculous heightening of the senses in which no single wild flower seems to grow without an intended beauty, and no branch to break into blossom without joy. They walked on a mossy path, bars of light lifting as Anne crossed them and sparkling over her as she stopped to turn to Thomas. He was drawn tight, but like a reverberating wire. They came on a clear space, bounded by a bank. The morning sun dwelt mellowly on the bank, though late primroses were clumped in the moist greenness of its shadow. Anne caught a bramble in her skirts as she mounted it, and Thomas stooped to free her. They looked at one another. He passed out of his command into a state that was boundlessly intense, with Anne borne to him in a similar intensity. As he looked he could see in Anne a new and singular beauty. There was hardly a mood in her that he was not aware of —he could catch changes with a half glance, and even when he could not believe her beautiful he found it ravishing to observe her, so suddenly revealed in one instant, or veiled and denied to him. Her instinctiveness always gave her power over him. Where he was so becalmed by the contradictory variety of the world, so forced to doubt himself and hold back, Anne possessed herself with ardour. Where he fumbled she drew a line so clear and free that he submitted to it as to a master's. It was herself she defined, out of her heart; and what she praised, what she condemned, what she loved, carried with it the keenness that is fresh from feeling; it was that living feeling, so faithful to itself, which never failed to prevail on Thomas. And now, when at last he seemed to become its true object, when he saw her eyes open to receive him with the consent of her heart in them and a meek expectancy behind her ardour, he was swept beyond himself. Anne was the first person he had known who felt into her whole world, and he, whom she once called "doubting Thomas," gazed on her with the eyes of worship, her gravity giving a beauty to the clear oval of her face that was beyond any he had beheld. She looked at him with a still look. It was so deep and unwavering that neither of them stirred; it was as if she were about to die, so great was this surrender. They kissed as they stood under the trees. And soon they went silent back to Hever.

## X

YET before the afternoon was out, when the royal party left Hever, taking Lord James Butler with them and the older Boleyns, Anne passed into a mood so perverse and brittle that Thomas was at a loss.

"Come," she said, "let's see the last of them," and she grasped him by the wrist.

"I still mark them!" cried Thomas. "A fume of dust!" He and Anne had climbed to the roof of the turret.

"It is unfair to be so small." Picking up her skirts, Anne stood on the parapet. "O, Altitudo!"

Thomas saw her danger. The earth beneath, precise and clumped and dotted and ribboned, was no longer a pretty miniature. It was a menace. He felt spikes of fear go through him.

"I shall not fall," she laughed. She looked fearlessly about her. "The higher, the better. I see no dust."

"It was a dry patch. They are gone," said Thomas. "Come down, Anne."

"Come up, Thomas."

Thomas saw her above him, gleaming and perverse. The parapet was about a foot high, and her skirts cumbersome.

"You are a-feared?" she said.

"In fear for you," he answered pleadingly.

"That I lose my head?" She teased him by the nonchalance with which she lingered.

"Your head, your heart, your every thing." He held out his hands.

"Thou'rt a sad fellow!" She jumped down without his aid. "I never lose my head," she laughed. And then, with a high wild laugh, "Neither my head nor my maiden-head. I saved it from Butler." With this, seeing Thomas's long, serious face, she threw back her head and pealed with laughter.

"Nay, Anne!"

She leaned against the battlement, exhausted with laughing.

"Not so sad, good Thomas! They tried me sore. What could you have done if they gave me to Butler, to foal an Ormonde? Have you no wit?"

Thomas watched her.

"Yea," she added, bright and bitter. "They were well concerted. The King, the Cardinal, Uncle Surrey, the Butlers, Mamma, mayhap Pappa. First not to take Percy, then to take Butler. And you, you, Thomas, nailed to your cross, never to rise again!" She gave a short, hard laugh. She went to him, her face changed, and laid her hands on his wrist. "You take not my black humour? What will become of me! I return to Court, and there—God knows!" Her face, amused before, was tragically grave. "Yea, for all you love me, you'll lose faith. Yet kiss me, Thomas, and love me. Never give me over."

With a queer, stifled cry Thomas took her in his arms. She loved him.

# Chapter 4

I N THE FIRST flush of her return to Court, Anne was irresistibly radiant. She was so steeped in the ways of the Court that the touch of it after a long absence was like the first feel of a ship to a returning seaman.

Greenwich was full of war excitement. An army was to cross to France as soon as the hay was in and the harvest ripe, and this movement of men and minds oscillated and swayed the Palace. For Anne Boleyn, however, Greenwich itself was the steady reality, anchored in a changing stream, and she lost the momentary excitement of the war in the immense personal reverberation of her return.

All that was quick in her nature was brought into play by the mere habitual Greenwich. She could not pass old Gibson, the sergeant at arms, without stopping to greet him. She knew individual yeomen ushers and all their history. She had strong likes and dislikes that ran up and down the scale, and this vivacity, this warmth of temperament, had a way of heightening her looks until she was rather beautiful. Anne's eyes could flash, and her breasts could heave quickly, and her body vibrate, without the least premeditation or conscious intention. She could give herself to the moment with a generous celerity, and since she loved to be loved this heightened the smallest incident of her return. The Boleyns were not on the right side, of course. They were too French at this particular minute, when an army was being led against France by the Duke of Suffolk. But Anne was too quivering with Greenwich itself to be stilled by this sobering thought. She was not only reinstated, she felt reinstated. She had triumphed over an excommunication. Her face lost its sombre look. She was all gleam and response, moving with the energy of the heart that is at home, and quickened by sheer relief from Hever's monotony.

The mere rustle of her queenly mistress, Catherine of Aragon, was sufficient to ripple her nerves. Anne got up, sat down, curtseyed, genuflected, promenaded and attended with all that inner satisfaction which is doubled after an experience of ostracism. It was not the King who uplifted her, though she beamed with young gratitude whenever he dipped his head to acknowledge her existence. She was back at Court; that was enough. She was gathered to the bosom, she could disport and comport herself in that suave element for which the atoms of her being had so long shaped themselves.

Somewhere in the twilight of her memory hovered the shade of Henry Algernon Percy. She was too hurt, even still, to think of him. But in her vivified spirit she scarcely admitted that she had been wounded. That was gone, a mist vanished from the clean surface of her renewed presence and her acceptance of Thomas Wyatt. She even wondered at herself, that a feeling so strong could leave so little trace —but she winced and did not dwell on it.

So far as Anne's companions could see, she had shamelessly recovered. They knew that Percy was now one of the palisades in the North of England, his father's heir and married to a shrew. But, probe as they would, Anne gave them no comfort. She glinted into Greenwich, they thought, like a fish into its native pool, twirling with joy to be back again.

But so obvious a lesson as her exile, and her brother George's sustained dismissal, certainly convinced Anne that to keep one's footing in this polished and slippery Court required a trick of balance. She had discovered from the long days at Hever that a single false step could have the dreariest consequences. The impression her friends had —that Percy had evaporated—was of course a false one. But if she had lost him, and been baulked before everyone by losing him, she had at least regained the Court. It was this that told her to guard her feelings. She could open her heart to Thomas, but Thomas must be her secret. She had suffered too much by the first exposure to give anyone the power to hurt her again. Her pride could not endure a new humiliation, but it heightened her spirits to think how much less frail Thomas Wyatt was than Henry Percy. Thomas, at any rate, would prove stedfast. And it was not in her nature to rest until he was part of the daily life that the Court was leading. To move on his behalf, when she was sure of her ground, would be her natural impulse. That, however, had to be governed by extreme caution, until she was really at home again, and had taken the full measure of everything and everyone, including her enemy Cardinal Wolsey.

## II

CARDINAL WOLSEY was himself quick to observe that the "foolish girl" had reappeared. The first fine day he arrived at Greenwich, after Anne's return, the Queen's attendants were filing out of the door on their way to the friary. He recognized the thin, black-eyed damsel the instant he saw her.

"Give way, sirs." The ushers shoved back the crowd with their pikes held lengthwise. "Back further, prithee."

A wide space in front of Greenwich Palace was thus kept free from the water-gate to the door, and it was here that the Queen and the Cardinal greeted one another.

By the pomp of the Cardinal's arrival the world was always impressed. He was an obese priest to be so regally escorted, yet as he slowly advanced, his eye prowling among the cavaliers who knelt while he raised his hand in blessing, no one could deny him commanding importance. Against his will even Thomas Wyatt was moved by this ponderous figure, and Anne was compelled to admit that he was still as dominant as ever.

His dominance was one of the facts she had to reckon with. It was true that the King had installed Mary in a lodge at Greenwich, that he had given Mary's amenable husband a sinecure or two, that he had dropped several of the Buckingham confiscations into her father's lap and promised, in spite of the Cardinal, to make Sir Thomas the treasurer of the household. Anne recognized all this, but with a certain bitterness. Her one unalloyed satisfaction was that she had triumphed over the Cardinal herself by refusing James Butler and yet was back again, under his very eyes.

He had, indeed, observed her; he observed everything. But Anne was too young to fathom how essentially insignificant he felt her to be. At times, to be sure, he hardly needed a hair shirt when he had a master who clad him in favourites like these Boleyns, but there were limits to the attention he bestowed on them. The fortunes of the Boleyn family did not loom large in eyes that strained so wearily across the narrow seas, scanning France, looking to Spain, peering into Italy.

Directly he left the Queen and entered the Palace, Wolsey learned that the King, contrary to his custom, was playing tennis in the morning. This he welcomed. As Suffolk was still at Court before he took his army out, and as the Earl of Surrey had not yet left to don his armour, Wolsey needed to prepare his mind for final decisions. Paris was the goal. If Bourbon rebelled and if the Emperor invaded from Spain, then Wolsey's career would be crowned by victory. He could already envisage himself as Pope, thus enabled to secure Henry's aid in wiping out Luther in Germany. Boulogne, exacted from France, would give England control of the narrow seas and so break the French link with Scotland. With such victories promised—the fruit of his career—a girl like Anne Boleyn was so trivial, so meaningless, to him that whether she refused to marry a Lord of the Pale, either on the Irish or the Welsh or the Scottish border, was scarcely worth a moment of his thought. What if Mary Carey was now the King's mistress! Mary Carey, Bess Blount, Jane Parker, Madge Shelton, Anne Boleyn, Beth Darrell—the King might sleep with all of them, have a child by any of them. What could that matter, in the name of Solomon? The Cardinal had greater things to concern him.

These greater things, on which his mind was dwelling while Henry finished his game, were so much the outcome of his planning from 1519 to 1523 that they were ever uppermost in his mind, if only because they involved a European war.

It was the last act of this Wolseyan drama that was now at hand. The previous act had been the Emperor's visit to Greenwich the year before. That visit sprang from the Field of the Cloth of Gold, which had blared the Cardinal's magnificent intervention into Europe, placing England as the mediator in the coming European war.

But to see a diminutive Anne as the Cardinal really saw her he had only to go back to 1519, from which followed the Field of the Cloth of Gold, and the young Emperor's visit to Greenwich.

These were the events that made him mighty as a statesman and left Anne a "foolish girl."

### III

IN THE YEAR 1519, to go back with him to the beginning of his great drama, Europe supposed itself to be at peace.

This unusual state of affairs was due to an accident. The Holy Roman Emperor had died in the January of 1519, and until a new one was elected no one could know who was to fight whom. It was a necessary breathing space. The greatest of the powers—France, with a population of twelve million—had recently won a war of conquest in Italy, and early in this year young Francis I hoped that he could add to his prestige by having himself elected Holy Roman Emperor. This would have made him invincible and insupportable. It was a hard choice for the seven Teutonic electors between the ambitious Francis and his juvenile Hapsburg rival, but they took bribes from all sides— all seven of them—and then they named Charles V, aged nineteen, to succeed his Hapsburg grandfather.

This meant that the state of peace that had been endured for a few years was certain to be broken.

The young Emperor had inherited the Netherlands from his father, and Spain from his Spanish grandfather. Now being on top in Germany as well he was able to lap France almost the whole way round. His election as Emperor, in short, gave Europe two fighting cocks instead of one, with Italy as their cockpit. By the time that Wolsey came forward, toward the end of 1519, the war was certain.

England at that time was still a green and relatively pleasant land with plenty of space for a human being to breathe in. Its population was well under four million—fewer people than has Ireland to-day, and in an area nearly double—while London had dwelling in it about one per cent. of those incredible numbers who now glue themselves into Greater London.

This was a thin population, yet not so weak in a military way as the mere numbers indicate. England, as Henry VIII put it, had a trench around it. And it was strong enough to hold Calais.

The coming war was no secret either to Henry VIII or Cardinal Wolsey. They had fought the French in 1513 and financed the old Emperor in 1516, largely because of their wool trade with the Netherlands. Their policy, on that account, was anti-French and pro-Emperor, but before they decided to support the young Emperor they meant to hold the balance as long as possible, and they did not propose to close their bargain until Henry and Francis had met at the Field of the Cloth of Gold.

The Field of the Cloth of Gold was already in view in the autumn of 1519. It was to take place the following June, and one of those whose mind was full of it was Anne Boleyn's father. Sir Thomas was leaving Hever, late in 1519, and he took Anne with him on this journey to the Court of Francis I.

Such was the excuse for that grandiose political picnic which was soon to be known as the Field of the Cloth of Gold.

And it was one of the bright chapters of Anne Boleyn's early life.

## IV

Not UNTIL THE EVE of the great festivity, however, was it made certain that Anne, the daughter of the English ambassador, could be included among the ladies to go with the French Queen.

For those ladies it was exciting enough—the rendezvous of King Henry VIII and King Francis I, but for Anne Boleyn it was doubly so, and when the actual morning of departure broke at Blois she could hardly contain her spirits. To take part in the Camp du Drap d'Or— that was enviable, but for an English girl to come with the French Court, to come talking French and to appear in a French style, no longer a child, several inches taller, with Mary and George and Francis Bryan and her mother and her sour aunt, all to be made fully aware of this high transfiguration—Anne was so gleeful that she had some difficulty in preserving aristocratic calm. Her term in France had, in point of fact, given her some of that subtle perception which subdues the enthusiastic, but she could not help leaping to this reunion, and while George's wit and her mother's wisdom might temper it for the family, Anne went to it in a quiver of anticipation.

In the great hall at Blois there was the glorious brio of departure and Anne moved into it with her big eyes dilated. Everyone was a little exalted, as on the eve of holiday; even enemies, before they could help it, spoke cordially. The scene was formless, quick with salutes and jests, darts and stops, forgettings and rememberings. There was no attempt at etiquette until Queen Claude arrived, and the King's mother and the King's sister moved among the flock like shepherdesses. It was a woman's hour, since King Francis and his band had taken another route before them.

Marguerite d'Alençon, the King's sister, was well under thirty. Her face was as salient as her brother's, but where his was adventurous with bold cheekbones and high colour, Marguerite's had a wistful cast, and from liquid eyes that had much suffering in them a look flickered over the company that was at once tender and amused. Anne gazed at her with girlish worship when Marguerite caught her eye.

"You come with us, ma petite Boullain?"

"Oui, Madame." Anne curtsied, and with such wild glee that Marguerite gave a little laugh.

"You'll see all your family?"

"Oui, Madame."

"You are unlike your little sister Mary; I remember her so well. She'll be at Ardres?"

"Oui, Madame."

"Voilà! But they cannot steal you, ma petite. You come back with us, no matter what!" With a gentle pat on Anne's cheek, Marguerite smiled again. "Now comes the Queen!" Then her expression changed. With a look of concern, almost as of a reverend mother, she exclaimed, "What has happened?" and went quickly forward into a sudden cluster. A glance told her everything: the Queen had fainted.

On account of Queen Claude's condition the royal physicians had been highly dubious about this rendezvous at Ardres. But Wolsey had so urged it, Francis I had consented, and Claude was obliged to make the effort whatever it cost. Beginning at sixteen, the French Queen had given birth to four children in the past five years, and the fifth was well on its way. The strain of departure had been too much for her. Squat, pale, corpulent, she reeled into the arms of the Duchess of Vendôme and was dumped into a chair in a complete collapse. At once the whole multitude was convulsed by fear. "She is dead!" one lady shrieked. Several fell to their knees. The sense of calamity converted early hilarity into a mob-like terror and pale guilt. But the King's mother, Louise of Savoy, red-faced and resolute, thrust her way to Claude's side. Marguerite followed, and soon, with a fish-like eye, the poor Queen took in the scene about her, pulling herself back to it by will. Nothing must halt a royal procession.

Anne Boleyn, herself as flat as a plate, had been feeling there was something absurd about a young Queen so forlorn and distended. Claude was four years older than herself, yet already a dropsical matron whose fate was sealed. How indifferent to her real martyrdom, how fresh and sparkling, Anne felt herself before the Queen fainted. But she, like the others, was seized by panic when death went through his pantomime before her. Anne cried, "Lord, Lord!" in an ecstasy of anxiety. She watched humbly while Queen Claude was slowly helped to her litter, but before they wound down the turreted staircase to the courtyard the hum of irrepressible life began again, and with shining eyes the young ladies awaited their palfreys.

When Anne's turn came she sat into the pillowed saddle on her own white palfrey, her clear face betraying no emotion; yet a zig-zag again jumped through her, mingling with sharp attention. The brisk, nervous harbingers were certain, to her shrewd mind, to put a dozen maids in a hovel en route, and none in a manor. Of this she laughingly assured her nearest companion: their mistakes were notorious. To and fro the sweating marshals rallied the line with shouts that ran through her fibre. Her eyes snapped as the cavalcade at last started through Blois, the far music crackling with expectancy.

But even when they began to move there was a fresh batch to gallop ahead of theirs: a band of courtiers. They whisked a salute. This amused Anne mightily, though their glances and their prances meant little more to her than a picture. To her they were not unlike dogs who can never help barking at a flying bird. She herself skimmed low to lure them, flew feebly to make them race, then pertly lifted beyond them, teasing and exulting. Her element was not theirs: they were on the earth, she in the air. Yet it was an instinct to make them pant for her and lose her: her heart was as free as a bird's.

But she had lent it to France. It was not that the French were four times as rich as the English, four times as numerous. Between royal habits at home and in France Anne saw little contrast: each had those of a Court with centuries behind it—centuries of grandeur and vicissitude. But an island is different from a Continent. Anne now took Europe to be her daily bread. The Papacy, for example, was no longer vague; it was a human neighbour, a fallible neighbour. The French Court still felt the shame of having given a royal cousin to a base Medici, the Pope's nephew. Here it was the lord despising the merchant, but the same incomparable hauteur marked its view of the German lordlings who came and were decorated and sent off pensioned. They were in pawn after that. Beyond French facility and franchise, behind the flirtation of the gallants and the lavishness of the châteaux, there towered Francis's bold conquest of North Italy. That made the nobles drunk with power. Their blithe tone with the maids of honour was the soldier's, though still there was something real about the French way with women. Anne was petted because she was English, since the French were courting the English, and she was picking up politics in the mood of alliance. But while she could not help absorbing current notions, just as she did costume and cuisine, the French touch said more to her than the latest head-dress. And while her inner loyalty remained unchanged she had lost her prudery, or thought she had. The Court did not go in for it.

She was only one of scores of "foolish girls" en route for the Field of the Cloth of Gold. She could not even imagine the multitudes who were rolling along the open road from every château—archers, footmen, gendarmes, cooks, farriers, gunners, gay ladies, priests, poets, beds, tables, chairs, the menagerie, the fodder, hundreds of horses, tuns of wine, mountains of baggage. All of this would be splendid, grimy and uncomfortable, but Anne could rise to any drama she had a part in, and this was a drama of King Francis's Court, his Queen on one side, his beauty on the other, and all the damosels, even her English self, dancing in the beam of his light, making his fêtes the most dazzling in Europe. He was only twenty-six. There was another life in France beyond the Court, from which Marguerite d'Alençon drew the sympathetic quality that everyone deferred to. The most frivolous paid her homage, and Anne glowed to have won her notice. But it was not Marguerite's starry seriousness that bound Anne to France, or the policy that enlaced her. It was its gallantry, its glory, its finesse and its discipline. Already, girl as she was, she read dozens of faces at the Court and caught the threads of their destinies. Some of them were mean, some generous. Her little namesake, Anne de Heilly, younger than herself, was already singled out by Francis. His *maîtresse en titre* he had snatched from a husband, but this was an old story and he turned to a new one. Anne's imagination flew from branch to branch in the maze of this courtly drama, the sky lost above it, the air enchanted. But at Ardres she would touch England.

## V

FROM DOVER, at the end of May in 1520, sailed the thousands of courtiers who were to glorify the Field of the Cloth of Gold. Thomas Wyatt barely arrived from Cambridge in time to cross the Channel.

It was not just a field, it was a camp, outside Calais. And here, by a stream, both English and French were pitching their tents for festivity.

It would have been more kingly under a roof, but under the sky it was exhilarating. The grass smelled sweet in June, and the horses were so at home on the turf that it made the blood race merely to see the gaudy companies go by. Here the world was gathering, the world and his horse, the French Court in one old town, the English Court in the wooden palace that three thousand slaving artificers had built, but most of the knights already under gilded canvas.

And Cardinal Wolsey had done it, had devised the daily tournaments, the banquets in the great pavilions, the knightly rivalry. From the tiny pages to the oldest varlets, from the least squire to King Francis or King Henry, the mood was aristocratic, guided and mastered by Wolsey. A hundred years after Agincourt the French were genial and welcoming. Cardinal Wolsey had secured this down to the last detail, and his magnificence was that of a third monarch. He had come with his own Court, his own footmen, his liveries, his choir, his army of chaplains and his chapel.

Anne was too young to understand this. She took the moment as it beckoned, the delight of festival crossed with farce, ceremony with circus, a fair in which the lightest-hearted spun like fireflies in the night, never aware till now that to camp in royal company for three weeks could be so delightful and so exhausting.

Thomas Wyatt, fresh from Cambridge, was in the thick of it, but he was with the Cobhams.

## VI

ALMOST AS NOBLY BEDECKED as his horse, Lord Cobham surveyed the brilliant scene with that ease in exclusiveness which is one of the charms of an aristocrat. "That was John Bourchier who left us. His Grace has bade him english Froissart. That is not what you aim at, is it?"

"My way is still to seek, my lord."

"But your French is good. Bess tells me you are quick at it?"

"Better at Cambridge than at Calais. And were I at Court . . ."

"You'll come to Court, my son Thomas. His Grace will welcome Harry Wyatt's son. Where is your father, by the way?"

Sir Harry Wyatt could easily be missed, though the June light shone clear. The air rustled with cries and shouts, distant calls and the hum of preparation. It was much like a camp, but so rich was each equipage, so powerful the glint of gold and the hint of inlaid metal, that its chivalric character flashed from every side. The squires and men at arms were often rustic enough, but this paddock revealed one countenance after another that had strength, surprising salience, and even beauty. They were fighting men, indomitable.

"Nay, I see not father," said Thomas Wyatt.

"He is much set on your marriage next month," declared Lord Cobham roundly.

"It is his dearest wish," affirmed Thomas.

Both of them still roamed over the crowd with enquiring eyes. Old Poynings went by, who had been ambassador with Boleyn. So did Sir William Compton, burly and hearty. With great resplendence the thin-featured haughty Duke of Buckingham and his many attendants rode out. Young Francis Bryan, Lord Berners' nephew, buzzed near them. They were all in fine feather yet mightily themselves as they strode or swaggered or waddled about, with nods of recognition or tell-tale flashes of the eye. It was a family of noblemen, their shrewd estimate of one another refreshed with bubblings of goodwill. And they seemed to flourish in this outdoor park. Under the horses' hoofs lay the grass of Guines, and between the stone buildings came the gleam of several thousand tents in the Val Doré. The air was so gently warm, the scene so bright, the mood so confident, that Thomas Wyatt was mutely immersed in it, feeling how sweet it was to be alive. His own young figure, clad in black velvet, with his auburn hair alight in the sun, was far from the least engaging.

His future father-in-law gave a final nod to his squire. Slowly he mounted, and from his elevation he spoke in a voice that sounded smaller.

"You go to the lists, Thomas?"

"Nay, Lord Cobham. I await George Boleyn."

"Kent all over again. Hever, Allington, Cobham. Good betide them! I must away. Ah, George Boleyn comes."

Lord Cobham waved his hand. Narrowly watched by his followers, the nobleman in his sumptuous apparel with his steed in trappers filed majestically away to take place in the royal pageant.

And then Thomas turned to catch George Boleyn.

## VII

GEORGE BOLEYN wore scarlet. With his leaping sword and his tilted chin he ruffled the world, and even his plumed hat was at a flaunting angle. A game bird that smites the eye, thought Thomas Wyatt as George skimmed past him.

"Fair sir, God save you," Thomas cried after him.

"Ah, there you are, Thomas! I saw all the plough horses of all the shires, but Thomas nowhere." He touched his little moustachio and the little beard that jutted from his chin. From these ornaments, within a century, would grow marvels, to match the wig.

"Are we still for Ardres?"

"Anne looks for us," said George, "but let's walk. The four-legged beast doth not amuse me."

They took the old highway to Ardres, with the myriad canvas peaks to the right, and the highway crowded. June sparkled. The road itself was quick with jaunting horsemen, companies in parti-coloured velvet bound for the tilt. The Burgundians in scolloped hose, with slits and slashes and puffs of silk, were already fantastically out of mode. Thomas Wyatt kept step with his swift cousin, who drew many a glance.

"Had they the Sweating Sickness at Cambridge, Tom?"

"Most horribly. They died like flies."

"The King is in mortal terror of it. And now you give up learning for marriage?"

"Yea," said Thomas. Bess Brooke, with her pale cheeks, came to his mind. She held aloof from him.

"You'll live at Allington. Your father is happy for it?"

Thomas nodded.

"That old oak!" said George gaily. "Oft have I mused on the good cat that brought him his daily pigeons in the Tower. Those were kind pigeons!"

Thomas looked vague. He reverenced his father.

"Yea." George noted the chill. "We are whelps of another age."

"You parley like King Richard III," said Thomas drily.

"Crookback? You flatter me. The Howards stood by Crookback."

"Yea, there's the rub. 'Why are you such a fool,' Crookback said to father. 'You serve for moonshine in the water. Your master is a beggarly fugitive. Forsake him and become mine. I can reward thee.'"

"And what did your father answer?"

"This he himself tells me, George. 'Had I first chosen you for a master, sir, faithful had I been to you,' he said, 'but the Earl, poor and unhappy, is my master, and nothing, by God's grace, shall drive or draw me from him.'"

"'Twere well," said George softly. "A stout man for father." He plucked his little beard. "And then the Earl became Henry VII and your good father was made for life! Yet how does this sort with the velvet tree at the tilt that has shields on it? We play at chivalry now. This is an iron age. You know the latest of Martin Luther?"

"How now!"

"I heard it yestereve. He is excommunicated. The young Emperor is to crush the heresy."

George was no longer jesting. "George," ventured Thomas. "Are you not as much a heretic as I?"

"Mistake me not, Thomas," George said quietly. "I am my King's poor minion." He took Thomas's arm. "Yet look at this." He waved his arm. "Here in this Field there is no heresy. This is not for bondmen. Here is a tilt under velvet trees with silken leaves, with princes and lords, fair ladies and the Cardinal. Here there spreads green grass with never a worm in it, flowers without dung, and pigeons without cats. Here the Cardinal, sold to the young Emperor, woos the French to bid for us. Here we blow our trumpet."

"Why should not England blow its trumpet?" Thomas wondered.

"But go abroad," George Boleyn spoke intently. "Go into the twisted streets, to the weavers, to the shoemakers. Go to the smiths and the fullers. They hate this Cardinal. They scorn this meeting of the princes. The Bible is in their hands, Thomas, food for heresy. They'll seek the divine inheritance. Men will die for this, and on this mayhap our Master hath not brooded."

"In Cambridge I met men who spoke fervent heresy. But the princes can crush it."

"The more they crush it the sweeter they make it. I am no oracle, yet we begin a Crusade. Anne must come home."

"And why?" asked Thomas.

"War."

"But here we treat of peace!"

"Universal peace," George corrected sharply. "In time of universal peace, prepare for universal war. We desert the French."

"We are to fight them?" Thomas asked incredulously.

"In my poor judgment. The Cardinal chooses the Emperor, who is to make him Pope."

"I am half heretic," said Thomas. "We groan under Wolsey. Shall the King be ever under his thumb?"

George Boleyn smiled. "To throw off the Cardinal"—he stood still —"the only way is heresy. Then, as the man said, we'll make him as red as his hat." He paused and pointed. "Here is the drawbridge. The password is Fraise. Now we have brewed treason, Thomas, and pulled long faces. Forget all this. Not a word to Anne. Remember!"

## VIII

IN AN OLD BUILDING at Ardres, at times used for a garrison, the French maids of honour were poorly housed, and there George Boleyn led Thomas. Under the archway they found a beaming, ruddy Frenchman who greeted George heartily.

Against a plaster that a garrison had battered and defaced, Thomas set himself to wait, letting George chatter to Saint-Même. How shabbily the grass sprouted in the paved courtyard, he thought. He heard a rustling sound, the swish of silk. In the wide low doorway three girls appeared.

Saint-Même uncovered with a sweep, kissing three hands in succession, and in some way appropriating the scene.

"Mary," George cried over his shoulder, "you see cousin Thomas Wyatt."

Mary Carey, who had been married to Will Carey a few months before, waved a cousinly hand. Her soft eyes were fringed with dark, long lashes.

As they billowed down the broken steps, a wave of silk and satin, Thomas marked Anne and the third girl, Beth Darrell. Beth had a kind light in her face and a certain happy nobility of carriage. She was dressed with the square virtuousness of Queen Catherine. Anne was in a daintier mode. If her gown had not been cut low, with the sleeves full and flowing, and if a breath had not ruffled severity into grace, Thomas could have seen her as one of a novitiate, with modest coif and habit still unworldly. Her silk was pearl colour, and her girlish slenderness stemmed from a high waist. They mingled greetings under the archway. As she turned to Saint-Même her little neck was touchingly young, and when she wheeled she intercepted the look that Thomas had for it.

"You lead, George," commanded Anne gaily.

"We have time to see the crowds on the heath," explained George.

"Worse than Cairo," laughed the burly Saint-Même, "lead on."

Before the bristling French captain waved them out of Ardres, he persuaded Saint-Même to accept an escort of five French soldiers with halberds.

## IX

OUTSIDE, on the heath, the Commons had camped uninvited. They had come to see the flower of French and English knighthood, and a gay multitude had swollen on the outskirts of the Field, a bright tent here and there, jugglers and hawkers in sight, bits of trash and rubbish on the trampled ground. French, Flemish, German, Burgundian, English thronged innumerably together, citizens that the pale boy John Calvin had seen ride through Noyon, scallywags that had made Rabelais smile, Gypsy and Jew, the wild landsknecht, the vagabond, all circling free under the sky. Patrols of fierce soldiers prowled ready to capture any thief and string him up. A fight or two had to be quelled at any moment, but it was friendly summer weather, flags were flying, there were snatches of folk music as courtiers and soldiers, beggars and children swarmed in the crowd.

The cavaliers and their ladies moved under guard. The crowd hardly noticed them. It was torn with pity at seeing a thief dragged to a gibbet, his grey face betraying his fear. They passed a brawl— two drunken men rolling on the ground, with beggars watching them, the beggars as terrible in their wolfish greed as in their syphilitic sores. A lewd disorder and brutality surged from dark depths, but with long pikes the French patrol ruthlessly pricked the rough ones out of their path. Rogues who were too slim to be captured twisted the simple out of their pennies and left them woeful of countenance, yet it was not this squalor that Thomas Wyatt saw. The sun was shining. The great crowd lay in the lap of mother earth, alive with a revel that few would ask to order in any other way. They took the moment as it rolled from the middle ages, for the most part sweet and full of relish, and Thomas loved the crowd.

In their path a fair-haired lad turned a handspring.

"This way," he cried, "this way to the Red Indian!"

"One of ours," laughed George.

"O Thomas, give him a penny," pleaded Anne, her eyes won by the youngster.

"Thank 'ee, sweet lady."

A wrinkled beldame, her head covered with a kerchief, advanced with a sort of whinny.

"Cross my palm with silver, lady," she said to Mary Carey. "Hansel, lovely ladies, and I'll tell your fortune. Your fortunes, sweet gentlemen." She was like an old witch, yet gypsy-like.

The fine young group, with its escort, came again to a pause, and in the centre of it, with her ingratiating smile, wheeled the beldame. Wrinkled, greasy, with beady eyes, she was just a spaewife at a fair, yet from one to the other she gave a look piercing with a brave vitality that neither time nor hardship could ever quench. She was burningly vivid, with her jagged grin. The greens and reds in her old woollens, her brown skin ingrained with dirt, her golden earrings, made her flagrant against the delicate smoke-grey young ladies. They watched her with a smile not a little nervous.

"See the savage Indian within, my lords," she nicked to the courtiers. "Give him a prick." She touched George's dagger. "Drive it into him, 'tis like your down pillow. He feels no pain, kind gentlemen. I tell the truth. Your fortune, pretty lady!"

"Do, Mademoiselle," said Saint-Même to Mistress Carey. "It could be amusing. May she be lucky in love, old mother?"

The beldame took the pretty, fair Mary by the hand. She gave a little cry. "Lucky in love!" She read the hand. "Look!"—her dirty nail traced a line—"you'll ever follow your fancy!"

Mary snatched away her hand. "Old wife's tale," she laughed. "And now my sister." She stepped behind Anne.

"No, she must not," Anne suddenly pleaded. She put her gauntleted hands behind her back and bit her lip. One fist, doubled up behind her back, was so clenched that it could not be unfolded.

"Nay, 'tis but in sport," Thomas urged.

"Sister Anne," said the rakish George, "let us know the worst. Let her read you."

Anne pouted and tossed her head. She flung out her free hand, uncovered. Her other hand moved nervously as her group bent to listen.

"See that line," mused the beldame. "Fortune, fortune, child of fortune." Her voice rose, as she bent and peered. Anne Boleyn stood tense.

The old woman, with awe in her voice, said, "Up, up, fair lady. The world at your feet!!"

Anne made a move to pluck away her hand. The old woman held it with a rude, strong grip. " 'Tis beyond cavil," she muttered. Then, with a rough lunge, she seized the hand that Anne had hidden. She tore the glove from it, and the deformed hand was exposed.

Her old face changed. She gazed up at Anne with dismay. "Mistress, I misdoubt. Could fortune be your foe?"

As Anne tore away her hand the young English boy rushed into the group with an excited cry. "Ho, ho! The oliphant!"

Out of his booth plunged the dumb Red Indian, in full feather. "Where be the oliphant?" he shouted, and bolted into the crowd.

To escape the wild rush George led them into a sandy wood. Here there was silence. Thomas saw that Anne was very pale, and he dared not speak to her.

They came through the little wood out on a road that passed an inn. Under a chestnut tree in flower an ostler soothed two magnificent stallions. A tall man and his soldierly comrade waved to figures receding in the distance. They turned back laughing. They stopped laughing as they saw the group emerge from the wood with a guard attending them.

## X

George boleyn promptly went on a knee, uncovering. So did Saint-Même and Thomas Wyatt. The three girls curtseyed to the ground. Before them, haughtily surprised at their intrusion, stood Henry VIII.

Henry was the first to recover. A man of thirty, or just under it, to Anne he was a gorgeous sight, ruddy, brightly blond, with his sparse golden beard. He looked at them, his blue eyes sparkling, with his air of well-being, noble breeding and confident authority. He could see their coming was an accident, and his slight frown gave way to a brief, courtly greeting.

"Who is the boy?" he quickly muttered to his aide.

"Young Wyatt," Norris told his short-sighted master.

"Forsooth!" He then waved to the road. "Ye come late," he said in his light voice. "I have paroled my French brother. This morning

he made himself my prisoner, in my own bedchamber, but, by my
soul, he paid good ransom." Out of his bosom he took a bracelet.

"Mistress Mary"—he laid it in her hands—"do you pronounce it
dainty?"

Mary exclaimed with delight.

Henry turned gaily to Saint-Même. "So, my friend Saint-Même,
you are in good hands."

"On parole, your Grace."

"And with an escort," said Henry. "You left London in my surcoat. Think you to step into my shoes?" And he glanced at Mary.
"He treats you well?" he said to her.

Mary shook her head, and Henry bent to her with a laugh.

"Now he forgets us," Harry Norris said to Anne, whose pale childlike face attracted him. Anne smiled faintly.

But Henry had not forgotten.

"All goes well?" he asked Saint-Même.

"Marvellous well, thanks to your Grace."

"You won at the lists?"

"In faith, your Grace, by a narrow chance."

"Bravo!" said Henry perfunctorily. "And now, on our way! We
dine at eleven of the clock."

On his great horse he was magnificent. He towered in the little
square, and his glance swept them, the ostler, the common soldiers, the courtiers, the girls. He poised with his weight free above
the hips, his legs gripping powerfully and with suppleness. He was a
master. Throughout the tournament he had met none to rival him. He
had proved his crashing strength, riding one horse till it died, shivering lances by the score, never shirking, never flagging. His vanity
had just been teased by the little visit from King Francis. He now
pivoted his stallion with superb dexterity, made it prance, and then
spurred wildly forward.

Mary took his parting salute.

"Lucky in love," smiled Saint-Même with his square not very white
teeth.

"How now!" said George. "Was he not bully?"

They stood gazing toward Guines, breathless with the accident
of meeting him, and the brilliance of his departure.

# Chapter 5

ANNE CAME HOME so tired that night she could have tumbled into bed anywhere and slept like a stone. Even the truckle bed that did camp service for minor beings like herself was welcome. The palliasse was straw, the sheets coarse linen, but her head soon lay in calm profile on the pillow, the quilt rising and falling as placidly as a summer sea at dawn. She was not naked in the bed, in spite of custom, but wearing a night-rail of fine linen, the last word in French refinement. Hers was a quick, piquant face in the day world, but under its frilled nightcap it was defenceless in the repose of sleep, childlike and inexperienced. Her thin arm had strayed from under the cover, and gave an involuntary jerk. She was dreaming.

The room was plainly improvised. The partitions were undressed wood, from which a medley of clothes was hanging. At a rude table stood a rush chair, under the window, and a mate to it had been jammed against the plank door to keep it from being unlatched and pushed open. The floor was bare. Against the wall opposite to Anne stood a second truckle bed, ready for the night but still undisturbed. Anne had surrendered to her fatigue without waiting for her sister.

As her arm jerked for a second time, in some quiver of her fantasy, the Watch that was ordered for the camp passed down below. *"Tout va bien,"* it chanted and faded.

Anne's eyes gaped open. Lifting herself on her elbow, she looked vaguely around, as if in terror. The unoccupied bed caught her glance. Startled, she sat up, brushed the sleep from her eyes, and looked again.

When she had made really sure that the bed was empty her expression sharpened indignantly. In a bound she leaped out of bed.

As she rattled the chair under the door to make sure it would hold, something that had stuck in the rush seat fell to the floor. Anne had to find a sharp bodkin to dig it from the planking. She picked it up, and carried it to the pale morning to examine it further. It was a fine bracelet, with a diamond in it, smaller than the King's. Her indignation gave way to close interest. She opened the clasp carefully, fitted the bracelet on her own thin arm, and then held it away.

"Who gave her that, I'd like to know," she murmured. "And not a word to me!"

She slowly took it off and dropped it on the table. Then she picked it up again. Turning back the covers of the fresh bed she triumphantly planted it between the sheets. As she did it she heard a sound. In a boyish leap she crossed the room and scrambled into bed.

The door was softly pushed inwards. It jammed against the chair, to Anne's delight. Again it was pushed without giving way, and she found herself choking with laughter. Only when the door was vigorously shouldered, and the stout chair fell back with a bump, did she grow serious. Though the hooded mantle was Mary's, this energetic body could not be Mary's. Then a hand lifted the chair: the hand was a man's.

Anne's body tightened with apprehension. The hooded figure was in the centre of the room and her eyes could not leave it. He gently righted the chair and jammed it under the door. As he turned she saw his quick eyes. It was Saint-Même.

*"Tiens!"* He came forward, Mary's mantle falling ridiculously from his shoulders. "I got here before her. And you are here, little Anne."

Anne saw his teeth flash in a smile. He tried to take her hand, but she swept it away, saying nothing, lying rigid.

He laughed. "You do not fear me." He leaned his hand on the wall and bent to her. "One kiss, and I go."

She could feel him near—warm, redolent, wine and perfume equally strong. He was a little drunk. "Only one," and his hand groped to catch Anne to him.

Anne stretched back. Her hand found the steel bodkin on the table. With a quick vindictive dart she drove it into Saint-Même's hand that was planked on the wall.

"Jesu!" he jumped. "You little devil!" His under lip pouted. "You could do that, you wasp!"

Anne's sharp face gleamed at him.

"Body of God!" he muttered, "this is too much. The devil! I must joust to-day."

Her eyes took in his consternation, but she was rigidly still. Then he was on his feet. With a contemptuous shrug he shook off Mary's cloak. He threw the chair from the door, and disappeared.

Anne began to tremble. A flood of frightening excitement ran through her, and she had hardly collected her senses before the latch lifted and in slipped Mary.

Round-faced and pretty, with her long dark lashes, Mary gazed rapidly about her. In the grey light she saw Anne sitting up in bed, holding a steel needle in her hand. The flush in her young sister's face, the dangerous sparkle in her eyes, astonished her no less than her own empty mantle on the floor. Around her shoulders she wore a long man's cloak, which she tightened involuntarily.

"Three o' the clock, Mary Carey," said Anne.

"What has happened?"

Anne's breast heaved. She said nothing.

Mary picked up her mantle. "You say nought," she pouted. "What care I! I make no secrets."

She took off her clothes with amazing swiftness, knelt to say a prayer, and stepped into bed.

Then she shrieked. "What abomination be this?" She plucked something from the bed. It was the bracelet.

"No secrets! No secrets!" Anne burst into shrill, childish, uncontrolled laughter. "Nay, not one secret."

Mary muffled her head in her bed-clothes. Soon she darted it out. "I am not the only one."

Anne stopped laughing. For a moment Mary hesitated, but the tell-

tale mantle caught her eye. "No one hath come from Kent for love
of me."

"Nor for me," flashed Anne.

"Forsooth! Thomas Wyatt is not here for you? Though he is to
marry Bess Brooke."

Anne had meant to fling Saint-Même at her sister, so recently married, but now she said nothing.

" 'Twere idle to deny it," Mary added more gently.

Anne stayed silent, though upheaval threatened her, a passionate
desire to let herself break into tears.

"Nan, forgive me."

Anne's lips trembled. Her sister married, made love to by Saint-
Même, flattered by the King, and now daring to reproach her for
Thomas Wyatt!

"It is nought to me," Anne flared. "He can abide in Kent for all of
me and marry Bess Brooke. But for you to say it!"

She sat up, clutching her bodkin, and again Mary hid her head.

## II

FROM THEN Anne avoided Thomas. Everyone was so active in festivity
that this was passed over, but Anne was outraged and harsh. She
despised Mary's fatuity.

Mary did give her a target. Mary's heart opened to any attractive
man like a door without a lock. Their courtly dissipation, their infidelity and wastefulness, she took them as signs of a free nature that
did not repel so much as touch her, so long as they were not cruel.
She really felt in them an appealingness, a richness of interest, that
made it easy for them to love her, and tender in forsaking her. She
fell but never crashed, and she could be endlessly tender. It revolted
Anne. That a man could sip her and leave her as Saint-Même would
leave Mary, made her curl her lip with contempt. Mary could read it
in her eyes. And she shivered at Anne's concentrated stillness.

## III

THOMAS WYATT could not understand why Anne Boleyn avoided him.
He felt at home with the Hever people. Much as he loved sober

Allington and worshipped his father, it was always with elation that
he had sought Hever. Theirs was a bright world, livelier than his
own. Life was sharper there, tongues quicker, eyes keener. And beneath this sparkle something appealed to him. They—the girls, George
Boleyn, Francis Bryan—were vividly at home in spaces that invited
him, moving in a newer world. Something in this was dazzling and
magical to him.

He was not completely won. George Boleyn and Francis Bryan had
unsparing tongues, and they often jarred him. George boasted he
could overcome any woman, a prowess that flashed in his saucy eyes.
Thomas heard him with envy and desire, but it threatened some
sanctuary in his life, and this laughing audacity to which Francis
Bryan gave rejoinder was brutally disturbing. Yet this shock to his
nature, this intimidation, was submerged in a hunger to share their
freedom; and he was frightened to be frightened. He could not hide
that the very language in which Allington was dumb, the language of
imagination, was possessed by these shameless devils who appalled
him. They were poets. It was this pliancy that excited Thomas.

Everything else was insipid beside this magic of the word. Here
was the accent of an age behind and beyond the pilgrims of Canterbury, an age of sinless marble and classic peace. Very little was
formed in his young mind as yet, but George Boleyn's eagerness and
a few books he had brought with him changed Hever from an
amusing home to an excitement that lured him. George Boleyn had
seen it the day he handed Tom his first book of French poems: imperfect though they were, he saw divinity descend on the lad in his
first startled comprehending glance.

Hever throughout the previous summer had been enchanting.
Francis Bryan picked up his lute on an evening, and then the birch
leaves danced against gold sunset no more sensitively than Thomas
Wyatt's beating heart. He was only sixteen. He could not dare to
play, yet once as he sat with the lute idle in his hands, alive to the
quick wits about him, he had ventured to sing a madrigal. He mastered it from the first, held his note, and, forgetting himself, brought
it to a graceful end. They broke into surprised, warm words, and
after that the group would sing together, taking him to themselves, in
the harmony of their taste, the springing of their nerves.

But it was not the lute and the madrigal alone that brought Thomas
to Hever. He could run or bowl or ride or shoot with any of them,
and he was never more at home than in the pantry at Hever, munch-
ing one of Sarah's apples. With his cap tilted back, and swinging a
long leg, he poised on the corner of the heavy table as he chatted
with old Sarah.

He looked perhaps two or three years older than he was, but his
simplicity was boyish. His full, shapely head was frizzed with auburn
hair that knew little of the barber, and the russet jerkin he wore, with
green leather hose, was well-rubbed and stained by usage. He was
prepossessing. What gave him freshness was the exceeding candour
of his hazel eyes, and their sparkle at whatever Sarah was saying. He
liked to quiz her.

"Time you was married, Master Tom," the abundant Sarah would
say, "I hold not with all this book-learning for a young gentleman of
your mettle. How many years must you to Cambridge? What are they
about, over there at Allington?"

Thomas could only laugh at her. At Cambridge, where he worked
hard, he enlarged his experience, but nothing at Cambridge—not even
Erasmus's remembered transit—was so close to his real self as those
hours inside Hever.

Throughout the summer, bathed in the group, he had swum in a
susceptibility. He believed, he almost knew, that Anne had shared it.
But now, with Anne withdrawn, and George occupied, and Mary
averted, this Hever security in which he had floated was gone from
him. He was reduced to a sharp need of it, but it had no sanction,
nothing to rest on, not even the least syllable, only an airy glance, a
fleeting smile, the most evanescent, intangible, fragile passages of
acquiescence, shining notes that danced away, the rainbow receding.

And even had Thomas wobbled, there was all Allington and all
Cobham to straighten him, not to speak of his father's close friend,
good Bishop Fisher. That, too, was pressing him into marriage. Had
he not gone to Rochester to be counselled by Bishop Fisher! Thomas
had dreaded to encounter him. Even after the shambling clerk had
taken in his name he beat around the cold room to find an escape.
But the name Wyatt was too potent for that: it was the Bishop him-

self who came out to him, and not a motion or a syllable of it had faded from Thomas's mind.

He could still see John Fisher. His face was worn to the bone, yet no weakness marred his tall, angular frame. He had no sooner entered than his dauntless eyes were fixed on Thomas with the flame that lives within. For a second he knitted his thick brows, peering hard at Thomas, and then in a magical voice, resonant as a viol, he made him welcome. "Is this Thomas?" he cried. "A mighty fellow like this? Come, you are cold here, come to the fire." With a bony hand light on Thomas's shoulder, he steered him to the next chamber.

This inner room was a long one. The candles that stood on the trestle cast wan light on many books, some in crinkled vellum, some squat volumes, some leather-bound folios. A pair of old slippers lay slack under the high chair. In the alcove Thomas could see a prie-dieu under a wooden crucifix, and against the wall a blemished statue of St. Andrew. The log-fire glowed kindly on the hearth, gilding the scoured planks and reddening the lime-white walls.

John Fisher seated his young guest and turned his unsparing gaze on him. Thomas felt how hard it would be to urge his own nebulous will against the dogged resoluteness of those jaws. This was the old, the faithful England.

"This is a welcome sight, Thomas, before you return to my beloved college. You go back on the morrow?"

"Yea, my lord bishop."

"And Greek takes root there?"

"Thanks to your lordship."

"Nay, Thomas. This we owe to Erasmus. A fretful soul, oft a torment to himself"—the Bishop gave a rugged laugh—"but our faithful bell-wether at Cambridge. Here comes a sup of wine. Refresh yourself, Thomas. Good cheer, my son."

Thomas took a goblet from the clerk.

"And now," when they were alone, "your road lies clear before you?"

"Save for one thing, my lord."

"What stands in your way, my child?"

"My good father speaks of my marrying Lord Cobham's daughter Bess."

"That lovely child? I know her from the cradle. These be glad tidings, Thomas."

Thomas bent his head.

"You incline elsewhere? You are otherwhere engaged?"

Thomas shook his head.

"Has there been aught elsewhere? A pledge? An overt act?"

"Not so, my lord."

"And your father's wish has weight with you, Thomas?"

"Yea, my lord."

"And so it should. Hark, Thomas, fond inclination is the mark of youth. Yet if your choice be made, God strengthens you to fulfil it. I have a friend, the best man living, who leaned to a younger sister yet chose the elder, and never hath ceased to thank his God for it. That good man's father, a merry sage, oft hath said that matrimony is a perilous chance, a blind bag full of snakes and eels together, and if you put your hand into it—it is seven snakes for one eel!" The Bishop laughed, somewhat gratingly, and Thomas winced a smile.

"Yea," he resumed his deep tone; "high or low, the heart is wayward, and without grace matrimony a vale of tears."

Silence fell on them, the Bishop cracking his bony fingers. Thomas gazed at the fire as it consumed itself in beauty, and such misery rose in him that he could not speak.

"I see your father in you," the Bishop had added in a quiet, gentle voice. "To obey him is God's bidding. Blessings attend you."

Thomas remembered watching the log crumble into the fire that it had fed. With an effort he had mastered his voice to thank the good Bishop. He knew no way to combat him.

This was not yet a year ago. And he was to be married in a few weeks.

## IV

THE PROSPECT of his marriage did not then revolt Thomas. Allington and Cobham always made marriages in this fashion, and Rochester always approved of them. But, in spite of his submission, the Field of the Cloth of Gold suddenly became dull for him.

Thomas was seventeen, the golden age, yet when he went out into the morning nothing could have seemed to him more squalid than this Field of Gold. Against this, at least, the nearest thing to him, he vigorously and blindly revolted.

He had a few duties in the Queen's chamber, as a minor clerk of the jewels. Then he escaped. From one quarter to another he strode restlessly, trying to decide whether to see the Boleyns or ignore them. He had a distaste for human society. He even laughed at himself, he was so inexplicably miserable.

He walked through the crowd, without seeing anyone, possessed by his young malaise. The parkways were still green, and the sod trembled with cantering squads of noble French and English. Thomas Wyatt did not see them. Their trappings were as superb as could be devised. Damsels would lean from the galleries to applaud them and the day would seem glorious to the victors. A trumpet bragged in the distance. It must be beginning. But he walked on, dull and desolate and contemptuous. He could imagine the lists, great names blown in the air like the wine tossing and looping from the fountains. To him it now meant nothing. Knights in armour rode by, high-nosed and hawk-eyed, their visors open, and behind them he could imagine manors hidden in the provinces where their lordship meant a grip on a few dozen fighting men, with sleepy villages nearby and rude fields bosoming the manor as the sea does a ship. Any one of them was happier than he, any one more fortunate. He could tell by their bearing that this tournament was their meat and drink. They pressed forward, flashing and undaunted. From early dawn, when the camp began to stir, to its last palpitation under the stars, these knights crackled with every little episode, every accident, as brave and stout at the end as the beginning. They and their healthy peace of mind were a million miles from Thomas.

He walked toward Ardres, his feet two traitors who heeded his disloyal heart, drawing him to the bitter medicine he craved for it. Already his prompt imagination had told him Anne could not help him. He hated himself for seeking her, but his heart cried to him from the chasm of misery, cried with a desolation he could not stifle. It was useless to see her, he told himself, as he neared her quarters. She would not be there. She would not see him.

She was not there. He went away dully.

## V

THOMAS WANDERED AIMLESS in the narrow streets of Ardres. The sound of minstrels playing brightly did not lure him, but as he turned a corner he saw them coming, wearing new gear of yellow and russet, with white damask. On their heels he saw revellers from far lands, with visors on their faces. They were ten young lords from Revel and Riga, a varlet told him. They wore hats made in Dantzig, with purses and girdles of sealskin, and their short cloaks of crimson velvet were scrolled. Thomas saw their curious shoes, studded with white-headed nails. After them came elderly lords with high velvet standing caps, in gowns of blue satin, and behind them were a third band in long garments of pale rich cloth of gold, the gowns lined with green taffeta.

These were "Esthonians" and "Livonians" on their way to the French Queen. It would be there, then, that Anne would be. They would dance with her, Thomas guessed, and feast on spices and fruits and jellies and rare viands. Then they would unmask, and everyone would be merry. It made his heart sick to think of it.

Next evening he stood under a gallery, at Guines, where they danced again. Anne had seen him, but Harry Norris had singled her out, and she and the older courtier were visibly amused in one another's company. He watched them bitterly. The music goaded him. The brilliant costumes rasped him. The melting grace with which Anne danced seemed to him coquettish and insincere. He was restless; enticed and antagonized. A combativeness rose in him that made him stay.

Beth Darrell, lovely in white and gold, saw him under the gallery. She beckoned to him.

"When go you hence?" she asked.

"On the morrow, Beth. I go to see Paris."

"And then the wedding, Thomas?"

"Yea, then the wedding."

Beth was silent. So was Thomas. He wanted to say, "Why is Anne angry?" but he dared not. Beth knew his mind.

"Anne felt mazed"—she spoke in a low voice—"that you never spoke of Bess Brooke to her. She knew naught of it——"

"But George knew, you knew, and Mary——"

"Anne knew nothing."

Then it was this.

"Speak to her to-night," said Beth Darrell.

Thomas waited until he found Anne alone. His face was peculiarly pale, his eyes darker than usual.

"You avoid me, Anne."

She looked at him coolly. "I, Thomas? I do not avoid you."

"I leave on the morrow."

"Then fare well, good Thomas."

They stood facing one another, their eyes wavering.

"And, oh, Thomas, God bless you!"

## VI

THOMAS WAS GONE. Mary was naughty. George was flighty. And yet the Camp du Drap d'Or was irresistible. Anne was in fresh high spirits when she joined the maids to attend Queen Claude to the great royal banquet.

King Henry was its guest of honour. He came from Guines just as the French entered the royal pavilion that connected with the banqueting tent, and Anne saw the sisterly kiss with which Queen Catherine greeted Queen Claude. The daughter of Isabella had much in common with the daughter of Anne of Brittany—equally pious, calm and solemn. Each had to keep the snow of purity white in the Courts around them. Anne felt the chances were not promising.

Magnificently clad, Henry filled the tent with his vigour. Anne could not tell whether or not he had seen her as, with an impatient hot glance, he scanned the tent. It had been a great day for England, and the victories at the wrestling had been liquidly celebrated. Anne saw him turn to Sir William Compton with his flushed, exuberant look, to make some remark that made them laugh. At that moment King Francis, no less sumptuously clad, advanced with his most gracious smile to greet Queen Catherine when, just as he was about to bend, the English king stepped in front of his wife.

"One last bout," he cried in French, "I would wrestle with you, brother."

This was a burst of energy on the eve of the banquet! Anne saw Francis step back, his eyebrows raised, his hands outspread, when, before anyone could think, the massive Henry clinched with him and held him in a bear's hug.

With amazing quickness Anne retreated. So did everyone else. The two grappling Kings were in a clear space in the little tent.

The grip Henry took was so strong, and his intention so brusque and so humiliating, that Francis's face became steel. With a quick, savage twist, he flung Henry across his leg, tripped him, and sent him sprawling.

Henry touched the ground. Anne felt it was shameful to have him thrown. He bounded to his feet, gigantic. He was out of temper and dangerous.

"Have at you again," he roared, and groped forward.

Before he could grip Francis both Catherine and Claude, in a common impulse, rushed in. Anne feared that the two men might forget Queen Claude, but she heard Catherine cry firmly, "Henry, it is time for supper." Marguerite d'Alençon laid her hand on Francis's arm.

Anne did not tremble. The polite surface had cracked, yet the girl's nerves were not shaken. "They are like that," she suddenly recognized, with a strange, hard practicality. Henry, Francis, Saint-Même—that is what men were like! Anne's eyes glinted, and she absorbed every move with intense curiosity. Francis muttered to his sister, *"Que veux-tu?"* Then, with a clang in their throats that was rasping, the silver trumpets sounded for the banquet. Henry forced a smile. He offered his arm to Queen Claude, who took it like a frightened little girl.

As they walked in, a procession from the main entrance advanced at the same time. Gentlemen in red and gold livery preceded porters carrying silver pillars and silver crosses. Cardinal Wolsey was also arriving.

## VII

HOWEVER they might glare and wrestle, the young barbarians, Cardinal Wolsey was well satisfied by this blustering June in France. In the coming war the French could not hide the fact that they had real need of him, and up to the last moment of his departure they courted him. Wolsey had discerned their two deepest weaknesses—their bad finances and their sulky Bourbon. He had pressed for terms without shame, and every old quarrel, every outstanding obligation, had been considered and revised in the light of the services that England might render. Even Scotland was to be sacrificed, if that had to be.

The Cardinal rode superbly to Calais. He was now armed for the next negotiation because there, with a small retinue, the young Emperor was waiting to meet himself and Henry VIII.

The germ of an alliance was in that second meeting. And out of it, exactly two years later, came the open espousal of the Emperor's cause. That was the sequel the Cardinal had worked for. It brought the young Emperor to Greenwich.

## VIII

THERE WERE PLENTY of Francis's pensioners at Greenwich, and they viewed the new alliance coolly enough, but the old nobility took it as the right, the natural state of affairs. Crecy and Poitiers and Agincourt were still in their minds. And Queen Catherine herself blossomed at this alliance with her nephew. His arrival at Greenwich in 1522 was perhaps the last high point in her life.

For his actual arrival she had to wait hour by hour, as he came up the Thames. A loud peal of cannon at last told her that the royal barges, thirty of them, were seen to be approaching. It had taken them five hours to toil up from Gravesend, and they were due at six of the clock.

The Queen, so calm as a rule, had never ceased inquiring the hour. Those who knew her as well as Lady Boleyn could read her mood, and even Anne marked the restlessness of her plump moist hands and the anxiety of her strained white face.

She seemed more Spanish than ever, forgetting her English after twenty years, nervously shepherding her child. But when the faithful Griffith whispered it was time to go down the Queen hurried with the Princess Mary to the hall door, to seat herself with majesty under the gilt canopy. On either side of the red carpet stood the nobles, and Princess Mary, seven years old, looked this way and that to study every feature of the arrival of the Emperor who was to marry her.

It was precisely six when Charles V stepped from the barge. He marched with slow paces to where his aunt was sitting. He knelt before her and kissed her hand. Catherine made him rise. Everything the exiled woman lived for was conveyed in her fond gaze and her trembling hands. She had adored her mother Isabella; here was Isabella's grandson, ally to her husband. Behind him, in the fleet of decorated barges that flowered in the river, were all the princes and all the grandees who were to accompany him to Spain, the Council of Castile, the Council of Aragon, the Council of Flanders, his chamberlains, his archers, his chaplains, several thousand persons. The hand she clasped, as he arose, would sign the treaty making Mary his wife; the Spaniard in Queen Catherine, the Catholic in her, the wife in her, the mother in her, mounted to supreme satisfaction as Greenwich opened to welcome this nephew of hers, the youth on whose Empire the sun could never set.

The ladies of the Court, several of them beauties who had come with Catherine twenty years before, stood gazing raptly at Charles. So did Mary, her pinched, white face tilted upwards. She screwed her little myopic eyes to see her future husband.

It was now the King's turn to do the honours. Henry's blond effulgence was notable as he came flashing in cloth of silver and shining jewels.

At the side of such a being the young Emperor was almost diminutive. In reality he was of medium height and erect bearing, but he wore black and had few jewels, and the sombreness of his figure was increased by his pale, immobile face. He was white-skinned, as if anæmic, and he breathed through his mouth, his projecting jaw somewhat askew. This gave his eyes a strained look, as if he were staring, but so cool was his pace, so measured the glance he bestowed on the sumptuousness around him, so serious his response to obeisance and reverence, that at once he instilled confidence in the Court. If there was no animal prowess in his modest frame there was a reserve power, the proof of a nature tenacious and sedate. Behind him lay Flanders, the Holy Roman Empire, and the heritage of Spain. The New World he shared with Portugal. Where Henry had need to promote his new monarchy, to push and improvise, Charles came from illimitable dominions, and a treaty with England was no proof that he was weak. Behind him were a host of advisers, some like Gattinara the match for Cardinal Wolsey, but already he was the captain of his ship. He had chosen the recent Pope and would name the next. Where Henry mustered thirty vessels, Charles had arrived with two hundred, and while he had never yet led a campaign or acted the Renaissance prince, he was a tireless worker, able to joust with the best of them, and learning patiently to twist his tongue around other languages than his native French. This devoted will that he brought to the discharge of his duties had been trained from boyhood. He was King of Spain at sixteen and Emperor at nineteen. He had never run loose, never followed his fancy, never gambolled. Both he and his ally Henry reinforced their kingly code by a Catholicism that had just lodged Charles at one Bishop's palace at Canterbury and next with Bishop Fisher at Rochester, with the Cardinal to greet him on Dover strand. But where Henry bowed to the Church, Charles held its reins, whipping the Pope to pull him over rough places. His was a conservatism that would ask much of a Europe beginning to read books. But since Charles V had been born to the sceptre he was unable to imagine the rude force that could dislodge a Martin Luther from tradition and drive him to rebellion. That self-identification with God which is so common with rebels who read a Holy Book is even more characteristic of princes whose holy books are furniture. Charles had doubts of others but little of himself. He was cautious, but not modest. His career was to impose narrow sovereignty on its widest basis, so that nothing could shake its rigidity other than endless series of hideous and inevitable convulsions.

It was to this guarded and laconic youth that Cardinal Wolsey looked for the Papal throne. And Henry hoped with this tight wedge to splinter the kingdom of France.

Thomas Wyatt, clerk of the jewels, had his place in the procession that entered the great hall. He searched in vain for a sign of accessible humanity in the young Emperor's pallid visage. He thought him cold and bleak and intensely self-important. Thomas thanked God that, instead of enduring a tedious month of ceremony, he was now to go at once to the Scottish border, where there was secret preparation for war. Then he was to go with messages to Calais.

It was on his return from Calais, early in 1523, that he walked into the heart that had never before opened to him.

And, early in 1523, Cardinal Wolsey was launching England into the great war.

# Chapter 6

GREENWICH PALACE, WHERE Anne was now so at home again, had aspects to which she was still blind. Placentia they called it, a place of pleasure; and by the way it received and banqueted an Emperor, by the way it greeted and entertained ambassadors, by the frolic at Christmas, the combats in the tiltyard, the drolleries, the masques, the music and the dance, it was indeed one of the merriest of royal residences. Hundreds lived there, in the simple long buildings that viewed the Thames. The country lay open behind it, the city came to it by road, and the sea and the river clasped within sight of it. But merry as it was, especially to so quick a temperament as Anne Boleyn's, to regard leisure as its mood and pleasure as its aim would be to see her in the falsest of settings. The Court was a workshop. Poetry and women were at home in it, but it existed to grapple with something besides poetry and women. It was a theatre of power. It existed for the State. The men who came there, gallants as they seemed, coated in gold or in satin, mounted and attended—the very picture of nonchalance and ease; they were soldiers, magistrates, ambassadors, governors, councillors, a host of willing and obedient servants. Anne Boleyn's life was now renewed at the very centre of a creative impulse. She was paired with the men who were at the helm in England.

Yet on this June day in 1523 they were directing it in combination with a game of tennis. In spite of the cool air off the river, the sunshine was kindness itself—young sunshine before the dog days, so full of balm that it was itself an invitation to play, amiable on the fresh leafage and the new-cut grass. And the game was in progress out of doors.

The King and Harry Norris were hard at it, while in the improvised gallery there stood or sat a throng of Henry's Court, some of them wearing the blue and black velvet coats that Henry chose for tennis players, but most of them costumed splendidly and waiting faithfully to dine at Greenwich. It was a day for the council, with the Cardinal to preside over them, and the campaigns to be finally considered.

Henry loved tennis so insatiably that he made the best of this temporary ground. He was sweating regally as he played, his silk shirt of a fair white that clung to him in patches of pink. He seemed, somehow, to become more red-haired and Celtic as he warmed to the game. He had a crashing stroke when the ball was at his mercy, was agile when need be, yet saving himself from running by foresight, with all the wile and precision of an old hand.

The men who now gathered about him were, for the most part, his soldiers, and they watched him with that sober satisfaction which quietens any social circle when the centre is acknowledged and stable.

Henry, to judge by his spectators on this pleasant morning, could afford to keep them waiting until he had finished his game of tennis. Above everything he knew how to hold and mould a Court.

They were all there—the sharp little Earl of Surrey, Anne's uncle, her somewhat oblique father, the stalwart Duke of Suffolk, with any number of the honest warhorses whom Henry employed in every office—Thomas Cheyney, William Kingston, Richard Weston, Wingfields and Guildfords, George Cobham and Anthony Brown. A number of them had been knighted for hardiness and noble courage the year previous, and now they were ready to divide themselves for the coming campaigns, the one against France and the one against Scotland. Useful with heavy sword or long spear, these were not only

courtiers but often landlords who could bring their little troops of followers with them—Marney, Powys, Curzon, Greville, Oliver Manners, Robert Jerningham, Edward Seymour, Richard Sandes. Through
them, so to speak, the land of England itself rose up and fought for
Henry. It was the ploughshare becoming the sword.

And this obedience, this hardiness and noble courage, Henry could
count on, after bloody years of doubt and confusion, years so terrible
that Henry could behead a Buckingham or any other servant of his,
and still be sure of this martial England he so adroitly and so know-
ingly assembled, an England happy for the buoyant giant who had
emerged as King.

They rejoiced in him for one thing: he gave them cohesion. The
sort of quarrel that divided Kildare and Butler in Ireland, Campbell
and Douglas in Scotland, or for that matter Bourbon and his master
in France—the bitter emulation of fighting animals—this sort of quarrel had, luckily for England, been worked to its dreadful end in
the bloodiest of civil wars, of which the older nobility, who clung to
Queen Catherine, still bore the cicatrice.

These Wars of the Roses had finally educated the ruling class to one
thing—cohesion. And Henry was the symbol of their will to cohere.
Through him they were making themselves a modern state.

Savage as their tempers could be, and violently as they ground one
against the other, they now had subdued their savagery and violence
to the necessity of a new system, this system of the national state that
Henry shaped for them, under Wolsey's masterly hand. Henry was
one of themselves by body, the most active of them, but also by his
brain and by his quick will, their commander at Greenwich and
Richmond and Windsor and Westminster, the captain of their habit
and their routine.

Even this tennis game was part of it. Self-willed as he was, he
knew what he was doing.

They were lords under him, territorial lords, land-lords, and because of this, war-lords. To employ them as such was as necessary as
to walk the dogs. Such lordship was not, however, a mere prowess of
brute property and brute strength, though this was the foundation of
it. These valiant land-lords and squires had also to give Henry his
councillors. He had to send John Wallop or the Wingfields abroad,

John Russell or William Fitzwilliam, Thomas Boleyn or Francis Bryan, Thomas Cheyney, Nicholas Carew or Francis Poyntz. Gentlemen at his own Court, they had to bear themselves proudly enough to go to a Valois or a Hapsburg or a Medici, to speak languages and write despatches, to be, in a word, Henry's spokesmen when they were not officers of his household or soldiers in the field.

Such flexibility widened their uses and multiplied the emotions that were appropriate for them. Some of them hated to be scribblers and dodged their brain work, but these found themselves set aside. The best of them were men of European mould. But besides this inflection —and Henry was an admirable judge of it—they were cohesive on other terms and inflected in other regions: they intermarried, they had establishments, their little wheels were cogged to fit into the other little wheels, and this machine of a ruling caste was intended to move as a whole, whatever fine romance and whatever gallantry they were idly inclined to. But, naturally, since they did intermarry and since the Queen's chamber was an integral part of Greenwich, the place of women in this world of male egoists was of immense importance, tempering and subtilizing and in many ways motivating the strange institution called the Court. For though it had its blood rites, though its best men had to kill, cohesion in that gallant society had other roots. The priests, dependent as they seemed, never ceased to exploit and insinuate their own ways of cohering, and the women divided into two groups: those who gained their ends by beguiling their males, and those others who, like Queen Catherine herself, while closing their eyes to many foibles, strove to bend the finer breed to other ends than amusement and even had gleams of another purpose than war. Thus there was an incessant swirl inside the Court, a ceaseless process of choice and many a shift in purpose, many a change.

The war-lords strained against the Priest. There were courtly bishops, amenable ones; but Thomas Wolsey, the son of a butcher? All their prejudices were aroused by this supple Chancellor. Yet Henry allowed this Priest to rule them. Powerful and genial, a warlord with themselves, he still was well-languaged, versed in the minor arts, a student, the writer of a book. Nothing said more for his power than that he could rule them through Wolsey. But even that was only secondary to his greater power—this power to mould a Court.

As for the People, they paid or resisted taxes. They were given the parliament to play with—the parliament of which Thomas Cromwell was a member and at which he had so recently smiled and shrugged.

The People! Even the Pope had just exclaimed at their arrogance. They were beginning to tell the Prince how to behave!

"I have never read, heard nor known that Prince's counsellors and prelates should be appointed by rude and ignorant common people." So Henry himself would come to exclaim. Brute and beastly people! "We pray unto Almighty God to give you grace to do your duties, and to use yourselves towards us like true and faithful subjects, . . . rather than by your obstinacy and wilfulness to put yourselves, your lives and wives, children, lands, goods and chattels, besides the indignation of God, in the utter adventure of total destruction, and utter ruin by force and violence of the sword."

The sword would answer the People if they should clash with their Prince. "What madness is entered into their heads!" Henry would cry out. Out of Luther, out of Wyclif, out of John Huss, must come such mischief, such folly and ingratitude and unkindness to their Prince and sovereign lord. Henry could be angry with his naughty children, the People.

## II

But, for all the loyalty he inspired, his tennis took too long.

Surrey tilted his sardonic nose. He gave Thomas Boleyn the edge of his glance. "Good God!" he groaned, as a new game began; and he deliberately looked away to accuse the too amiable sky.

He was the old Duke of Norfolk's heir, still waiting at fifty for the church bells to ring his father into Heaven and himself into the Dukedom. He was proud, he was poor, and he was caustic. He liked to sting his brother-in-law Boleyn.

Thomas Boleyn, Anne's father, was correct as a yardstick and groomed to the last hair. He had eyelids that drooped petulantly and he could be quite rude and disdainful, but he was afraid of Surrey.

"You stand about like this?" Surrey muttered in his acrid way. "Then I marvel not at the things that are left undone. God knows what will happen when his Grace be entirely at their mercy."

"Whose mercy?" mumbled Boleyn.

"These gentlemen of his House," sneered Surrey. "These dancers and dicers who never leave him. His Household. You know them all, I wot."

"But he must have a Household. He must have his game of tennis."

"Yea, and we pay dear for it."

"Is he not well served, my lord?" Boleyn asked with his oblique dart of a look.

"He'll not be well served if this endure," said Surrey curtly. "The day of battle comes, Master Boleyn. Men without experience of war shall do small service, and experience of war will not be had by carders and dancers and dicers. It will not be had without it be sought for and adventure given."

"Oh, the day of battle," muttered Boleyn. He knew these old soldiers. "Ah, now, methinks, the play is over."

There had been a purse under the rope, and the gamesters were in a group, Francis Bryan and half a dozen of them, with meek Will Carey at their heels and the Duke of Suffolk going forward.

A tall, graceful man, Suffolk did not press to reach the King. He looked down at the eager group with his drowsy eye and, when they caught sight of him, passed through to Henry with his smile.

Brandon he was born, son of the standard bearer whom Richard III himself had slain, and brought up from the first as Henry's "fellow." He was agreeable to look at, his cheeks tanned, his hair a golden thatch, his eyes blue as the sea. He had mown down many women before he proved irresistible to Henry's seventeen-year-old sister Mary, and married her out of hand. The Norfolks had been furious that this Brandon made himself brother-in-law to the King, and but for Wolsey he had been beheaded, but now he was back in favour, and so at ease in Zion that even Surrey could not upset him. He was taller than anyone else and Henry brightened to see his fellow. "Later, my lord of Suffolk," he nodded. Then he turned to Harry Norris, another tall man.

"A stout battle." The King slapped Norris's shoulder.

"You showed no mercy, sir," murmured the equerry, who had won the purse.

Henry made a disowning gesture. He glanced at Suffolk. "Our next game will be in France," he cried. "But now"—he heard the clock—"by the Mass, I do delay the Cardinal." With brisk, impatient nods he smiled his way clear of everyone, flinging his tennis things to the keeper and hurrying to change.

## III

"BRERETON!" he called as he swept through ante-chamber and privy-chamber.

His bedchamber, the door closed by Brereton, was bright in the sunlight, but garnished in a ponderous style, with a crucifix prominent and many religious symbols.

"Those doublets," said the King. There was a humble throne by his bedside, but he was soon on his feet and a dry shirt was agreeable to his warm, strong body. He flapped his arms like blunt wings, to feel at ease. In a moment he was trying on, and discarding, his pompous doublets, muttering comments. He studied his figure critically in the long glass, standing this way and that, talking in jerks, spurts of positive force, a play of observation on his face, despite a certain wilful and gusty expression.

"It doth become me? It sits me well?"

"This one could not be bested, your Grace."

"So methinketh. An English cutter, Brereton. The French may do women better, but for men we outdo them all."

He examined himself. "Yea," he mused, "the French have an eye for women." This profound truth he liked so well that he repeated it. "Mistress Anne Boleyn brought pretty coifs from France."

"I did not know, sir."

"Mistress Carey's sister. Whom doth she affect?"

"Mistress Carey, sir?"

Henry shot a glance at him. He compressed his lips. "Mistress Anne."

"I know not, sir. Be this to your Grace's liking?" He held up a surcoat.

"No. That one with red. You gave word to Mistress Carey?"

"In sooth, your Grace. At two of the clock, in the Model Chamber." He sprinkled perfume on his master. "Your Grace's handkercher."

"Now for the Cardinal! I would not have delayed him."

Brereton, a small dark youth with a hot face, went to his knee as the King passed from the bedchamber.


## IV

HENRY WAS SHOCKED as he entered. Often as Wolsey was ill his recoveries were quick, and it was only the other day that Henry had seen him. But so faint was the voice that now greeted him, and so grey with fatigue the face, that he made the Cardinal keep his chair. Himself fresh from tennis, abundantly vigorous and his appetite healthily edged, he had a slight revulsion, which he concealed.

There was a strain at the beginning, due to this unspoken check, and Wolsey felt it. He was a careworn man by the side of a master so robust, and he flagged after his morning's toil. He had told the Commons that he would rather have his tongue plucked out of his head with a pair of pincers than to move the King to take any less than the enormous sum he had demanded—a fifth part of every man's goods and lands—but the insuperable difficulties of war taxation were preying on him. Yet as he droned about the Duke of Suffolk and the Earl of Surrey a flick of a smile crinkled his face; Bourbon had sent word he would receive John Russell. The French King's cousin committed himself to revolt, to burst the seams of France.

Wolsey's drooping eyes kindled as he mentioned this, and the change was extraordinary. It was as if a sombre mountain, crouched dully between its paws, was touched swiftly and emblazoned by the sun, throwing off its mantle without a move, erecting its head, enlivening its body. The light from this mobile countenance that until now had been a clay mask shot into Henry, whose heart bounded with reassurance. His Cardinal could think for him and plan for him. They were in harmony.

Conscious of this renewed sympathy, Wolsey's voice became firmer. He touched on the prospects of a war that he himself had manipulated as peacemaker. He revealed that he meant to consign Surrey to the humble war against Scotland rather than the glories of capturing Paris. To this Henry agreed. And then so deftly did he paint the approaching conquest that Henry's face suddenly flushed. He stood up and burst into speech.

"They name Madame Louise as governor of France!" He bared his teeth in a short smile. "Marry, that needs not be."

The Cardinal looked at him expectantly.

"I trust in God to be their governor myself," said Henry loudly. "Let them make a way for me as King Richard did for my father!"

That was good enough. The Cardinal considered Henry to be at the right heat for his Council.

## V

THE COUNCIL was meeting when Anne descended into the garden, to find Thomas at the fountain.

"What is afoot I know not," she said hurriedly, "but Mary is sore troubled."

"You have seen her?"

"For a moment. She was most distant and unnatural. Oh, Thomas, sometimes I cannot breathe here."

Anne was so troubled herself that Thomas exclaimed, "But this morning you were merry!"

"So was I. I had not seen her." She bit her lip, and then quite abruptly broke into tears. She sobbed in his arms.

"Cannot your mother——"

"Oh, mother"—Anne shook her head—"father! mother! Will Carey!"

Anne's misery stopped her voice. She could not control herself at first. Then she pushed him away and looked at him.

"This is an affliction to you. I have no right to afflict you."

Thomas smiled. Then he murmured, "Is it his Grace, Anne?"

Anne nodded. "Mary is distraught." She dabbled her hand in the fountain and stroked her eyes. "This has affected me, I know not why." She gazed at Thomas wistfully and pleadingly. "You are also a man—and yet!" She kissed him.

This was so unlike Anne's earlier moods, and so painfully moving, that Thomas mused over it when she left him. He had never given much heed to Mary.

## VI

IT WAS TWO MINUTES before two when Henry let himself into his little armoury, crowded with models of ships, models of siege implements and implements of war. Here he was himself designing new armour. He glanced at the clock and then at the new headpiece he was shaping, by which he was so fascinated that Mary Carey had slipped secretly into the room, carrying a basket, before he had even heard her.

"This," he said, "is a new harness of my own device and fashion. Here, you may mark——"

Mary did not see anything. She gazed at him.

"What have you there?"

"Strawberries for her Grace," she said. "They came from Hever."

"Are they ripe?" His face was brightly eager, though the basket was closed.

"How now!" Henry opened the basket. "You'll allow me?"

Mary's eyes followed him as he began to eat the strawberries.

"Come, my pet," he said generously. "They are so wondrous sweet."

This kind offer Mary ignored. Usually quick to sparkle, she now stood mutely before him. She seemed to seek for something in him, but hopelessly, as by dumb instinct. Then, putting her hand over the basket, she pleaded, "They were for her Grace."

"You are pale," he saw. "You are not yourself."

Mary bent her head.

"Come, let us sit down." They sat on the day-bed. He patted her shoulder. "Head high, Mary." But Mary still bent her head, with her lashes black against her cheek.

"How now! You were not like this before," he said. "Be it that you are with child again, *m'amie?*"

She moved her head and pressed it against him.

"I'll send Mother Butts to you, dearling. 'Twill be for your greater ease to be near her here. Yes, and you have the house here."

It was, indeed, convenient. Henry had provided the house. He had provided Will Carey. He would provide Mother Butts. Yet a void there was which, had she the words or the courage, Mary would like to convey. But he was too dominant, she feared him. Her father, her mother and Will Carey owed so much to him.

Henry loved Mary's unspoiled nature, and the absence of guile in her. All the Boleyn women were different: the mother as cool as a pearl, Anne clear like a diamond, and Mary opaline. But this muteness troubled him.

"You must not fret," he said. "Be brave, my little one. And you'll call him Henry if it be a boy."

"May I?" She brightened.

"By God, you must," said Henry proudly. "He'll be my jewel."

One of her hands clambered up to his shoulder and she propped her head hard against him. Henry was touched.

"God will protect you," he said. "I'll have the Observants pray for you."

It was now half-past two.

"If you wish to catch her Grace with those rare strawberries." Henry slowly disengaged her. "I must to my Lord of Suffolk."

Mary watched him rise, and as he did so her rounded, somewhat immature features were convulsed by a sudden grimace. She was about to cry.

"I'll go first," he said hurriedly.

"Only yourself," Mary broke out, "always yourself."

"But, Mary!"

"I know I am nothing. Forgive me, sir. But this time I feel so hopeless."

The tears like clear water rolled down her cheek. Henry's jaw dropped. This was very painful to him.

She waved him out with a kind of childlike desperateness.

## VII

BUT MARY, whose desperateness could not find words, had little power to act on it. She was in a net, and as she struggled she wearied herself without freeing herself. Her mother could see it. Mary was not her fresh self. She had lost her light charm and sparkle. It was best, then, since the Court was soon emptied of its fighting men and Henry about to go hunting, that Mary should be taken to Hever.

Lady Boleyn had her own permanent apartments at Greenwich, as lady-in-waiting to the Queen, but she was aware that the little Carey household was tense with an obscure emotion, and Mary was summoned to her mother as often as possible.

Very soft and dimpled was Mary, pale as she was, by the side of her mother.

Lady Boleyn could cool Mary's fever merely by asking her to her bedchamber. By the time a crystal flask of toilet water had been sent for and bobbed into the room by a housekeeper and received by Mistress Jane Parker and passed to the carved chest that served as a toilet table, Mary was no longer congested with inconvenient and inappropriate emotions. This life of the emotions!

Lady Boleyn had just passed forty with an erect chin. She was as clear-featured as if carved, but it was a fine mask that she presented to her mirror of polished silver. With slow movements she patted her face, the shell of her beauty exquisitely intact, and with a practicality that was almost rude she tugged and moulded her low-cut bosom into a sort of proffered bouquet. "Announce me to Sir Thomas, Jane." It was a voice of metallic precision. When Jane returned her mistress was quite ready, as composed as she was stately. She wore life as proudly as she did her diamond collar, moving with unimpeachable magnificence.

"You are at last alone, Thomas." She entered slowly.

He blew his nose, too loudly, but fortunately he had a handkerchief. He had been reading a book.

"You are coming to Hever, Thomas,"

Lady Boleyn looked at him as if across a gulf that had never been bridged. Obviously that fine wrinkle of uncertainty on his porcelain front was Lady Boleyn's hallmark.

"Mayhap, Elizabeth. Within three days."

"Mary is peakish. Have you marked it?"

"I? Nay. Methought she plumped out somewhat."

"She could come to us. Is all well with Carey?"

"Carey? Was ought amiss?"

"Did his Grace lend him the thousand pounds? Mary is so dejected, I cannot see why."

"Oh, that was done a week since."

"Well, if his Grace permit it, let us have her at Hever," concluded Lady Boleyn decisively.

"And the child as well?" asked Boleyn.

"How else? The child must be fed."

Sir Thomas had forgotten. "Yes, yes. Then Mary and the child."

"What is your book?"

"His Grace's book on the Seven Sacraments. You know, his book against Luther."

"That beast!"

"Yea, that dreadful fellow. A pestilent fellow, his Grace calls him."

"Is it a good book? You can fathom it, Thomas?"

Thomas Boleyn, curiously enough, could fathom every word of it. "A shrewd answer to the heretic, Elizabeth, most cogent, most powerful."

Lady Boleyn was impressed for a moment. Impressed, that is to say, by Henry's prowess. It was not the branch of Henry's education in which she herself had helped, but she believed in him in any field. Then she reverted to Mary.

"It is so weariful to have Mary a mope like this. We must aim to restore her."

## VIII

Hever restored mary, to Anne's astonishment. "She is her lovely self again," observed Beth Darrell to Anne, after the hunting season returned them to Greenwich.

"Mary? Yea, fresh as a blossom!"

"You missed it!" laughed Anne's cousin, Madge Shelton, who sat in the window.

"Missed what?" asked Anne.

"In the near garden. I saw a youngster come along and he fell in love with the lavender bush."

"At first sight?"

"He stroked his fingers on it, he popped his nose in it, and then he ran his cheek along it with ravished eyes."

"The imp!" said Anne, "but I cannot see him."

"Oh, he gave a hop and a chirp, and disappeared."

"You knew him not?" Beth Darrell asked.

"Mark Smeaton, the choir boy—scarce higher than the table."

"Lord," exclaimed Beth, "to be that age! Ten years hence he may not be so blithe."

"Pooh!" Jane Parker said, "ten years hence he'll have a new love."

"He'll forget the lavender," said Anne.

"Not he," exclaimed Madge stoutly. "He'll dream of that for years to come, just as I dream when rain plobs on warm nettles. The nose is a faithful fellow, Anne. Thomas should write him a poem for fidelity."

Both Beth and Anne ignored this mention of Thomas, but Jane Parker was less delicate. "Thomas keeps his pen for another theme," she said slily.

"What's that?" Madge asked.

"Infidelity," Jane rapped out.

"The more fool he!" exclaimed Madge. "But for that brat of theirs he could marry again."

"And go against his honoured mother?" Jane asked sourly.

"Honour Thy Son and Thy Daughter, for a change," Madge retorted.

"Yea," Beth murmured, "but Thomas is no rebel, Madge."

"Then give me a rebel! Anne here stood rebel against the Cardinal, and she's with us again."

"And lost Percy," said Jane maliciously.

Anne flushed, but held her tongue.

"And lost not much, methinks," scoffed Madge Shelton.

Anne glanced from one to the other. "I am departing," she smiled.

When she had left, Madge turned to Jane Parker. "You seek to be loved?" she asked drily.

"I give as I get," snapped Jane. "Let the Boleyns bring George to Court. Then I'll love them." With this sally she too departed.

"A very dove," Madge shook her head. "But, Beth, are not all women droll? Anne was never so gay as to escape James Butler, yet I could love that hot-eyed Irishman. Now she's like ourselves, a green old maid."

"Not like her sister Mary," smiled Beth.

"Mary!" laughed Madge. "Was it not bold to name the first one Catherine? And now she'll have a Henry."

"Oh, Madge, you think——?"

"What you think, dear. A boy it must be. Then George will come back to Court, Sir Thomas will step up, Will Carey will have more manors, and Mary more jewels. All for a boy!"

"And Anne?"

"Anne will hold the baby at the font. Old maids are always godmothers."

Beth Darrell smiled. Then she looked serious. "Thomas Wyatt has no proper room at Court," she said. "Yet no one deserves it better."

"Then twit your cousin Harry Guildford," said the red-cheeked buoyant Madge. "Thomas should be named to the King's Chamber since John Russell goes abroad. Speak for him."

"Would I dare?"

"Dare! Is he not a right man and meet to be a squire?"

"That he is," Beth smiled. "Yet dare I do it?"


## IX

THOMAS came up from Allington with his father, as clerk of the Court jewels, and the free air of Kent still clung to him. He carried it into the great hall at Greenwich, where he moved broad-shouldered and limber, with his smile hovering on his lips. He had that indefinable look in his face: he was not a wild man, yet he was unbroken. By the side of his good father, so massive and sage, Thomas was still the unbridled colt, but they made a noble pair as they worked their way through the thick mob infesting the public chambers of the palace.

The Spanish ambassador was departing. The Cardinal's ushers were standing about mingled with stolid red yeomen ushers of the King's household whose numbers had been much increased since the war. Thomas's father stopped to speak to the marshal, and Thomas scanned the throng. The feeble old Duke of Norfolk followed his footmen, who cleared a passage with difficulty. It was a motley mob. A tattered man gazed about him with imbecile brightness, a priest at his elbow. Broken veterans stood in a silent group, their wounds set out like begging bowls. A press of people, some scrofulous, some bunched in rags, some thick in brocade, made the hall smell like a cathedral plugged with graves, and yet the place swirled with dizzy movement, with character and colour. Thomas's nose, however, was less tolerant than his eyes. He was grateful when his father stopped talking and led him along the rush-strewn gallery to his own treasurer's chamber. This was the sanctum of gold and silver plate, hushed like a private chapel, with attendants smooth as green baize, who included Thomas in the obeisance they made to the father.

## X

THEY had no more than settled to their tasks when the controller of the King's household arrived. This was Sir Harry Guildford. Heavy of jowl but with gentle eyes, he flung himself into a chair. He was yellow in the face, quite out of breath.

"I perish for a drink," he confessed. While Thomas fetched it and the clerks bowed out, "God's wounds!" he cried, "his Grace can well be vehement!" He paused to drink. "I've had one hour of it, worse than a joust. Ah," he gave up the tankard, "thank'ee, Thomas."

"He can be roughcast," he continued ruefully. "What have we in the Palace, he demands of me. Confusion, annoyance, infection, trouble, dishonour! Sickly persons about the Court, rascals, vagabonds —noblemen oftentimes disappointed of their meat and drink because of them. Lads and rascals, greyhounds, ferrets, hawks, spaniels—these all lodged in Greenwich! So he cries high. Ferrets, if you please! Only the ladies to have their spaniels, he saith. He laid about him with a vengeance, and now it must all go to the Council. We must have Orders on it."

"Is it without his chambers, Sir Harry?"

"Without and within. Good friend, he gave out reams. In his own chambers they disturb his retirement, they meddle with his dressing, they jangle, they touch his person. They are not humble, blithe and merry in his chambers. So his Grace heaped it on my head." He mopped his brow.

Thomas Wyatt smiled, but Sir Harry frowned. " 'Tis ill-found, mayhap."

"To say truth," Guildford observed slowly, "there's somewhat in it. Our youngsters can be light. We must rub this into them. We must polish or tarnish. Master Thomas here!" He laid his jewelled hand on Thomas's arm. "Would he be answerable?"

"With his Grace so vehement?" Thomas smiled.

"Oh, well," Guildford shrugged, "that has its causes." He turned to the father. "The waiters are beknown to you—John Russell, Harry Norris, Will Carey and the rest. Will Brereton is his favourite groom. Young Weston is the page. All friends, mind well. These of the privy chamber must be friendly to each other and keep secret all things done there. They must never inquire into the King's absence, where he is going, or talk about his pastimes. Nay! 'Tis patent. And if any use unfitting language of the King, that must be immediately reported. Thomas," he turned to Thomas, "are you up betimes? Some of these young gallants dice and game till all hours, so to lie yawning in the privy chamber of a morning, with their nightgear strewn about long after his Grace hath risen. Sometimes their good companions resort to the privy chamber of an evening, so that his rest is broken. But you are sober and discreet, Thomas? You can be reverent?"

"For that I can answer," said the father, "but the wardrobe, Sir Harry? That would confound me. He was given a hundred shirts last Christmas, each more sumptuous than t'other."

"That would not trouble the squires," Guildford reassured. "The garments are brought to the door of the privy chamber by the yeoman of the wardrobe of robes. He hands them to a groom, Will Brereton or Walter Walsh. The groom warms the clothes, but on no account must he touch his Grace without special command. He hands the clothes to these gentlemen," he gave Thomas a little tap.

"But how do these gentlemen know to enter the bedchamber?"

"He calls. Will Compton was wont to enter himself, to rouse his Grace, but with his leg he can no longer bide there. Now Harry Norris will give service in the bedchamber, and two of the squires must lie on pallets outside the door to be on hand at night."

"Poor Will Compton," Sir Henry Wyatt exclaimed. "His leg!"

"Yes," said Guildford drily, "he is infect. His Grace cannot have him longer. And when Penny the barber comes to comb the King's head and trim his beard, he too must keep his person and apparel clean and not go in company with vile persons or misguided women. Else the Italian shall be punished. And he must be all in readiness with his water, his cloths, his basin, his knives and combs and scissors. This keeps his Grace in humour."

"Oftentimes the King is up before seven?"

"Still Penny must be ready. But no one is to rush in to the King. None of the chamber is to press him with suits. The nearer they are to his person, the more humble they must show themselves. And that, my Thomas, is but meet and proper."

Thomas's assent was prompt. To be a squire for the body, when Anne was maid to the Queen, was to be certain of seeing her. As for reverence, he looked his thanks to the Controller. Then Sir Harry Guildford lifted his bulk from the low chair. "So you'll have further word," he beamed most cordially.

Sir Henry Wyatt rumbled a grateful, easy word.

As Thomas showed him out, the Controller came to a stand.

"By the by, I saw a strange friend of yours from Cambridge t'other day. What did he call himself? Tyndale. His face twisted like a tree-root, and his manner, by my soul, rough as the bark. He is in mind to translate the Testament."

"So he once told me," said Thomas.

"Yea," mused Guildford. "He mounts a strait path. I know not how wise he be. I sent him to Bishop Tunstal."

## XI

By becoming a squire for the body Thomas Wyatt was never absent from Court, and not a day now went past without his seeing Anne Boleyn.

He had come to the privy chamber by the right path, proved loyalty to the Tudors. The full-blooded Will Compton had betaken himself to Compton Wynyates. That good comrade to the King now retired to Lady Hastings, a veteran whose iron constitution and iron conscience proved that on certain females time cannot bite without breaking its teeth. Harry Norris, who succeeded Will Compton, was far more akin to Thomas Wyatt. He was one of those whose quiet manner goes with a shrewd experience of men and women, uniting sensitiveness with a clear, hard vision of the courtly world. Norris was of moderate ambition, and no detail was too small, no attention too

careful, in his personal service to the King. He was quick to welcome
Thomas Wyatt, a deft man for the jousts, sure to win him the King's
favour, and Thomas Cheyney, an older squire, married to a Boleyn,
hinted that with his literary bent, Thomas was no less fitted for
diplomacy than arms. By entering the King's household, Thomas was
sure of a career. His wit, as lively as it was amiable, made him loved
from the start. The estrangement he had felt from such a courtier as
Suffolk never affected this inner circle. He was at home in the privy
chamber.

But his charm, his prompt amiability, revealed little of the inner
Thomas. The whole of his existence was bound up in Anne. By the
degree to which this was secret, with prying eyes around them, it had
to compress its intensity, which gave it a fierce vibrance. He began,
in consequence, to know what it costs the nerves to lead a double
life.

Every day he looked for the moment when the Court's activities
brought him near to Anne. Then the least flutter of a look turned
dark into light. He could stand like a tower, correct and dumb, but
under this stilted presence, which he mastered for her sake, there was
a whirl of rapture. The dark tower of himself, wrapped in dignity,
was a shaft of singleness behind its bolted door, a blaze and concord
of such force that it immolated his being. He followed Anne's movements with apparent immobility, yet each of them, the least of them,
could quiver through him with a sting of delight. He had ceased to
have that dominion over his will that a man enjoys whose imagination
is lent to a definite purpose: it was to Anne, incalculable and unsub-
dued, that he gave the energy of his imagination. Whatever she did he
magnified for delight or for suffering to the fullest capacity of his
nature. He did not try to reconcile the conflict that was forced on him
by circumstance. What now held him was so poignant that he surrendered his will to it. Knowing that he was not free to marry Anne,
since he could never divorce his wife, he still gave himself to rapture,
and this was favoured by a chance word from unsuspecting Beth
Darrell.

"I have just come hither from Northcote," she told Thomas, who
inquired into her absence. "I was with my brother Francis."

"And Bess was there?"

"Yea, Thomas."

"Tell me, how was she? In God's name, do not fool me."

"Thomas, she was as shy and happy as a bride."

Thomas gave a short nod. "Honest Beth!" He heaved an immense sigh and then smiled. "God be with her."

Until Anne was absolutely sure that he no longer thought of his wife, she could take no deep happiness in his enslavement. But once she knew from him again that Bess was consigned to her Darrell, Anne herself drew a deep breath. From that moment, to Thomas's astonishment, she was gentler. Because she had stood away from him at times he had suffered with the tragic susceptibility that could make him a poet. But now he was in reach of her. And just as he heard, like a rumour in a distant wood, the clamour of more honest and subtle tones than English had yet captured, tones no longer formed under the dome of a cathedral but brought into the communication of man and woman, so he worked with his imagining of Anne. That became the quality of his living. His father was master of the Mint, he sought to become master of this other mint. And to reach Anne, in spite of his inability to marry her, was an urgency like his desire to sing. Where George Boleyn was dionysiac in pennies, Thomas hoarded his intensity. Gradually, by the touch of a finger or the glance of an eye, he knew that Anne shared this intensity, and in some ways these days of probation were the happiest of his life.

# Chapter 7

Neither anne nor Thomas, in this autumn of the war, could get it into their heads that they were concerned in it. They were fighting on the Somme. They knew this, and they knew that Surrey was yelping for the dancers and dicers to help him on the marches of Scotland. Francis Bryan, who had been serving with the tall ships, was told to leave for Scotland with Nicholas Carew and Edward Baynton. Anne could judge by this that the war was serious, and her tone became sagacious and full of weight and foreboding. But there were brilliant banquets to come at Christmas-time, when the weather would be too foul for war, and meanwhile she saw Thomas every day. Her mood was wholly untroubled.

The campaign, however, was not so remote from either of them as they imagined. It was staggering along by the means of what was delicately called Anticipation, which is to say, payments taken from the commonalty before their season. The Cardinal had even to borrow money from the King to keep it going, and he was hard put to it. And just at the moment when the hill was heart-breaking, when the tug brought Wolsey to the last pang of his force, his ally the young Emperor treated him to a species of diplomacy which was so childishly dishonest that, from then on, Wolsey became his secret enemy. It concerned Pope Adrian's death and a new Papal election. The promises the Emperor had given to Wolsey after the Field of the Cloth of Gold were fulfilled to the letter. Only to the letter; and his literal letter was deliberately held back at Barcelona until it was too late to assure Wolsey the votes he had been promised. Pope Clement VII was elected. Wolsey was baulked of his life's ambition. The alliance was, to that extent, fruitless. And the campaign correspondingly lost heart.

But even without the Cardinal's slackening of effort, even without that feeble succour which Anticipation could give, Suffolk's advance to the Somme was a minor triumph. He had started forth with standards, banners and pennons. To make strong war on the realm of France was his full intention. He was ever looking for battle. But the French were content to exhaust the invader by retreating, by wasting the country and burning the towns. It was wet weather, and by the time it reached Bray on the Somme the army was discouraged. If we pass the river, pass over the great river of Somme into the realm of France, some of them said, we are past all succour and all supplies.

"Sirs," Lord Sandes cried to the half-hearted men, "behold what I do." He took a banner of St. George. "As many as love the King of England and be true to him and to the Crown, follow me!" He and Sir William Kingston set forward and passed the water. Then the others plucked up heart and followed, with the guns and the supplies.

But Montdidier was its halting-place. The great rains had ceased, the winds had fallen, but came a frost so sore that many a soldier died for cold, some lost fingers and some toes, many lost the nails of their hands to their great grief, and even the wretched bill-men grudged and muttered more and more. The adventurers were for hanging them. They cried "Hang! Hang!" But the fingerless and toeless, the nailless and foodless, set out a shout and cried "Home! Home!" That was the Cardinal's fault, according to many of the command, but morale was broken, and the harried remnant retreated, while Suffolk sent Lord Sandes to Windsor, to tell Henry how it was.

"They abide in much misery, sir," reported Lord Sandes. "The weather is wet, the ways deep, long nights and short days, great journeys and little victual, which cause the soldiers daily to die."

"Yea," said Henry with a frown, "but these be the chances of war."

"But, sir, we trusted when we passed the seas to have had aid of

the Duke of Bourbon, and we have never had a word of him, wherefore the Duke of Suffolk and other nobles of your army have sent
me to your Highness to declare their state and condition, their goodwill to tarry, and the evil chances which daily happen to them, by
God and not by our enemies."

"Well," replied Henry, "all this we knew before your coming. We
are sending six thousand men to the relief of our army. For we will
in no wise that the army shall break."

But by that time, in spite of Henry's valour and resolution, only
a quarter of the army still existed. The rest had died, there was no
food, and in fact the soldiers would not abide.

So the Duke of Suffolk made his way to Calais with the other
nobles, to wait for the storm to blow over.

Henry was furious. The Welshmen were blamed for it. Bourbon
was blamed for it. The weather was blamed for it. God was blamed
for it. Suffolk was blamed and the Cardinal was blamed.

Suffolk's friends did not dare sue for his return. Henry was too
chagrined.

## II

AND YET THEY DANCED. Christmas at Windsor was a Christmas for
lovers. Thomas followed his master to Windsor, Anne followed the
Queen, and they took part in those solemn banquets that always
ended in a dance.

During each dance where they could be partners, Anne was charged
with a fire not hidden from Thomas. She gave no direct sign, as she
whirled to him and away from him, but he had stolen into her blood,
and as the evening wore onward a glow, subtle as a whisper, in-
sinuated into her delicate pallor and transformed it from the wistful
white that was habitual into a tinge so exquisite that her flesh became at once lucent and transparent, like the petals of a rose. Her
ardency spoke first in her lithe body, in suave movements and lumi-
nous eyes. As she flashed through the round dances, sparkling with
silk and jewels, her beauty was a pulsation. She hardly knew that her
glance glistened in the whirl and swirl of the evening, expectancy
quivering in it. She danced inexhaustibly, with swaying grace, and
no man who saw her that evening could be unaware of her. There

were ladies in the company who stood cool as the lily, and to them she could not be compared. Beauties of a finer ripeness came in Catherine's ranks, and several of the younger damsels scintillated no less. Young Simon Langton from Ireland stood dazed to see the glory and luxury about him, the wealth spilled from every golden vessel, from every moving limb and jewelled breast. But in the midst of these shining splendours, where human beings were intoxicated by so many primitive appeals to their senses and by direct allurement, even the Irish squire saw no one more compelling than this young girl whose head was carried with such poise and whose body was so supple. Each time she came to view she tormented his eye. But Thomas, who danced well, knew that Anne's coquetry had passed into a contagion beyond her will. She had opened like a rosebud in the evening, and she turned to him with her defences down, vulnerable and almost pleading, as a woman who might have danced in a glade on the edge of time, her eyes saying everything the lover longed for. Thomas worshipped her anew.

### III

THIS MELTING MOOD was new to Anne herself. Her whole life was a schooling in diplomacy, and this had been quickened since she returned to Court: she could feel that events were at last favouring the Boleyns. She was by nature of that lean, black brightness which takes life as pressing and immediate, bringing everything to a point that demands to be driven home. Combined with heart, this power can make a heroine, as with intellect it can make a pioneer. It is a quality of will that can even give eminence to a whore. But by itself it is a force that does not pierce ahead, and Anne was not, so far, enlightened to Thomas's nature. She was only half-aware of it. He was revealing to her, not so much his own sensibility as the power she was wielding over him, and that she had scarcely known herself to wield. He was, in this sense, a new world conquered. She was so entranced by the ardour he gave her, however, that she could scarcely resist it. She was invaded by a tenderness less nebulous, more physical and more aching, than any that Percy had aroused in her. It was a torrent she had not known to exist in her feelings, one that no firmness or precaution seemed able to stem.

She could not live without seeing him. Time and again she took risks, but fortune was kind, and his gentleness encouraged her. She was pursuer and pursued, unable to divide one from the other. They had the same fire, and neither shaded it. But, unlike Thomas, Anne could wonder at times what the penalty would be. She was watching her sister Mary. She knew of Bess Blount, discarded by the King. Sir William Compton's friend, her own cousin, Lady Hastings, was not lost to sight. Her uncle Thomas was living with Bess Holland, and when the Duchess learned of it there would be a famous eruption. The fixed ideas by which the ordered women condemned the others were not lost on Anne Boleyn. She had lived long enough in France to witness the revolt against such matriarchs as Anne of France and Anne of Brittany. Yet without a name intact, without impregnable reputation, what could a woman do in a tight world where all the unscathed frowned on a discovered woman, and all the men smiled on her. Anne held up her deformed hand and looked at it. If her name were like that, it would be the first thing seen, or not seen. On a cool morning, with Thomas out of reach, she took a long look at her hand.

Yet the hand itself longed to caress him. As the weeks drew into months, and they learned their signals, Anne undertook the passionate discovery of her heart. It was no longer the dream of early years, or the tentative hours with Percy, but a continuous acquiescence in which, quickly as she could withdraw, it was never beyond pursuit. Thomas's love had no withdrawal. Whenever the cruelty of their incompleteness made her cruel to him, by recalling his marriage, he could only suffer it, condemned in his own eyes. Yet if she did not spare him this excruciation, she could recompense him by disclosing that little existed beyond him, and by moods of contrition that dissolved him. They lived in an excitement that came with hazard, darkness, the mystery of two beings who give themselves to a discovery. They had no chart in this voyage.


## IV

ON THE RETURN from Windsor to Greenwich, Anne felt gay enough to visit her sister Mary.

Mary's lodge had the advantage of isolation, even in the grounds of the palace, but Anne seldom went there by impulse. Mary was no longer the rosebud of earlier years. Since this second child began to come she had been a subdued matron, still naturally sweet, but with an air so preoccupied that Anne stifled in her presence, and never could wish to see her unless she felt high-spirited.

Her spirits were dashed the instant she came in. The King was in the house, and, with consternation in his face, met Anne in the hall.

"Your sister hath fallen in a swoon," he said, firmly enough, yet big man as he was, filling the hall with his immense shoulders, his eyes were helpless and rounded, like a hen's. "We must find vinegar and—and——"

"Where is she, your Grace? Above?"

He nodded. Anne mounted to Mary's chamber. Mary was fully dressed, on her bed. Anne loosened her clothes. Mary's head lolled on her supporting shoulder, then slowly the pale eyelids lifted and the forlorn eyes stared blankly. The King watched the sisters with mouth compressed.

"I'll bring her to," said Anne, over her shoulder. "The ewer."

Henry brought the ewer. Anne slapped a cold flurt of water across Mary's face and neck. "All's well, sir," said Anne, with a twisted bow of her head. "She pressed my hand."

"God be loved," breathed Henry. "She did fright me."

Anne gave him a sweet, enveloping smile.

"Now I may go," he said half asking her, and when she nodded he departed.

"I felt pains," Mary murmured, "and then I fainted."

"What?" said Anne sharply.

Mary lifted her eyes. "Ah, the relief," she sank to the pillows. "I was laced tight, I scarce could breathe." She closed her eyes. Her wan young face, pale to the roots of her black hair, slowly revealed a tinge of flowing colour.

Anne watched her with a curious look. This, then, was the price of new estates in Buckingham. She studied her oblivious sister.

## V

THE CHRISTMAS FESTIVITIES had been diversified with interludes and disguisings, banquets and plays. So enlivening was it, and so encouraging the King's New Year gifts, that Thomas thought to plead for an unfortunate Easterling who, in a trade dispute, had been forced to take sanctuary at Westminster.

"He hath nothing, your Grace," said Thomas, "save four pieces of Arras he brought with him. Master Cromwell is his sponsor. Mayhap your Grace could like them?"

"Their value, Wyatt?"

"More than a hundred pounds they cost him."

"My Lord the Cardinal desires them not?"

"I wot not, your Grace."

"Offer him a pound apiece."

"Your Grace?"

Henry smiled frugally, two teeth showing.

"What be the subjects, Wyatt?"

"They are of the Passion, your Grace—Christ bearing the Cross, Christ praying in the Garden."

"Say five marks each," said Henry, and Thomas bowed to him.

After Christmas, at any rate, Thomas could think of something besides the Court. He found his way to Westminster, to see the man in sanctuary for whom he had spoken. He was, no doubt, a Lutheran. There Thomas espied Skelton, the priest who had rhymed himself out of favour, and the mere sight of the old poet sent Thomas to St. Paul's to see the bookstalls. There, on the same quest as himself, he ran into a Cambridge acquaintance, William Tyndale.

They made a quaint pair, Tyndale and Thomas, each with a vellum-bound volume in his hand. That they had come to the written word from opposite ends showed in every line of their bodies. Thomas had an apparent serenity that made Tyndale look grotesque by contrast, so knotty and rumpled was his countenance.

Thomas's glance at him took him three years back to Cambridge where, on the eve of leaving it, he had first encountered William Tyndale.

There had been times at Cambridge when Thomas felt he had eyes but could not use them. Cranmer, Gardiner, Foxe, Latimer, Frith, Tyndale—all were there together, at the time that Thomas was student. But where they had seen Luther smash the pane, Thomas was still gazing through a stained glass intricately and reverently pieced together by scholastics and grammarians, just as opaque, just as cluttered and twisted, as the thousand-year-old Latin grammar with which he was struggling. He was fettered, and the freedom he knew to exist, the freedom of which Erasmus had spoken, was in his college still the topic of gossip and sneers.

One sunny morning he had flung his Priscian down. Outside by the river the grass was young, and no donkey condemned to hay could have felt more aggrieved than the young man who had been devouring this fodder. Why was it dead? He cursed the tortuous grammar and the lubbers who taught it. He hurried into the fresh open. There, at any rate, he could wrestle with the realities of his growing years that kept surging beneath.

His boundless impatience drove him for miles. Only toward evening, after a great assuaging walk, could Thomas wheel homeward to St. John's. He strode freely at last, singing for his solace, when an unexpected man came out of a field by the river. Thomas had seen the little bearded man before his sudden emergence brought them face to face. Each eyed the other. They nodded and awkwardly fell into step.

"You are Hutchins?" Thomas looked askance.

Hutchins glanced up. He was a pale, under-sized man, poorly clad and dingy, with a brow too big for him. He had lines in his face, a severe, almost morose expression, but the eyes he raised to Thomas Wyatt were infinitely good, and it was their look that drew Thomas to him.

"Yea, and you are Wyatt?"

Thomas nodded.

"You are free this day?"

"Nay," laughed Thomas. "I wearied of sophists and their sophistry. I am mitching. My Latin was too much for me."

"And your Greek?" the little man smiled.

"My Greek! Methinketh you are master of yours?"

"Far from it. Yet shall I master it, God willing."

So earnest was his tone, so unfathomably earnest, that Thomas was arrested. He cocked his ear as to a song in the hedgerow, holding still lest he should frighten the bird.

"How so, Master Hutchins? Is Greek so living?"

Hutchins, who almost trotted by the tall youth's side, could hardly control his voice. "The living word is found in it," he said thickly. "Would I could set it out in the mother-tongue."

Thomas halted. "The New Testament?" He said it as if a document so fiery must be named with care.

"Aye," answered the shabby student, "the New Testament." He was so sombre, so ungainly, and yet so powerful in manner, that Thomas stood waiting. Hutchins burst out: "Your sophists! Have I not known them all my years at Oxford? The enemies of truth! What care they for the lay people? They think only of pride and place. They wallow in desire and superstition. Unless the Scripture be laid in its truth before the plain unlearned people, they shall forever be deluded by these owls who dread the light!"

They were alone in the road. Above them the evening sky was high and seraphic, spangled with the fairest blue and rosy light, the hawthorn breathing its scent into the coolness that rose from the earth. The bells from Cambridge tolled across the fields, so peaceful that for a moment Hutchins's phrases seemed raucous. Yet these words had pierced the evening, a sharp, far-off trumpet. That instant Thomas Wyatt knew that he too dissented from his fathers, yet he was so alive to them he cried, "Soft, Master Hutchins. These be dangerous words!"

"God's word is life," replied the little man. "If He spare me, ere many years I'll cause a boy that drives the plough shall know more of the Scriptures than does many a priest."

To Thomas the ploughboy was another, an unknown order of being. But as his companion spoke, his burning word flashed across a peopled abyss and in broken hands Thomas saw the book of a redemption. "Their Redeemer liveth." The thought blazed through him. That lasted an instant. No sooner had he assented than his natural obedience, obedience to his King, overcame an instinctive deference to Hutchins. He made an abrupt move. They fell into slow step again, plunged in thought.

"Your words sink in," said Thomas in his firm, manly voice. "Here they lie buried."

Hutchins bowed. On the threshold of St. John's, Thomas held out his hand.

"I cannot lie to you, friend," the little man said. "I came hither from the hypocrites of Oxford. My true name be William Tyndale. God save thee," and he disappeared.

That was Thomas's last evasion before Commencement. It was as a Master of Arts that he soon hurried to Kent, to accompany his father to the Field of the Cloth of Gold.

And now, over the bookstall, he saw Tyndale again. He himself was no longer a student. He had become a courtier, who spoke with gentle mien, who had the air of a fortunate zone where men were pleasantly inclined, where women were tuned to them, and the human spirit civil. It showed in his free limbs, in the light touch with which he slung his sword to one side, in the fine fingers that turned a page as, with a hovering smile, he had looked up and caught sudden sight of Tyndale.

Tyndale's nose was burrowing in his book, his brow furrowed, his hair and beard as rudely clipped as the country hedge, his fingers thick. He was a blunt, curt stump of a man, in the black of a priest, with no hint of propitiation in him, but the intensity of a small, powerful engine, a sturdy crane or a snub cannon. Even when his eye alighted on Thomas, his smile was reluctant. His body did not budge.

But Thomas's heart warmed at the sight of Tyndale. He closed his book, and stretched out his hand.

"How fared you with the Bishop of London?"

Tyndale's face opened. "Bishop Tunstal? You know I saw him?"

"Sir Harry Guildford told me."

"I fared ill, then. I asked but for a place to do my work of translation. He walked to and fro with sullen countenance. 'Is everyone alive,' he said, 'translating the New Testament?' He could support no more, but was sure I could readily find help in London."

Thomas knew the Bishop of London, a polished gentleman, a faithful diplomat, scholar and mathematician. An uncourtly soul like

Tyndale might well expect rebuff from him. Thomas shook his head.

"Bishop Tunstal? Nay. I know the man for you. His name is Poyntz. He is a grocer in Antwerp."

"Out of England?"

Thomas nodded. In England, with Luther's name anathema, it was idle to seek freedom to translate the Bible.

Tyndale brooded. "Farewell to England," he broke out, "mayhap forever!" The torture in his face was all the deeper because he did not move a muscle. "You commend this Poyntz?" he searched.

"From my heart. No better man lives. He is in London now."

The little priest allowed himself to look at Thomas. "Well met, friend Wyatt. I thank God for you."

With a queer feeling that he obeyed a clairvoyance, Thomas thereupon took Tyndale with him to meet John Poyntz's brother.

Poyntz, as Thomas knew, was already near to Luther.

As they went together, Thomas suffered the pangs of doubt. The old religion, in which Tunstal and Wolsey and all powerful prelates magnified themselves, was no longer an institution to which he clung; and he saw how easily a true religious man like Tyndale would be shoved aside by worldlings who incanted phrases. But divine truth, for which the new religion searched, was something that Thomas himself sought as a poet seeks, in the travail of his private soul, in the delight and anguish of his senses, in obedience to instincts which, in the religious world, still writhed in original sin. The poet in Thomas strove for another dispensation. He was a child of the Renaissance. It was this bitter struggle to express himself, in a poetry that came painfully from his experience of himself, that had sent Thomas to St. Paul's Churchyard to grope among the bookstalls. In this search for significance he could have little help from any priest. He was himself writing a testament. But the labour with which he bent his thought and turned his phrases made the soul within him more akin to the tortured Tyndale than his graceful figure gave a hint of. He had distant kinship with the pioneer, and stayed long enough to see that good Poyntz, the merchant, was happy for his bringing William Tyndale.

By this means, within a few months, Tyndale and Luther were to come together.

## VI

ANNE drank up Thomas's account of Tyndale. She was weary of Queen Catherine's friars. She longed for a Court like the French Court where, together with the religious feeling of Marguerite d'Angoulême, there could be an escape from primness and austerity. If the New Testament was to be in French, Anne saw no reason why it should not be in English, and while she dared not speak out for Luther because of the King's book she shared Thomas's enthusiasm for this solitary adventurer who was now to be in exile. Just as Nicole Bourbon, a poet at the French Court, who linked with Marot and Rabelais, could stir Anne's interest and sympathy, so, in her lightning way, she responded to William Tyndale. Her antipathy to the Cardinal, and to most of the bishops for that matter, was the note of her lively generation.

But the Cardinal was so powerful that Anne had to guard her tongue. His influence had been exercised on Suffolk's behalf so skilfully that, after his delay at Calais and a gloomy homecoming, the King at last could take his French campaign in good part, and soon Suffolk was well received, once more in great love, favour and familiarity with the King.

So great was it, indeed, that it carried him over a moment that would have seen another man banished or destroyed.

The tiltyard at Greenwich had been idle for some months, but Suffolk was at Greenwich again, and a joust was arranged between Henry and himself, to test the new harness that Henry had been designing.

"Sir," said a gentleman to the Duke, "the King is coming to the tilt's end."

"On my faith," murmured Suffolk, "I see him not. My headpiece takes my sight from me."

Henry, at the other end, was handed his spear, and then, with the visor of his headpiece still up, he entered the lists.

"His face is clean naked!" a horrified courtier observed.

Suffolk saw nothing. When his gentleman said, "The King comes," he set forward and charged.

"Hold, hold!" cried the spectators.

Suffolk neither saw nor heard, and before anyone could interfere his spear crashed into the King's open headpiece. It caught Henry on the brow, right on the coif or metal edge to which the headpiece should have been attached, and bore back the visor so hard that the headpiece was filled with splinters. An inch lower, and the King was killed.

By the time Suffolk learned what had happened, he instantly went to the King, speechless with the shock. With trembling hands he showed him the closeness of his sight.

"I swear by the Saviour I'll never run against your Grace more!" he blurted out.

"Nay, nay," said Henry, "none is to blame but myself."

"But my lord Marquis delivered your spear when your face was open," said Suffolk in bewilderment.

"Even so," Henry reassured him. "I was to blame. I intended to have tried the sight by myself."

The courtiers who listened muttered their horror. Had Suffolk injured the King at all they would have put him in danger of his life. But Henry was serene.

"Come," he said to his armourers, "put all my pieces together."

This time, with the headpiece closed, he ran six courses very well.

But the shock to Suffolk was worse than the loss of his army. So noble and gracious a master! There was never man, he once had said, that had such a loving and kind master, or ever had a truer servant than himself. "For the passion of God," he then had cried, "let it not be in your heart against me, but punish me rather with prison or otherwise." And it was this master he had nearly killed!

## VII

SOMETHING of the same devotion inundated Mary Carey, who had been delivered of a son. The boy was duly named Harry. She was soon well enough to go to Hever, and she did it in the glow of the King's grateful munificence. The properties to be granted to Will Carey were impressive, and Lady Boleyn had an inkling that a high honour was on its way to her husband. George, too, was no longer in disgrace. He joyously returned to Court. He, it seemed, could now pluck up heart, in spite of Queen Catherine's nephew. Hope ran through the household, and even Jane Parker, who became George's wife, at last gave an acid twinkle.

Anne held herself somewhat apart from it. The glimpse she had had of Henry at Mary's bedside made her wonder at Will Carey, and she shuddered, as though she had touched a worm.

"Why didst shiver?" asked Thomas in a low tone.

"Someone crossed my grave," she smiled. She looked at him, thinking, "You're no Carey."

"How much, Thomas," she asked, "wouldst do for our master the King?"

"He hath my life at his beck."

"And your honour?"

"I might lie nobly for him," smiled Thomas, "in the manner of good ambassadors we know of, and eke poison for him were it in fashion, yet some things could I do for no man."

"Couldst lay down your wife for him?" Anne whispered.

"My wife? I have none!"

"How sad you are! I tweak you. You are a clerk at heart."

"And you my darling, are a goshawk. Eyes watch you."

"Would we could be alone, my Thomas."

"That cannot be," groaned Thomas. "We are hedged with thorns."

"Yet it could be," Anne played with a tassel. "I could find you this night."

"Where?"

"In your chamber?"

"Mad."

"Heed your zany, then. You are in the little chamber alone. Leave your door ajar. Promise me. On the latch."

"What time?"

"When the mice steal out, until the cock gives alarum. Strain your ear to the silence, Tom. Shall your heart beat?"

"If I heard you a mile away."

"I'll steal to you. Hear my heart beat now." Her eyes bent on him like a midnight sky.

"Down. We are watched."

Anne bent her head, to hide her lips quivering. "Am I bold?"

In a thick voice Thomas answered, "No more. Come when it fortunes you."

## VIII

THE YOUNGER MALES at Hever caroused in the great hall swathed in thick air and the fumes of Gascon wine. Thomas Wyatt was enough of a poet, however, for Anne to tuck him away by himself in a little room in a tower.

When he had undressed and put on a quilted robe, he blew out his candle and sat by a window.

The night was clear. Not a breath of wind stirred the idle branches of the trees. The stars hung in them, scarcely more palpitant than the sky itself, which was pale and faintly lucid. Its vastness, with the bare trees so proud, gave Thomas the peace outside him, the immeasurable night so mild in the lap of Kent. He trembled with its loveliness. He gazed long into the unfathomable, limpid night. Its brimming silence began to tingle in his brain. Somewhere he heard a dog give a treble bark. The dry boards gave a sudden creak, and mice ceased to nibble. Breathless, the night tightened for him like a string, his heart leaping as a sound plucked it. He heard everything: he heard nothing.

From time to time he trembled, almost uncontrollably. He had a strange impulse to pray, but for the most part, strained to the uttermost, he listened. The minutes no longer moved for him. They became dense and palpable, as if inelastic, and he endured them like pain.

At last, infinitely gentle, he felt rather than heard the slow opening of the door. Anne was inside, her nightgown clinging to her, her hair loose, her bare feet on the rushes. She placed a tiny handkerchief under the iron latch, and clicked it firm.

## Chapter 8

Anne had gone to Thomas in a veiled moonlight. It was completely dark when, with a finger raised in warning, she closed herself out of his room, on the turret stairs.

It was not only dark but quiveringly silent in the sleeping castle. Her passage from Thomas's turret to her chamber down below was an adventure she had not counted on. The watchmen who were now on their rounds inside Hever—strangely enough, Anne had never given them a thought as she set out to join Thomas, but coming away from him it dawned on her that it was only in order to see him that she could possibly have visited the turret. Barefooted and cautious she crept down the cold stone steps. The further she stole from the turret the more her body grew tense, her feelings suspended, gripped by anxiety not to betray herself, yet possessed inside by that secret exultation which came from having defied the rule-makers.

A terrifying moment arrived: she had to cross the great hall to reach her own chamber. This, too, had not occurred to her. Anyone—a page or a guest—might be asleep there, tossed down in an odd corner with the casualness common to great houses; and Anne stopped before she entered. She was a somewhat ghostly figure in her flimsy nightgown. Under her black hair Thomas had lovingly caressed her head, holding it as the wealth of her hair rained over him, and in those moments she had known bliss. Now, with a summary hand, she gathered it back, while with the other hand she lifted the folds of tapestry. She could spy no sleeping form in the clouded gloom.

Halfway over the hall, however, came a sound like a shot: an oak log in the fireplace was expiring. The alarm of it pierced her, but she held herself upright. Once out of the hall a long bended passage would take her to her own room.

As Anne escaped into the passage, nearing the moment that she lived for, the moment of safety and release, a light sound reached her, one footstep and then another, unmistakable, coming toward her around the elbow of the passage. She stopped dead. But as the quick footsteps approached she decided to go boldly forward. In the bend itself, a dim candlelight revealed the pointed features of her sister-in-law, Jane Parker.

"Anne!" Jane exclaimed. "Whatever did become of you?"

"Nought untoward," whispered Anne. "I had to cross the hall."

"Yea," said Jane, "but in the dark? And three hours since?"

"Nonsense," said Anne firmly, "I have been afoot several times."

Jane peered at her incredulously. "I could swear"—she broke off —"I heard you but the once."

"Hist!" whispered Anne. "Why wake the Castle?"

"Then you are sure you are better?"

"Much better, thank God," said Anne. "Good night."

Jane turned back with her. "I was alarmed for you, sister. God rest you!"

Anne was bitterly disturbed by this encounter, but, after all, Jane must believe her. At last in bed, its coldness made her shiver. Again and again the shivering fit gripped and shook her. Yet in time her nerves gradually eased, she forgot Jane Parker, and her body became wrapped in calm. Wholly exhausted, yet humble and triumphant, she at last lay back to possess herself, to resume her existence.

Her return in the dark, with its ugly surprise, had sharpened for her the dangers that must threaten Thomas and herself, and this thrust her once more against his marriage. But painful as it was, she no longer sought to think of it. She had broken through it. She could feel. It was this that her night visit had given her.

What had driven her to Thomas was the warmth for which she starved. She had refused him, inside her heart, as long as she could. He had sung in the garden, pursued her to Hever, lingered and hovered and pledged himself. Anne had thrust it away, with every force of her will, every atom of her reason, since it gave nothing that her own and her world's good sense laid down for her. But at last, and in spite of herself, she had bowed to an imperious need for union with this subtle, dangerously tender, human being.

There is a marvellous complexity in the surrender of a being whose capacity for love has been governed by pride and calculation. It is another person, the child of another set of ancestors, who at last asserts itself in the group that has made the individual, and its sovereignty is the more overwhelming because the subordination has been so perfect. Anne had never given scope to the naïve woman inside her, the creature of feeling. This starveling now emerged with generations and æons of primitive felicity to capture, and Anne shuddered as the force of her feeling for Thomas took impetus from the hours they had had together, hours borrowed from another plane of existence, borrowed from eternity. In those hours she had come into something of her own buried self—almost as if she had learned to walk or learned to talk. The proud woman in her, as well as the calculating, gave way to a creature of blinding tenderness, and this sweeping tenderness rolled through her, ran ramparts that advanced as they mounted, one surging on the other, until they broke with the dazzling submission of a wave. It was a succession of rapture she had not been prepared for. She was stunned by it, yet ached to return to him through it. And as the light slowly died from these ecstasies, the fragility of her bond with him invaded her. Having left him so soon, she might lose him. The bare possibility of losing him alarmed her. The urgency to regain him was already alive in her, and each word he had murmured was a secret to be captured again.

## II

FROM THIS NIGHT at Hever her intimacy with Thomas took hold of her life.

There was a quality in it that went deep. Nothing mediæval held either of them, in principle or practice, yet their love lost every semblance of Court gallantry. In Thomas, faithfully as he had pursued her, there was a natural illimitable reverence for the creature who is loved, and in this Anne felt solace for her pride. Her progress with him, in spite of her first audacity, was by no means headlong. She fell into reserve at times, even holding him at arm's length. But the bond was unconquerable, and when she abandoned her reserve only his firmness and precaution stemmed the torrent. She was capable of extreme recklessness. Time and again they took brilliant risks to snatch a meeting. It was a period of such dissembling, such passionate union, such renouncements and attachments, that she wondered how she had lived before, and wondered how she could go on.

She had never looked so beautiful. An expression came into her eyes less acute than before, a brooding light in it, a hint of pathos and wonder, that completely changed her glance. When she had cared for Percy she was no less moved, but passion was quiescent. Now she was fully aware. There were times when this again became as hard as it was brilliant, but in this subdued rapture she found herself so consumed that the world she had composed herself with her secure place in it, threatened to lose dominance for her. She had to bridge a chasm to reach Thomas, but sometimes she did not believe that she could ever hold away from him. She felt as defenceless as Mary. At other times, seized by weariness and desperation, she was no longer sure of herself. She felt her strength leave her. Then she went cold, like her mother, and the pitiless chasm widened.

### III

DURING these enchanted months, when Thomas had it in his power to give her everything but marriage, Anne saw and knew little of the great change that was impending in Europe, and consequently at Court. For herself, on the sunny slope of the volcano, it was the uncertainty of her immediate fate which occupied her and drove her from mood to mood.

Thomas made a figure at Court that was promising. He was so alive and unspoiled that everyone could like him. He could enter the lists for a joust or for a tussle of wit. He was in favour with the King, and through his father he would be wealthy. Anne's circle, in short, had few young men in it so well looked upon as Thomas, and had it been in his power to divorce a wife who had left him for another man, Anne could have taken him. This was what agonized her; the sweeter she found him the worse she revolted.

But revolt was useless. A divorce was possible for an amorous lady like the King's sister, who was Queen of Scotland. Margaret could get rid of a husband on plausible grounds, to take a lover; that the Pope could arrange under suasion. But Thomas Wyatt was politically unimportant. Thomas was tied for life. Anne was forced to enjoy his sweetness in secret, or else to break with him. And secrecy, sooner or later, meant scandal.

When the new Pope's ambassador came to Greenwich, to talk of peace, Anne's hopes rose for a moment. The new Pope was a Florentine, a Medici, and reputed to be pro-French. But Henry quickly drew himself up and declared himself to be the inheritor of the realm of France by blood. That meant a further campaign in the coming summer, and Anne felt additionally discouraged.

And even later, when the Pope sent a rose of gold for a token to the King, Anne observed it without joy. It was a tree forged with fine gold and wrought with branches, leaves and flowers that resembled roses; this tree set in a pot of gold which had three feet of antique fashion. The pot was of measure half a pint, the tree was of height half an English yard, and in breadth it was a foot. It was sent to declare the good mind, love and favour that Pope Clement VII bore to Henry. Anne examined it at leisure when Thomas received it on behalf of the Master of the Jewel House. The sapphire as big as an acorn in the uppermost rose was a lovely thing. She admired the token, but what was the good mind, love and favour of a Pope who granted no divorces to unimportant persons? The Pope, the Pope!

They wandered in the farm garden at Hever during the summer and stopped to look into the beehives.

"What might that be?" Anne demanded in her clear voice.

The gardener's helper gave a grin. "That there, my lady?" He poked a huge lump that cluttered the hive. "That there, with respects, be a dead mouse. She was stung to death, I durst say, and when she took to rotting they lapped her up." He chuckled amiably at the embalmed mouse, and looked for high praise of his bees.

Anne and Thomas exclaimed as they should, and as they walked away, "That there mouse," said Thomas, "is in my own hive."

Anne started, and then laughed. "You could not drive it out?"

"Nay. But it is sealed in forever, and I still make honey." His lips quivered as he spoke.

Anne looked at the ground. "Thomas," she said in a low voice, "you cannot move a mountain. And so you suffer."

"I suffer because of you."

Her face hardened. "I should find a Will Carey, and be a Mary to you."

Thomas winced. They walked out of the garden and stood in a little grass-grown lane. Anne held him at arm's length to look at him. Her eyes were not tender. Something deeper than tenderness was in them, some recognition of Thomas and herself that went beyond desire and accepted the fatality of their existence in this place where they found themselves.

"We are doomed," she said, and suddenly caught him to her, her long slender arms about him.

"But you love me?" he asked desperately.

## IV

EARLIER IN THE YEAR, leaving her at Greenwich, Thomas had run into a surprise. He was walking along the wharf to the water steps, his heart full of his tenderness for her, when a hurrying figure jolted him, only to pass on with a gruff word. Thomas was incensed. With a powerful grip he caught the boor's arm; the man turned abruptly. It was George Boleyn.

"Thomas!"—he gave a short laugh—"that were a rude jostle! My old grandfather hath just died. I bear tidings to the Cardinal."

"What!" said Thomas, "my boy's godfather, the Duke?"

"Yea," said George. "Let you join me. We'll tell the Cardinal together."

"This comes late for my Lord of Surrey," murmured Thomas on the barge.

"Over fifty," agreed George, "and sour as a crab."

"But no one so hard to down, and now he's Duke."

"Yea, and his wife is Duchess, with the brains of a flea. My good mother is content, but what's it to me? So long as Queen Catherine is a Spaniard, I am in the shade. There's no hope for George Boleyn, married to a shrew, without one penny to lay on another, yet born to love and to spend."

Thomas laughed. "You are in sad case. But why to Hampton Court?"

"Not to Hampton. To Dr. Lark's nest in Southwark. I know more than my prayers, Thomas."

The house in Southwark was a respectable one, since Dr. Lark was prebendary of St. Stephen's. After a short parley the two courtiers were admitted.

They were scarcely inside when a quick step was heard on the stairs. A youth was running up.

"Oh ho," said George quietly, "not in bed yet!"

The youth stared at him, then smiled. "I study late," he blushed, and disappeared.

"The Cardinal's boy," whispered George. "The Cardinal had a Lark, then Winter came."

"Look up again," warned Thomas.

Thomas Winter had come back to the banisters.

"Master Boleyn!" the youth called softly.

"Yea, my merry man?"

"A friend of yours is here from France."

"So ho? Who's this?"

"Hush!" The boy slid away.

George turned to Thomas. "See here! A Frenchman with the Cardinal, though we be at war."

As he spoke a dark-clad man, massively built, with a bulldog jaw, came from under a hanging. It was Thomas Cromwell. In his train, his cap on a level with his nose, stepped a foreigner who wiped the courtiers with an obsequious bow.

"Why," exclaimed George Boleyn, "it is the maître d'hôtel, John Joachim," and he advanced to greet him.

John Joachim, his eyebrows startled, took a step backward. He was a lean, knife-faced man, his skin the colour of dingy biscuit, with eyes like knobs of onyx. He wavered as he retreated, and then his face changed. "My friend Master Boleyn," he gleamed, "my old friend."

They both laughed.

"This is a dark secret," the stranger held up a finger. "I am not here," and laughed again.

"Nay," said George, "and Madame Louise hath not sent you."

Cromwell looked from the Italian to George Boleyn with a sort of brutal authority.

"Ça va, ça va!" said John Joachim to Cromwell. "Master Boleyn is one of us." And with that he led George to the far corner.

"So!" scowled Cromwell, much perturbed. "Why are ye here?" he turned on Thomas.

The question was so rude that Thomas stiffened.

"Master Wyatt!" Cromwell understood. "I should not question you." He stood closer to Thomas. "Your servant, sir, now and ever, Master Poyntz may well assure you. But to-night you have happened on a close secret. The Cardinal hides this Frenchman."

"We have not seen him," Thomas bowed.

"Then may I shake hands on it?" requested Cromwell humbly. "You come to his Grace?"

"To bear melancholy tidings. The Duke of Norfolk hath died."

"Nay!" exclaimed Cromwell. "One of the old school! He gave me my seat in parliament."

George and the nimble Italian came toward them. "We are intruders," said George, clearly excited, "but fain would see his Grace."

"I'll tell him," said Cromwell.

As Cromwell disappeared and as John Joachim withdrew, George flung both arms round Thomas and danced a step or two. "The war is over, the war is over!" he whispered. "And I'm to have my pension! Ha, ha!"

"The Cardinal goes French?"

George nodded again and again. "It may take months, but it's over. We'll all be French in six months."

"Hush!" said Thomas. He had heard Cromwell.

And then, with a long face, the Duke's grandson broke the melancholy news to Cardinal Wolsey.

## V

"THEY CAUGHT OUR CONY, Thomas?" the Cardinal said to Cromwell as soon as they were alone.

"Yea, your Grace, but we have nothing to fear. He gave Master Boleyn his sop."

"Ah, and Master Wyatt?"

"Have no fear of him, sir. He is straight, your Grace. I'd trust my life to him."

"That's rare, Thomas. You to have downright faith in any man! Now, where are your lists?"

"Here, your Grace."

Cardinal Wolsey took them—a score of small monasteries listed. He probed them one by one. "Yea, when we break these houses," he murmured, "we'll build the goodliest college in all Christendom!" He handed back the parchment. "You'll be my hammer, Thomas." He pulled his fur tighter round his neck. "Is there a draught? I feel an icy wind."

Cromwell pulled a small carpet to the door and fitted it against the sill. The Cardinal watched him, one eye open, the other hooded. He shifted a great candle to have a proper look at his counsellor.

"Glad am I you are admitted at Gray's Inn," Wolsey said thoughtfully. "Your eye is trued for this. They will hate you, but never stint that tax on eminence, Thomas. Learn to be hated."

"In that I was schooled," Cromwell glittered.

"Yes?" The same candle illuminated Cromwell's face, smooth as a bastion tower, and the Cardinal's fevered and blemished countenance. The two men had been underdogs. As a youth Wolsey had sat in the stocks, punished by a bully, and each understood that the other had known degradation, contempt and shame. This bitter initiation is never forgotten. It flashed unspoken from one to the other, and moved the older man to bare his heart.

"Who is more hated than I am?" the Cardinal demanded in a hoarse, low voice, his eyes fixed on Cromwell. "It is my daily portion. Hampton Court is his Grace's any day he speaks, with every ounce of gold in it, and yet they hate me for it. They hate me for my noblemen and gentlemen. Thomas, they hate my mules."

"Wherefore, your Grace? You are the King's best servant. Is there no sense in them?"

"At times there be, since the prelates forgive the Chancellor and the lawyers condone the Legate, but when he that is first in Council be both Chancellor and Legate, it puts a strain on charity. To outpass custom is to outpass most charity, till enmity borrows courage from its host."

"You are too brave, your Grace. You should flatter them by feebleness."

"Yea, and be meek. Hark to me, Thomas, I'll name you my offence. His Grace's grandsire was a slothful man, and his good father sidled like a crab. From this I studied to advance his Grace by boldness. They hated me when my Lord of Buckingham met his doom, yet for rebating Suffolk's life they also hated me. They could not judge which was the traitor and which the servant. I have lifted England from an angle of the world to set it in Europe, so that the Crown is high above them. They cannot touch it, but they can see my cross and pillars and hate my mules."

"You hold the whip," grinned Cromwell.

"No, Thomas," the Cardinal rebuked. "Confound not the master and the servant. This I durst say, the trash of Europe littered this Court when I was in youth. Now one embassy treads on another, suing for his Grace's aid. I demanded this. I set beacons on the coast to blaze his name. But for whom is this? His is now the glorious name."

"Then what is their plaint, your Grace?"

"That I rule him for my ends. Heed me, Thomas, our nobles would fain devour us. They'd clamber on one another's backs to strip the Church as they have done in Germany, were I not here to tame them."

"But these abbeys!" Cromwell quietly lifted the parchment. "Forgive me, your Grace, but is this not blood on their tooth? You teach them this trick. Do you not fear it?"

"Fear?" The Cardinal opened both eyes. "Not while I live."

"But you attack the monasteries?" Cromwell persisted.

"Unless they yield colleges, to house the New Learning, the Church goes down. We have no clerks. We must milk these abbots."

"War has milked them, sir."

"But peace is nigh."

"John Joachim?"

"Yea, Thomas." The Cardinal picked up a goblet, took a drink, and looked at the candle through it. "Last year we should have taken Paris, but Bourbon and the Emperor saw it otherwise. So be it. The young Emperor!" He slapped down the goblet. "The liar! Were we not bound to him or to his scoundrel of a Chancellor, and that ribald aunt of his, were we not bound to him by our own Queen, I'd show what our King could do. He is a Prince by nature. But we are lamed by this alliance, outwitted by this cheat, sharing pains and no gains to show for it."

"But," said Cromwell slowly, "if Queen Catherine can never bear children more . . ."

"Who says so?" blazed Cardinal Wolsey.

"No one that hath call to say it, doubtless," smoothed Cromwell. "No one may pronounce on it who is not beyond cavil."

The Cardinal shrugged. "We have five royal physicians, but what do they know? One is more fear-full than the other. Master Linacre is dying. Doctor Butts holds that she hath passed the age."

"Doctor Butts!" Cromwell raised his eyebrows. "Mother Butts, no doubt. But Doctor Butts?"

"Well, who's his match?"

"I know one in Antwerp," Thomas Cromwell said coolly and gravely. "A man beyond price. He is at the Regent's Court in the Low Countries. And if the Regent's physician should pronounce, who could carp?"

The Cardinal watched Cromwell stedfastly.

"Well, if she be sterile, as her age leads me to fear . . ."

"Then divorce her, and the Emperor with her," said Cromwell boldly.

"Good God!"

"Why not?"

"You mean divorce, Thomas?"

Cromwell shrugged. "Divorce, your Grace? Let the good Queen retire to a convent, to make her soul. This hath been done."

"Yea, when Alexander was Pope. Now we have Pope Clement." He picked up the empty goblet, and then laid it down again. He stirred in his chair. "Nay," he exclaimed, "this is a stroke. If the Queen be sterile, so to a convent. Who knows! Who knows! How is this man named you spoke of, this physician?"

"Master Salmon, your Grace."

"Doth he know you?"

"An old friend. I knew him in Rome."

"Send for him. Nay, go for him." He opened his table with a key around his neck. "Here is this purse, and here's my signet ring."

Thomas Cromwell stood up to take them, the Cardinal fumbling to remove a ring. Cromwell watched him intently. He was sure of Master Salmon.

## VI

THE CROMWELL who now set out for the Netherlands to fetch Master Salmon was no stranger to the land he was about to visit. Some years before he had been a wool stapler there in a declining business, and only five years before, on the chance word of a wretch named Ned Lark, he had set out for Antwerp to grasp at a connection that might lead him to the Cardinal's service. His cousin, agent for York Place, had whetted his desire for that, but so grim were his needs, so low his fortune, that he had to stake everything on one journey. He could afford to think of it now, with gold in his purse and the Cardinal's ring on his finger, but so horrible was the memory of his predicament that he only adverted to it to savour his present security, as a man marvels at the ground under his feet when he has cleared a chasm.

Yet this New Man, this upstart who was to mean so much in Anne Boleyn's life, this Columbus who had set forth from Fenchurch Street to reach the fabled wealth of Hampton Court—he could never bury that first adventure which saved him from the gulf of squalor.

## VII

IN MIDDELBURG it was cold in that mid-winter of 1519 as only the Netherlands can be cold. Outside the town the earth was no longer ridged with crops; it stretched flat and desolate, for miles around, no longer the bottom of a shallow ocean but still little better than an earthy sponge soaked with glacial moisture, its dampness oozing up and standing icy in the air.

At a late hour the reluctant sun had crawled aloft. Through the vapour that hung on the plain it shed a glare at once dazzling and feeble, the scene too dreary even for the morose crows. Middelburg was pleasant of a summer, with its red brick façades, its burghers' gardens and the fine trees that shaded the Abbey, but now the roads across the low island were ground into slime, the gardens lay dead, the trees dripped tears. Even the brightest windows gazed out discouraged.

Off the Market Square, in a street room that served as an office, sat Thomas Cromwell. The light was grey in the room, and it smelt of musty wool, but so intently was he scowling over his ledger that he did not notice the chill. An hour before, by candle, he had breakfasted on warm ale and slabs of corned beef. Since then he had been delving in his accounts as a wool stapler. His square finger ran down a column of entries, his lips pursed anxiously. Once he shot a reproving glance at the veiled sky and gave a shrug, only to plunge more deeply, wetting his thumb as he flicked his ledger.

At last he rose. He threw a glance toward the door thinking to summon his cousin who had charge of the business in Middelburg. He shook his head and stood brooding. With a sudden stoop he whipped a small rug from the floor, picked up a sunken ring in a trap door, and dragged up a heavy metal box. His face still red from effort, he took a key from his bosom, opened the cumbrous lock with it and pulled out a sheaf of bills. These he rapidly scanned. He took them to the table and made memoranda in his book.

"The devils," he muttered. "They leave me this one chance."

He darted a look at his parchment book, compared it with his papers. After a sustained glance he slowly closed his precious book, stooped ungracefully to replace the bills and shut the metal box with a crunch. In a moment he was kicking the little carpet into position.

He sat down, set out the ledger before him, and then raised his voice in a loud bark.

"Willum," he shouted. "Willum."

A door covered with baize slowly gave way and in peered Willum.

He was exceedingly long, pale and limp, with wide-opened doleful eyes of the fish family.

"Meinheer," he said in a sepulchral voice.

"Imbecile," retorted Cromwell. "Tell Master Dick to come to me."

Richard Williams, sallow with black hair, came in directly.

"I go to Antwerp, Cousin Dick," said Cromwell shortly. "There I'll try conclusions."

"Never too late, Cousin Thomas," Dick Williams smiled sourly.

"Never too late? You sit bare-arsed here in Middelburg, yet sneer at my venture. I see the way out."

"Nay," Cousin Dick answered. "That I see not."

"Think you I'll yard white cloth all my life, for you to moon in Middelburg? Soon you'll see."

"And how about me, Cousin Thomas?"

Thomas Cromwell snapped the ledger shut. "You are done with Middelburg, for good or ill," he snapped. "I have my man. I seek him in Antwerp."

"And will London not look into the ledgers?" asked Richard Williams with a sneer.

Cromwell flung on his cloak without answering him.

## VIII

BEFORE THE NEXT DAYS were out Cromwell had scoured the thriving city of Antwerp. Much useful information he gleaned, yet nothing vital, and had he not come into the field with a clue he might as well have gone home. But for a week before leaving London he had wrung Ned Lark until, drop by drop, every leakage from Cardinal Wolsey had been drained from him. It was so little, at first, that it was maddening, but at last a scrawl that the Cardinal supposed himself to have mislaid for a day gave Cromwell the light he needed. All the great bankers—the Fuggers, the Welsers, the Hochstetters—were engaged to advance money to the young Emperor. But there was one man not yet engaged by the Emperor and attainable by England. To reach this man, to catch him before Richard Pace's arrival—that was Cromwell's plan, with all his inner knowledge of the Hansa Towns and the London Steelyard. His share might be a small one, but to pull out of the hole, to pave his way to Cardinal Wolsey—that was the chance he looked for.

Cromwell sought it grimly. He had battled with adversity all his life. Four years previously his drunken father had lost his last feeble clutch on the family holdings in Putney. From his uncle, Archbishop Warham's cook, he could hope for nothing. His father-in-law was a cautious wool merchant, and the portion his wife had brought to Fenchurch Street amounted to little. He had three children, many poor relations. He was an outsider in finance, in the wool trade, in brokerage. To lift himself from the ruck a brilliant stroke of fortune was needed.

Cromwell was as resourceful as he was tough, unsparingly active, but of common stock. He was a low-born Englishman. He had small access to the aristocracy that controlled privilege. He had no leaning to the Church, and no share in its prestige. If he wanted to make his mark, it must be in the new field, the one the bankers were opening, with merchants and adventurers to abet them.

Here Cromwell had no backing. He was nobody. Ambition, driving and unsatisfied, was born in him. Dissatisfaction at home in Putney had driven him from the blacksmith shop even in boyhood, to fight in the Italian wars, but that dissatisfaction had found no outlet in the smithy of soldiering. There too the aristocrats controlled. He had been a menial with the Frescobaldi, the bankers in Florence. Then, with his father-in-law to help, he tried his hand as a wool stapler. But with Wolsey's policy, trade was uncertain. So long as the powerful in England closed the circle so tightly, what hope had he, or the likes of him?

He was not a priest like Wolsey, a great one of the law like Thomas More, a learned secretary like Richard Pace. He was an upstart. The lowest rung of the ladder, in truth, was still out of his grasp. It was not the dizzy heights that intimidated him, it was the short reach of his arms, the hard thrust, the swing that must jerk him above the mob, out of the mud that clung to him.

He was too urgent to be at home in the warm mud of the mob, but it was not livelihood alone that was difficult, it was paying for separateness. He was one of those who rip out of community, who have floating friends and allegiances, who risk being outcast. The skulking tribe that had to shift for itself in the dark vaults of the Savoy, as afraid of daylight as the rat, were not all recruited from the poor in spirit, but also from the baulked and malignant. Strong, unsatisfied, detached, they slip into that slime of anonymity in which the monsters breed. In that ultimate dismay into which his own father had crumpled, Cromwell might prey on weaker men for a time, but what he craved was to go forward, to strike out, to employ his powers. He had seen the rough side of life. He was not afraid of change. By the luck of the age he was living in, perhaps he could grasp fortune. This little adventure, the chance to lay hands on a few hundred ducats and worm his way into the affairs of England—would he miss it? He hurried around Antwerp, his blood fevered, his eyes restless, his lips tight. He made an excuse to visit the handsome mansion that the Fuggers were just finishing. He went to the English House. He knew a scrivener who worked for Spinelli, the English agent. He had a chance acquaintance with the Welsers. But the man he needed to find was as far from him as ever, and he dared not be direct: even in a town so thronged with strangers he feared to stir suspicion.

## IX

INTO THE INN YARD, late in the afternoon, came a strange figure of a man. He was bent over, leaning on a stick. His voluminous black mantle half swathed his white face, while his big hat came deep on his brow. He moved with effort, intently and slowly.

When Cromwell saw this man from the window of the common room he gave a cry. He rushed from the room and out into the yard. Holding out both hands, "Of all people," he exclaimed; "ho, my Master Salmon!"

The lame man tilted his dark head to give Cromwell a piercing look. Then he recognized him. "Ah, Tomassio!" he said gruffly in Italian. Exchanging his staff from right hand to left, he held out a withered claw. His melancholy gaze rested on Cromwell as a slow, benign smile melted his expression.

"My old friend"—he let Cromwell greet him with both hands—"impulsive as ever."

"You heard I was here?" beamed Cromwell.

"No, Tomassio. I come to the inn to see a patient. Yes, I am a physician now, my friend," smiled drily. "So do not let us stand here in the cold. That nook inside the door—anywhere will do. Let us be in quiet."

Inside they went, and into an embrasure in the common room. Allowing his mantle to fall into a long drapery, Salmon seated himself opposite Cromwell, his face outlined against a dark panel.

Of all the faces in a town where men had gathered from Europe and Asia, this must have been one of the strangest. Master Salmon's pallor was intense. It was a waxen white, almost silver white against his pitch black hair, with his large eyes dull as dark velvet. He leaned back at first, to regard his old friend Thomas Cromwell. Then he crouched forward, sideways, with both hands resting on his staff, and in this posture he was unforgettable—the nose cuttingly aquiline, his lips blood-vivid, his intensity almost rapacious—not cruel, perhaps inhuman, with a formidable remoteness.

"It is years since we met in Rome," said the sombre physician in his slightly nasal voice. "But I have not forgotten, Tomassio. I owe you my life."

This was literally true. A mob in the slums of Rome had waylaid Salmon. Already they had injured him and would have killed him had not Cromwell arrived, to brave their insane fury and rescue Salmon. It was the beginning of their friendship, but to have it mentioned made Cromwell uncomfortable.

"Oh, that story," he smiled; "you'll drink with me, old friend?"

Salmon shook his head. "And things go well with you, Tomassio?"

"The world wags along," Cromwell shrugged.

"Girolamo Frescobaldo is here. You have seen him?" Salmon lifted his thick eyebrows in inquiry.

"A shrewd hit," said Cromwell admiringly; "I see him on the morrow."

"Why not?" smiled Salmon, pleased at his own insight. "You are not here for your health, or you'd be consulting me. But the Frescobaldi are out of it?"

"Wiped out. They lent to our King, and he told them to collect from the old Emperor, Poco Denario. Then they went under."

Salmon made a grimace. "They will not play together, these Italians. Genoa goes one way, Florence another, Venice looks after itself, and the French take Milan. Between the lot of them it can only end one way: either France or the Empire is going to have Italy."

"Why not the Pope?"

"Ah, the Pope! You did not know, my friend, that I was made for life had Pope Julius lived. That is true! I became his physician. There was a good prince! But he would not obey his physician. Too bad!"

"And the present Pope?"

"Medici, flabby like all the Medici. You know the Cardinals hired a physician for him—to poison him. True! But that is Rome."

"The Holy City," laughed Cromwell. He leaned forward. "You and I saw it together, Master Salmon. Was there any city like it—new palaces springing up, statues, jewellers, painters, perfumers! And such fat cardinals and beautiful women!" His ironic contempt, his gross disillusion, wreathed his face in a bitter smile, but it faded as he recalled Rome itself, the light in which it dwelled, its nobility, its glamour. His voice softened. "I loved Rome. Pagan Rome was not more magnificent."

The man whom Rome had crippled answered drily, "It was much the same, a stream of gold from every province and Rome wallowing in it."

"And so it goes on," mused Cromwell.

"Goes on? It is ended."

"How so?"

Salmon looked at him mournfully. He spread his palms. "Every prince in Europe wants the wealth of the Church, and every prince who cannot take it will favour heresy." He scrutinized Cromwell. "And your King? What will he do? Will he remain Papist?"

This question struck Cromwell forcibly. Salmon, deep as a wizard, watched him closely.

"We are as Catholic as Spain," replied Cromwell.

"And your King?"

"He is all Catholic."

"Has he children, then?"

"Not many," smirked Cromwell.

"But in the marriage bed, Tomassio?"

"One miss, and many misses."

"Ah ha! The Queen miscarries? What causes it?"

"I am no physician, good Master. The clerks say the marriage is cursed because she was his brother's wife before him. But why do these babies die, Master? What is the true cause of it?"

"How can I say?" Master Salmon answered. "But this is serious. Is she young?"

"Older than the King by six years."

"And what age?"

"Let me see. I am thirty. She is five and thirty."

"So!" Master Salmon pouted. "She must hurry. And he is a healthy man?"

"Strong as a bull."

"He'll find another woman. I should go to England, perhaps I could cure the wife," he mused. "But I may not leave here. I have to stay by Margaret of Austria."

"The Regent?" Cromwell's eyes opened wide.

"Of course. Cardinal Schiner brought me to her."

Cromwell's eyes glittered. "Then," he said bluntly, "you must know all about the Empire."

"Naturally I know all about it. What do you wish to find out, Tomassio? Why are you curious about it?"

As Master Salmon was speaking a flood of emotions rushed through Thomas Cromwell. Here was a man like himself, but not only a bondman, an alien as well, and yet he had made Europe his own; he talked of the Pope, of the Cardinals, of the princes, with perfect calm and knowledge. He was inside. Not merely this, he was at home at Malines and Brussels, where King Charles's aunt was Regent. Then Master Salmon could set him straight, he could put him on the right road, and this journey would not have been wild and foolish.

"We have lost the Frescobaldi," Cromwell said quickly. "What banker is there for England to deal with?"

Master Salmon reflected. "Herman Rynk," he said.

Cromwell bounded in his seat. "How do you know that?"

Master Salmon lifted his weary eyelids. "Still young, Tomassio!"

"I want to meet him. Do you know him?"

"He is my friend. Would you like to meet him on the morrow?"

"Yea." Cromwell moistened his lips. "That would I."

"*Ecco!* I have forgotten my patient." With great effort the physician pushed himself upright.

"To-morrow? I'll send word to-night. Depend on it."

They clasped hands and parted.

## X

A WEEK LATER a small trading vessel stood down the river Scheldt. It was the *St. John of Barcelona,* bound for London. In addition to its captain, its mate, and a crew of four, it carried a single passenger—Master Thomas Cromwell. He had come aboard wrapped in his heavy cloak, with a satchel tight in his hand. Now he lay stretched in the dark bunk assigned to him in the common cabin. His body was uncomfortable, but his mind was so busy he hardly knew whether he lay on planks or on clouds.

He reviewed the last week stage by stage. Master Salmon had been as good as his word. Together they had gone to Herman Rynk. Every fact that Cromwell exposed to the banker showed him to be correctly informed. Rynk's confidence was gained. Cromwell was frank to say that he bore no credentials, that he merely had Cardinal Wolsey's private ear, and that England might pay twenty per cent. for a loan of, say, half a million, or even a million. Rynk had agreed that such a loan might be arranged, and Cromwell advised him that Richard Pace could be expected. Then it was that Master Salmon had talked privately to the banker. And now, in the wallet in his bosom, Cromwell held the proof that his errand had not been fruitless.

At last, he told himself, he could approach the Cardinal. He came from Rynk. No longer did he fear the brand of the rogue. Hope was born in him. He could be in the thick of things, and he planned each step with buoyancy.

The stout bark passed from the smooth Scheldt into the bitter sea. It meant nothing to Cromwell. He heard the smash of the waves with exultation, and then he slept inordinately.

But it stormed cruelly. He was happy when they made land. Day was falling as they came up on the tide, and a cold wind blustered on the river, shattering its surfaces and spewing the deck with spray. The smell of London river greeted him when he came on deck. It was a friend. He went below for his satchel as London Bridge was sighted, and in the wan light in the cabin he settled with the mate. Then they hove to, and a row-boat pushed out to them.

His satchel was lifted from his hand, to be plopped on to a coil of rope as he climbed down to the row-boat. The master of the ship looked over, giving him a salute in silhouette, a stately Catalan to whom his boat was the fixed order of things, who dropped a passenger as a tree might lose a leaf. They parted. Before he had broadened on his seat Thomas Cromwell had forgotten the *St. John of Barcelona*. He was thinking of London.

The Thames clapped the row-boat roughly, and winter tore the air with wet hands and whirled it wild across the blackening crags and hollows of the water. Down the river, to his right, the Tower rose up sullen in four points. Cromwell gave it a glance and smiled: some kept their treasure there, he thought; he would lend his own out at good interest. And the whole city, implacable when he left it, now appeared to open its arms.

The two stalwarts had to land him near St. Paul's. As they rowed they mumbled in their minds how much he was good for. They judged him to be nobody in particular, substantial and no fool. They were right. He was nobody, but at the moment he felt an emotion rise unbidden within him, a surge that mounted and enveloped the whole of him. All the time he had been absent in the Low Countries, all the time he had been in search of his man, he had clamped down the being within him that could feel. But now, sitting in a wet row-boat, the dark vacancy of the waters slapping into him, the bridge speckled with evening lights in front of him, the stream sucking him between the piers and carrying him breathless under the bridge, with splash and slide until they emerged and the Gothic bulk of St. Paul's gloomed for an instant, all an incoherence of time and space that he was sharing with two dumb watermen—he let this passivity take his body, while his mood seized his spirit, shook him from head to foot. He had come through. Now he could command. Not a trace of his apprehensions or his anxieties remained to taint the ecstasy of this untrammelled moment. All was consumed in a burst, a flame, of confidence. He relied on nothing outside him. He asked for nothing but his footing. He was coming ashore. The tension he had held was released. It

flooded him, transfiguring his grim calm as the blast melts dead iron.
No love, no principle, no faith, could have exalted him as this molten
transfiguration, for he could say yes to himself, himself alone, to resist
the world that had pinned him down. He could do it, do anything. A
sense of illimitable power seemed to gather him up, and to illumine
him in every recess of his being.

The oars grumbled as the boat headed for stiller waters and the
wharf. He saw that they were at the landing. He opened his string
purse for small coins.

## XI

IT TOOK Thomas Cromwell months to reach the Cardinal. But at last
a summons came. On a private barge that carried several lords and
their attendants Thomas Cromwell was rowed from Westminster to
Hampton Court.

Through one sumptuous chamber after another he followed his
usher, a hush of luxury about him. The apartments themselves were
shapely and they enchained magnificence. He was left standing in a
superb ante-chamber that held him immobile. Try as he would, he
could not help feeling plebeian.

He was admitted. The Cardinal's sonorous voice told him to be
seated, and he had to remind himself of Lark, and Lark's sister, before
he could be capable and alert.

The interview had long preoccupied Cromwell, but it was the
Cardinal who gave it shape, and what stamped itself on Cromwell's
imagination, the moment Wolsey spoke of his service, was the reasonableness, the simplicity, with which he suffused his mighty authority,
for not even the thought of Lark and Lark's sister had diminished the
Cardinal. Thomas Cromwell was amazed, near at hand, to see how
heavy and dropsical he was. His face, against the red of his robes, was
of a slate grey, or bluish-grey, and one eyelid hung down, giving him
a lewd or sinister appearance. The whiteness of his teeth, moreover,
against his leaden hue, accentuated the unhealthy, livid aspect of the
great churchman. Yet when he spoke, in solemn measured phrase,
Cromwell instantly deferred to him. His pomp was the natural accent
of his being. His was the voice of Church and State, laden with the

dignity of a Cardinalate and the consequence of his Chancellorship.
If the ante-chamber had been encrusted in pride, Wolsey's immobility
was still more stately, inordinate, imposing, but what he pronounced,
gazing straight at Cromwell, was inescapable, disinterested fact. He
caught the inner man in Cromwell within a few sentences. His voice
grew supple and warm. He no longer stood outside Cromwell, but
sat above him, Hampton Court grouping itself about its creator with
a perfect appropriateness, and the Cardinal no more revolving around
the King of England than the King revolved around the Cardinal. It
was this sedateness, this adequacy, that won Cromwell most of all.
The largeness of the Cardinal's style and the ease with which he bore
it, it lived for him. This was no grand vizier. This was a master. And
in Cromwell's soul there leaped the desire to be his servant.

And Wolsey knew, within a few minutes, that the man at his feet
was malleable and eager. Here was no hereditary lord stiffened before
a butcher's son. The resistance that infuriated Wolsey was the tacit
resistance of the older nobles who still emulated the King. Their pride
aroused an anger in him that knew no bounds, and few could tower
in anger like Wolsey. But here was a plebeian, a useful man, capable,
concrete. Wolsey had intended to smite him for the little intrusion he
had been guilty of, to send him away empty, but when he saw this
round-headed, crop-eared block of a man, with his hard, clear eyes,
he understood him. He sunned him. Cromwell melted. And as he
melted the Cardinal mentally enrolled him.

There were so many clerks who came to him, intelligent, delicate,
bookish, but who were these witty gentlemen, after all? Men of the
long robe, chanting of life as it should be, of plants in a garden to be
sheltered and cared for, of seasons observed and under control. They
were benign, no doubt, serene and sweet, living on a patronage at
which they would be sure to grumble, innocently indulging themselves perhaps, but protected, talking of a protected life. What was this
Cromwell? A young dog who had been flung into the river, to drown
or swim. What did these saintly men know of the cut-throats and
bullies who seethed in a stricken land like maggots in a dead horse?
Could these clerks measure the passion that fumed in every ambitious
man, every ruthless woman? No, they lived in a gentle mist that veiled
the sun. Wolsey knew of Cromwell—the handy tool of a trader in

Venice, a lynx-eyed agent, a trader, a go-between. Yet was he a Pope stooping to make war, like Julius? A poisoner, like Alexander? A common cheat, like the Emperor Maximilian? The Cardinal frowned, and then sighed. The inordinate nature of man, why disguise it?

"I shall have work for you. Return when I send for you." He dismissed Cromwell.

Cromwell had tasted the vintage. He went down the Thames to Westminster, his brain racing.

### XII

THAT WAS THE BEGINNING of Cromwell's acquaintance with Cardinal Wolsey. The Cardinal was then preparing for the Field of Cloth of Gold, and it was not long before he called on Cromwell to make purchases for him.

Though Cromwell permitted himself many a despairing groan at the Cardinal's endless fantasy and shocking extravagance, he marvelled at the many inventions that tumbled from his master. He saw the purpose of this royal interview, to dazzle and bemuse the French, and he admired the audacity of it. It entailed a preparation that went down to the price of a cabbage and rose to the King's latest refinement. The first task was to carry it over and supply it without a hitch, find labour in England and on the spot—horses, wagons, ships, cranes, good roads, good harbours, the men to guard them, the eyes to superintend them, the paymasters, the accountants, and furniture for ceremony so gorgeous that it would live in memory for hundreds of years. It must prove itself no less lofty in worldly pretensions than the French, no less suave in the social arts, no less generous in hospitality, and ready at the barrier to reveal to observant Europe the advent of a renewed power that must be reckoned with, not less in the prestige of its ancient houses than in the clank and the chink of its gold. Wolsey meant to scintillate from Calais to Naples, and not merely Francis but the young and needy Emperor would have to blink at the resplendence which England was to parade to the saluting sun. To go back to Flanders to buy tapestries, to order timber, gave Cromwell his chance.

With this success to build on, and his relentless energy to count on,

Cromwell paved his way to Hampton Court. Slowly but gradually his name passed into circulation. He did services for people who looked to the Cardinal, for Lady Dorset, for the Archbishop, for the Duchess of Norfolk, for those who were in trouble and sought ease of one sort or another. He picked up a client here, an acquaintance there, found a tool or an accomplice. He could do honest jobs without a slip. He knew the law, its hardships, its delays, its anguishes, and those who feared its caprices he could steer through subtle channels. The Cardinal learned to depend on him, a quick-witted, sure-footed agent who was flexible and audacious. Bit by bit, between pauses and hesitations and surprises, he made this knowing man the apprentice of his mind.

Hence the Cardinal could trust him to return from the Netherlands with a physician who would answer to his purpose. He might doubt the honesty, he could never doubt the ability of Cromwell.

## XIII

AT GREENWICH, in obedience to the Cardinal, three of the royal physicians were ready to meet Master Salmon.

One of them, the elderly Chambers, was doubly regular, a priest as well as doctor, and with him were the stately Butts and the astute Cromer.

They waited for Master Salmon with the slight stiffness of the honourable and orthodox about to be associated with a stranger. Like the eminent in any profession, they were ready to respect an outsider who was sufficiently formidable, but they based themselves on Galen as Holy Writ, and would be quick to see that any departure from Holy Writ was the mark of a quack and a charlatan.

"It is the first time you have been in England?" Chambers smiled, speaking in Latin.

"The first time," answered Salmon.

"But you have known Master Cromwell elsewhere?"

"It is years since we met in Rome," said the sombre physician.

"You were a physician in Rome, then?"

"That is so," responded Salmon. "Pope Julius's physician—as one your honourable selves, a household physician."

"And later you went to Malines?"

"Quite right. Now, sirs, her Grace your Queen?"

"Yes," answered Dr. Chambers solemnly. "We have the honour of consulting with you."

"From what I understand, to examine her Grace . . ."

"Oh," Chambers raised both hands.

"Mistress Butts, methinks," suggested Dr. Butts, "could give our friend the necessary information?" He looked at his colleagues. "You have never been with us before." Dr. Butts looked extraordinarily handsome and reproving as he said this. "You do not know us English?"

"Only as anatomies," said Salmon. "I have carved up the dead, who seemed like other corpses."

Then he dissected! The silence was dense.

"You have always attended the King?" Salmon turned to Chambers, as Dr. Butts went for his wife.

"And his father before him."

"And what serious illness has he had?"

"His Grace?" said Chambers. "It was her Grace, I thought——"

"Are they not one flesh?" asked Salmon grimly. "Has he not had illnesses?"

"Blessed with perfect health, thanks to God."

"No podagra?"

"Gout never troubles him."

Mistress Butts, a portly matron with a face as shrewd as it was good, had now arrived. She plucked her husband's sleeve. "His measles, my dear!"

Dr. Butts murmured to Chambers. "Ah!" said Chambers, "ten years since he had an attack of smallpox. He was secluded until he recovered, and not disfigured."

"Smallpox? Was there an epidemic?"

"Oh no!"

"Where did he contract it? In the palace?"

"In France, as I believe. He was sequestered with it for five or six weeks."

"The usual treatment, Doctor Chambers?" said Salmon. "No baths? No mercury?"

"Most certainly not."

"How old is he?"

"Thirty-three."

"And bald since his smallpox?"

"Here I cannot help you, Master Salmon. We must ask his barber."

Salmon looked round. "And now, Mistress Butts." He slowly pushed himself into a standing position. Taking her by the arm he said, "Now I must lean on you." And he cross-questioned her about the Queen, her miscarriages, her normal child-bearing, the twin that had died in the uterus, the other twin that was delivered, every detail of her history as a female. Mistress Butts was thoroughly versed in her subject, clear, candid and commandingly sane, with that presence of mind so characteristic of sea captains and midwives. Salmon heard her with perfect patience, questioned her searchingly and exhaustingly.

"What is your own opinion?" the physician asked at the end.

"Short of a miracle," Mistress Butts stoutly declared, "her Grace cannot bear again."

"A miracle?" Salmon screwed his eyes half closed. "That is an event whose laws are not yet apprehended. But the Queen is only thirty-nine. Ten years older, and even then a baby might be no miracle."

"It is not her age," said Mother Butts decisively. "She is plainly diseased." She then murmured many details to her husband, who communicated them. Salmon heard, cogitated and inquired.

"The salt of the earth," said Salmon to Mistress Butts, "a sensible woman. Her days as a mother are over, you say, and she can never bear again, if what you say is true. But of myself I still know nothing. Now let us return."

After a long discussion between the physicians, the Cardinal sent for them. Then the King arrived. He took Salmon into his privy chamber. Their talk was prolonged and, to judge by Henry's flushed face, not without excitement. They parted with solemnity, however, and Cromwell, waiting outside, escorted his crippled friend back to the Three Cranes.

## Chapter 9

While the cardinal and Thomas Cromwell went about the King's business in their own practical way, Thomas Wyatt was called upon to take his part in the tournaments. The Christmas feasts were to be elaborate, for the benefit of Scottish envoys who had come to Court, and Thomas was one of the chosen.

He was young enough to delight in it, and happily a right man for it, but in the midst of these preparations and Anne's pleasure in them, he pursued another existence. That had been startled into life by his chance visit to the Cardinal's.

He was honest with himself, the Cardinal lived in a real world; his own was the ideal one, formed for him by Bishop Fisher and Cambridge, by his father and mother, by a general preference for those spirits he was drawn to. But this ideal world, glowing with loyalties, could not contain the enemy's agent. It had cost Thomas agony to turn against the French after the feast at Ardres, but Crécy and Agincourt and Poitiers were no dead names, he had seen great horses led out and the companies take ship, he had carried messages to Berwick and to Calais, and he foresaw what King Henry foresaw, the augmentation of the realm. It had grieved him, during the summer, that

Marseilles should have successfully resisted Bourbon; and the descent
of Francis I into Italy, with the beginning of the siege of Pavia, caused
Thomas a melancholy that Anne shared. The King, clearly, was unhappy at French prowess. He talked impatiently of it, and scorned
all suggestion of peace. Yet Thomas, with his own eyes, had seen the
sallow John Joachim who came to connive at peace with the Cardinal.
This was a contradiction, and Thomas ached to explain it to himself,
since it would not sit down at ease in his moral universe.

He was inclined to ascribe it to Wolsey's deceit and treachery. Yet
George Boleyn smiled when he said so, and laid a sceptical finger
against his nose.

Thomas then held his tongue. He needed a stedfast world, where he
could love and hope, yet by leaving the old discipline he seemed to be
plunged into uncertainties. He did not know what to think. He
yearned for certainties.

He felt, at any rate, certain of his own heart, and of Anne Boleyn.
And Anne was clear that if the Cardinal was doing anything under-
hand, it was out of his base nature that any contradiction arose.

## II

THE SECRET CAME OUT. Everyone soon gabbled that John Joachim was
in London, just as they admitted that John Joachim's master, Francis I, was sitting down in front of Pavia, hoping to blast the Spanish
out of it and so to fling open the wide door to Italy.

A great contingent of landsknechts, mainly Lutherans, were being
recruited by Bourbon to attack Francis in the rear. John Russell was
with Bourbon, Pace was with the Imperial troops, Clerk was with
the Pope at Rome, Sampson was with the Emperor in Spain, Wingfield was with Margaret of Austria and Gregory Casale was in the
camp at Pavia. Hour by hour their reports reached Westminster, to be
hurried by Wolsey to King Henry. As the parchments were unsealed,
despatches scanned even in the middle of dinner, Cardinal Wolsey
knew the worst tortures of the gambler. He had prepared for every
contingency—for Francis's victory, for Francis's retreat, for Francis's
disaster. He could imagine no outcome he could not manipulate.
Never had his imagination been more brilliant or his resources more

artful. England might be exhausted, so far as finances went, but it was Francis that was pinched between Bourbon and the imperials, it was Spain and Germany that were gushing blood and gold, it was Italy that lay prostrate as a battlefield. Yet the Cardinal moistened his lips and drank his barley water, too worn out to enjoy the roast eels, the fresh salmon, the baked oysters or the fried pike with which he was regaling the Council. They might be jolly enough to guzzle eight fat conies and three dozen larks, pheasant and partridge, and a pestle of pork, but the food on which Wolsey fed was his own fevered flesh, diseased by anxiety.

### III

AND YET this dreadful tension, which had continued from October to February, was nothing in the lives of most of the courtiers. It had, so far, made not the slightest impression on Anne Boleyn.

Before Christmas she had happened to meet old Gibson, the sergeant at arms, hurrying through the long gallery at Greenwich. And Anne stopped him, knowing that Master Wyatt was to be one of the sixteen to display themselves in the tiltyard at Christmas.

"Well, Gibson," she beamed, "this is to be a pretty revel!"

"If I can get my paint, Mistress Anne." He was a plump little man, his dried red face puckered like an old apple, with eyes as bright as a squirrel. "But with this war, all is beyond price, so monstrous scarce. I have work even to build me mountain."

"A mountain at Greenwich?"

"Yea, ma'am," he twinkled, "a mountain of brown paper glued to lathes. 'Twill cost a penny, mark you, even to tote it from the workshop. And we edify a castle, ma'am, to be assaulted by these here noble lords that would capture the ewnykorn."

"You have a unicorn, Gibson?"

"Yes'm," Gibson gave a toothless grin, "with a wooden tail and a prick of timber for his horn. She'll be a champion ewnykorn. But now, with my respects, I must to Cripplegate for the metal bell."

"And don't forget my hair," cried Anne.

"Nay, me lady. Mrs. Pyke of the Chepe supplies all the ladies' hair. Though your own—'tis a crime to hide it."

Anne sent him away with a wave of the hand.

The festivities could not have been more splendid, with interludes, disguisings, plays and banquets. Thomas was mighty with the lance and the two Poyntz brothers fought like lions. George Cobham, Francis Bryan, George Herbert and William Knevet besieged and defended the mountain castle with zeal. The New Year's gifts of 1525 were scarcely less encouraging, even though money was so scarce. The King had ninety-four new beautiful shirts to add to his wardrobe, some of them stiff with embroidery, and the few who did not give him shirts gave collars to his greyhounds.

Considering the war that was bringing Wolsey to the verge of prostration, the Christmas was wondrous merry.

And after the ambassadors from Scotland had seen the King and Suffolk dance a great season with Anne and other damsels in the Queen's chamber, they went away to bed almost too full of thought for sleep.

"Are ye as merry as this, all the war time?" a lank-jawed Scot asked Thomas.

"You find us merry?" smiled Thomas.

"Such joyous pastime to-night, such royal household and so well apparelled!"

" 'Twere ever thus," nodded Thomas.

"In our country in time of war," remarked another Scot, "is nothing but wailing and mourning."

"And is the realm of France a realm to sport with and mask with?" asked a red-haired visitor.

"We set not by the French King one bean," responded Anthony Brown.

"There is a brag!"

"Why so? Our King, the King of England, may sit in his chair and yet damage the French King. And another thing, we win by the wars of France."

To that the Scots had nothing to say. They mused and went their way to bed.

## IV

EASILY as these courtiers talked of beating the French, the Cardinal thought better of making a treaty with them. He believed Francis might win at Pavia, and to bring John Joachim into the open seemed at last propitious after eight months' negotiations. Wolsey had gradually condensed the French terms into hard cash, and, in spite of the brave festivities, hard cash was bitterly needed. He made up his mind, after consultation with Henry, that he could publish the fair prospects of a peace with France. He gave word to John Joachim to don his best garments and ride to Windsor.

After eight months under cover John Joachim was happy to be free. He mounted his horse at Southwark with a glance of satisfaction at the little troop the Cardinal was sending with him. To skulk like a spy had been no pleasure for this well-born Genoese, but his hour had come, he emerged as ambassador, and the King was to receive him at Windsor.

He and his troop had got as far as Holborn when they heard a shout. "Halloa! Halloa! Halt!" They pulled up, wary and alert. John Joachim fixed his eyes on the oncoming horseman, while the stragglers of the village gazed on them. It was a courier from the Cardinal, waving a paper.

He had barely uncovered before the story of Pavia stabbed the ambassador in a single sentence. "The French King is taken, 10,000 are killed, most of the nobles of France are killed or taken." The Genoese read it a second time, his face grim. He looked about him, at the thatched houses, with hens on the road, the wayfarers snugly clad against the cold. Without a word he folded the paper. Then he wheeled his horse, signalled to his troop to accompany him, and turned back to hiding.

## V

AT WINDSOR, a few hours earlier, Henry had been roused from bed to hear the news of Pavia. It was brought to him from Margaret of Austria.

"I must talk to the King without delay," said the messenger, "I bring him news from beyond the mountains that will rejoice his heart."

The King was waked by Harry Norris. When he heard the imperialist's name he flung on his furred night robe and ordered Norris to bring him in.

Margaret's messenger went on his knees in the bedchamber, and a candlelight was held for Henry to scan the despatches.

"What are my good friends doing beyond the mountains?" asked Henry, before he read a word.

"Sire," said the envoy in a voice that trembled, "if you read these letters you will see clearly in what a state they are."

Henry opened the first letter, started to read it, and as he read it began to weep for joy.

"My God," he cried, falling to his knees before the crucifix, "I thank Thee. Thou hast sent the news that I badly needed. Thou knowest and understandest all."

He stumbled to his feet and embraced the messenger. "My friend," he cried, "you are like the Angel Gabriel who announced the coming of Jesus Christ. This news tells me what I ought to answer to the French about what they are asking me, which has weighed on me terribly. And the news is such," he added, "I won't have to make any answer to them. Brereton!" he called. "Wine for the Post!" He drank to the messenger's health. "And you yourself were at Pavia? And did you see the King of France in the hands of the Viceroy of Naples, as this letter testifies?" Henry asked with opened eyes.

"I helped to disarm him," said the envoy. "He was on the ground. His horse was lying on him. The men who surrounded him were about to kill him, Sire, when one of Bourbon's gentlemen recognized him and ran for the Viceroy. The Viceroy hurried up, and kissed his hand. The King of France handed the Viceroy his sword, and the Viceroy gave his own sword to the prisoner. The French King was wounded in the cheek and on the hand, but slightly. As he lay on the ground, everything that could be taken from him was taken by his captors, every plume of his helmet."

"How did you leave the army?"

"Ten thousand French slain. Only fifteen hundred of ours were slain. Master Bonnivet dead, and scores of nobles with him. The rest of the French nobility captured, save the Duke of Alençon, who fled."

"And Richard de la Pole?"

"The White Rose, Sire? Dead in battle."

"Did you see him dead?" darted Henry.

"I saw him dead with the others."

"God have mercy on his soul! All the enemies of England are gone. Give him more wine. Entertain him well."

## VI

IN THE NERVOUS DAYS before that battle, wise men had shaken their heads, all their prognostics carefully guarded. The Cardinal had not dared to be sure in advance. He had waited with a lily in one hand and a pomegranate in the other, to be ready for either victor, and he was too seasoned a politician to risk his opinion.

Even during the actual battle there had been moments when the Fates seemed to fold their hands. But once the balance shifted, once Francis himself was captured, the event spoke with a single tongue over the whole of Europe, its bell tolling a calamity of the first magnitude. Francis sat at a table in ash-coloured garments, with Bourbon to wait on him. The event slowly pierced his bewildered heart. It was studied by all Europe in every aspect, red from the battlefield, grey in retrospect, but palpable to all, not to be palliated or concealed. Francis was in the Emperor's hands, and so was Italy.

What then?

To Paris, shouted Henry VIII's instinct. Cut them down. Carve them up. Serve them to Bourbon, to the Emperor, to himself. He exulted like his bonfires.

But to carry out this operation on the fallen enemy, in obedience to primitive instinct, required a knife. This was the Cardinal's gloss on it. At least 30,000 men would have to cross the Channel, and he had no money. The King had no money. This meant another appeal to England.

It was Henry's faithful henchmen who had to go directly from Court to the people in their country towns, to break the news to them that his Grace was ready for another subsidy. The Duke of Norfolk, the Duke of Suffolk, Sir William Compton (ten years a sheriff without showing his nose), Sir Thomas Boleyn—Henry's close councillors had this ugly responsibility laid on them. The war had dragged along for three years, and now the people must dig down and hand out their pennies. On to Paris! The royal inheritance!

The people of England met Henry's councillors in public places, eye to eye.

"What befell you, Boleyn?" they asked Sir Thomas at Windsor, where he came to see the King.

Sir Thomas's cheeks sagged morosely.

"They were like to pull me from my horse," he said. "I never saw most of them before, but I could do no good with them. We cannot drag a copper from them. How were they in Norfolk?"

The Duke drily scanned his brother-in-law: he could fancy how Sir Thomas had sung low when the scowling fellows crowded about him.

"We fared well not long since," said Norfolk in his harsh voice, "but now they jib. One of them came into the open. Captain Necessity, he called himself, sent forth by Poverty. It smacked of Lollardy, methought. He lodges in the Fleet."

"A weaver?"

"So I was told. We'll weave hemp for him. And you, my lord of Suffolk?"

Suffolk was fresh from a similar encounter. "I? Oh, ah, I made no great headway. I never met such stubbornness, in truth, but no one is blessed with a penny. The Cardinal, meseems, must climb down."

At these words, by a trick of mental contagion, the same thought entered three minds. If the Cardinal did climb down they would all resume their welcome French pensions. That could not decide them, yet the thought was natural. To lose a pension is to forfeit a blanket in a long night, and this war had gone on for three years.

A little later, as the Cardinal wheeled the Council toward a peace, the same thought occurred to himself. He and John Joachim, in fact, had been agreeing on a colossal pension.


## VII

It was the young emperor, however, who brought it home to Henry.

Though the loan had collapsed so utterly, Henry still remained sanguine.

"Ha," he exclaimed to Wolsey, "you dare not say my nephew will make terms without consulting us. I believe, now that he is a prisoner, we ought to ask for the French King."

"So we might, your Grace," said the Cardinal, "but your ambassador has just written from Spain."

Henry took Bishop Tunstal's despatches from the Cardinal's hand. His face clouded. "So!" he exclaimed. He read them word by word. "This is it."

"Another King Ferdinand," the Cardinal said drily. Queen Catherine's father had deceived Henry ten years before.

The King made no comment. His face had lost its geniality. He went back over the despatches.

"We cannot send an army all by ourselves," commented the Cardinal.

Still the King said nothing.

"The Emperor means to help himself to all Italy," said Wolsey. "The Pope stands in utter terror of him."

This picture of his ally was not lost on Henry. He brooded as he read, and the Cardinal watched his face slowly redden, and the veins thicken on his forehead.

"This is our thanks," reiterated Wolsey. "Our aims pushed to one side, our gold pocketed, our men wasted, and your daughter the Princess cast off. At last, your Grace, we may open our eyes."

The King laid down the despatches. "My lord Cardinal," he said harshly, "we trusted our nephew." He stood over the Cardinal. "I could have remitted his debts and borne his refusal to meet me with an army in Paris. He is penniless. But, by God, to lodge his prisoner in Spain, to make terms behind our backs, and to marry his cousin of Portugal! This is a friend!" The King gave a short laugh. "Now may her Grace vaunt her nephew." He rounded on the Cardinal. "He takes Burgundy as well, and sends his Spaniards into Italy. This you feared, you said so from the start. I refused to credit you. You know I have never loved the Frenchman. I refused to see this John Joachim of yours. On my knees I thanked God for Pavia. And then our nephew disowns our daughter!"

"You never thought of him as other than your beloved nephew," said Wolsey.

"He rewards me well."

"You took her Grace to forge a perpetual link with Spain. Though God hath not blessed your marriage with a son, you still revere her, doubtful as it seems that you were rightfully dispensed to wed your brother's widow."

"Doubtfully?" The King's face changed.

"That dispensation, your Grace, hath never had your scrutiny?"

"It was from Pope Julius. Has anyone cast doubt on it?"

"Your Grace, I am not to trouble your conscience."

"My conscience? Could this be matter for my conscience, my lord Cardinal?"

"Only your own confessor could answer that, your Grace. But we have strayed from Spain."

"Nay, by the Cross!" The King gazed at Wolsey. He walked to the window and returned. "Let us be plain. Were this dispense invalid, the Princess is a bastard?"

"She was born in good faith, your Grace. She could be held legitimate."

"But it could be open to doubt? Speak. Mince no words."

"Open to every doubt, if your brother knew her Grace carnally."

"But he did know her. They lived together. I can prove it."

"Then, your Grace, your marriage is in doubt."

"Mind what you say, my lord. These words will be engraved in me."

The Cardinal faltered. "You made protest in your nonage, as Archbishop Warham can declare."

"While you speak I think," the King said with brutal frankness. "God hath blessed me with a son. If Mary be a bastard, she is no more and no less my heir than my boy Harry. Then shall I give him my first title. We'll name him Duke of Richmond." He stuck out his jaw. "We'll signal that to Spain," he said. "This to begin with. My wife's bed will never know me more. We'll remove Mary from her. Let us start anew. We'll sign our pact with France and win the Pope. Then we'll answer the young Emperor."

## VIII

HENRY DID NOT RUSH to tell Queen Catherine about his plan for his illegitimate son. Though the ceremony of creating this boy a Duke would have to resound through Windsor, Henry wished to avoid the pain of breaking it to her. He was not sure how she would take it.

Catherine was above everything a loyal wife. She had bowed her will for years. She had condoned infidelity. She was, indeed, a partisan for Spain, a proud and loving aunt. She had never ceased to extol and to pray for her nephew. And when the battle of Pavia gave Francis into Charles's hands, literally delivered him, it seemed to Catherine like a judgment, an intervention, of God, coming as a thunderbolt— and on Charles's birthday. Hers was not a political mind in the detached sense. It was a theatre in which political happenings presented themselves dramatically in all the simplicity of her brave old world, wearing the badges of friend or enemy, of right or wrong. To this her heart was devoutly alive. That Francis, in the throes of defeat, could send a token to the Turk—that was the sort of black treachery in which Queen Catherine could believe. The French, the Turk, the Devil—these, together with the Jews and the Moors, trooped across her stage in the guise her heart allotted to them, all blackened with the same brush that was now daubing Martin Luther. Hers was a Crusaders' soul. Her mother had fought a Crusade, and Queen Catherine herself, over a decade before, had mounted a horse to crusade against the Scots. Her soul was pure in these matters, her temper gallant, and her brain uncomplicated. When Luis Vives had just written to the King not to destroy the French, not to put out "one of the eyes of Europe," Catherine had recoiled from him as from a renegade. But this loyalty, so dynamic and so honest, had not been suffocating to Henry, and Catherine relied on his Spanishness, as she had relied on the Pope, and on her nephew.

But within a few days of Henry's talk with Wolsey, sitting in her inner chamber, the Queen had a rude shock. Her face shadowed darkly when Lady Willoughby knelt to her and in low voice said rapid words in Spanish.

Lady Willoughby was Mary de Salinas, one of the maids of honour who had sparkled around Catherine when she first came from Spain. For over twenty years, married to Lord Willoughby, she had remained the Queen's closest companion. Statuesque, dark and aquiline, with Spanish pungency as marked as her Spanish breeding, she was in physical contrast to her mistress, whose blue eyes had still the hazy bewilderment that is so touching in a baby but whose body, flaccid and distended, went with her pale, fat face. Yet washed-out as Catherine looked, she was royally self-possessed and irreproachable, as her friend poured out her heart to her.

"His Grace has not told me. He is to name him with his own father's title, Duke of Richmond!"

"So it is," said Lady Willoughby. "And, your Grace, more is afoot."

"What else?"

"They are to establish the Princess Mary on the borders of Wales."

"But her marriage? We prepare her for our nephew."

Lady Willoughby looked to the ground, unable to control herself. "It is because the Cardinal was not named Pope," she blurted out. "That is the reason of all this. He has contrived—no, it is too much." Tears actually gushed from her eyes. "Your Grace, they force the Emperor to give up Princess Mary."

Queen Catherine half-rose. Her eyes had a bruised, affronted look. "You are not clear." She waited. "Tell me clearly, Maria. Control yourself."

"They have learned in Spain about John Joachim. They trust us no longer. The Emperor is to espouse the Infanta of Portugal."

Queen Catherine sat still. "Calm yourself, Maria. These things may not be true. His Grace can explain them."

But his Grace, unfortunately, could only confirm them. He did it brusquely, at a sad disadvantage. It was exceedingly painful.

So was the Queen's parting with her daughter. She feared the dampness of Ludlow Castle, where her first husband had pined away and died. She had been teaching Latin to Mary, and this was another reason she grieved to see her go. By these events she was quite bewildered.

## IX

As ANNE BOLEYN said good-night to her mother, that elegant lady took a look at her younger daughter.

"You have *bonne mine*," she said.

"Oui, Mamma," smiled Anne.

"You may as well know," Lady Boleyn remarked, "that your father is to be made Viscount Rochford."

"Nay! When?"

"In a week or so. When his Grace makes his boy the Duke of Richmond."

Anne heard this with a throb. "And Will Carey?"

"He is to have Beaulieu."

Anne took this budget of news to bed with her. As she unravelled it, she grew more and more astonished. How could Queen Catherine yield to it? If the King were to make his boy the Duke of Richmond, that threw everyone else in the shade. Anne could not honestly admit that it threw her sister's boy in the shade. She could not honestly admit that the King was the father of Mary's boy. But her suspicion of it illumined the honours that were to fall to Will Carey and to her father. *"Pour consolation,"* she murmured. She understood that. But her mind returned to the King's extraordinary act, in treating his bastard as his heir. This could only mean that he expected no other heir, that something had happened between the King and the Queen.

These things, as Anne knew, were loaded with significance. She promptly supposed that the Cardinal had contrived to ween the King away from the Emperor. As a Boleyn, bound to the French, this made her rejoice, and she was all agog for what might come next. Her spirits rose at the prospect of a new, entirely new, situation at Court, where the Queen's party would no longer frown on the French party, and where opportunity would widen for everyone—for George, for her father, for Francis Bryan, for Will Carey.

Young as she was, Anne's grasp of Court intrigue was instinctive, and her excitement at the change was almost passionate. She could read the tiniest sign as a hunter can go by a broken twig or a feather. The prominence that the King meant to give to Bess Blount's child —that was no whim. That was a turning-point, and decisive. Anne could not rest when this sort of thing agitated her. She sat up in bed, her knees tucked up so that her chin almost rested on them, her eyes sparkling in the dark, as lean as a witch, with one idea chasing through her head as fast as another followed it.

In all of this Thomas Wyatt was promptly and completely forgotten.

When she remembered him it was only to fit him into her scheme as an ambassador. But her scheme, her fantasy, had leaped to a full blown French alliance, with the King dominating it, the Cardinal dragged behind, and her uncle Norfolk superseding the Cardinal. So was the deck of Court cards well shuffled and dealt. Anne could not see Queen Catherine a mere dowager, yet she imagined a union with France that would bring her own sympathies into play, and pay off scores that had mounted. Her glee at this prospect was as cheerful as it was malicious. Behind it was a feeling that the Church, on which Queen Catherine and her allies based their whole superiority, should be rocked to its foundations by the Lutherans. There, too, a score asked to be settled. Anne scanned a total reversal of policy. All depended on the King. She wondered how deep his resolve had gone, and how far he would go forward.

The whole Court was made aware of Henry's change of heart by this ceremony that created little Henry Fitzroy the Duke of Richmond.

## X

"AH, HA," said Anne eagerly to Thomas, "my lady of Salisbury takes the Princess Mary to the Marches of Wales. How is that for a change? And I hear Dr. Butts is to stay there. He is to have a green and blue livery."

"It is not the only change," said Thomas.

"You know of one?" smiled Anne.

"Yea," said Thomas, "and so doth all the House. His Grace is to couch by himself in his own bedchamber."

"What?" Anne had a way of tilting back her head so that her nose seemed keen and cruel, and her eyes no less so. "Methinks her Grace cannot welcome this sign of indifference."

"But she says nothing? She is not angry with the French?"

"Not a word so far, but at the next banquet we may see. She may refuse to meet French ambassadors when they come."

"That will be untoward."

"The King must go his way," said Anne decisively.

"Yea, but she is still his wife."

"Wife!" cried Anne. "That gives her no right to hamper the King."

Thomas shrank, she was so terse, and Anne broke out laughing. "Do not fear for her, dear. The King stands in great awe of her."

Thereafter Anne watched Catherine with the merciless curiosity of the young, but it was as she had told Thomas, not a sign that the King and Queen were at cross purposes. Still, the French party took heart again, and Anne was scarcely surprised when her mother, who was now Lady Rochford, told her that the King was to visit them at Hever. As she had judged, he was once again at home with the good "French," and she picked out her loveliest French gowns, aware of an extraordinary elation.

The charm of this particular visit was its wholly private character, its intimacy. But this time Henry found a new quality in it, a special sensibility.

Hever had never been so congenial to the amorous and pleasure-seeking man in him. To be so superb as he was without having a private titillation of it would have been as meagre as being a Persian cat without something to brush against, and Hever seldom rubbed him the wrong way. It understood his habits, his humour and gal-lantry. He could never have chosen, as did his recent visitor Chris-tian II of Denmark, to impose on his nobles a mother and daughter of another class and race. Henry loved appearances. He was expansive and free, but he was the creator of a Court, and he dared not be so free as to invite familiarity or hostility. He detested the least sugges-tion that he was the victim of favourites. This was a touchiness that the Boleyns had always understood. They did not dispute the space his ego must be free of, and by not pressing on him, by lulling and soothing him, he became capable of a gentleness, a felicity and even a humility that he dared not indulge at the Court itself. Mary never ruffled him. George was amusing. Lady Rochford was his oldest friend in this kind of intimacy. He was at home with them. And after Catherine, of course, it was a great relief. He had many men and women about him in his active life and had come to present himself in an expected form, not merely the King who tilted and played tennis, met ambassadors, talked theology, went to Mass and was a good father. All of this, with his great proficiency, he threw himself into cordially and vigorously, but he was also a God-fearing husband for whom Catherine was a central loyalty. Under her frowns he had cut away Bess Blount and edged Mary Boleyn off the scene. He pre-served the façade of monogamy, and he did this because it worked better than the loose French way, or Christian II's way. Henry was, first and foremost, practical.

But with a wife so astringent as Catherine, he knew precisely what joys he had forfeited. He had given them up after several snatches of intimacy in which his ego had found indulgence and a new resonance. For the sake of politics, and of posterity, he had made this compromise. And, full-blooded as he was, he had continued, with whatever excursions and lapses he could not avoid, a loyal husband from eighteen to thirty-four, wedded not only to Catherine but to the Spanish alliance.

But it was to beget children and to assure himself against the French that he had held to Catherine. That was the other side of the bargain. And since it had been made clear to Henry that the Emperor was no friend, since it had been shown that Catherine could no longer give him children and could no longer claim him as husband, his central loyalty to his wife had received a fracture. For the first time in his life he felt unmarried, aware of his unconsoled existence, and in this mood, nebulous as it still was, he came to Hever.

## XI

It was a short visit but, under the circumstances, a moving one.

Henry's tenderness for Mary, who was nursing her child, did not preclude a very vivid feeling for her mother. Lady Rochford was, of course, a few years older than Catherine, and perhaps nine years older than Henry himself. She was, at this moment, about forty-three. That, no doubt, was old, and Lady Rochford, looking at two young daughters, felt with some asperity that it was toward them rather than herself that Henry must naturally direct his longings. Lady Rochford, however, was the first member of this family who had caught and held Henry's fancy, and it was still in her power to evoke the young man in him. Ever since he came to the throne Elizabeth Boleyn had been in constant attendance on the Queen, and her thin lips had given many an icy smile in those sixteen years, but so cool was she, so perfectly under control, that never had she lost for one instant the accord which, when he was seventeen, she had created by a swift and complete response to him. He was then the most radiant of young men, rising golden above the horizon, with all the freshness and sublimity of his hour. She was a matron in the twenties, and her peculiar quality for him was perhaps the Howard darkness in her, the fine fierceness in her blood, and the utter comprehension of her own part in this brief and fugitive embrace.

The liaison was known to very few, though Thomas Wyatt's mother had never forgotten it. She had always regarded the Boleyn lady with a fascinated horror, and the mere thought of Allington allying itself with Hever, which would have been natural when Thomas's father and Anne's father became joint constables of Norwich Castle, aroused her inflexible opposition. But Jane Wyatt, who avoided Court, meant very little to Elizabeth Boleyn. That lady glided effortlessly into her duties as lady-in-waiting, once Henry had married Catherine, and she exerted no pressure on the youth who then became her sovereign. Her whole family was always his to be at home with and to count on.

So when he came to Hever, relieved from formality, with just Francis Bryan and Will Carey to attend him, he did it in obedience to old longings. While the war lasted, and while Catherine lasted, there had been little surge of adventure in him, but now he fell into the arms of Hever, enveloped by Elizabeth's solicitude and tenderly welcomed by Mary. It was quiet and kind. Its acquiescence made the most of him, heightening his spirits as the day lengthened and drawing forth the private resource in him. All the doors seemed to open, and he could feel Hever invite his mood, though Anne, the liveliest of the three, kept somewhat withdrawn. This detachment had an effect on him. She was alive to him. Her eyes faithfully attended him. She pondered him, and he could see sparks of assent in her, and feel the occasional pang of conviction that answered his own. But, while he existed for her, and her charm rapidly conquered him, she had not admitted him as Elizabeth and Mary had done. And that made him exert his powers as seldom before. The mother and the two daughters might be three separate persons, each utterly distinct and even opposed to the others, yet to his released imagination they made an appeal, one after the other, as if there was an element in each of them so sympathetic that it must be known to all three. By some alchemy the intimacy with the mother seemed to give him a certain persuasiveness that even Anne was aware of, and to carry this further, so that no resistance remained in any of the three, was the urgency that took possession of him. How to do this, without sacrificing Elizabeth's constancy and Mary's submission, was a difficulty that unconsciously allured him, a temptation to extract the last ecstasy out of his precious insubordinations. He came to it, not by direct perversity but by the pursuit of delectation in a field that was his own, a preserve that Thomas Boleyn and Will Carey could keep for him. There were others who would suspect it, but all of them were either cousins of the Boleyns or closely allied with him, and unless Henry could pursue his adventure so that it had depth, so that he could prolong the tête-à-tête until he was wholly engaged and appreciated, his emotional hardship would be too great. He was not made merely to swig and guzzle. Hever offered him something else, offered him a perfect, a unanimous acceptance.

But to approach Anne directly was not so easy. He went through various stages of indecision and hesitation. His instinct told him that a single false step would startle her for ever. He put it off. But by putting it off he discovered that she was the only thing he could think about. Hever was no longer Elizabeth and Mary and Anne. It was Anne alone. The Castle ceased to be a building. It became a lair in which Anne was able to retreat to hidden caves, and yet stalked to the drinking pool, slimly alone. He was no longer a calm and complacent guest, a King who condescended. He was a male who had suddenly lost peace of mind. This was the deepest obsession that had ever seized him.

On the eve of speaking to her, however, he felt the propitious warmth that her mother and Mary had provided. He could not fear Elizabeth, after sixteen years' clemency, and Mary was born submissive. Were Anne to love him, in this so perfect retreat, it would exalt his heart not because of any voluptuous daydream but because of the amorous quality he detected in himself as he experienced their presence. This, after so many years of Catherine's proprietorship, was a burst of violent protest, but in a region that time had sanctioned for him.

Anne dropped her handkerchief, as it happened, while she was alone with Henry in the window. Before she could stoop for it, the King himself bent and picked it up.

So swift was this that Anne blushed to the roots of her hair. "Your Grace," she cried in a low voice, and stepped backward to curtsey.

He stood into the dark embrasure. "I am your friend," he said with passionate warmth, "and, were you mine, you had no servant more loyal."

Anne was pale again. "It is for me to serve you, sir. That is my place."

"If you please to serve me as I could wish, then be my mistress and let me be your true and faithful servant." He sought to take her hand.

Anne sank to her feet again, to prevent his touching her, and as she rose she said, "I cannot hear you more," and stepped from behind the hanging.

Henry could not keep her from leaving him. For a second he breathed hard, gazing into the dark, and then turned with a forced smile to join the company.

# Chapter 10

Next day the King left, and Anne had soon to follow.

She first went to the garden to cut late roses for the Queen, and as her eyes chose the good ones and her hands deftly clipped them, she had that absorbed look which came from Henry's approach to her.

It had been raining. The rain lay on the petals, little globes of grey water, and stood blobs of pure crystal on the green leaves. Anne's feelings were just as disparate, seen against the King or against Thomas. She shook the rain off, delicately and surely, but wary in her movement to save the roses that gave promise of beauty, and with her emotions she was no less wary. She held Henry apart, and in her face there was the hunted look, the slightly equivocal darkness in the eyes, that declared she was troubled, perhaps even frightened.

It was her fear of the King that gave her this look. She was returning to Greenwich perforce, where he would be unavoidable and where he would pursue her. She did not fool herself, he meant to make love to her. He had not, so to speak, brandished his antlers and bellowed. He had, on the contrary, been meekness itself. But their encounter, brief as it was, left no shadow of doubt in her mind. Her eyes were opened to him.

Up till then, the King had been in another realm. He had existed for her as a master and a lord, but not as a person. She was wholly absorbed in Thomas. The King had kissed her publicly at the Camp du Drap d'Or, but it was Mary who truly knew him, and her mother; to him she had been nothing, and she had never seen him as a man, never perceived him either with her senses or with her heart.

Now, with that signal of his glance, he was made clear to her. She saw him formidable and yet insinuating, his small prudent mouth, his strong hands, his neck with golden hairs on it, and that searching, suppliant gaze. Before this he had always impressed himself on her, because when he entered any room or any hall he displaced everything else, like a royal barge in a narrow canal. But now it was another being, it was the man himself who came close to overshadow her. Anne turned it over, rapidly and breathlessly. And no matter what she did, she must return to Court and face it.

"Are they meet for her Grace?" she looked at her roses. "The rain did not spare them!"

## II

YET it was not so bad in actuality. Anne did not find herself madly pursued by the King. He was continually occupied with the French, with the slow process of disentangling himself from the Emperor without separating himself from the money he had lent to the Emperor. And Anne was once more elated to find that the Boleyns were seriously in the heart of things. It was her father who had to lead the Spanish ambassador to Greenwich, and Will Carey who had to house him. This was the sort of ritual that established Lord Rochford's new importance. But it brought Anne into a smaller circle, one in which Thomas Wyatt was not fully at home. He was still "young Wyatt," and Anne was often forced to leave him on the outside when she and her family were in demand.

Thomas himself could see that Anne's time was no longer her own. Lord Rochford as treasurer of the household was brought closer to the King than Sir Harry Wyatt as treasurer of the chamber, and the delicious multiplicity of encounter that Anne had contrived a year before became hampered.

"The devil is in it, Thomas," Anne lamented, "we seem to be more in the presence. And so our proper hazard is greater."

"You must have me in the interludes."

"So I will. But we must not be caught, dear."

"You turn predicant, Anne."

"Yea, my love, we must be reined by reason."

"So I ever told thee! Send me away."

"Nay, stay. But we do lend ourselves to evil tongues, and——"

"All cannot be to our fancy! So farewell." Anne saw him laugh at her.

"You fool with me," she pouted. "But look beyond the minute. Jane never ceases to watch me, and now, when the Queen is so prone to suspect—oh, God, Thomas, cannot you divine?"

He saw she became troubled. "But, sweet Anne, you doubt my obedience!"

"You are not injured?"

"Injured? My life is yours."

"Yea, but I ask for less than that. Only to have care. Look not so crushed, my darling."

So easy to say, it, and to kiss him tenderly, but when she had really to make it clear, one time after another, that she would have to neglect him, he was hurt, in spite of himself. She had a greater capacity to detach herself than he had, yet when they were together she could not steel herself.

In company he was more easily leashed, too schooled to reproach her, yet he suffered to an extraordinary degree, trembling with eagerness to reach her, a poignancy of love behind his good behaviour. Anne, in truth, shared this tension that shook him, but she had made up her mind to have no accident disclose that Thomas loved her. The cruel thing was that at times when they could be alone he could not speak their bodily language unless she answered unequivocally. She suffered, to disappoint him, yet she dared not see him break through every restraint.

### III

YET, when she had no excuses, she listened to his pleas with only a pretence.

"But for an hour!" he begged.

"But so late, love. We'll be caught!"

"Not so." Then Thomas smiled. "Fear not! I have no base intent."

"For shame!" She came with him. "Where do you lead me?"

"Hush! The yeoman of the guard." They passed two yeomen.

"Treasurer of the household's daughter," said one of them.

"Treasurer of the chamber's son," mumbled the other.

"In there," said Thomas, opening a small iron door. He had a great key for it.

Anne gazed at him, alarmed.

"Go within," he nodded. He lighted candles from his torch, setting them on a green table. Anne sat rigid on a bench. Thomas took another key, to open a black metal chest. Then he said to her, over his shoulder, "You forgot I am clerk of the jewels."

The chamber had that lowering presence of darkness which candles shine against, but the table lay islanded in light, and Thomas came to it with a tray that drank this light into a thousand splinters of colour.

"Lord!" cried Anne, her hands lifted, "those are not jewels."

"Carcanets," said Thomas, "collars and neck ornaments."

Anne pointed to one. It dripped a pearl.

"Yea," said Thomas, "that should have two and twenty diamonds, and three and forty pearls." He swung it so that it glistened.

While Anne gazed from one to another of these gawdy collars, in which great rubies, pearls and diamonds encrusted the enamel, Thomas returned with a huge handful of bonnets.

"Over two score," he said, "and some of them right merry."

They were velvet bonnets, for the most part, though a scarlet nightcap was among them, and the brooches in the bonnets were nearly all in diamonds—a lady holding a crown, a man standing on a faggot of fire, a lady leading a brace of greyhounds, a lady holding a heart in her hand, and still another lady holding her lover in her lap, at which Anne pealed with laughter.

"But his chain, Anne!"

Thomas held up the King's gold chain. "This object," he said, "weighs 124 ounces." He hung it round his neck and groaned. "And this collar!" He picked up the King's diamond collar. "There's the Great Mirror." He ran his finger across pointed diamonds, table diamonds, long diamonds, square diamonds, triangle, heart-shaped. "This weighs 88 ounces."

"But those emeralds," cried Anne. "Let me have them close."

She bent over them, passing from them to the pearls. "Those are matchless," she said with reverence in her voice.

Thomas could not bear to tell her that they were suspected of being false. He took off the eight-pound chain and set down the half a dozen pounds of diamonds.

"Here are girdles and wreathes and backplates, all bedizened," he said. "Now you have beheld our treasure."

"Not all," said Anne.

"How now?"

"Not the Queen's jewels."

"Ah," rejoined Thomas. "How dull I am! These mean but little to you, and yet I only have these since Amadas comes to clean them."

"Then," said Anne, "the Queen's jewels must be for later."

"Yea, I'll show them you myself. Was I not dull to disport these." He looked at Anne across the table.

She put an elbow on it, and gazed at him, fingering the jewels idly. "Nay, my sweet, you give me the treasures that you have." Then she went to him, folding her arms about his neck. "Think of his Grace with but a chain about his neck," She gave a wild laugh and clasped Thomas. "Am I not a fool!" she said in a low, thrilled voice. "I am drunk with jewels."


## IV

ANNE did not raise her eyes to Henry the next time he entered the Queen's chamber. In spite of this evasion he came over to her.

"Here, Mistress Anne," he cried, "Erasmus has sent me his book on Free Will." He held up a pamphlet. "I was reading it at Mass."

Anne had feared he would speak to her. She had caught the Queen's look as Henry approached her, but was astonished that Catherine was benign. There was no hostility. Then Anne understood: in the Queen's eyes she was simply his new fancy, her sister Mary's successor.

Anne arose from her curtsey, stonily calm.

"Her Grace," she said demurely, "hath named a subject for Erasmus."

"How now?" Henry turned to his wife. With a frank matrimonial surprise he asked, "What may be your subject?"

The Queen drew all eyes. She remained in her seat, heavy and placid, her face powdered thickly in the Spanish mode, leaving her eyes circled by dun disks of flesh.

"I wish Erasmus to compose a treatise for us," she said bluntly, "on the safeguarding of marriage."

Every woman in the chamber winced, the wife so characteristically blunt, and the husband so young, evidently in the fulness of his powers.

Henry took it without a qualm. He could come to woo Catherine's maid-in-waiting under his wife's very eyes, for the sole reason that she repulsed him, and yet smile as if perfectly decorous and unperturbed. He looked about him with a snap of light in his eyes, twinkling into a smile. God's anointed as he was, severely dominated by the dignity and superiority which brocaded and jewelled him, he yet had a certain impudence, a mixture of pomposity and audacity.

"Yea, by God," he said for the whole chamber. " 'Twere time Erasmus expounded marriage. Luther hath put off his cloak and his beard to marry a young nun. That makes a pretty picture!"

With this, and thrusting his book on Anne, he fetched off his bonnet and left the chamber.

## V

ANNE HAD BEEN DEMURE enough while he took notice of her, and her companions were not certain what to think of it. They imagined that by this time he was becoming tired of Mary Boleyn. His manner had become not more positive, because one of the exciting things about Henry was the degree to which he was always wholly alive and present, but it had become more sensitive to the persons who touched him in passing, and perhaps more open to invitation. He was their King in this sense as well, and by the light of his eye he could choose, and stir, and even enlist the most honest of the Queen's ladies. He fluttered them by coming among them with this bold air he had, and

when he liked he could be dangerous. How dangerous, the little Duke
of Richmond was there to make clear. Almost no royal house in
Europe could close its doors to Bess Blount's son, should Henry ask
for a bride, and yet Bess Blount had been picked like a rose in the
garden, out of invitation no less casual than yesterday's. Yet Anne
Boleyn had been so cool, she was so natural in his absence, and her
gaiety so unconcerned and unforced, that no one took the King to be
seriously smitten by her. Her manner had that breath, that breeze, of
spontaneity which enlivens the company, and when the Queen took
her for her game of cards, the others quite forgot the King's passing
notice of her.

Catherine liked her young maid-of-honour. Anne's deference to the
older woman was, in some girlish way, unafraid yet humble and affec-
tionate. She was unflagging in her good humour, which the Spaniard
in Catherine rejoiced at, when it went with correct form, and Anne
never failed in the form she had learned at Blois and Amboise. The
game they played was a very simple one, Catherine's card sense being somewhat ponderous. Anne's was dazzling, but she subdued
hers to encourage her mistress, and she was sly enough to deal with
magisterial solemnity. They were a couple that, so far as age went,
might have been mother and daughter. In temperament, however,
they were as different as earth and fire—Queen Catherine solid, compact and sedate, with her face so beautifully candid, her brow clear,
her mouth sweet, and dignity inherent in every line of her, while
Anne Boleyn, flashingly quick, had so flexible a body and so vivacious
a face that she gave no impression of weight but seemed to live in
motion, to be as quivering and restless and intense as fire. Her intelligence, however, signalled the stable character in her, and was at
once attentive and sympathetic in her eyes. She went on dealing her
cards with the gravity appropriate to that ceremony. All of the pack
were face down till the last two. Catherine's upturned card was a
low one, and then Anne turned up her own. It was a King.

"My lady Anne!" Catherine looked at it seriously, "you have good
hap to stop at a King."

Anne glanced at her mistress sharply. Catherine met her glance with
a steady look. "But you are not like others," she said in a friendly
voice, thinking of Mary, "you will have all or none!"

Then Catherine took her loss, and they matched the next cards.

Anne remembered her words as she undressed that night. "All or none."

"That was wondrous!" she reflected. "She saw straight into me. All or none! I am like that. Like that, with Thomas. Like that, with Henry."

Her mention of his name, silent as it was, brought him livingly before her. She was physically aware of him, not as a human being with whom, as with Thomas, she could forget her own existence, but as a human being who could arouse in her a powerful sense of his physical presence, a vibrant, almost brutal desire for its communicating itself to her so that she wished to yield to it, yet refused to, no matter how powerful it might be. Anne did not hide from herself that she was alive to him, but to resist him was her strongest instinct. With Thomas, whose pursuit of her had been no less ardent, she had never felt danger. With Henry there was a will that threatened her own, that aimed to subject her, however lovingly he approached her. She invited and yet repelled this danger. It was a danger to the innermost conception she had of herself, a danger to her integrity. And yet she held Henry to her. The conflict was dear to her, and the certainty that he would renew it was absorbingly intense for her. She could repulse him for ever and for ever.

## VI

ANNE HAD SOON good reason to know how constantly he was aware of her. He drew her to his presence on the flimsiest pretexts.

She did not recoil from it. There was no surprise now, no moral shock, in this caprice of fortune. The surprise was within herself, where she guarded the final consent that a human being gives, or denies, to his destiny. And in that sanctuary, to which she had admitted Thomas Wyatt, she inwardly confessed, without the same alarm as at Hever, "This is happening to *me*."

Her interest in it had lost the first sensation of fear. Henry's docility, each time she rebuffed him, had lessened her fright, and what was growing in her was an excitement that had a faint tinge of female pride in it, in spite of her contempt for the rôle he proposed for her.

Out of all the damsels at Court, and all the beauties among those damsels, she was the one he chose. But why *me?* she asked herself. What is there about *me?* This she had no clear answer for, until her mind roamed to Mary, and then a painful blush, so hot that it was conscious, mounted to her forehead. "He is tired of her," she thought. "I am another Mary."

Her flattered credulity, which had moved her to artless response in spite of herself, coldly dissolved in this cruel perception. Pale and severe, Anne turned against herself, the blush that had stained her dying utterly. That she was not such as Mary—not only did she know it, he must know it. But until every trace of doubt were wiped out, Anne saw that the King's approach to her was a danger and a degradation.

These whirling thoughts never touched Thomas Wyatt. She was more perfectly aware of Thomas than of anyone else. He knew more of her than anyone had even suspected. The richness of his nature, the energy of his feelings, the delicacy that persisted until everything that had limited her was liberated—these had given her a possession of herself that was life to her. But this peculiar power of his tenderness left Anne unsatisfied in the glowing immediate region where fortune had placed her, the life of the Court. She saw Thomas not as a poet who was a courtier, but as a courtier who wrote poems. The region of the imagination, on the shores of which he faltered, was as meaningless to her as those actual undiscovered lands to which adventurers were voyaging. It was no voyage that won her inner allegiance. Poetry was a dreamland, at best a prettiness and a facility, but nothing to grapple to, in a world of reality, of tangible values, and of power. Anne was at home in the thick, concrete world, where the King reigned, where he perceived her. Thomas's world, strongly as he allured her to it, thrust her back from its threshold. She could hear its music, distant and plaintive, the voice of those generosities that made their beings sing together, but to follow it blindly would be to lose her way. Anne drew back from it. The possession of herself that Thomas gave her, from that hidden region, was in itself delusive. She could not trust herself to it. Her anchorage was at Court.

Yet neither could she let him go from her. She held him. She held him back.

This impulse to keep Thomas was native to Anne's heart. The habits of the Court, and the training of the Boleyns, fostered in her a quick discernment of such a rôle as the King's mistress. She had seen Anne de Heilly elected to it in France, as well as Mary at home. Her mind had a stall in it for such a notion. But the aliveness that drew Henry to her came from the elemental nature in her that Thomas had evoked—evoked, in spite of his disability to marry her. This aliveness, both to Thomas's tenderness and to the King's power, gave Anne a mortal dilemma, but she refused to see a dilemma in it, since the King was plainly pursuing her as another Mary.

## VII

YET HENRY REFUSED to leave her alone. It was a "still" Christmas, because of the plague, so that Anne was spared the usual courtly masques, but he did not desist. Even in the gallery he sometimes had a word with her. And one day, hearing soft footfalls on the rushes, she turned to discover him behind her.

"Well met, Mistress Anne," he exclaimed. Mighty as he was, tall and golden ruddy, he was less self-possessed than the girl, whose curtsey had floated her like a water-lily at his feet.

"We tilt to-morrow, and 'tis for you," he shot out, bending to her, "so be advised."

Anne's eyes gravely questioned him. "The Queen attends, your Grace?"

"Yea. I am her servant to-morrow. You ladies honour me at a banquet. But the tilt is privy to you and me."

She could not rebuke him, he was so hotly earnest. With a faint blush she curtseyed again. What could he have imagined for her?

The tilt at Greenwich was always magnificent, but Anne went to it with tingling excitement. Thomas and Francis Bryan were to have their part in it, as well as the King, and she sat by the rail of the Queen's gallery with her eyes gleaming and her lips parted.

The band that was to contest with the King included Thomas. Anne saw that they had symbols embroidered on the bards and on the bases of their horses' coverings. As they drew up, to salute the Queen, Anne discerned the device: a burning heart, and over it a lady's hand coming out of a cloud, holding a garden watering-pot, which dropped silver drops on the heart.

Anne's eyes sparkled as she deciphered it. Courtship by symbol was no novelty to anyone at Court, yet she could not guess the further signallings of the King.

He and his own band were superb in gold and silver, as against green and crimson. But Anne only spied out his trappings. There she could see a man's heart on fire, held in a press, and it had a legend. Anne peered at it. *"Déclare je n'ose"*—declare I dare not. She sat back when she had puzzled it out, aware the King was saluting her.

While she was fearing what the Queen would make of this protestation, and what Thomas would take it to mean, a sudden breaking noise, and a cry of horror, brought her to her feet. All of the ladies, with the Queen herself, were on their feet in the gallery. One of the Knights opposing the King had been stricken. Anne's heart was wrenched with anguish and guilt. It must be Thomas. The victim was helped from the ground, his armoured body bent over. Someone cried, "Francis Bryan, 'tis Francis Bryan!"

A page hurried to the gallery. A splinter had struck up and pierced one of Bryan's eyes. The King's physicians were with him.

The tilt was heartily resumed. But Anne could no longer follow it, though the King pounded triumphantly through course after course, looking to the gallery for admiration. She was fond of her cousin Bryan, the "vicar of hell," whose scabrous tongue went with high animal spirits. She dreaded this accident, lest it be an omen. But it was her own pang of guilt that most disturbed her.

"The eye is destroyed," Beth Darrell whispered to her. She was grey with pain.

But the banquet was so luxurious that even for Anne it dulled the shock.

"I am your servant," the King bent to wait on her. His words were no less devoted than his look. Anne smiled palely and averted her head. She saw his disappointment, but this time she truly held aloof from him.

## VIII

THAT EVENING Thomas came to her after she had danced.

"There is no place for me?" he bowed.

She begged him, "Not so close, Thomas."

"I have tidings," he murmured. "Thomas Cheyney goes ambassador to France."

"In faith he does? Then God speed him!"

"And takes me with him."

"Nay!"

"In truth."

"Thomas, how wondrous!" Anne was resplendent. "Here, sit by me. This is merry news." She made room for him. "You go promptly? At once?"

" 'Tis urgent. The King of France is at a point, to be delivered out of Spain."

"Oh, were I a lad, to bear you company to France."

"Needs not to be a lad."

"Yea, but you'll see his sister Marguerite, who was widow both for Alençon and for her brother. They brought him to death's door in Madrid, and now he's King again, he's free." Anne was alive. "Thomas, I envy you. Now you'll touch the quick. Now you'll go forward. You'll soon be ambassador, who knows! This is your day."

"But I am leaving you."

"Nonsense."

Thomas's face was grim. "You care not!"

"Not a jot," Anne smiled.

"You are as hard as flint."

"Then be steel and strike fire from me. You go but to Bayonne or Bordeaux. You'll be at home to see the may."

"The may!" Thomas was bitter. "Is it the virgin you speak of, or the blossom."

"So you revere me," Anne flamed. "You are perverse. You speak thus to me!"

Thomas bent his head. "Forgive me, Anne." She could hardly hear his smothered tone. "My heart is in torment. I find no peace. Every step from you will be agony. We are at a pass. My absence will be sorrow. I can bind you by no promise, but my lovely desire for you—have you no word?"

Anne looked down. "Here, in this glare?" She lifted her chin, as her mother might have done, with eyes like black ice. "You fill your heart with mistrust. You wrong me."

"Mistrust? What would I not give to prove how I trust you? France would I give if it were mine."

"I ask it not," Anne laughed cuttingly, "not even our antique realm. But do not cloud our parting, Thomas. You are on your first embassy. You must wing home to us."

Thomas watched her. She shed his gaze as if she were a statue, and yet he kept searching her for a quiver of tenderness.

She walked by herself under the pleached trees when he had gone. The light from the torches lay in bars under her golden slippers.

"Why did I speak thus?" she asked herself.

## IX

ANNE would have found it doubly difficult to answer her own question had she understood what the real motive of this embassy was.

She could see her cousin Cheyney as an envoy to congratulate Francis. Thomas Cheyney had married a Boleyn. He was a brave, jolly, confident knight, one of Henry's solid captains, gifted with a warm heart and a superb digestion. Anne always felt her spirits mount when she thought of cousin Cheyney. But to go behind him, to see what the Cardinal was really up to, did not occur to her.

Several months before, as Wolsey started for his afternoon walk, he stood a yard or so away from Thomas Cromwell.

"Eh," he shook his head, "you have come on, Master Thomas. You are far from the novice that first I knew." He gave a sigh. "Walk a space with me in my garden."

Cromwell's effort to look modest was never highly successful. There was an indescribable energy in him, a bounce in his manner, and an air at once sly and bold that took away from his formidable reserve; his face and his neck had, unfortunately, something of the pig's embarrassing nudity. By his side, slowly as he progressed, the Cardinal

looked noble. He was a wreck, tattered like a stormy sunset, but while
he toiled in his paces, so that Cromwell had to hold back, the Cardinal still dominated the younger man by long habit of authority, his
eyes looming out with that challenging power which he fed from a
fire within, from his turmoil of emotions and purposes, his un-
scrupulous zeal born of a worldly urgency that still wrestled with
wide reflectiveness.

"We are now at a point," brooded the Cardinal. "You brought us
Master Salmon, and now we have to act on it."

"How, your Grace?"

"Take a long view, and tell me yourself."

"The Emperor has deserted us," said Cromwell, "so we must turn
to France."

"Right so far."

"And the Emperor offers King Francis his sister. We must counter
that." Cromwell cocked a bold eye.

"A shrewd hit. The sister that's offered to the prisoner is skin and
bone. We cannot let him have this skelet in his closet, Thomas. We
must bind him to us."

"With whom, your Grace? Princess Mary is but a child."

"So the King complains, but we'll send her portrait to tempt the
Frenchman. And we'll do more, but that you cannot guess." The
Cardinal halted, to pull his fur about him. The wettish grass, the
matted path, and the disconsolate bare branches of the garden would
have chilled any but the most fervid. He saw none of it. He saw
only Cromwell. "We'll also," he rumbled, "have his Grace's effigy
taken. But for whom?"

"That is beyond me," said Cromwell frankly. He was puzzled.

"So it should be," retorted the Cardinal. "It is my private fantasy
and yet as solid as my house there. We'll wed the King to King
Francis's sister. She is a widow. She is ripe for him. I married King
Louis to a Tudor. Now we'll give a Tudor to the French King's
mignonne, his only sister. There is a match for you, Master Thomas.
It rivets us together. It binds Scotland to us. Let the Emperor tear
that asunder! I see no flaw in it."

"But our Queen, sir? The divorce?"

"It must save the Pope's existence. I am broaching the divorce to him. Once Marguerite sees his Grace's portrait it will be as good as settled. She was greatly taken with him at Ardres."

"And his Grace? He is willing?"

Wolsey's face became softly illumined as from within. "Willing, willing? God willing, Thomas. No Princess is more worthier. She is a poet, a gentle soul, meet to have children and affectioned to the King. What more is needed?"

Cromwell could not keep his mouth from twitching, while his eyes raced here and there in the bare garden.

"Yea," Wolsey observed, "it is bare now, but it is seed-time. Where is the Emperor if we plant two French marriages? France and he can never be joint against us."

"It would crown your politic," agreed Cromwell, "and only one obstacle to it."

"Name it."

"The Pyrenees, your Grace."

"Be this a riddle?"

"No riddle, sir. If King Francis come out from Spain, he must give hostages. His sons are the apples of his two eyes. The Emperor will hold him by his heartstrings."

The Cardinal pondered these words. "We'll ransom them at a million apiece. The Emperor is penniless." He dragged his footsteps back to the manor, the only sound for a few moments.

"King Francis is all too human, Thomas," said Wolsey. "That is the lameness in our structure. But since he must fight to remain France, and since we free him from Madrid, he becomes our hostage, and I'll tempt him to marry us. My bait is the greatest in our realm, the King himself. That will make them brothers." He paused. "Now we'll sound him out, when he is fresh from prison. We'll probe him to the bottom."

# X

THE TWO ENVOYS started for France, Sir Thomas Cheyney and Thomas Wyatt. An old dog like Cheyney took his time about teaching the young dog tricks. He said nothing about Marguerite d'Alençon to Thomas. That was the big secret. But he was studying his young man, whose charm in the privy chamber had won him.

Thomas was unhappy. He burned with Anne, but he was not hardened in the furnace, and even if he were setting out on his first mission to a foreign Court, with a companion whom he wished to please, he was too absorbed by her division from him to give himself happily to his adventure.

Too much a poet to live on the surface, he knew cruelty and terror by intuition, and he was young enough to think of the remorseless end of things. His gaze had in it the melancholy one may see in a mariner, as if he had looked too long to the horizon. But this mood had no anger in it, no knowledge of defeat, nothing that forced Thomas to bare his claws, or tussle with naked, harsh and inexorable enmity. He was a Wyatt, taught to be loyal and endure, steeped in the benignity that had fashioned him. He was not made for hate. His gentleness was native to him, and even were his faith betrayed he perhaps could not destroy. But he could suffer, which made him a poet.

Sir Thomas Cheyney, on the contrary, was not afflicted with compunction. He looked on the world with eyes that had merry wrinkles. Just as he would have liked a good sheep-dog, he liked Thomas Wyatt, but he judged that, so far, Thomas had never encountered wolves, and he longed to train him.

"That bawd of a secretary," droned Cheyney as they rode by themselves, ahead of their company "He held me down to nothing. 'Tis all one to you, Wyatt?"

"Faith no, sir," said Thomas. "I never have a penny."

"What, you wastrel! You'll need them now. They scupper you in France." The heir of Allington disappointed Cheyney. "Yea, by my soul," he drawled, "they pack us off without a by-your-leave, without a full wallet." He was a soldierly man, with a keen eye to the main chance, yet soon he smiled broadly. "Last time I went to France, 'twas to Lyons, to declare war to King Francis. Our herald near turned tail, he was so frighted." Here Cheyney chuckled. "Four years afore, George Boleyn, Francis Bryan, King Francis and myself rode through Paris in our masks, pelting the citizens with eggs and apples. That was a drunken bout."

Thomas grinned feebly. The older man sobered. "Those were gay days, before the war. Now it's all to do again. We have much to glean, Wyatt. His Grace talked to me privily."

Thomas was deeply attentive.

"His Grace hears that Bourbon now splits the royal house in two. You are quick of wit. You'll see signs of this. And then, doth Francis's next Queen come out of Spain, the Emperor's sister. His Grace much fears it."

"So can I see."

"All turns on how the Emperor will have served his prisoner at the last," said Cheyney. "We must not chafe against the Emperor, lest they made friends. We must begin with congratulations. We are not to hide the great love we have ever felt for France."

"We hid it three year since," said Thomas.

"St! None of that! Now he's our darling. We must cocker him. We must show stupefaction withal, and marvel at the great and high conditions imposed by the Emperor, the like whereof have not been heard. Then, if he's frank, we must ask, with vehemence, does he feel bound in conscience."

"That spells another war," said Thomas. "Is he for war again, think you?"

"I doubt it," said Cheyney. "They say he has the pox. We must find out if they have sweated him."

"But how?"

"One of his Scots will tell us. We have friends at Court, and this cannot be kept dark."

Thomas was silent. He thought of that lithe prince at Ardres, before the war. Then Pavia, then prison, then the pox. The journey into France, merry as it sounded, led into murk. Yet he himself felt that his own great love for France could never be quenched by any storms or clouds. Anne Boleyn was no more a Frenchman than himself. He was ready to spy out the truth, and serve his King by it, though it meant huddling with a Scottish archer who had made friends with the apothecary.

"So we'll proceed," confided the straight-backed Cheyney, his glance on their county of Kent. "A backward spring this year. We cannot make war right soon. How is my eye, prithee? 'Twas swollen from a rheum. Is it unsightly?"

"Not one sign of it," said Thomas.

"That cheers me," smiled Cheyney. "In truth, I feel game as a fighting cock." He rode ahead, with his slight unconscious swagger. "At Cognac," he mused, "I may have a shot at a deer. But first, Bordeaux. We cannot do it under eight full days, not possibly."

## XI

THOMAS had not been prepared for so startling a change. At Ardres the French King had been a galliard. Since then he had been defeated, in prison and mortally ill. He had been forced to sign a disgraceful peace, giving a free hand to the all-triumphant young Emperor. Now, at Bordeaux, his cheeks were sunken, his eyes were feverishly bright, and his nose seemed longer and more questing than ever. Thomas, who could observe him while Cheyney interviewed him, had difficulty in seeing the same man in him. He was more like an older brother who had been on the rocks, and his glance was eager and yet uncertain.

Tears came to his eyes as he talked to Cheyney. One of them rolled down his nose and dropped off as he was saying, "Yea, by my soul, I am greatly unkind if ever I forget their goodness." He could not say enough in favour of the English, especially Wolsey. "If we continue in this amity," he laid his hand on Cheyney's sleeve, "we'll give laws to all the world, or my father the Cardinal will, for I am a very son to him." He piled it on, until it was necessary to smile, and yet its ardour was, at the moment, convincing.

Louise of Savoy hovered near her darling, and Marguerite of Alençon was by him, the devoted sister who had planned his escape from his dungeon.

Their yearning for the man who had been at last released—"they menaced to lay irons on him," Marguerite was saying—gave Thomas the deepest impression of gentleness. The two women were separated by more than years, the mother testy and gouty, the sister a woman of sublime nature, with depths of sensitiveness and poignant emotion, yet quick, rich humour.

They knew, of course, that their beloved King Henry had only been kept by the danger of revolution at home from sending over a great army to smash up France. That they knew, perfectly well, while Francis poured out his gratitude.

Yet all three—mother, son and daughter—were so tuned to one another, so finely allied, so acute, that Thomas's first untoward impression was dissolved in the sense of their refinement. It passed anything he had ever before experiencd.

They were somewhat shabbily robed, if he went by Greenwich standards, and they were casual and unceremonious. But to be with them, even as a stranger, was to see the efflorescence of natures that had reached a consummation of intimacy, in ease as well as discrimination, which gave Thomas a curious sense of their tolerant power— power to apprehend all round, power to foresee, to bend, and to assert themselves. It was at this Court that Anne Boleyn had been at home. Yet it was not their power that most impressed Thomas. He perceived something else, some essential in them, that made him feel like the member of a younger race. They were, in some way, alive to everything—to religion, to war, to politics, to art—as a complex that they mastered, not by pedantry, but by susceptibility, and for the sake of this consummate social intimacy he was observing.

While Thomas mused on it, the King and Thomas Cheyney and the Queen-Mother drew away. Marguerite then came over to himself.

"So," she said quietly, "you are the poet. I have known of you."

Thomas blushed.

"It is of you that la petite has spoken. La petite Boullain. You must tell me of her."

Thomas bowed. Marguerite had strange eyes. They seemed to have a film over them, giving them a melancholy and mysterious expression.

"Come," she smiled when Thomas had spoken of Anne. "I have something." She led him to a window-seat, on which a box was lying. She searched about in its warm disorder. "This is desperate," she said. "It is a manuscript. We have travelled so much, I cannot keep things in order. You write now, Monsieur?"

"At times, Madame."

"Had we time! You know I saw the brouillon you sent to la Boullain?"

"You remember that!"

"I have not forgotten it, though my English! You are enviable, Monsieur."

"But it is so painful to try new forms."

"Birth is painful," she looked at him with a light smile at her platitude. "They conspire about you over in the corner, to send you to England to-night. And when you come back, you are to meet Bourbon, Nicole Bourbon, and Marot. We'll talk of the Italians."

Thomas, so alive to her, had already stirred that mobile imagination. Everything in her life depended for her on her brother, to a degree that nothing could limit. Her devotion was unimaginable. But if he wanted her to marry Henry VIII, she was ready for it. She was one year younger than Henry, and the thought of it was amusing, were it not that she was so wedded to France and to Francis.

Her mother called her. Then Thomas learned that, in the interests of the new league, he was to depart instantly with a despatch for England.

## XII

NOT A MOMENT was squandered by Thomas Wyatt in posting home from Cognac. He brought the last word of King Francis's intentions. He was entrusted with gifts. And every day counted, because every day threatened the outbreak of another war.

By nature one of those footloose men who roam the world, disarming it with a smile, Thomas saw many a place he would have loved to linger in, many a broken soldier or sage innkeeper with whom he would have chosen to gossip. His quick eye read every sign of a coloured and inviting life. France, with its brave folk and its gracious distances, worked in his blood. He sighed as he came on one happy surprise on another, the sudden sight of a castle, the glory of a Gothic church, the moulded styles of long civilization. These he had eyes for, as he had ears for the language. But he had no right to loiter.

As he pushed forward without mercy, he never lacked for admirers, but this, first of all, was for his royal companions: two mules from King Francis to King Henry, magnificently caparisoned, the most elegant and ennobled of mules.

Never had Thomas had passports like these. If the girls threw a look at him, it was the mules they began with. Priests stopped to look at them. Burgesses steered swelling bellies to a halt, to have a full view of them. The mules took it in. They had long, nervous heads, like officials of the inquisition, and they sidled with disdain. But from these sumptuous animals, who established Thomas's status, the French did in the end cast a glance at Thomas himself, and that tall young figure, amiable and lambent, made even fishwives mellow, and induced gaping boys to forget the hoofs of mules. Was he a lord, or a young prince? No, he did not impose himself, yet they felt he was Someone, and knew he was benign.

The impression he gave was nothing to Thomas, since he and his mules had to speed on. "On, on," he spurred himself: he was a courier.

The King was not at Greenwich. The King had gone hunting. So Thomas, throwing a weary leg across the saddle, turned his horse's head around. He was one of thousands who had hoped to rest their limbs when they heard the Master was out hunting.

He had been out from five in the morning, so Thomas was told at Penshurst. Thomas waited. His sweat dried on him. His delight in his own quickness sank low.

Henry, weary from the chase, put in an appearance as daylight faded, about nine o'clock.

"By the Mass, you lost no time!" Henry greeted him cordially, laying a hand on his shoulder. He took King Francis's own brief letter, nodding as he read it, and he brushed Cheyney's despatch with a hasty look.

"In the morning, then, we'll study this." He was famished with hunger. "Come to me, after your supper." He had first to hear evensong. He bustled into the manor, while the carcase of a deer was taken to be prepared for Cardinal Wolsey. His presence brought everyone to life, and as Thomas found his way to the squires, Henry went to be freshly attired before he prayed.

Once Thomas related to him all that he had learned (not after supper, since the Queen was too much there, but in the morning) there was place in him but for a single thought: to go to Hever. He knew he had made a fair impression on the King, who had jabbed him with questions, but in the few days, or even hours, that were left to him before he should return, he wished for Anne Boleyn. To display himself, to tell her of Francis and Marguerite, and above everything to see her. He thirsted for her with that exquisite anguish which, painful as it is, may have in it a promise of heaven. His impatience blinded him as he spurred to Hever.

## XIII

A LATTICED WINDOW stood open as Thomas waited for Anne.

"His Grace was with her yesterday," Sarah had told him, as he passed a word with her in the pantry. "He blew his trumpet in yon wood, then here he was, like he was yourself." She waved a cloth. "I hate flies! 'Tis the second time his Grace come in eight days. One of our family I call him, Master Tom. How he's gone to flesh! Not like you, Master Tom. You're thin as paper!"

Thomas had left her to wait by the window. A rose came above its ledge, and lifted its blossom to the light. It was a glowing pink, though in the outer leaves it whitened to a tender hue, a mere tinge of violet.

A bee sailed into the room and zoomed unheard by Thomas's ear. He did not see the delicate rose that nodded at him, or heed the bee. Bathed though he was in the enticing sun, he brooded on the scene with an eye that seemed glazed. His face was ominously pale.

"Wake up, Thomas!" Anne spoke from behind his shoulder. "You grew deaf in France?"

He turned abruptly. Her smile rained on him.

"The King was with you yesterday," he rasped in a queer, dry voice.

"Thomas!" she stepped back.

The blood flared into Thomas's head as he gazed at her. Up till now he had not admitted his suspicions, even to himself. They had pressed against his intense feeling for her, and he had forced them back, and his repression had dazed him. Now, within reach of her, this sweet water he had thirsted for was bitter, and his doubt of her mounted to such a height that it flooded him with a wave of accusatory warmth.

"You are seeing him alone," he flamed, his eyes sharpened to pinpoints.

Anne gazed hard at him, her bosom rising. "This is no trifle, Thomas. Come! What do you mean?"

With her eyes full upon him like this, and her voice hard and cold, the fatigued wretch was suddenly seized by the danger he was running. Their eyes met. He wavered.

"Nay, but this is grave, cousin," said Anne with icy coldness. She turned to lay aside her gauntlets and her flowers. He saw her profile in its severity. Then she turned to him again.

"It is he, not you," said Thomas. But the words he had spoken were silenced by Lady Rochford entering the hall.

## XIV

HIS RETURN TO COGNAC was speedy, but he was allowed to go back without any kind word, or any confidence, from Anne.

She foresaw a whole summer in which she would be out of touch with Thomas, and in close touch with the King. This was because the King intended to go on "progress," in a circle at about a day's ride from London, hunting from the manors and the castles of his most favoured subjects, and doing as little political business as possible. He was devising every means, as became an ardent suitor, for making his visits through the home country coincide with Anne's presence. Her father was in his entourage. He was taking George with him. He was weaving Anne into his fatherly meeting with Princess Mary and into his occasional reunions with the Queen. So Anne could not hope to avoid him. She could pit herself against him with all her skill, counting on her feline agility and even her claws to protect her in case of necessity. But unless she pleaded illness, or went into a convent, she was attached to the Court like a tail to a kite, and when the rope pulled, up she had to go and soar and follow.

It was painfully clear that Thomas had lost faith in her. His visit— she had deplored it, she cursed it. But as he had actually not seen the King, she did not feel forced to explain that it was he who was pursuing her. To excuse herself would be to create a tension that the long summer would make intolerable. Her motives for silence were not clear, even to herself, but they were as powerful as they were obscure, and before Thomas returned she was braced to evade him, and to say nothing.

So it was then, for the first time, that he really learned to suffer.

Once he was home in England he again hastened to Anne to bring her a fine flagon of perfume from Cognac.

"I cannot linger," hurried Anne. "Your tale may wait." She stood about to wing away.

"I lived but to return," cried Thomas. "I burn to see you."

"We are about to leave," she smiled. "His Grace goes on progress. Now I fly." She receded, to wave farewell.

He followed her, his face aflame. "Be not so cruel, Anne. I am parched. Give me a word."

"Nay," she murmured, "you are galliard from Cognac. These are French practices." With these teasing words, Anne fled. Thomas was at a standstill.

To be evaded, when he had so much to tell her, churned him into a frenzy. He had caught fire at seeing her. But instead of anger he was filled with a mad longing to melt her. He went to his home with a desolation so absolute, and so helpless, that he flung himself down and ached for tears, the vision of Anne taunting him like a goddess who never can have mercy.

He reached a state where life itself became a waste land, though the cause of his misery passed into insensibility. He made little effort to see Anne. He heard of the Great Death, the plague, with a melancholy contempt. He was no longer suffering acutely. He even, for brief spells, could chat and laugh like Thomas Wyatt.

But this grey respite was the only relief that he was to know for many months. Instead of avoiding Anne, he was ready, as winter approached, to resume his effort. His will was firm. He was determined to make her speak to him.

She was no longer at Greenwich. She had left for Hever.

To follow her was impossible. That she could have escaped him, and that he had relaxed his efforts to be with her, mounted for him into an infidelity for which he could not cease to reproach himself. He blamed himself for this; for his jealousy, and for his unworthiness. All the grief of a sinner who has committed the unpardonable sin— Thomas experienced it. He began to work round in a groove of self-reproach with the haggard aspect of a slave. He milled incessantly in this fever.

It was a kind of living death that he was enduring. He ate, he drank, he rode on his horse, he went to the jewel house, he talked of France, he even joked and took part in games, and watched the others enjoying themselves. But his disease was almost like the loss of honour, it penetrated him irremediably. The love that Anne had given him was no longer a solace. It was the memory of light to a man suddenly blinded, never to enjoy it again, something the very thought of which was immeasurably empty. Anne had disappeared from this souvenir of their being together. Her essence escaped him. He was searching for something for which he had no name, some meaning in things, some core in existence, something that could give him a feeling. Nothing but Anne gave him any feeling, and to be without her was incomprehensible.

## XV

With christmas she returned. She avoided him. And then he learned that she was to be Venus in a pageant.

He made his way to her apartment at Greenwich.

"And you will be party to this festivity?" he demanded.

"Unless your Highness forbid it," mocked Anne.

"I bow to your true Highness. You are to be one of the damsels mayhap?"

"A maid, you mean?"

"Why not?"

"No more a maid, you fear?" she jeered.

"Then perchance you are Venus herself?"

"And wherefore not?" Anne laughed harshly.

"Doth his Grace require this of you?" Thomas asked with savage seriousness.

"Oh, God, be not untoward!" Anne changed at once. "This is but mummery. I can endure your frown no longer, Thomas, you are my true darling. Speak. Have mercy!"

"You are to be Venus for him in this pageant?" Thomas repeated bitterly.

"You need not gaze on me."

"I, with their eyes upon you, to strip you with the others?"

"Were I without a stitch, I still am yours," Anne's lip quivered. "You drive me from you with your anger. What if he lay this upon me? He hath sent compasses to father, all new gear, for the boat *Anne Boleyn*. He heaps up the measure. How can I say nay to him? Can I repulse him, other than I do? You are never mine, never can be mine. Oh, God, now I melt. Now I betray myself. Had you a heart, or brain, or good sense, you would not break me. What if I be Venus? 'Tis in play."

"Not for this I plead with you," groaned Thomas.

"God pity me," said Anne, sobbing.

"This I cannot bear," said Thomas.

"Say nothing," she tried to stop her tears. "This is the worst." She turned away from him.

"What have I done?" he moaned.

"Alas, what ails me!" She stamped her foot, her tears mastering her. Thomas put his arms round her, so that she twisted to him and embraced him. "I can do nothing," she sobbed. "I was so well off with you, and now—now——" He held her, while her tears fell on his neck.

"Nothing can help," she wailed bitterly, and quivered in his arms. "I cannot stop it now." She buried her face against him, and wept so terribly that she scarcely could speak. Her words were so tender, so desperate and so full of anguish, that he was tormented beyond words. To hear her sob and groan made him curse his fate in such a frenzy that at last she pushed him. "Go hence, my Thomas, my love. I can endure it no more."

He heard such despair in her voice, and such mournfulness, that he resisted, but her hand spoke to him, and he left her.

## XVI

HE HELD TO HIMSELF on the barge, but in spite of himself he could not help seeing Sir John Russell, whose cloak was heavy and who wore riding boots.

"Whither bound, cousin Russell?" Thomas was forced to speak.

"To Italy," came the cool voice, "sent by the King."

At these words Thomas's heart gave a mad leap. Before he knew what he was doing, the skin of his face drawn on his bones as if by some torturer, he turned to Russell, "And I will, if you please, ask leave, get money, and go with you?"

"No man more welcome," said John Russell in a surprised but happy voice. "But there's no time for banquet or pageant, friend Wyatt. I part on the morrow."

"All the better," cried Thomas. "I'll meet you at whatever hour, by London Bridge."

"Well said, it must be seven of the clock."

They parted with a handshake. Thomas rushed to his father, who saw the King for him. With his purse filled, his gear ready, and well mounted and attended, he joined John Russell the next morning.

# Chapter 11

B<small>Y THE TIME</small> that John Russell and Thomas had come to a halt at Canterbury, cold and mud-stained, their fellow-courtiers were arriving at the palace on the Thames which, in the January dark, was ablaze with festal lighting. Barges followed one another to the water-gate, while torchbearers attended the Cardinal's guests to the main entrance. They were gathering for a banquet, and to see Venus bestow her nymphs on her favourites.

These guests had scarcely seated themselves at table when a roar of cannon was heard beneath the windows of York Place.

"What is this?" exclaimed the host. "We attend no guests. Prithee," he turned to two of the royal household, "tell me who arrives."

From a window on the river, "Noblemen," said Lord Sandes, "I see them. They are at the water-gate."

"And a score or more of torches," added Sir Harry Guildford.

"Ah," exclaimed Wolsey, "ambassadors, forsooth! Since ye speak French," he smiled to the two royal officers, "take pains to go down to the hall and do them fitting honour. Let us bid them hither." He looked at his company, and then, with a sweep of the hand, "Let them sit down with us and join these noble personages who make good cheer. Yea, conduct these strangers to our fare and pastime!"

This liberality was scarcely uttered before a swirl of music burst from below, to stop all talk, and with fife and drum to lead them six and thirty torchbearers mounted the broad stairs, parting to admit the strangers. Two by two, they advanced to make reverence to the Cardinal. They were tall bearded men, wearing high caps and flashing cloaks of gold and crimson satin.

"They be strangers," Lord Sandes explained for them, "and speak no English."

Everyone smiled at them, but waited for further explanation.

"Hearing, my lord Cardinal, of this triumphant banquet and such a number of excellent fair dames assembled——"

The excellent fair dames were not captured so easily.

"——they could do no less, under permission of your Grace, than hither to repair, as well to view their incomparable beauty," Lord Sandes bowed, "as to play with them at mumchance——"

Mumchance! They were amused at this.

"——and after to dance with them, should your Grace so please to licence them."

With a ripple and a glow of pleasure, the guests heard Wolsey. "We are well content to welcome ye."

So the maskers did their duty. They greeted and kissed the ladies. One of them opened a cup of gold. Out of it they picked coins, and cast dice with each lady. A couple of hundred crowns remained when all had played. With a large gesture a masker emptied the cup before the Cardinal and bowed low to him.

"At all!" the great gambler spilled the dice. In this single cast the Cardinal won, and everyone broke into applause.

"So there!" The Cardinal wiped his nervous mouth, grinning triumphantly. "Now, there should be among them one we should honour above the others. I would most gladly, if I knew him, sur-render my place to him, according to my duty."

Lord Sandes made an inquiry. "Sir," he reported, "they do confess there is a noble personage among them. If your Grace point him out he must disclose himself and accept your place most worthily."

The Cardinal rose and, squinting keenly from those with gold-wire

beards and silver-wire beards to a black-visored giant with a black
beard. "Meseemeth," he proclaimed loudly, "the gentleman with the
black beard should be even he." He unctuously removed his cap and
indicated his high chair.

The massive personage bowed low and sat under the cloth of state,
wearing his visor.

A gale of laughter came from another of the guests. "By St. George!"
he exploded, like a schoolboy, plucking off his own visor and then the
honoured guest's. The Cardinal had picked Sir Edward Nevill in error
for Henry.

The mistake was so amusing that, under cover of repeated laughter,
the maskers left. New and perfumed cloths were spread, a fresh banquet was rapidly laid, and by the time the King appeared in court
apparel a splendour of costly dishes with meats of rare device came
to the table.

After the feast they went down to the hall, where a stage had been
raised. Here a comedy of Plautus, the Menæchmi, was recited by
actors, each of whom came kneeling afterwards to the King, and
reciting Latin verses that praised him as richly as the Cardinal had
feasted him.

But these praises Henry scarcely heard. The whole evening he had
waited, and his moment was at hand.

"Tell them to douce the lights," he barked at Harry Guildford.

Only the stage was left bright. Then a high curtain fell away, to
music of viol and flute, while high above the audience, softly lighted,
with six damsels at her feet, sat Venus enthroned. So startling was
this apparition of a beauty in golden tresses that Henry never noticed
three naked boys who pulled in Cupid on a chariot, with six of the
strangers drawn after it by a silver rope. As the trumpets gave a
flourish, Henry turned to Harry Guildford.

"What is this?" he cried. "This is Madge Shelton, not Mistress
Anne Boleyn."

All he had craved to enjoy was stolen from him. The Venus before
his eyes was as lovely as could be desired, but as she bestowed her
nymphs on the forlorn strangers, each couple dancing away to the
trumpet, Henry looked restlessly from side to side. Anne was nowhere. He was so disturbed by this that the chamberlain had to come

to him. Then he opened the dance, and it did not cease until day was breaking over the Thames.

## II

THOMAS'S DEPARTURE for Italy had come so suddenly for Anne that she pleaded illness to her cousin Madge Shelton, and herself hurried home to Kent. Up to this she had been blithe. So long as he was near her, no matter how hurt he was, his love sustained her and she was able to evade, or even coquette with, the King. But it struck her a cruel blow to have him desert her in the dead of winter. It left her without a shred of hope. She cared nothing for Henry's anger or disappointment. She only yearned to be alone, to escape to Hever.

She had never let herself realize that she must choose between them. Each of these lovers, after all, was married, and with a touch of malice that sprang from her own plight she had watched them struggling in the toils of disability: it was not her fault if they were unhappy in pursuit of her when they had no right to pursue her, when they had no honour to do her, nothing to assert but their love which, as each of them knew, was not put to the proof in public, and never could be.

But this was the play of a malicious spirit. When Thomas actually left of his own desperate will, to go to an Italy ravaged by war, the comedy ended. The sustenance he had given her heart—it was all the true love she had. It was all that made her a being who could feel, believe in her feelings, and believe in herself. Thomas was not only a palpable man to her. He was warmth, indulgence, adoration and life. To have him go away from her, in despair, was the death of every hidden hope. She did not say to herself that with Thomas she could have flown beyond the bounds that Hever set to her. She did not give it words. But the strength she had drawn from him, from that clouded yet faithful attendance on her, no longer existed. He was no longer there. She had been swept by a storm of emotion when she knew he would go. At that dreadful moment, defenceless and honest, the very roots of her heart were torn by anguish of separation. Then she became numb. He was gone. There was nothing to do.

Yet for the time being she lost power over her will. She refused to obey her mother's urgent summons and return to Court. She was not violent, she was immovable, and Lady Rochford knew her too well to put pressure on her.

## III

The king was astonished and almost humiliated. He had taken it for granted that Mistress Anne was to appear as Venus. He sent Lady Rochford to Hever, but day followed day and they did not come. They were not coming. This extraordinary defection was not the sort of thing that happened to Henry VIII. He found himself moved by amazing apprehensions. What had he said? What had he done? He could hardly bend his mind to the necessary negotiations with France.

Cardinal Wolsey had pushed those negotiations to the utmost limit. The new seal of England still named Henry King of France, but the extinction of all old claims was nothing, to Wolsey's mind, if Francis would be bold to break off clean with the Emperor and give Marguerite, his own sister, to Henry VIII.

Every day, as Thomas Wyatt and Sir John Russell pushed forward with succour to the Pope, Wolsey waited fretfully for news from Paris that King Francis had been won over. This French alliance was now Wolsey's master ambition. He cared nothing for the legal or theological obstacles that stood in the way of discarding Queen Catherine. The Emperor's aunt was now no bride for England if he could secure Marguerite of Alençon. Her consent the Cardinal was sure of, if Francis would agree. Never had it been so painful for Wolsey to sit at Westminster while his ambassadors fumbled into the French mind. The one argument against him, he knew, was the imprisoned children. The Emperor held Francis by that, yet he would do anything to please England. His heart gave him, he sent word, that he should find himself a true brother to Henry. Yes, yes, but his heart also gave him that the Emperor held his two boys. No father could dare to displease the man who, by a single word, could sentence those children to undeserved death. The Emperor's own father had been removed from the scene in Spain, and Wolsey no more doubted how it had been done than that the Princes had been murdered in the Tower. He groaned at his impuissance. Save for these hostages, he could make certain of this French marriage. And this was the great crisis, the pressing moment, the chance for a true union.

"What is to come out of it?" the King nervously asked Wolsey. "We make great offers, my lord Cardinal."

"That we do, your Grace. Methinks he may turn to us as the broken man to the Samaritan, and beg our aid against the Emperor if he refuse to restore his sons."

King Henry stirred impatiently. "But the Duchess of Alençon? She hath had my likeness."

"The post arrives, your Grace. Hark!"

The Cardinal opened Clerk's despatch with trembling fingers. He read it in a sweeping glance, and then coughed. He scrutinized Henry anxiously. "King Francis thinks to invade Spain from the north, should the Emperor remove to Italy——"

"Yes," snapped the King, "but is Clerk a fool? Doth he say nothing of our marriage?"

"He says, your Grace," replied Wolsey in his gravest voice, "that on Wednesday last past, the Duchess of Alençon was married to the young King of Navarre."

"What!"

"Yea, your Grace. He would not wait for us." With a limp hand Wolsey dropped the parchment to the table, and looked at Henry.

Henry looked stonily at the Cardinal. He was touched to the quick, outraged and humiliated, but his pride compelled him to hide it. He picked up Clerk's despatch with a quick move and pretended to study it. The Cardinal looked at him from under his eyebrows, almost as an apprehensive wife looks at her young husband. He saw Henry's resentment, and the fury with which his ideas were revolving. But well as he knew the King, he could not fathom the sudden emotion that was flooding him.

"That was the young prince who escaped after Pavia?" Henry said in a choked voice.

"The same, your Grace."

"And the French choose to recover Navarre through his aid rather than marry us?"

"Navarre is their dearest care, your Grace."

"Yea," said Henry, with intense quiet. "Yea, by Jesu, this may not be so untoward as it seem."

"But, your Grace," Wolsey brooded, "this stroke we fancied."

"No, by God," flared Henry. "The lady is well. I say nothing of that. But I never chose it."

Wolsey turned pale. He half raised his hands. "And now you will not meet them. You will not give Princess Mary to King Francis?"

"She's eleven, my little girl." Henry stuck out his jaw. "Mayhap two year from now."

"But it is at a point." Wolsey made grimace. "The King of France's mother urges it."

"How now?"

"She was married in her eleventh year, your Grace, and many over there are married at the same age without evil following."

"Who knows that?" sneered Henry.

"When our Princess comes twelve, her ladyship thinks, she might be delivered six or seven months thereafter without danger. She trusts we will not stick in this matter. She sees no danger."

"Married before thirteen?" Henry glared at Wolsey.

"It is to make sure," said Wolsey slowly, "that neither party should vary." He tapped the table with a finger. "Wait a year, the Emperor may have triumphed. Join them when nature allows, and we are one."

"But Mary is a child," the father demurred. "You must respect that."

"That is so," the churchman deferred. "Yet Madame Louise is of our mind, and herself hath sketched a course."

"Let's hear it," frowned Henry.

"After the marriage solemnized at Calais, the King might abed himself for an hour or less, with my lady Princess. The King her son, she saith, is a man of honour and discretion, and will use no violence, especially the father and mother being so nigh."

Henry removed his bonnet and scratched his bald head. "I do not trust them," he said. "Do you like this of yourself?"

The Cardinal pondered, his grey cheeks hanging down. " 'Tis displeasant," he said, "yet I entertain it. Your Grace, so much may hap."

"Yes," Henry grunted, "but he cannot marry her, not till she is thirteen, full thirteen."

## IV

STILL SEETHING with resentment, Henry left the Cardinal, and instead of turning to Harry Norris, he set off as if busy. A King has no freedom unless resourceful, but Henry frowned his way to the royal Chapel, and no one ventured to follow him.

It was empty at this hour, melancholy in the flat grey light, with shadows cumbering the vaults, and sounds expiring in that hollow vacuity which is still so full of dullness. Before the lonely altar there hung a lamp, a sole witness to the living faith.

Henry entered his oratory, knelt to breathe a prayer, and then drew into protective solitude to meet his agitated mind.

His fury at the slight that had been given him, this marriage of Marguerite to a princeling, was something against which it was his instinct to batter himself, in all its outrage to his pride.

But no sooner had this been born in his soul, with a rush of overwhelming feeling, than his pride again was troubled. For over a year he had been in love with Anne Boleyn. The depth of this, strangely enough, was mingled with tender moments he had never forgotten with Mary and her mother. This was incongruous, but it was so. Yet however powerfully he was moved to her, he was still uncertain of her, and his mind was torn. Might she, by accident, have learned the great secret, his suit at the French Court? The mere chance of it made him groan. "By God," he thought, "that may be it." He wanted to rush out to deny it. "But wait, wait," he reflected, "I must think this out." He leaned forward, breathing hard, with his face in his hands.

Had Anne not absented herself, her place in his heart could never have been so painfully known. Her refusal to leave Hever, couched humbly though it was, alarmed him even more than her defection as Venus. She was outside him, beyond him, unattainable. Would she have him, even if he were free? So intolerable was this question, so sharp his longing and his doubt, that Henry could not endure it another hour: he would write to offer himself to her, come weal, come woe. That alone could settle it.

This determination, inchoate for weeks, at last burned clear. Perhaps she had something against it. Perhaps she would refuse him. But he had no need to reflect longer. He would end the hell of doubt by writing plainly to her. Then, God willing, he might have the woman he honestly desired, be blessed with a son by her, and defy all of them.

So great a sense of freedom did his resolve give him that the rest was nothing. If she consented. If only she did that, the trouble of the divorce would be no great thing, the Cardinal would be well able for it. Anne was the daughter of a Howard and had royal blood in her veins. She was a good Frenchwoman, and on that side would be welcomed. But all these usual points, her rank, her fortune, her fame, her nation—all of them sank into nothingness for Henry when he knew that he loved her enough to make her Queen and mother of his heir. Only he could know this. Only he had the right and the power to take so bold a step. It bloomed for him into a sudden glory. He would write at once, but cautiously, and send Brereton with it to Hever.

He started to leave the royal oratory when the door pushed against him. There was the Queen.

"You, Catherine," he exclaimed.

"Henry!" Catherine's face expressed wonder, a wan and pathetic radiance transforming it. "You came to pray alone, Henry?"

"Why not," he growled.

"I begin a Novena," continued Catherine eagerly. "And you?"

"Pray take your place. I am on my way." With his little grunt, he bowed her in, and closed the private door. He hurried away to write to Hever.

## V

ANNE had promptly greeted Will Brereton and sent him to refresh himself while he was to wait to take back an answer to the King. She was now hidden in her room with Henry's letter in her hand.

"If it shall please you to do me the office of a true, loyal mistress and friend, and to give yourself up, body and soul to me who will be and have been your very loyal servant (if by your severity you do not forbid me), I promise you that not only shall the name be given you, but that also I will take you for my only mistress, rejecting from thought and affection all others save yourself, to serve you only."

She read it again and again. Outside the sky was soft with the grey plumage of January. She went to the window, cool and abstract, yet feverishly occupied within. Her figure was slender. No one could have thought her a voluptuous or dazzling female. She was slightly built, but in the poise of the small head, in the beautiful modelling of her features, and in the dauntless eyes, which were not only steady but of a black magnificence, she incarnated a primitive force that could bring any man to his knees. Her sex had none of the tenderness that made Beth Darrell or Madge Shelton so sweet. It was a flame within her, yet did not force her to yield. She had aloofness and disdain, an awareness of desire that resisted while it attracted, but there was also a power that Thomas Wyatt had felt from the beginning, the promise of completion that only a nature so ardent could possibly give and redeem.

Henry's letter to her was directly addressed to this power that she knew herself to possess, "body and soul." He had hunted her, and he had cornered her. "Beseeching you," she glanced again, "to make me answer absolute to this my rude letter." Yes, answer absolute. She could not, like a hunted deer, find another opening in the wood. She was at a stand. He had closed in.

"Of necessity," she glanced once more, "I must ensure me of this answer, having been now above one whole year struck with the dart of love."

Struck with the dart of love! She now saw him, clear in her mind's eye, and she believed that he did love her. He was ready to give her everything.

That the King of England should be at her feet, should promise to reject all save herself, and serve her only, was a triumph that literally made Anne tremble. A sombre, metallic brightness in her eyes proved what it meant to her pride. Her uncle Norfolk had disdained her. Her father and mother had deserted her when she was banished from Court. The Cardinal had publicly humiliated her. These were things she could not forget, and to step from despised obscurity to a position they must bow to, gave her a fierce pang of satisfaction. But everything, even this satisfaction, especially the gratification of revenging herself on Wolsey, depended for Anne on a man who proposed to make her his own. It was this that held her so tense in the window.

She asked herself, Dare I? And she did not know the answer.

What pleaded for Henry, as she mused on those same bare trees that Thomas had seen one night two years before, was not the caress he could lavish on her. That did not melt her. What touched her was not his force. Though the glamour of Kingship bathed him, that was not speaking for him. Yet she could feel something within herself plead for him as she was driven to renounce him.

He was himself so strong that he could scarcely imagine the opponent he could not down. None in the tiltyard could hope to resist him, and this not in his young manhood but as he neared five and thirty, and as she saw him year by year. This powerful and sanguine Henry was not Anne's Henry, brave as she reckoned him. Suffolk was brave, yet Anne despised him. He was nearly a match for Henry at the joust, yet in council he could only beat an obedient drum and recite his orders. And though Henry infinitely surpassed Suffolk in his brain, even his brain did not awe her. She had seen flaws in many a lofty argument of his. But his powers of "singular love," his dependence on her, his faith—they pleaded for him inside the defence from which she had fought him back. She had felt and seen a large nature in him, a morning brightness in him, something that could rise over and beyond the sons of disillusion who attended him. He had a zest that could carry her away. When he was a small boy, he once had told her, he had found a bit of stone at Westminster. He drew it across a slab. It made a mark. He scrawled with it, a few wild lines. That was a ship. "The stone can draw," he cried to his grandmother. "It can draw, the stone can draw." He had invented art, and his delight he had never forgotten. That was in him, strange in his domineering nature, where there were so many graces and surprises. All of this moved Anne. All of this, prompted by his letter, beat against her heart. She could see him, humble, pleading with her, and overwhelming her.

She suffered, not in her heart, in another depth, some unnamed region where it was shame to admit the choice that the King forced on her. If she left Thomas, it must be in his absence. She had not the strength to do it otherwise. She was not strong enough to wait for him or to endure being near him without having him. She had to put an end to it.

She walked to her table, hesitated, and returned to the window. But Brereton was waiting. She quickly sat down and picked up a quill. In a few rapid words she bowed herself humbly to her tremendous lover. Now it was done.

## VI

THE ROADS FROM HEVER were sodden, the night foul and dark, but Brereton did not spare himself in returning with Anne's answer. He knew, when she gave it to him, that it must be most personal, since he had orders to deliver it into the King's own hands. Good servant though he was, he was no eunuch, yet he was just as remote as one when he delivered up Anne's reply at Eltham.

What he could not guess, however, was the exact state of this courtship between the King and his subject. Even Henry, tremulously eager for Anne's reply, did not know where he stood with the girl he was courting. He had required her to answer him, yes or no, but he could not be certain of her.

As he read it, his eyes dimmed with tears and he was flooded with tenderness. Exceedingly humble, exceedingly flattering, she submitted to his will. In every line there was the glow of her youth, a freshness that to Henry's heart was inexpressibly touching, and the knowledge that she was to become his own, body and soul, when for so long he had been in doubt of it, spread through him with a sweetness that submerged him. He instantly thought, "What can I give her?" Some jewel, some token worthy of her submission to him, must at once be dispatched to Hever. He could not, of course, consult Queen Catherine, with whom he usually debated these extravagances. No, not Queen Catherine. But he could pick out a token himself, and then, with a letter to convey his happiness, she would be assured of him till he had the joy of seeing her.

This was Henry's first impulse as a lover, and he yielded to it unreservedly.

"My mistress and friend," he wrote to her, deploring her absence, "seeing that I cannot be personally present with you, I now send the thing most nearly thereto appertaining that it is possible to me to send, which is my picture set in a bracelet, with the whole of the device which you already know, wishing myself in their place, and it should please you."

## VII

ANNE COULD NOT DOUBT, from this picture that Henry sent her, how utterly he was committing himself to her. She had caught herself brooding on Thomas Wyatt, but it was now too late. Looking among her own things for a present to convey her state of mind, she selected a boat with a solitary damsel in it, tossed about on a diamond sea, and this, with a letter of even greater submission, went on its way to Greenwich, to convince Henry that her fate was in his hands.

Soberly as Anne looked at this, knowing her essential helplessness before so powerful a man as Henry, her mind was by no means as quiescent as her spirit. Henry promised to "serve her only." This meant that the Queen's false relation to him would have to be made clear, both in obedience to his conscience and this promise he was giving her. And, as Anne reflected on this, her mind leaped into extraordinary activity. Her long tutelage at Court and in her diplomat family made her see in the proposal conveyed by Henry's letter not any vague or sentimental offer but a definite, a binding promise.

Had Anne consulted her heart, she could not have readily submitted to Henry, but her separation from Thomas closed her heart, and it was with her reason that she took the promise, the contract, so eagerly urged by the King. Her horror of what had happened to Mary, her exasperation at what had happened to herself with a man under Thomas Wyatt's disability, as well as her sullen anger with the Cardinal over the humiliation she had experienced on Percy's account —all these blended into an emotion so strong that nothing could satisfy her except a fulfilment of Henry's pledge to give her the first place in his life. Her injured pride asserted itself, beneath the helplessness that she honestly felt in submitting to the King, and no sooner had the messenger departed with her jewel than she began to examine the steps that they must take, to secure Henry's divorce and their marriage. This was a project she had never set out with, but she seized on it with a surprising vehemence, and with a vision as sharp as it was unwavering.

Anne was a Boleyn, to be sure, but on her mother's side she was a

Howard, a member of the foremost military family in England, whose prowess on land and sea had been affirmed repeatedly within a few years, whether in the victory at Flodden, the savage raids on Brittany, or the epic naval battle when her uncle had been a heroic sacrifice. It was in their spirit, and not in her father's, that Anne gave herself up to the goal which alone induced her to accept Henry, the goal of becoming Queen of England.

She could see the field as plainly as her grandfather saw Flodden. The pivot of the divorce must be the Pope, since Henry during the summer had revealed to her that the existing marriage was invalid. The Cardinal would hate her: but he had no way of defeating her if they secured the Pope's consent on theological grounds. He was the Pope's legate, as well as Prime Minister, and he was committed to the divorce. Young and disillusioned, Anne saw no reason to temper her harsh and exultant view of the difficulty in which Wolsey must find himself. She had only to be fully certain of the King to force this action, and on this she felt clear-headed and spirited.

Her gift gave intense delight to Henry, as well as her letter. He thanked her right cordially for both. She was too humble, but this he set down as her great benevolence and goodwill, "for which I have sought, do seek, and shall always seek by all services to me possible there to remain, in which my hope hath set up his everlasting nest, saying *aut illic aut nullibi.*"

"Henceforth," he added, in a rush of generous exaltation, "henceforth my heart shall be dedicate to you alone, greatly desirous that so my body could be as well, as God can bring to pass if it pleaseth Him, Whom I entreat once each day for the accomplishment thereof, trusting that at length my prayer will be heard, wishing the time brief, and thinking it but long until we shall see each other again."

Thus he pledged himself with pious fervour, and then, urged by the same passion which possessed him as a boy, he traced a heart at the end of his script, with A.B. quite filling it. "Written with the hand of that secretary who in heart, body and will is Your loyal and most ensured servant."

No, Anne could no longer doubt it. The King was hers. But it was not to God she prayed to bring it to pass that she and the King be united. Anne could not leave it to Providence.

"The King must not let the Cardinal know of it," she told herself. "He must appeal straight to the Pope." And with her mind made up, so strongly that she was diamond-clear, she at last felt it would be safe to return to Greenwich.

One thing, however, had to be done. She went to her mother.

"Mamma," she said, "what has come to pass may not be hid from you." She gave her Henry's letters and walked away from her.

Lady Rochford read them slowly and unflinchingly. Then she called Anne and looked at her without wavering. "He means to marry you."

"So I believe," said Anne quietly.

"Would you that I said nothing?" Lady Rochford held the folded letters.

"I pray you, Mamma, give me your counsel."

"He loves you," she said, "as perchance he never loved in all his days. So much is certain."

"That I feel," Anne murmured.

"Would you marry him?" Lady Rochford gave her a piercing look.

"Yes, Mamma."

"Most women would. I wish you well of it, Anne."

"You fear it for me?" Anne was cool.

"Men are so covetous, it is seldom safe to gratify them, yet his Grace may grow in love as he possesses you. Have you thought of this?"

"Of everything, Mamma."

"Then the Queen. I cannot stay by her longer."

"Let this wait, if you please, Mamma. So much may hap."

"I fear this for you," said the mother.

"Wherefore?" asked Anne, astonished. "A divorce must be decreed since his Grace's marriage is void. So saith the Cardinal."

"Yea, but her Grace." Lady Rochford was stern. "She will never yield."

"But she hath no choice, Mamma. The Cardinal's Court here will pronounce on it." Anne was genuinely hurt.

"Can his Grace be sure? The Cardinal is no friend. Is he not rash to venture it?"

"Rash? Is he not best judge of that? It is his doing."

"And who's to counsel you, Anne?" pursued the mother. "Your uncle Norfolk gives not a fig for any Boleyn."

Anne lifted her chin proudly. "I require no counsel but yours."

Lady Rochford looked at her daughter. "Here, child. Pray take your letters." As Anne curtseyed, her mother waited to embrace her with a sudden fierceness. "Come what may, I wish you well, dear. Remember it."

Anne left her, somewhat disturbed, but at Greenwich her fears vanished. Henry's longing for her was evident when she came, and his confidence in the future changed Anne's disquiet. With head bowed down, she told him in tender and faltering words how unworthy of him she was. He answered her from a full heart. His marriage, he now saw, had never been lawful. He had been living in incest. The Cardinal viewed it thus, and as he had sent John Russell and Thomas Wyatt with 30,000 ducats as earnest goodwill, he felt sure the Pope would confirm it. He was, in fact, so buoyant that he gave Anne assurance. From childhood, unimpaired, Henry had kept his zest. It was perhaps his greatest characteristic.

And he had no reason to doubt his ability to deal with his Prime Minister or his Archbishop of Canterbury. His confidence was founded on deep experience of power. He had now been reigning nearly twenty years. He had discovered, in that time, how to bring his nobility into dependence on himself for money. He had studied theology, which enabled him to combat his priests on their own ground. He had manipulated parliament, so that when the country was really against him he could submit without loss of prestige, and when it was not solid against him he could impose his will on it without dissent. This flexibility in government he had attained by his devotion to government. He had gone down to parliament to address it. He saw delegations from the City and from the burgesses and from the lords. He knew the prelates. He dealt direct with ambassadors. He was a captain among the soldiers, an admiral among his sailors, a lord among his ladies, a patron among his people. His own desires and his own purposes he was seldom in doubt about. He could be brutally direct, especially with foreigners. But human beings found him tractable if they took pains to study him. His Council could always speak straight to him, and he went far out of his way to

win men of learning; experts and disinterested citizens who commanded respect and guided opinion. He was, in this respect, almost
as shrewd as his father. All of this flexibility and deference did not
mean a real concession of his will. It meant that he could temporize.
Much as he bowed to Cardinal Wolsey, for example, on the vast
schemes of policy when Wolsey was master and he apprentice, he
kept a firm grip on those intentions that were inward and original.
Anne Boleyn was too close to his heart to be debated with the
Cardinal, and he had not the slightest doubt that he, as King of England, could prevail on the Pope to accede to him, without the help or
even the knowledge of the Cardinal.

Henry, however, was thinking of the Pope as situated when John
Russell and Thomas Wyatt started out to see him in January. Without his knowing it, that day was over. By the time Anne and Henry
had met at Greenwich, their Pope was no longer free to help them.

### VIII

"YEA," said John Russell to Thomas in February, "what can now save
Rome? Bourbon is advancing. I've laboured endlessly with the Pope
to return him to the war, but he is timid and bankrupt. He'll endure
any knavery, he'll try any truce, rather than resume war. We cannot
waste further time with him. We must leave him and nerve Venice."

Thomas heard these words with that submission to a new world
which often begins an education. Ever since his departure from
England in January he had been discovering a continent—the vast
continent of his ignorance. He was still so impressed by it that he was
teachable.

When he had left Anne for Rome, he carried a wound with him. So
far as his body went he was lean and wiry. He and Russell started off
in the best of spirits, Russell an erect, bearded man with a cold blue
eye, and Thomas his match in height, open and eager by nature. Yet
under his free talk, which Russell enjoyed, he suffered a pre-occupation
as ceaseless as a disease—his separation from Anne hurting him in
proportion to his illimitable feeling for her. He had lent his wonder
to her, had given her that trust which has in it some of the child's
dependence on a mother. He had worshipped her as a man worships

his Madonna, and by bestowing herself on him she had unlocked him.
His marriage was nothing, an obedience to the rules of his tribe, to
his father and mother. But what had he done to protect his heart? It
was this that secretly ate into him. Anne had parted from him in such
distress that every league he travelled was a widening of the gulf.
They were divided from one another. He had given her all his
ecstasy and surrendered his pride, yet as he and Russell pushed farther
away, down through France, to Chambéry, and across to Savona,
every town he saw, every mountain and every river caught echoes
and gave him symbols of a deprivation that mutilated him. He saw
dogs whose legs had been sawn off to keep them from hunting. He
saw thieves whose ears had been cropped and thumbs amputated. On
their breasts were burned the marks of shame. But these wretches
were no more mortified than himself, and in spite of his ability to
share the road with John Russell, he often wished he could dismount
to abase himself at a wayside cross. Yet his true agony was that he
clung to her. She was with him. He loved her. He could not renounce
her.

With Cheyney, on the road to Bordeaux, he had had at any rate one
minor comfort: he could scrape his wound against a surface: Cheyney
was married to a Boleyn and the Boleyns were, therefore, a fair topic
of conversation. Thomas had brought up the Boleyns as often as he
dared—and he had soothed himself by this. It was a wretched, excruciating pleasure. But even this salt satisfaction was impossible
with John Russell. Russell, unfortunately, was at loggerheads with
Cheyney, on this very issue of the Boleyns. A dispute about Russell's
stepdaughters (valuable cattle) had almost brought them to blows.
Anne was warm in support of Cheyney and Thomas could not dare
to expose Anne to Russell's dry and caustic tongue. So he heard
nothing of her and said nothing of her. He was immured, without
light or air, while he migrated as if a carefree young courtier. It was
no play to him, no erotic comedy. He was ready for any jest, but this
was a merciless one, stopping his heart when it came back to him, and
leaving him agonized.

Still he was out of England, he was on the road, and Europe waved
to him like a ragged banner. Soldiers everywhere. France full of
straggling soldiers. Italy full of soldiers. Hordes of Germans, "filthy

hordes of Germans" as John Russell said gruffly, on the way into Italy. Europe convulsed, writhing into a new shape, contorted by war and hate, murderous, destructive, mad to secure power according to private patterns, and regarding these patterns as public and reasonable, necessary, and worth fighting for. The hospitals were full, the surgeons' saws were busy, Rabelais was at Lyons, Erasmus was at Basle, thinking of his excoriated bladder, Machiavelli was at Florence, Benvenuto Cellini was in Rome, Guicciardini was captaining for the Pope while Michelangelo was planning for the Republic, and, in the midst of it, Francis I was wondering whether he could ship a load of wild boar to his brother Henry. "The hunting of them is very pleasant, and a King's game."

The most dreadful of all things had happened to European society. Gunpowder had been put into the feudal system, and that system had exploded. The Church had exploded with it. About this convulsion, neither John Russell nor Thomas Wyatt could have very clear ideas. They had their mission. They were carrying 30,000 ducats to the Pope. Henry VIII had actually been reduced to tears when he learned the plight of Clement VII. So had Cardinal Wolsey. Both of them understood that, since the battle of Pavia, there had been nothing to stop the young Emperor from carving up, swallowing and trying to digest Italy. Everyone could now see it. Machiavelli saw it and hated it. Michelangelo hated it. So did Guicciardini. Benvenuto Cellini thought of gold in its plasticity and the gaiety of form, but even Benvenuto, beautifully absorbed, could feel Italy tremble under his feet. The old house was coming down. The old faith was crumbling. Once more, the end of a world was nigh.

Seen from England, where the Cardinal had tilted the landscape to catch the dying sun, there was, as yet, no question of Martin Luther. Luther, making a mistake and supposing that because Henry was against the Emperor he must now be on the right track, wrote a clumsy eager letter of conciliation, to which Henry replied by telling the reformer that the more Luther and those like him abused Wolsey, the dearer Wolsey would become to him; England was well rid of apostate friars who, deserting his Kingdom and Christ's faith, were wallowing in lust with Luther; let Martin give up his wife, bewail his errors, and either preach the truth or retire to a convent. So Henry

thumped it out. He could privately marvel at the variableness of the
Pope, whom the Imperial party had raided and befouled at Christmas,. but he was at one with Wolsey on the Pope's misfortunes, and
the proof of it was the condolence that John Russell was carrying to
him.

But no one in England, where there was still good game and rec-
reation, cared to imagine the tragedy that impended, unless it was
Wolsey, who was European. When the King of Hungary had been
defeated and slain by the invading Turks in September, Wolsey could
understand why the Pope, in great trouble, and weeping bitterly,
besought the princes to sign a truce. His Italian agents made no bones
about it. They reckoned that the Pope was bankrupt, that the
French were slack, with little care for their serious interests and none
for those of Christendom, while the danger of the Turk was as
great on one side as the cruel and insatiable ambition of the Spaniards on the other. If they do not help the Pope, Wolsey was told,
they themselves, the English and the French, will be considered the
most blind and the most cruel of living men. Henry heard this,
though he did not see why he should break off hunting Anne to do
anything about it, and meantime, as the Pope quaked and fidgeted
and vacillated at Rome, Bourbon recruited the Lutherans to advance
on Italy.

"Woe to us, woe to the Emperor, if those Germans and Spaniards
get the upper hand."

So quailed the Italians, when Bourbon and the Germans began to
descend on them in the interests of the young Emperor, the Most
Catholic King.

While Francis hunted Anne de Heilly, in short, and encouraged the
Turk, Charles V employed the Lutherans to break the Pope. It was in
this crisis, being so deeply moved, that Henry had despatched his
30,000 ducats.

Few of Henry's ambassadors was more keenly aware of the impending clash than this shrewd, wary John Russell, whom Thomas Wyatt
accompanied. They reached Savona just as the hordes of Germans
were sighted, and left four hours ahead of them. It was Russell who
had been Henry's secret agent with Bourbon when that embittered
duke decided to ally himself with the Emperor, and John Russell had

from Ferrara, and he dreamed of a gracious court, like Mantua and Urbino, where Ariosto was the great name, as Rome had insisted to him.

It was Il Libro d'Oro, the Golden Book of Baldassare Castiglione, that had flooded his imagination with the thought of Ferrara, sister to Urbino. It would be a Court, he hoped, where the influence of women had created a sphere in which every human inflection, religious, artistic, philosophic, was valued for itself. This was what he had derived from Castiglione. He never had read a book that evoked so marvellous a picture of men and women in civilized communion.

But the Ferrara with which Thomas collided was a military headquarters, not a court. The Duke received him instantly, in a grim red-brick building, but they were interrupted by messages from the Imperialists, which were impossible to conceal from Thomas. Bourbon had not a penny for his troops. Could the Duke of Ferrara send him 100,000 ducats on account? Could he send provisions, and medicines, and pioneers? Could he send him cannon?

Alfonso, the duke, had been married to a famous lady, Lucrezia Borgia, but she had died half a dozen years before. Now he was in the market for a bride for his son. He looked high, either the Pope's niece Catherine de Medici, or the Emperor's bastard Margaret, or the King of France's sister-in-law Renée. This was the poetry that sang in Alfonso's soul. Ariosto was a warbler who cost him a few crowns a year, a supernumerary.

He had, in fact, no mind for anything but the present moment. Allied to the Emperor, bid for by the Pope, pressed by Bourbon, the Duke saw himself magnificently situated to extract the last honour and the last reward out of his military advantage. Ferrara could gather in Reggio and Modena, perhaps Ravenna, to control the eastern approach to the Apennines. The elimination of Milan and Pavia forced invaders to take a route that pivoted on Ferrara. Hence the renown that had come to the name of Este from Leonardo and the rest, a cluster of genius, was nothing to the European prospect which the invasion of Italy opened to Alfonso.

That night at Ferrara, however, Thomas forgot Ariosto, the Duke of Bourbon and the troubles of Italy. A queer feeling in the calf of his leg, like a red-hot needle, brought him to a waking state. He searched for the needle without success. Then he was stung on the arm. He found nothing. So tired was he that he put it out of his mind, but not for long. He sat up in this castle of Ferrara, in the dead of night, convinced of the existence of demons. He lit a candle from the fire. Small molehills rose up on his arms, his thighs, his calves, his belly. To him, as he gazed on them, these molehills were mountains. In Bordeaux, he remembered, he had been nibbled, but here he was devoured. All the troubles of the world, the disharmonies of the imagination, the miseries and disappointments and despairs to which he was so alive—they narrowed themselves to this diabolic discovery that he was no longer a unit, but a host in himself, himself an in-vaded Italy. His blood seemed to be running in veins that shrugged. Sitting up in his proud bed, with canopy and all, his candle a halo in the dark, he saw his naked body with a disowning, shameful look. Was this indecency Thomas Wyatt? And then he decided, with a flush of anger, to find the enemy that had made him their food and their victim. He turned back the heavy covers, and spread the sheets flat, kneeling naked in the middle of the bed, with his nose pointed downward. Nowhere, on this dingy snowfield that the candle ex-hibited, could he see a speck of black, but Thomas was so full of hate and so anxious to avenge himself that he settled down to his hunt as remorseless as a god. At last, in the shadows of a foothill, he saw a flea. It was a slow, plethoric flea, round with satiety. To Thomas it was ducal. But even when he had killed it, staining Ferrara with it, he dared not deliver himself again to its blood relations.

He came down, still able to grimace but unable to smile.

"You had better have my safe-conduct," said the Duke. "You'll go through the Duke of Bourbon's encampment."

Thomas fabricated a smile. He was miserably happy to leave Ferrara.

## XI

IN SPITE OF THE SAFE-CONDUCT, Thomas now rode into the worst danger he had yet encountered at the very centre of the storm that was brewing for Italy.

As he left Ferrara, to reach Bologna, he met an increasing number of Imperial soldiers. Their condition was appalling. Their hunger stared from their hollow eyes, they were ragged as well as unkempt, and in a state so dejected that no one asked for his safe-conduct. He could not be sure what was in store for him. The sour weather, the foul roads, and these straggling men gave Thomas a sharp sensation of unrest. He kept straight on, his eyes well open.

The town he was approaching seemed to have no civilians in it. It was a wasps' nest, he thought to himself as he halted on the outskirts; there was such a going and coming at the mouth of it, such fierceness in the movements about him. But no one spared time for him. The rattle of distant drums, menacing, impatient, never ceased in the centre of this occupied town, and from every side, out of lanes and up cobbled streets, men hurried of every race and description, some of them uttering hoarse shouts, cursing and glaring, while certain of them broke into a run.

Thomas and his little company thought it better to dismount, but the host that assembled was so impassable he made a detour, and by another way came to the open place from which he heard the beat of drums.

By a side street he approached the open space now thronged with the soldiers. They were all Spaniards, he thought at first, but soon he detected an admixture of Italians, and then he discovered that at least half of them were German. There were thousands of them—perhaps twenty thousand, so far as he could guess—and a fiercer group he had never imagined. Their commander, who stood on a barrel above the drums, was calling to them, "My sons! My sons!" He spoke in German. His face was red with shouting; a powerful warrior, obviously accustomed to dominate and lead them. There was a brief lull, but before his first sentence was finished in his great guttural voice a terrible shout of wrath, a clamour in every tongue and at every pitch of human or half-human voice burst from these wild, disordered, ragged, frenzied bandits. The commander heard it. He raised his arm, lifted himself to his full height, and roared with the power of a bull. The storm that this provoked was a mad cry, "Kill Bourbon! Kill Bourbon!" For a moment the leader's eyes blazed with astonishment, mortification and fury. A vein in his forehead swelled. His face became purple and, with a single gurgle of inarticulate rage, he fell over the drums.

This collapse of their leader was the loosening of a linch-pin. The

mob churned and roared. Lances shot up into the sky. "Bourbon!
Kill Bourbon!" In a few moments a lane of figures swirled into motion
and bore out of the crowd toward a clump of tents. The ringleaders
burst into the one that had Bourbon's shield on it. He had fled, captain
though he was. They emerged without him, waving in their hands the
first possessions they had grabbed from his table and his bed. This
was a signal for more raiders. Meanwhile the Lutheran chief, stricken
by apoplexy, was carried from the centre to a house in the square.

So much of this happened so rapidly that Thomas hardly compre-
hended it. He knew that Bourbon from Milan, and Freundsberg from
Germany, had been waiting to converge their forces in an attack on
the vulnerable cities of Italy, beyond the Apennines. He could not
know that the Pope had been frightened into a truce, and that these
emaciated invaders, whetted by one postponement after another,
starved, denuded, perished by cold, and promised the satisfaction of
every craving, the release of every lust, had now been told that, for
the sake of a few ducats not certain to be delivered to them, they
must forget the prospects painted so glowingly, and trail their lances
in ignominy back over the wet mountains. This news, the result of
haggling and bickering and deceit and compromise, was barely
breathed to them, like cold air into burning metal, before they had
flamed into uncontrollable explosion, with which they still boiled while
Thomas Wyatt, trembling with excitement, saw them rush forward
and backward, intent on capturing and murdering Bourbon.

So intent was he on this blazing drama that, forgetting his own
uninvited presence, he pushed forward into the fringes of the crowd.
From this new position he saw even better how magnificent and how
predatory this army of destroyers could be reckoned. They had been
fined down to skin and bone, but they were ravenous and merciless,
nothing clean about them except their weapons. They flashed an
occasional scorching look at him, since he was obviously well-condi-
tioned and a stranger. Perhaps his benign detachment might have
saved him, but from the wavering mob one fellow emerged, an aquiline
Spaniard, who roughly seized his bridle. "Arrest him!" he cried. "This
is a spy!" Before Thomas or his escort could say a word, they were
torn from their horses and dragged to a stone house, hustled into a
dark chamber with an earthen floor, and the door slammed on them.

To find himself in the hands of this enraged and leaderless army was enough to daunt any young man. Thomas was unshaken. He still had his precious safe-conduct, his wallet and his warrant from John Russell. He only needed to reach the captain of the company that held him.

"We are in no danger," he told his escort. "But if we are separated, take orders from any messenger who has my ring," and he then removed his ring and hid it in his boot.

By that time the door opened, and Thomas, demanding the captain, was led alone to a bare chamber high above the street. It had an alcove, heavily barred, with a dirty mattress on the floor. He was closed into it, and a heavy iron bar dropped into the sockets at the other side of the door.

The daylight had completely died from this chill, empty room before a soul returned. Then came a Spanish captain, with a man who held a lantern. He examined Thomas's papers and folded them away.

"Who wishes to see them?" Thomas asked in French, and then in Italian.

"The Duke of Bourbon," said the captain.

"He is still alive, I trust."

The captain made no answer. "Cesare," he said to his escort, "you are responsible for him. Take charge of him."

Cesare, a block of a Spaniard with a bold carriage, saluted his young superior, and they left Thomas. The thud of the bar as it fell into place was the last sound of contact with his keepers that night. He was already famished and horribly thirsty. His bones ached, and his feet were ice-cold, but there was no help for it. He groped his way into the alcove, his foot slipping on filth before he reached his mattress. An indescribable disgust and shame, mingled with anger, made it impossible for him to rest. He could not see into the street, though he heard the tramp of feet and harsh male voices, until at last, frozen to the bone, he lay down. It was a night that flowed forward in painful jerks, with halts prolonged into maddening inaction. Thomas, for the first time in long months, could extract no pain from the thought of Anne Boleyn. She came to his mind, but it was a whisper in this new clamour of sensations, and that clamour deafened him. He wondered whether he could ever be warm once more, or endure until they came in the morning.

Long after daybreak the bar lifted, and Cesare entered with black bread and a jug of wine. He was himself as hard as the bread and as sour as the wine. He was about to depart when Thomas, hoarse as a crow, said, "Where are my papers?"

"The captain has them."

"Will he return?"

Cesare shrugged. "God knows," and he stepped outside.

"Are you soldiers or bandits?" cried Thomas. "This is worthy of the Inquisition."

To his immense surprise Cesare grinned. "Signore!" Cesare's teeth were white as ivory, and his grin made him human.

"This filth!" said Thomas. "No blanket! This cold!"

"It is not an inn, Signore."

"But I am no enemy, Cesare," said Thomas.

Cesare shrugged. "That is for the captain."

Before noon the captain visited him, bearing all his papers. "You are to be held for ransom," he drily informed Thomas.

"To what sum?" asked Thomas.

"Three thousand ducats," and the captain departed.

Thomas was then left to meditate. "Ten like me," he thought ruefully, "and our 30,000 ducats would go in smoke." But paper and pen were brought to him, so that he could send letters to the Duke of Ferrara and Sir John Russell. Before he delivered these letters he demanded to see the captain. He was unaware how wild the camp was, and how uncertain Bourbon's own position. Twelve leaders had been chosen among the men, to lay down the law, and in the interval, before Bourbon knuckled under, the uproar never ceased. But, when his jailer returned, Thomas was able to exact a few necessaries, a couple of coarse blankets for the night, a block of wood for a pillow, some water, and a rough towel. A slightly milder Cesare brought him more bread and wine and a bowl of soup.

By night-time, on his fourth visit, Cesare took occasion to linger. "Your escort," he said, "are sent on to Rome. They have no money."

"Could you give them this?" asked Thomas, bringing out ten ducats.

"Not impossible."

Then Thomas said, "Close the door."

Cesare closed it.

"I need a file," said Thomas.

"Yes," said Cesare.

"And a rope."

"Bah," the Spaniard said, "that rope would serve me." He pretended to garrot himself. Then he opened the door.

Thomas handed him fifteen ducats. "Buy them food," he told Cesare.

It took several days before the captain brought word that the Duke of Ferrara had sent a protestation against Thomas's arrest. As the Duke sent no ducats, everything now depended on John Russell.

That evening, consumed with boredom, Thomas tried to detain Cesare.

"You are a soldier," he said.

"A man who fought at Marseilles," Cesare answered, "may count as one."

"At Marseilles?"

"Yes, and at Pavia."

Thomas's eyes widened. "You saw King Francis at Pavia?"

"Saw him, Signore? Saw him! I took him prisoner."

Thomas laughed.

"You do not believe me? You laugh at me?" Cesare stepped up to him, bristling.

"The Viceroy, methought, had that signal honour."

"The Viceroy? That traitor who now sells us to the Pope? Body of Christ! Was Signore by chance at Pavia himself?"

"Neither before nor since."

"Then he knows nothing of the battle?"

"Nothing."

"I believe it."

"But, Cesare, since you took the French King prisoner, why still—Cesare?"

"In this world, Signore, does anything astonish you?"

"Forgive my laugh. What happened at Pavia?"

Cesare glanced around, to make sure no one was listening. As he did so Thomas darted his foot behind him and gave him a terrific push. In a flash he was outside the door and dropped the bar. Cesare thumped on the door. Thomas heard him shout, but faintly, through the thick wood. Picking up a sword that stood against the wall he stole downstairs. The house seemed quite empty. The front door was not even locked. Thomas was in the dark street, and free. No one had seen him.

He was dressed like any captain. Walking coolly through the streets, he saluted the guard at the gate, trusted to luck to make his way in the direction of Castelmaggiore, where the Duke of Urbino had his camp. It was, at best, only a day's march. By hiding in a wood for the first daytime, Thomas was able to make the most of the dark hours, and he arrived at Castelmaggiore without encountering his pursuers. All he regretted was not to have learned how Cesare had captured Francis at Pavia.

The Duke of Urbino, who commanded the Venetian army, was a sallow, laconic general who, for his own reasons, wished to see Pope Clement chastened. He received Thomas, heard with sober interest the disorder among Bourbon's followers, and gave King Henry's envoy an escort to Bologna.

It was in these days that Bourbon's wolves, belly to the ground, resumed the chase to Rome. They smelled its blood from far off, and their gallop knew no halt. Urbino limply followed them.

By the time Thomas reached Rome it was clear to John Russell what must happen. They had begun by burning churches and pillaging abbeys and convents. They cut the crown off a priest and planted a crucifix in his brains. All they asked was "monies and towns to sack." By the intervention of the Duke of Urbino they were diverted from Florence, but by agreeing to spare Florence, Bourbon left himself with nothing but Rome with which to assuage his ferocious horde. Pretending to hold them back for a stipulated sum, he doubled his demands on the Pope at the same time that they sped forward.

"We are bankrupt," the Pope wept to Russell.

"Raise more money by selling Cardinals' hats," urged Russell.

But no Italian wanted to pay full price, even for a cardinalcy.

On the eve of Bourbon's arrival John Russell saw it was hopeless. He and Thomas Wyatt had scarcely received the Pope's feverish blessing and directed themselves to Civita Vecchia, to go north by water, when Bourbon was sighted at Acquapendente. Then it was that Pope

Clement VII tasted sorrow. He had pledged his niece, Catherine de Medici, to King Francis. He had sealed his pact with England. But the Italians themselves had meanwhile bared Rome to the murderous dagger. A Colonna led the way. A Gonzaga followed. Ferrara had replenished the bandits. Urbino folded his arms. And now the Pope was to become the Emperor's hostage.

A couple of days after Thomas's departure began the Sack of Rome.

# Chapter 12

THOMAS WAS SAFELY at sea, in a Genoese galley, when the Sack began, and this was to the good. On May 6, as the city lay in a morning mist, Bourbon had led the assault which alone could crown his march on Rome. Himself fatally wounded by a shot that perforated his intestines, he was carried into a church where he died raving, "À Rome, à Rome!" His men went on without him, and after two hours' fighting they were inside the walls, and nothing to bridle them. Their privations had maddened them so that loot was not enough. They had other arrears to make up: they wanted the pleasure of dealing death, of gratifying malice and revenge, of raping the women, of cowing the weak, torturing the proud and disfiguring or destroying the beautiful. By nightfall thousands had been murdered and new possibilities began to open. In Sant' Angelo Benvenuto Cellini plumed himself on having fired the shot that killed Bourbon, as a cock on a neighbouring dunghill plumed himself on the next sunrise. This new dawn the weary Pope greeted with a low heart. He was a prisoner in his own fortress. Rome lay broken under him. He could no longer go to St. Peter's, where horses were stabled. Humiliated by his flight, beggared by defeat, the Holy Father at last knew that neither the English nor the French had acted in time to save Italy from the Holy Roman Emperor; and he, the inheritor of a spiritual dominion, must be bent to the Emperor's will.

On the same night, at Greenwich, there was an unusually splendid banquet. Confident that time was no object, the French and the English had been haggling for months over the details of an alliance, even over so small a detail as a tribute of salt. "Pah," said Henry, "I often lost as much at play." But at last Henry had put his arm around a delegate's shoulder. "I'll ask the Cardinal to be reasonable." So they came to sign, and the happy event was being celebrated at Greenwich in ignorance of the unforgettable lesson which the Emperor was teaching Pope Clement.

## II

ANNE TOOK HER PLACE at the great banquet with a glowing heart. At the centre table, under the canopy, the King was seated. The Queen was at one side of him, to honour this French alliance, and Mary, the "French Queen," Suffolk's wife, was at the other side. Anne Boleyn, from her lowly place, had no envy of them. She had been torn by anxiety until the treaty was signed. This banquet was, so to speak, a landmark she had set for herself, but once she reached it, once it was past, she comforted herself as people always do when their own point has been met, even though the point was an absurd one.

And nothing could have convinced Anne that hers was absurd. From the time that she had clung to Thomas in the agony of parting, she had no longer allowed herself to waver or weaken. He was in Italy. She was in England, and the fact that the King was resolved to marry her, no matter what stood in their way, had gradually taken absolute possession, not merely of her heart but of her will. She would never have been Henry's mistress, and never would be. But to be his wife, to be established as his wife before everyone, was a triumph that meant so much, in so many different ways, she could hardly allow herself to contemplate it. She had not been a day back at Greenwich before Jane Parker and Nan Cobham had contrived to slight her because she was still unmarried. Their superiority as matrons was dear to them, and her failure to appear in the rôle of Venus was taken by them to have been a proof of disfavour. Anne could not retaliate too soon, but as she looked over the new banquet house with Henry's roses and Catherine's "pomgarnets" decorating it, the secret meaning of the banquet house made her inwardly smile. Henry intended her to have a private apartment in it, away from prying eyes. Anne gazed at the long rows of torches, in "antique" candlesticks, that threw their light on the pretty ceiling, and she admired the tapestries that hung under the high windows, with the history of David told on them. But it was her secret, and the French treaty to back it, that made her glow.

Mary, a queer, precocious little sprite, was at the banquet. She was now destined to be married to Francis's boy Henry. Earlier in the day, to gratify her father's pride, she had answered French to one address, Latin to another and Italian to the third. She had also performed on the spinet. Anne was not so captivated by this performance as the father was. She knew by what tutorial methods these great accomplishments were reached—taunts, threats, pinches, nips and bobs. Anne looked at Mary less as a performing animal, a Talking Dog, than as a princess to be married, and for that, so much more to the point than any language, Mary was too thin and spare to be considered. Anne deplored, almost as a step-mother might, that this wretched child could not possibly be married for three years. But the French treaty, to which Queen Catherine was so submissive, did not stand or fall by the marriage. It went into effect without that, and for Anne it meant triumph, the triumph of Henry's private, as well as public, intentions, the break with Catherine as well as with Catherine's nephew. For Anne the banquet acquired its lustre from such secret significance, with action in the Legate's Court to be begun in a week or two.

No commiseration for her mistress came into her young heart. Her feeling for Queen Catherine as a person had never been really strong, and neither she nor her family had ever been reckoned true members of her camp, which was the imperial, the ultra-pious camp. A man like Suffolk, who was a cousin of the Wingfields, could be both a new man and attached to the Queen, but Queen Catherine had always singled out the flippant younger men for her reprehension, and since Anne was strong in personal loyalty above everything, it was to Thomas Cheyney, Francis Bryan, Nicholas Carew, Edward Baynton, George, and the other frivolous ones that she privately and tenaciously adhered.

It was because Henry was really at home with these men, the dicers and dancers, that Anne detached herself so easily from the matron under the canopy. A whole generation, in any event, divided them. Queen Catherine did not dance.

Anne's prejudices, in this respect, went even further. Thanks to Master Hans Holbein, whose services had cost Henry about thirty crowns, this was rather a beautiful banquet. It was the young German's superb architectural sense that made it so memorable, and Henry was exuberant about it. Holbein had worked over it for weeks, and already the Venetian and the Milanese ambassadors had said a good word for it, even before seeing the great work of the evening, for which Master Hans had had £4 10s. 0d. extra—the *bonne bouche*. But, unfortunately for Holbein, he had come to Henry from the imperial side, from Sir Thomas More, and one of Anne's first impressions that evening was an invincible one—no Holbein! She did not want him if he came from that side.

Thomas More, as Anne perfectly knew, was the certain partisan of Queen Catherine, he and old Fisher. They were the backbone of the Church. And even before she had risen from the banquet, to go into the companion house that Henry had also erected, she was certain she was not going to like Holbein's decoration on the far side of the arch.

Holbein had certainly imagined a fine arch, and cleverly moulded it in papier mâché, set into a frame, with "Dieu et mon droit" on the front of it, a balcony on top for the musicians, busts of emperors in the niches, and three vaulted passages in the arch itself. No sooner had the guests washed in rose water and started through the arch than the King, limping in a velvet slipper, turned and said, "Look back." On the whole of the rere of the arch Master Holbein had spread the siege of Terouenne, very cunningly wrought, and in vast dimensions.

The point of this painting—to recall a military victory over the French—was not lost on any of the ambassadors, nor on Anne, but they walked through the gallery into a new chamber that made them forget so crude a breach of taste.

Banked up on either side were three tiers of seats. The ambassadors, the nobles and the guests were at one side, and on the other two hundred ladies. It was perhaps the diffused brilliancy of the lights, and the exquisite variety of the ladies' costumes, that astonished the incoming visitors. Without the least confusion or delay, in perfect smoothness, form and silence, the whole company found itself at ease to contemplate the latest entertainment. The ceiling, quaint with the zodiac, the harmonious colours, the sweet perfumes, the glow, the polite hush and the expectancy prepared this company for a moment where, under a gracious arch of a single span, the spectators were enticed to expect marvels. The arch itself was all gilt with fine gold, and decorated in low relief with lovely figures. Beneath it, in angelic colours, came singers, ranged on either side. A youth, in light blue taffeta, had the centre. The songs were so sweetly sung, and the processions so artful, that it made little difference whether it was Mercury, or Plutus, or Cupid, or Justice who was given the word. Even the final verdict in their dispute, left to contending knights in white armour, for whom a bar was lowered down in the centre of the arch, was only of interest to the literal. The opening of a cave behind, peopled by a group of damsels who came forward, gave merely another occasion for music and dancing. When little Princess Mary, with a profusion of silver tresses falling over her shoulders, said good-night to the French ambassadors, the entertainment concluded. Then, under the arch that recalled Terouenne, the whole company returned for supper, and continued dancing until daybreak.

It was Italy, now in the throes of agony, that had taught Henry how to felicitate his guests in this enchanting style. Naples, Florence, Genoa, Milan, Venice, as well as Mantua and Ferrara and Urbino, had lifted this exquisiteness to human lips and trained the palate to discriminate and to savour. But the creators had now invited their own destruction. And their allies, their beneficiaries and inheritors, were so tardy about helping them that a new power, more primitive, more impatient and more resolute, was at that very moment smashing the source from which this enchantment had flown.

Yet the alliance was secure, and Queen Catherine under its heel. Anne danced with her lover repeatedly. Except for the siege of Terouenne, about which she was to make him uncomfortable, the evening was auspicious for her.

Had it not been for the Sack of Rome, indeed, it would have been Queen Catherine's last public appearance. Bourbon had saved her, in so far as the imperialists could save her—Bourbon, with his Lutherans, his renegade Italians and those Spaniards among whom were so many Jews and so many Moors.

## III

HENRY had only waited to be sure of the French to begin his private and secret suit for divorce.

As he went up to the Thames about it, he said not a word of it to Harry Norris. This was a divorce with a difference, and all that was needed was the Cardinal's final word. As the Cardinal knew nothing of Anne Boleyn, he had been considering Princess Renée as the right bride for Henry, and Henry did not undeceive him. He was content so long as Wolsey should arrange for the Legate's Court. Archbishop Warham would be assessor. Henry himself, the man guilty of incest, would assent to have the lawfulness of his marriage looked into, for the sake of public morals and the good of his soul. Then Catherine's advocate, appointed by Henry and without her knowledge, would plead against him and the case would go through.

As he passed Lambeth he congratulated himself that the Archbishop had from the first questioned the dubious dispensation that had enabled his brother's widow to marry him; and as he passed Chelsea he reflected on the possible opposition of Sir Thomas More. The Queen was not without friends, either among the clergy or the nobility, and the mere project of a divorce might arouse feeling at home, not to mention the Emperor's resentment. But Henry VIII, on this cold spring day in 1527, foresaw little difficulty so long as he had the Pope's Legate to serve him. He depended on this legatine authority in England to free him from a marriage which was abominable. His use of a Legate, when the legatine authority was also abominable, was not the sort of thing that, in a moment like this, he cared to dwell on. It was practical for him to plead his conscience on one point at this juncture, and not on the other, and that was enough for him.

It was also enough for Wolsey. The divorce, as Wolsey saw it, was purely political. Catherine would go. Renée would come. The Empire would be countered. He told Henry that he would open the Legate's Court at York Place on the day that suited him, and Henry returned to give Anne the happy news.

It was in the disused banquet house at Greenwich that Anne hid herself to wait for Henry's return. The Cardinal was the one person she feared, and she suspected that he was stronger than the King. If he failed Henry, she saw no prospect of the divorce.

Henry was late. Anne knew he would be, but explained it to herself calmly and convincingly. He was bound to be late.

The instant he reached her, however, she broke into a smile. Victory beamed from him—victory, tenderness and pride.

"Sweetheart." He kissed her.

"Oh, sir!"

"There is nothing more to be done," concluded Henry firmly and gaily. "Now we are sure of it."

For the first time, and with a surge of joy, Anne really knew it. They parted with a kiss, and as Henry was going he stopped for a second.

"Oh, the Italians are returned—Russell and young Wyatt! Till to-night, my darling!"

So great was Anne's elation that she could not go into the Palace. She needed to savour this. Until now, a gate had been locked, but at last the path was hers, the endless admirable vista. Her eyes dilated with an almost innocent exaltation. She was not the poor man's daughter whom the good prince was taking to wed, but her heart filled with Henry's courage and aplomb. He had not betrayed their secret to the Cardinal.

As she reached her favourite walk, by the fountain, a figure in black stood there already. She drew away, but she too had courage, so she went forward. "Welcome!" she cried laughingly, and waved to Thomas.

Thomas stood rooted. Of this he had not dared to dream. He did not even bow. He looked at her. They were in the same garden.

"Behold the English mode." Anne gave him a royal curtsey.

"You are merry?" He steadied himself with his hand on the lip of the fountain.

"You are home again," smiled Anne.

" 'Twere long," he muttered.

"Nay, nay," she said quickly. "We have made peace and feasted every hour. Time flew." She prattled hard, not watching his face. "And

now, like time, I fly. But it is home, now you have come." She waved
again and turned.

"Anne."

He drew a casket from his bosom. "From Venice." Anne feared it,
because of Henry. She opened it. It was a lovely small Venus.

"Oh!" She gave Thomas her hand to kiss. A little miniature dangled
from her, and he seized it. It came away with its chain. "You will
give me this?"

"Nay!" she shrieked. "You cannot."

"But I have it." Thomas thrust it behind him. "We cannot battle
so soon."

"Thomas!" she demanded.

"Take it," he said.

"Oh!" She bit her lip in anger, and left him abruptly.

When he saw her vanish he cast down his eyes on this miniature he
had snatched so rudely. He opened it. It was a portrait of the King.
He closed it.

If only I have patience, his mind cajoled him, as the mind cajoles
the mortally wounded. Within a few moments a thousand suspicions,
resentments, memories and desires wheeled through him, until he
stunned himself into numbness. He would not, he believed, struggle
again.

Then he hung the miniature round his neck and buried it in his
bosom. He had first had an impulse to kiss it. That made him smile.


### IV

EVERYONE WAS HAPPY to welcome Thomas. The old father hugged his
son with simple love; Sir Harry Guildford was as warm as the sun;
Lady Rochford, Cheyney, Madge Shelton—they all, in their cordial
way, gave him a bit of their heart. Beth Darrell was quiet and unfeign-
edly happy. Thomas took it all to him, and let it all slip from him. It
could not touch him. He hated himself for his incapacity, and prayed
for the wealth of life. How long, he wondered, was this servitude to
endure, and what could end it?

But it was not as before. Now he was not a suspect young poet. John
Russell had generously told of Thomas's quick help, his journey to

Venice, his fate as a captive, his lively escape, and the appalling ransom he had evaded. Francis Bryan, turning his diabolic blind eye on
him, chafed him heavily about Venice, where there were reputed to be
20,000 prostitutes to every yard, dancing, apparently, like angels on the
point of a needle. Thomas, as he grimly admitted to himself, did not
use jesting, but he tried hard. He felt more at home, strangely enough,
with the familiar curtness of the King.

Since his foot was still troubling him Henry could not play tennis,
but he had to have some game.

"Come," he called to Thomas. "You are worth your weight in ducats.
Be one of us at bowls." It was a compliment to the returned courtier,
and Thomas obeyed him, while Suffolk and Francis Bryan strolled
with them to the green.

The King chose Bryan as his partner, while Suffolk, clapping
Thomas on the shoulder, said, "Now we'll give them a fight."

The game was lively, but at the height of it, when Thomas's cast
was clearly better than the King's, "it is mine," cried Henry in his
stoutest tone.

Even Suffolk was astonished. He looked at Henry with amazement.
"With your Grace's leave," said Francis Bryan, "I think not."

"What!" He turned on Bryan. "How can you tell?" Facing round,
he pointed at the bowl while fixing Thomas with his glance. "Wyatt,"
he said meaningfully, "I tell thee, it is *mine.*" With this he stooped
and pointed with his little finger. Thomas saw why. He was wearing
on it a ring that had belonged to Anne Boleyn.

"It is mine, I tell thee," Henry repeated, leaving no doubt what he
meant.

Thomas put his hand in his doublet and unchained the miniature.

"If your Grace give me leave to measure it," said Thomas, "I hope
it will be mine," and he stooped to measure the cast.

Henry recognized his miniature. His smile died. Just as Thomas laid
down the chain Henry kicked away his bowl with royal rudeness. "It
may be so," he glared, "but then I am deceived," and walked from the
green.

While Thomas stood among the bowls Suffolk hurried after Henry.

Suffolk had little animosity in his nature, and none for Thomas, but the moment he saw Henry spurn the bowl he was moved to run to his master.

He pulled a long face when he came up with the King, who gave him a thunderous look.

"Meseems, your Grace," he blurted, "that Wyatt should tell all."

"Tell all? Tell what?" Henry walked on. "You deal in slander."

"Slander? Exempt me, sir."

"Then what is it?"

"Things I have heard at firsthand, and from Hever."

"To what effect?"

"That the lady hath known him too well, or I am greatly mistook."

Suffolk followed Henry, whose face was a thundercloud, while Thomas and Francis Bryan watched them.

"La! La!" said Bryan to Thomas. "He braved Paris from Montdidier. He braved his Grace from Calais. Now what does he do?"

"We'll soon know," said Thomas.

In a moment Suffolk came out. "His Grace," he said with his little lisp. He was quite affable, debonair Suffolk with his soldierly bearing and his good manners. Stout and yet pliant, he fitted his master like a glove.

Thomas hurried to the King. He noticed white tense lines in the King's otherwise ruddy face.

"Wyatt," the voice was cool and curt, "how came you by this tablet?"

"To say truth, I snatched it from the lady, your Grace."

"Ha! Not a gift?" He paused. Then, with somewhat more heat, he said, "But she hath favoured you in other wise?"

"I have always known her," Thomas replied quietly.

"Attend," the King said, fixing the younger man with sternness, "this touches me, and you must give me truth. How well have you known her?"

Thomas raised his glance with some difficulty and their eyes met. This man was the King who exacted the truth, who had a right to it, and on whom Thomas's life and well-being absolutely depended. In Henry's implacable look, and his direct question, Thomas saw nothing untoward, no more than if his father questioned him. But he was aware, in every fibre of his body, that a man who loved Anne Boleyn was speaking to him. In a voice that trembled slightly, "I have loved her these many years," he said.

"Yea," said Henry. "And hath she loved you?"

"In my plight I could never marry her."

"Is that an answer?" Henry demanded violently. "Beware. You have been seen without marking it. This is no play. How have you known her?"

Thomas looked Henry in the eyes. "Not as you intend, sir," he said.

"Without subtility?"

"Since I am accused by my lord of Suffolk," Thomas replied hotly, "and since this touches your Grace, I pray to be confronted."

"Not so. You give me your word. You have never known her. Beyond that, I do not press. She is young, you may have caught her fancy. But you have never known her in that fashion?"

"Never," repeated Thomas.

"Then wherefore brag, she is mine?"

"By your leave, your Grace, I said I hope she is mine."

"Even so."

"But that was in the play."

"Nay, even so. And you snatched it from her." Henry's small eyes snapped as he looked at Thomas. He was beside himself with rage and could hardly speak. His cheeks puffed and sagged, and his two teeth showed.

"Give me that tablet," he said.

Thomas took it off.

"Get thee hence!" said Henry. "Let me not see your face again. Go till I send for you."

Thomas knelt to him and bowed. Then, with head down, he backed out of Henry's presence.

## V

THE INSTANT Thomas was dismissed from Court, with this abruptness so characteristic of Henry, he had only one thought. To go to Anne would be fatal: it would be seen. To send her a word in writing would be insane: a single phrase would damn her, and no page could be trusted. Torn by confusion, as he penetrated to his father's apartment, he lost precious moments, unable to think or scheme. "Fool that I be," he halted in the corridor, walking to a window to avoid a halberdier. He twisted his cap in his hands. "Ah," he clapped it on his head, "I have it."

"Beth," he explained at her door, "I am dismissed from Court. There is no time to clear it. List, go to the Queen's chamber. Say to Anne Boleyn, from my mouth, 'Thomas was true.' No more. I must avoid. Wilt do it, Beth?"

This harsh demand, flung at her without an instant's warning, with Thomas standing on one foot, left Beth Darrell speechless. Doubt shook her, but his face was argument enough. She raised her blue eyes. "I will." He snatched her hand, kissed it honestly, and was gone. Beth hastened to the Queen's chamber, only to meet Anne, who left it in train of young Francis Weston, the King's page.

"You sally forth?" cried Beth, as if aggrieved. "You have my sampler still in hand! I have three words to say"—and she added, with a stabbing glance of caution—"from Thomas."

"I cannot tarry," frowned Anne, turning her back on the page, "but say that that you must."

"'Thomas was true,' he said, no more. He is dismissed from Court."

"He will not tell," breathed Anne, indicating the page who gazed out the window. "Till anon, sweet Beth. And thank thee." She flew away.

Henry was in the banquet house before her. When Anne came up alone, he dangled the miniature.

"How, sweetheart, came you to relinquish this?"

"Ah, you have it," exploded Anne with an angry smile. "Wyatt stole it, the wretch. Would I could slay him."

"We spoke of you privily."

"And good, I hope, sir."

"That you loved him heretofore," said Henry soberly, but evidently moved, "he did confess to me."

"He was ever fond of me," said Anne quite simply, "since we were children. We were as close as Hever is to Allington."

"No more?" Henry breathed heavily.

"Your Grace, he chose his part. I hold him bound to Bess Brooke in conscience."

"But he hath left her, Anne."

"He cannot leave her, and your Grace may heed, I am stiffly framed in this. I could not suffer his or any dalliance. This you may grant me."

"Yea, but where are you inclined?"

"Where think you?" Anne lifted her eyes to him. "Do you doubt me? The spring that holds my tablet is not yet true. It slipped to earth. He seized it, and by force he held it. Was I remiss? Am I so light as to bestow you on a squire who frequents you?"

"Frequents no more, by my soul," snorted Henry. "By God, to leave his wife like this. Let him go to her." With this he put his arm round Anne. "When the spring is righted, you will wear me here." He slipped his hand to her breast.

Anne looked at him severely. "What tale comes next?"

"I never doubted you, my sweet. I never doubted you."

"That is easy said, your Grace"—Anne disengaged herself—"but hear me speak. Tale-bearers and informers are not unknown. I could name a score of them. Against them, what cure have I? You give me credence now, when you are fond, but how will it be when I am familiar to you and malice takes lessons? My sovereign lord, I'd be a poor woman without your love, but what is it unless you trust me? Pack me away, as you do silly Wyatt, unless your faith is whole. That were but plain charity."

"Nay, sweetheart, my faith is perfect."

"Then you are there." She placed his miniature between her breasts, and looked at him.

## VI

Anne's stiffness with Henry had an effect. Harsh as he could be with Suffolk, who turned to him like a sunflower, he was submissive to Anne, and Thomas Wyatt was never once mentioned in reproach to her. So strong was Anne, indeed, that he consulted her after every sitting of the Legate's Court. The news of the Sack of Rome had come with a crash into England. Wolsey had concluded, after the first sitting, that, in view of opposition, he must get as many bishops as possible to join himself and Warham in pronouncing the marriage null and void. This was a serious hitch. Anne warned Henry it was dangerous, because of Bishop Fisher. The French alliance was not popular, and scurrilous sheets were being circulated against Wolsey. But to harry him, under such pressure, would be to lose everything. Rather than do that, Henry believed he could end the matter by going straight to Catherine.

Anne took these difficulties hard. Her hopes had rushed up when Henry had Wolsey's concurrence fresh on his lips. Her eagerness for the prize had made her forget the complications. Now her suspicions of Wolsey redoubled. The glamour that he seemed to possess for Henry as the Pope's Legate had never existed for her—she was not a Defender of the Faith, had never received the golden rose, or written a book against Luther. She was of a younger generation than Henry, and, so far as the Church went, disillusioned and disaffected. But her lover chafed as much as she did; between him and herself there was difference neither in ardour nor policy; so Anne made up her mind to take a better occasion for scraping the gilt off Wolsey, and she seconded Henry by urging him to go to Catherine himself.

Henry went to Catherine in her privy chamber, to break the news of her impending divorce.

It was only a few weeks since they had throned it in the banquet house at Greenwich and shared their pride in Mary. But in those weeks messages had been carried to Catherine. She knew they were true as soon as Henry came in and closed the door.

They were seated. He spoke quietly. "This is painful," he said slowly, "but my confessor tells me I must speak to you. My conscience hath troubled me of late that we have lived in mortal sin these many years."

In spite of herself, the sound of these words unnerved Catherine. Her tears could not be held back. She broke down.

"We cannot avoid it, Catherine," Henry went on resolutely. "I can no longer remain in your company. You must remove from Court."

While Henry spoke, and Catherine wept, the unalterable facts were evident to both of them. Her failure to give him a male heir was a national misfortune, and a humiliation to so stalwart a male. She was in a weak position as his brother's widow. She was a Spaniard, on whose nephew he was preparing to levy war. And she was six years older than himself, looking fifty as she wept, rather than forty-one.

So weak was her position—her isolation, her sterility and her superannuation—that Henry believed she must yield to him, especially on the grounds of his conscience.

It was, however, that admirable discovery, his conscience, which gave Catherine her only weapon—another conscience, just as good as his. He was planning to annul their marriage and to make Mary a bastard. To do this, he intended to recruit bishops against her and appeal to the Pope.

Catherine was an honest Catholic, a naturally stubborn Spaniard, and the daughter of Ferdinand and Isabella the Catholic.

"We are man and wife, Henry," she said at last. "And that we have ever been, with the full sanction of the Church and of the world."

Her tone, sober as it was, arrested Henry. He had not expected this. "But my conscience——" he began.

"My own conscience does not sleep," said Catherine proudly, "and I am ready to submit it to God, and to the Holy Father who is his vicar."

At these words, delivered in a voice that he had known ever since he was eleven, the King quailed. Catherine meant it.

"I only wished you to know that I have mooted the question. It had to be threshed out, nothing more." So said Henry solemnly, blinking his white eyelashes at her. "But, prithee, talk of it to no one."

So saying, and then repeating what he had said, as was his habit, he left his spouse.

## VII

So soon as henry had broken the news to Catherine and encountered her resistance, he reported it to the Cardinal.

"John Fisher!" ejaculated the Cardinal. "He is priming her. I'll halt at Rochester, your Grace, to read him a lesson."

The Cardinal was to leave for France, to bring sixteen barrels of gold to King Francis, who was now ready, at long last, to push an army into Italy. Lautrec was to lead it, and the Cardinal had to scrape this money together to avoid raising an army, but he intended to secure payments of old debts from France, and to assure his master of Madame Renée. That Henry had another plan for marriage never entered the Cardinal's head.

"But it is not only John Fisher we have to think on," said Henry, "it is Master More."

"Have a word with him, your Grace," advised the Cardinal earnestly; "he is even now in the gallery."

Henry found his councillor outside in the sunny gallery. "Walk with me"—he took him round the shoulder—"there is a matter I would share with you."

More, broad and under-sized, gave a look at the magnificent being who thus cajoled him. It was an astonishing look, at once eager and apprehensive, quizzical and respectful, humble and audacious. There was a quick, a lively play both in mouth and nose, and the whole face, its reds splashed with blackness of hair and brow, had the utmost mobile intelligence in it, but beyond that, beyond the wary tightness that at once repressed the mouth, the eyes had a dark splendour and the voice a timbre of its own. Rather untidy, or at any rate careless in his attire, and with uneven shoulders that suggested the studious man, More's was a presence in the gallery of Hampton Court that was as enlivening as light in a house or water in a landscape. He did not stand out from the others, he soared out. Against Wolsey himself, against Henry, against Norfolk, or against the underling Cromwell, here was a figure of the first order. And it was on this sincerity of More's that Henry was about to press his conscience.

But there was nothing comic for Thomas More in this gesture of conscience. His was a character mordant and sincere. It was also reverent. Henry was God's anointed. He took him with a submission that verged on abasement. All that splendour in his own nature, his mirth as ready as his wit, went with a tragic awareness of forces, moral forces, which can never be played with. Those eyes had a watchfulness in them, a merciless insight and a promptitude of judgment which forced him to relate himself to the sovereign who addressed him, one immortal soul relating himself to another immortal soul. All the flexibility and passion, all the paradox and vivacity, of this ironic nature had its origin in the adventure of immortality on which it believed itself to be engaged. The Round Table had merely preceded him, and the Holy Grail was only in new terms for him, but he was a Knight who barely succeeded, by force of reason, in keeping from an escape into the desert, where emptiness is at last vast enough to fill itself with God. And now, as Henry took him up and down the gallery, he felt that there was something in his master's conscience which was like the howl of a lion in that desert. How could he, a layman, go forth to face the lion?

"Your Grace, I am unmeet to meddle in such matters."

But Henry pressed him. He urged certain places in scripture.

Thomas More was more alive than ever to this ravening lion. He pleaded that he could not answer until he had talked to Clark, one bishop, and Tunstal, another.

So far, so good. Henry had boarded More's conscience; and from that conscience, as from Catherine's and Bishop Fisher's, he knew he had something to contend with.

## VIII

IT WAS NOT to be too easy for him, or for anybody. It was not to be simple for Anne to become Queen of England.

Before Cardinal Wolsey got so far as Rochester, on his way to France with the nine hundred (only nine hundred) who attended him, two earnest men sat buried in talk. They were in the plain workroom where, eight years before, Thomas Wyatt had sat by the fire.

The Bishop, John Fisher, had been so concerned about the divorce that he had persuaded Thomas More to spend the night at Rochester before joining the Cardinal. The divorce was so radical a step, so far-reaching in its consequences, and so deep in its roots, that the two good friends could not exhaust their discussion in an evening. Now, after Mass, communion and breakfast, they sat in privacy while morning sunlight fell on the window sill and lapped the long table.

"The Queen is on safe ground," John Fisher reiterated. "My dumb friends here support me. I have no doubts. I cannot see it otherwise."

More shook his head. He revered his venerable friend, their hearts warmed by years of cordial interchanges, by love of Erasmus, joy in Greek, their common faith, and their hatred of corrupting wealth. But where Fisher shot up, bonily upright, a Gothic spire, the knowledge of the world possessed by Thomas More made him infinitely less detached. Often as he was quizzical and sparkling, now his grey eyes were clouded by trouble, his whole expression harried. "What

ground is safe?" he queried. "The Cardinal goes to France. There
he will cut it from under us."

"But the Queen sends a message to the Emperor," John Fisher
chimed out. "That I know."

"At your behest?" More rapped out anxiously.

"I have not seen her yet."

"To stir the Emperor—that may well be treasonable. Who is to
guide her? You dare not see her, my lord Bishop. His Grace is
rampant."

"But the Queen must stick fast," John Fisher urged. "And the
Cardinal cannot decree, the Pope hath the final word."

"Yea, my lord Bishop, yea," More smouldered. Then he blazed:
"Should this divorce be pressed, it may carry to lengths unknown.
We'll have to meet the devil's argument yet."

"I am not shaken, good More," Fisher laughed affectionately. "The
marriage is beyond argument."

"Mistake me not. So I believe. But were the Church beyond censure,
I were not uneasy. Hath not Erasmus put his finger in the wound a
hundred times? Wealth has corrupted the Church, heresy breeds and
feeds on our corruption. So comes the devil's argument, straight from
Italy itself."

"Which of his myriad arguments, good More?"

"The Crookback argument, Bishop, that the commonwealth is above
all law. It's up again."

"The Pope rebuts it," John Fisher rejoined grimly.

"So I humbly trust, through God's pity and mercy. But since the
commonwealth be brought into peril because no son of hers lived, so
may the Queen be cast out and another found for the purpose! The
argument is as old as Cæsar."

"Faithless and unkind."

"Aye," said More fiercely, "and to speak as a lawyer, which I must,
there come others in its train, a whole tribe of them. Mark what must
recruit opinion in the end—the scourge, the rack, the wheel, the
thumb-screw. We'll spy, we'll bribe, we'll torture and kill. To save the
commonwealth on this pitiless ground we'll call in murderers——"

"Some one knocks!" In his long bony stride John Fisher reached
the door.

"Call him in," More said heartily.

"Pardon, my lord Bishop." Master Thomas Cromwell, a deferential smile on his white face, bowed gracefully to both of them. "My lord Cardinal nears Rochester. I am his humble harbinger."

"Well met, Master Cromwell." More gave him his hand. "You came at a point."

"My poor house awaits ye all." John Fisher broke into a nervous laugh. "Ye number thousands, I am told. God bless ye all, and welcome."


## IX

JOHN FISHER was visibly frail, as he came out to welcome the Cardinal, and yet between the great churchman who had ridden into Rochester in royal trappings and this sparse, clean-lined bishop there was a contrast as between visible and invisible. Wolsey brought multitude with him, colour and the resonance of his commission to a King, but Fisher had a flame in him, a commission to another king that stripped him to the bone, refining appetite away, the senses chastened for the sake of this more perfect mutation. Wolsey, powerful and heady, greeted Thomas More and hailed Sir Harry Guildford, who brought him reports of the shire. But his real object was to see Fisher alone, who now offered him the hospitalities of the palace, with that ring of gaiety in his ascetic voice which, to rich Wolsey, was like the clang of a village belfry.

"So you do not hesitate." Wolsey at last could take soundings. "You think the dispensation is within the Pope's power?"

"That is my poor opinion," said John Fisher.

"Tell me, how can the Queen have heard of the matter? Has she sent anyone to you?"

Fisher paused. "She sent a message."

"By script, my lord Bishop?"

"By word of mouth."

"And the message?"

"Certain matters had happened between the King and herself, she said. She desired my counsel."

"And you answered?"

"In such matters, I told her, I could only act upon the King's commandments."

"Be plain and frank with me, my lord. What deemed you this matter to be?"

"I could not know for certain, but I took it to be of a divorce."

"What made you think of that, my lord Bishop? She had said nothing to you."

"A tale my brother bore from London, your Grace, who in a certain company heard things noised to such a purpose."

"Ah! Then, under oath of secrecy, I will reveal to you this matter of his Grace's conscience." He then gave Fisher an account of Henry's talk with Catherine, such as he and Henry had agreed on in York Place.

"And," added Wolsey indignantly, "the Queen said it is by my procurement and setting forth that this divorce is proposed between her and his Highness."

"That is most blameworthy," deplored Fisher. "If I might speak with her, I might bring her to submission."

"Nay!" Wolsey lifted a hand. "Not a word, unless the King command it. Do nothing, say nothing. Nay, nay."

So, having convinced himself that in this business of Henry's conscience there would be something to grind against, Wolsey went on to Canterbury and Dover.

At Canterbury, where the feast of St. Thomas halted him, he had the choir chant a special litany for the imprisoned Pope.

As he knelt at the choir door, wearing his Cardinal's hat, he leaned forward at a form carpeted and cushioned, and as the monks chanted in the body of the church, the sound swelling in its spaces, Wolsey bent his face into his hands, his body shook, and he wept very softly.

So he left England. And in spite of his spies and his allies, he had no suspicion yet that his master was deceiving him, and meant to marry Anne Boleyn.

# Chapter 13

HAD ANNE DEVISED it herself, she could not have done better, to get rid of the Cardinal. All the time he was away, making peace and aiming to become the Pope's surrogate, she was free to see the King. Summer had driven him from putrefying London, and it was easy for him to ride over to Hever. Every time her great lover came, he announced himself by a blast of his horn, and then Anne left the Castle to meet him under their tree—the tree where Thomas had kissed her for the first time. There they could be tenderly at home, and plan the divorce. Her lover brought the world with him, and he was easy in it, a master who could laugh and make merry and, courtly as he was, often as pleased as a boy. Long after he left her she quivered with him, just as did the Thames when one of his ships passed with flying pennons and full sails. Her life, so slight before, was grand with promise. Their Court could be a joy. Anne had seen enough of France to wish for a style as subtle, and with Henry to love her, with fortune to favour them, she foresaw a Windsor and a Greenwich and a Hampton where all could be moulded to their will. Her companions, and she forgot none of them, could fill the places nearest to the King. She had a liberal hand and longed to employ it. Even Thomas Wyatt—when all was sure, she could love to see him in her train.

But these dreams of the future, with children to fill it and friends to enhance it, were more buoyant than any Thomas Wyatt could indulge in.

Since his dismissal from Court he had gone home and stayed there. For the time being he had no more to do with Anne.

It was quiet at Allington, with that smooth and steady hum of a great house grooved in its methods and wisely supervised. Lady Wyatt, tight-faced and serious, was only confirmed in her earliest misgivings by Thomas's dismissal. When she contrasted her husband's faithful occupation with the fitful employment given to Thomas, who to her mind was equally worthy, she felt bitterly about "the black one," as she called Anne privately. Lady Wyatt knew whose fault it was, a certain acidity in her expression was considerably deepened by the spectacle of this disused human being, who was naturally endowed to pursue a career, and acquire honour, and shed lustre on the name of Wyatt. Margaret, Thomas's sister, was less impelled to judge the black one. She was not sure that Anne was at fault, but she pitied Thomas, though neither she nor her mother had the stupidity to remind him of his deserted wife, or to try to condole with him. They treated him rather like a sick animal who goes to and fro at a thoughtful pace, hangs his head a little, flops lumpily into his old basket, and, with a kind of religious intensity, licks his wounds. That was Thomas. He was, socially, a loss.

Yet not so dead a loss, in the final sense, as his good mother supposed. Thomas had fled to Italy, worn out by his struggle to win Anne, and his desperate attempt to meet Henry's rivalry on the bowling green was his last effort to overwhelm the difficulties that were beating him. But the heart that he had set on winning Anne was full of nothing else. She was not an incident in his life, an object he could either acquire or not acquire. She was the meaning that life held for him. It was his love of her beauty that had drawn him into the mood that forced him to write poetry. When he had met Mellin de St. Gelais, and Nicole Bourbon and Clément Marot, when he had learned of the Italian versifiers, it was Anne who fired him. She moved him by some primitive urgency such as the salmon feels, or the frog, or the eel, but with this urgency went his need for a thousand gratifications and ratifications, to follow from the instinctive leap in his blood whenever she even passed him in the gallery at Greenwich. To see England rhythmic in the ever-shifting, ever-striving dance—that was a need for Thomas Wyatt, but this England was, as he saw it, an inner swirl of other dances, and when it came to a private rhythm he was driven by greater forces than had sent him to Italy. One was an instinct, to shape the creation of a society, and the other was an instinct, to take each thread of impulse not yet understood or acknowledged and give them the tender twist that is the law of the poet. There was no crude impulse that Thomas did not feel—to injure Anne, to get drunk, to whore, to fight, to splinter and shatter the reflection of her in his own wounded soul. But, where his father had stood by the Tudor out of sobriety, so Thomas struggled with the same sobriety to respect his feelings—hopeless pangs of loyalty, despair, cutting sighs, eternal hope, blind aspiration.

His father, who had heard of his dismissal with a mute distress, came home to learn what he could of it, but this was in vain. Thomas could not speak. Neither Lady Wyatt, nor Sir Harry, nor Margaret, had any positive account of it.

## II

Lady Wyatt hated Anne Boleyn for it, yet this hatred touched her own conscience, since it was she who had prevented her husband from matching Thomas and Anne Boleyn.

Well she remembered a night, before Thomas was married, when he had gone over to Hever at daybreak, to say good-bye to the slender Anne, who was leaving for France.

That night the sound of his horse's hoofs had wakened her. She lay listening as the beat of the hoofs receded to the west, followed by dog barks on the frosty air. For a few moments her own heart beat so much faster that she could hardly think. "Tom is for Hever," she had said to herself, and her brain began the sickening moil that for so long had dizzied her. This time, however, she could hold back no more. She gave a cough and waited.

Sir Harry's head was covered. His nightcap was about his ears, and he made not a stir. Though he had been early to bed, he still lay ocean deep in oblivion. She coughed again. And that had its effect. Still under the transparency of sleep, he opened his eyes. Above him was the ceiling of their four-poster, a tester of the rising sun, and from the mere shape of it he seemed to say, "This can't be Norwich!" Slowly he came to the waking surface: he was at home in Kent, and with that he had thrust out his hand to her. His was a nature rooted in fidelity. There she was, they had this last gratuity of the night to share, he had feasted on sleep till the peace of his spirit flowed into him, and he gave her hand a squeeze, and heaved a sigh.

"You did sigh, Harry," she had said to him.

"Not sadly, wife."

"We have good cause to be happy, thanks to God," she murmured. "But now we are awake, you still threaten to leave?"

"My hands are full. I must away."

"It is the jewels?"

"Yes, his Grace hath plainly charged me with plate and jewels."

"That must take you to France, dear? Would that Tom were old enough to help you."

"We must not press him. 'Tis time enough."

"Yea, but he is old enough to have this matter of his marriage taken to heart. This we must face, husband."

So she had broached it. She had waited for his silence, but with his hand engaged, she let him feel he must answer.

"Must we speak of this, Jane?"

"I see not how we can avoid it."

"It is the Boleyn girl that perplexeth me."

"Do I not know!" she pounced. "But you keep me in the dark. Can you not open to me?" And when he said nothing she had added, "I should not have to urge the boy to take Nan Boleyn. Yet, on my soul, I cannot bring myself to urge her. Is it not strange?" And her grip had tightened involuntarily. He still gazed above him. She could feel the stubborn power in him that nothing could ever shake, and for a moment her fear gripped her. Henry was Constable of Norwich Castle with Thomas Boleyn, and if he never spoke of Lady Boleyn it was out of loyalty. That had long kept Jane Wyatt from risking a disagreement, but for weeks she had been pondering her son's fate until at last the omens of the declining year, of endless dripping days at Allington, with young Thomas Wyatt in Cambridge, her husband at Court, and this question gnawing her nerves, was more than she could bear.

"What think you?" She had turned to him.

His happy mood was gone. He tossed his nightcap awry and sat up a little. He was troubled, uncomfortable.

"Does he see anything of Elizabeth these days?" she had had the temerity to pursue. The dark emboldened her.

"Elizabeth?"

"By Elizabeth I intend Lady Boleyn," she said calmly. "Consorts the King with her?"

That question broke into the attic of matrimonial reticence, the twilight room where inconvenient things huddle in the dust. Neither Sir Henry nor Jane Wyatt made bonfire of its awkward bits. They took their lives as a whole. But one item, unmentionable even in the privilege of the bed, was Lady Boleyn, half-sister of his former wife. She had scorned Jane Wyatt from the first and Jane only avoided it by avoiding Court. She had no doubt about her own feelings. Her pride had been too great to permit a fretting antagonism, but now neither pride nor placidity could smooth away the obstacle before her. The mere thought of Thomas becoming allied with Hever and the Boleyns had aroused in her a fierce will to declare herself before a step were taken. Her husband might be slow to reveal his feeling. Anything that touched the Howards made him bluntly silent. But it was Thomas the mother was thinking of, so she had bravely renewed her question.

"Does Elizabeth still hold the King, Harry?"

"That I cannot say, Jane," Sir Harry had replied. "Lady Boleyn is in constant attendance, the Queen hath her in favour. But no, she cannot be in his graces. His fancy is somewhat for Mary."

"Mary? Mary Boleyn? The elder daughter?"

"And why not?"

"Why not, forsooth? Like mother, like daughter. Yet had I only come so far in the lesson as Bessie Blount."

"You are in retard." Henry Wyatt chided a wife who did not come to Court. "Bess Blount nurses her boy now. She is no longer at Court."

"The King's fancy is nimble," said Lady Wyatt drily. "Yet Mary is under her mother's eye. She is to be married anon."

"So be it. The King hath a passing fancy for her."

Thus it had been exposed, and as her husband waited Lady Wyatt spoke finally her mind. "Nay!" she exploded. "Nay! This Boleyn family cries to heaven. They are not for our son Thomas."

"How now, wife?"

"My will is yours, Henry, but, if it please you, my love for him is touched. I do beg of you, speak out to me. Could he incline to Bess Brooke, 'twere for our contentment. Thomas Cobham is our good friend. The child is comely. She is a winsome child. Speak out to me."

He had heard her broodingly. In the domain of his boy's life he had no guiding star. No one could meet a crisis with greater calm than he, or untie a knot with greater wisdom, but his wife was seeking a clarity that was beyond him. His boy Thomas was his pride, but Thomas's was a new world. Its obscurity, its intricateness, its hidden laws, its strange allegiances, baffled him without cease. Still, he had promised her to approach Lord Cobham, and it was after this fateful talk with her that he had sent Thomas to Bishop Fisher.

Yet, well as they had meant, Bess was a failure. What was to happen now? If only Thomas could forget it, and be at home at Allington.

The master of Allington, oddly enough, never suspected who made Thomas superfluous there. It was himself. Even when he came back for a few days he gently brushed Thomas aside. He was the patriarch.

He never could idle. From early morning he gave himself to crowding duties with the patient good sense that was native to him. It was not for nothing that the first long gallery in England had been built into Allington. Cast away on an island, Thomas's father would have made capable shift before the sun went down. Tucked away in Kent, he was no less thorough. He was stonemason and saddler by sheer instinct, fletcher and armourer, ploughman and jeweller. The stuff he worked in, its laws and limits, he bent his faithful will to it, weighty, firm and obedient. And he bulked large in the family vision.

Unlike Thomas, he wrought within tradition. Things had to be fashioned by hand, or with feeble use of mechanic power, and many of the ways at Allington were simple and rude. It did not do to be too sensitive. A faint odour of wool fat, of stale sweat and unwashed brocades, hung about the rush-strewn chambers, which the dogs were at home in and the servants could not easily air, the windows being fast, the flambeaux mingling fumes every night with the prevalent, sweetish exhalations of perfume and putrefaction. This was the conglomerate which would blend, with the warming sun, into the terror of sweating sickness, and even in winter the sparing use of water and the simple methods of cleansing made every old building a nest of infection. It was nobody's clear business to dispose of waste, and the knightly costumes were worn over an epidermis polished to new surfaces, rather than soaped and rubbed.

What was amazing, with the conformities that still encased a knight like Sir Harry Wyatt, was the heroic patience inside the armour of habit, and the jointed armour's flexibility. Dutifulness goes far, and he had it. He was born to inspire faith, to win love, to respect his kind. Yet he had no way of reaching Thomas outside the routine way, and he was just as much in the dark in 1527 as he had been in 1519. He wagged his head mournfully as he departed for Greenwich. "I'll leave it to the women."

## III

MARGARET, younger and less troubled than Thomas, rode to London with her father. In a few days she came back with a budget of news and a budget of purchases. Spices, drugs, silks and some cutlery were of intense interest to her home-keeping mother.

"How was London, dear?"

"London stinks," said Margaret in her dry manner. She had a sharp, clever nose, a clear brow, and a manner youthfully sedate. She was three years younger than Thomas. "London stinks, most fearfully, mamma. They fear the Sweat, as ever. The King is on the wing. Yet the deaths are few thus far."

"You were with your father?"

"Yea, as he had to visit the Archbishop of Canterbury who sends out new coinage. Metal is scarce since the Cardinal cleaned us out. There's to be sanctuary no more, for fear of plots. Master Cromwell hath been too smart in pulling down the monks. Let's see, what more? Oh, Pappa saved a poor man from the gallows."

"An innocent?"

"Well," laughed Margaret, "to say truth, he had stabbed his wife."

"A guilty man?"

"Nay, for he succoured her, and she forgave him."

'Margaret, you jest!"

"In earnest, mamma. That's all, methinks. Nay, the divorce!"

Lady Wyatt looked at Margaret. They were both serious. "The Queen is incensed. She will resist it."

"Spoke the Archbishop to your father?" Lady Wyatt asked.

"That I could not know. But Harry Lee confides that my lord of Norfolk had angry words with the Cardinal. Now the bishops are at odds. The divorce must go Romeward."

"Nay, but this cannot answer," exclaimed Lady Wyatt. "The Emperor will prevent it. This must unsettle England."

Margaret heard her mother with calm attentiveness, and held herself proudly as she listened.

"How is Thomas?" she asked casually.

"Mewed in his chamber," Lady Wyatt replied.

"And he was in full course! All went so galliardly in Italy!" deplored the sister softly.

"Why is she unkind to him, Margaret?"

"Anne? She hath ever been my friend, mamma, but here I cannot answer for her."

"What can it be in her—a witch, like her mother. What is her lure, dear? You are almost her companion in years. What do they see in her?" Lady Wyatt asked this outright, her face pinched with anxiety. Margaret had never known her to be so pointed.

"Mamma, 'tis in her eyes. She is no more to look on than a hind, and yet they'll hunt until night falls."

"But she is cruel. I have no fathom for her."

Lady Wyatt looked grimly out, and the young daughter could tell that she was thinking of Thomas. When at last she turned her mourning glance to Margaret their thoughts met. "He wears that old cap of his," the mother said, "sallies out without his sword. He halts, stares, then starts furiously and disappears. He is beside himself."

"Have you marked his bearing when you speak to him?" asked Margaret. "He is never stockish, yet he's at pains to hear. He waxes thin."

"And flushes!"

"Nay, this is not our Thomas," exclaimed Margaret, "yet I'd court his anger were I to speak."

"Oh, Margaret, he is in torture. Speak. Break this spell!"

There was no rumour of Anne and the King, so far, only of Anne and Thomas.

## IV

"Brother," Margaret clasped her big hands and looked direct at him, "you have regard for me?"

"That you know," said Thomas uneasily.

"I am eager to go to Hever on the morrow. No one, here or there, will waste a thought on me. Have a message ready, so I may bear it." And with a casual small gesture Margaret left him, her footsteps inaudible.

This temptation was too great for Thomas. Before morning he had written Anne Boleyn. How well, how long, how faithfully he had served her! "I have never swerved," he swore. "Why are you then so cruel?"

With easy simplicity his sister took the sealed message, and no one at Hever saw it pass to Anne. When the right moment offered, Anne hid herself to read it. "Assuage me! Succour me!" It was a cry from the depths. Anne frowned as she read the tender and urgent words. On letting Margaret depart, however, she pressed her hand. "Come soon again. He must not pine, poor Thomas!" That was all. Even Margaret could not see in it the palest glimmer for her brother.

## V

When Margaret had left for Allington Anne sent for her French maid. As she sat later by her mirror, implacably aware of herself, her breast mounted and fell with the sharp disturbance of her thought. Thomas was battling for succour, for assuagement, though the hour for him had passed. Why should he be such a fool as to pursue her?

Anne's profile might have been cut by a knife. She turned her head slowly, back and fro, to see her coif, her brows arched in inspection, her throat beautifully supple.

This suppleness, it was in her whole body as she rose, and in the
long hands that rippled as she moved them. She sent away her maid.
Then she crossed her chamber with a grace peculiarly her own. She
moved as if in fusion yet detached, a leaf on water, gliding effort-
less. Already, as she opened a hidden panel and took out a casket, her
face had become absorbed. She had lost contact with the commonplace
of Margaret Wyatt, her companion in years. She was in another
element.

"I send you this letter," the King had written, "praying you to adver-
tise me of your well-being, the which I pray God may endure as long
as I would mine own." Anne bent it to the fading light. "Written with
the hand of your servant, who oft and again wisheth you in your
brother's room." George was by his side as they hunted buck, and yet
the King would have her in George's place, to be near him. Her eyes
marvelled over her "servant" as she returned the casket to the wall.
Not one grain of uncertainty existed in her regarding the King. He
and she were bounded by a complicity more exquisite than words. Before her she could see him in his overpowering presence, his eyes
searching hers, his lips compressed, each discerning the other. This
was no longer Mary, the wild rose. This was herself, leaf folded into
leaf, secret, and inviolable. His letter was as fervent as she desired. In
that, and it loomed magnificently in her life, she had achieved Henry.
She passed her two hands from her breasts, down her body, and drew
in her breath, exhaling it in a sigh. Yet her sigh ended in impatience.
To possess her King and her Kingdom she still must climb a mountain.

What this meant, while Henry kept on the move, the Queen by
his side, and her father and George in attendance—at the More,
Beaulieu, Enfield, Hunsdon—was something Anne's sigh could
scarcely utter. The resistance to conquer was still so huge that she
ached to attack it. She sighed in the captivity of decorum.

The Cardinal! Anne had deferred to Henry within her own heart,
and was reluctant to press him, as when the Cardinal had opened his
favourable Court. But Henry's talk with the Queen had startled Anne
as a declaration of war. She knew Queen Catherine. She had served
her with that vigilance of eye, that hunger of curiosity, which any
Queen whets in a young attendant. Catherine was a Spaniard of high

royal blood, Spaniard in her taste, piety, food, dress, doctor, cook, Spaniard in stubbornness. The Spanish ambassador was her spy, her advocate and partisan. To meet all this, when the Emperor had been invoked, called for drastic steps, could not wait on the delays that the Cardinal had pondered and pampered.

And the Emperor, as Anne knew, had been invoked under Henry's nose. The Queen's sewer, her maître d'hôtel, Francisco, had asked to go to Spain, to see, of course, his sick mother. Yes, Catherine had pretended it was against her will and asked Henry to detain him, but Henry, afraid he could not do this without implying suspicion, gave Francisco a passport, meanwhile instructing Wolsey to have Francisco stopped and searched in France. Wolsey had answered, sensibly enough, that Francisco might go by sea. Francisco did. And just as Wolsey was carefully assuring the Emperor that the rumours of divorce were "entirely without foundation," Francisco was by his side, and spent a whole day telling the Emperor—what? Naturally, that this divorce was not a pure scruple of conscience but a plan for re-marriage. In a week, perhaps in a day, the Emperor must learn the rest of the story.

Anne's imagination was less benumbed by age than the Cardinal's, less bemused by wine than her lover's. Her head was clear. This case of Francisco Filippo, or Francis Phillips as he now was, showed that their war was on. She could not rest until they, too, despatched their messengers, but not to the Emperor: to Rome. She chafed. She clenched her fists. She grew sharp with impatience.

Anne's vision was not at fault. A mountain stood in her path. But to sight so keen as hers, and so unsparing, the mountain top seemed almost within reach of her quick hand. She could not understand why her King should be put off and set back by the dead intervening plain that lay at the foot of it. This was her inexperience. Her sharp wit, however, could sight so many stupidities that she almost planted Rome in Greenwich, to be won by a word. For this she had her plan, feverishly reasoned.

Thomas at Allington had no clue to this. He knew the King was courting Anne. He had no inkling that it was Henry's intention to marry her. Hence Anne, before she hid Thomas's poem in a book, had a wave of anger against him. He was battling for her, when she had ceased to be there, and though it was herself who kept him ignorant, she was angry at his ignorance.

## VI

THE IGNORANT and trustful Thomas had waited for his sister's return in a state hardly controlled by reason. Anne was so vivid to him that she seemed to be within him, yet unable to speak, and not until Margaret sanctioned it from Anne's mouth, might they resume their eternal confidence. Why it had been suspended, even in view of his banishment, Thomas could not grasp. He never supposed that, divorce or no divorce, the King would seek to marry Anne. The King's marriage, every courtier knew, must be political. What he feared was Anne's alienation for a term, but they had so often talked of Mary Carey, and Anne had so scorned Mary's subservience, that Thomas kept hope alive, though its flame bent and lay down.

Margaret could not persuade herself to look on Anne's quip as any answer to Thomas's letter. From Hever to Allington she turned it round and round, to give it shape. It had no shape, so she decided that, since Anne had been so little at peace, Thomas must postpone all present answer. This she told him. She proposed to visit Hever again, and invited him to use her as he did the first time.

Thomas struggled with himself, but at last consented. By his blazing exigence he had forced his sister to yield up the miserable pinch of sand that Anne had sent him, and to search it for the least grain of comfort. But though she had given him so little, she was within reach by this honest courier, and he bent himself to plead. I must remain your thrall, he repeated, I restrain my liberty for your sake. I have no power to move your heart, I cannot restrain your cruelty, or force you by my goodwill to favour me again. The only reward I have deserved is to serve you without reward. I see well that by your high disdain you will grant no more. But at least, this poor and small request you must grant: do not rejoice at my pain!

This wounded, agonized message was carried to Hever under seal. Anne became rather pale, and even hesitated to receive it. She was on the eve of seeing Henry, who had written to her with undisguised

longing for her return. "What joy in this world," he cried to her from
nearby, "can be greater than to have the company of her who is the
most dearly loved, knowing likewise that she by her choice holds the
same, the thought of which greatly delights me." Were Henry, for an
instant, to suspect her of a message from Allington, all that was so
near consummation would be shattered. Her father, moreover, had
come home, to take counsel with her. A false move, a moment's dis-
traction, and Henry might reject her. Yet, angry as this made Anne,
the unopened message in Thomas's hand was more powerful than
her will. She took it, hid herself, and tore through it. Then she descended, white-faced.

"This must cease!" she cut at Margaret. "Mother is ill. Father takes
me to Court on the morrow. Were his Grace to hear, he'd call me
traitor. Thomas has no right to do it."

"You fume, Anne. Has he otherwise offended?"

A gush of angry tears came to Anne's eyes. "Offended, nay. But bid
him take thought. I too was banished and restored."

"Can I say more?"

"No more. No more." Anne quivered and parted from her.

## VII

THOMAS GAVE NO SIGN of being hurt when his sister brought this
answer. He took it with a little jerk of the head, and a short smile. He
murmured his thanks to Margaret and went away, as if to feast on it.

But while his pride lasted long enough to see him to his turret, it
served only to convoy him. Beyond that, proud as he was, he dropped
without defence into the abandonment he had fought against. He
had hoped for a token, a word of true consolation, even a chance to
see her again. His hope had still been vigorous. But when Margaret
gave him the truth, and he was alone with it, he struggled no longer.
He admitted defeat. Behind his barred door, a voluntary prisoner, he
beat out the flame of his heart with violent blows.

"I die, I die, and you regard it not!" So he cried, and so forced himself to sing, like as the swan towards her death. My hope hath abused
me, and vain rejoicing hath fed me, but I was wonderly mistaken, I
am comfortless, I remain all comfortless. What death is worse than

this, he cried alone. I seem alive, but my weal, my joy, my bliss, is gone from me; my heart is hence, my life is death.

This consciousness of death within himself, in the heart surrendered to Anne, was after a little time no hot and passionate truth against which he was rebel. He had expected to weep when he barred himself in, and this was shameful. But after a few days he no longer was feverish. He was able to rejoin his family more frequently. He admitted that Anne had left him.

Thomas then imagined that the circle was complete, and he felt calm. But the least reminder of Anne, in the next few weeks, had the power to renew pain surprisingly. And when it was renewed, with excruciating force, he broke into piteous reproaches. Your unkindness, he cried, hath sworn my death. Your fault has forged this. I die, I die, and you regard it not. So he repeated the wildness he had thought exhausted. He could not sleep, or if he slept he dreamt horrible dreams of bloodshed and despair. To punish Anne for her cruelty he thought continually of killing himself. To see me bathe in blood, to content your cruelty, would do your heart good! You could ask no more! His mind brooded on her unkindness, and he wished he could gratify her by killing himself, to make certain she would be defamed for ever.

I served you, he raved, I served you with all my power, as faithfully as any man might do, and claiming nothing as my right. Now I burn in this fire by cause of you. If you sleep, forbear awhile, hear me, it is the last trouble you shall have, pity your poor unhappy slave, I am in despair, I faint. It is not now, but long and long ago I became yours. Awake, hear me! Since so often you have kept me awake in tears, do not be angry if I am forced now to break your sleep, crying, I die, I die.

This agony, pounding itself day after day, night after night, against Anne's silence, could only end by reducing him to submission. He was incapable of wishing to injure Anne. He was not vindictive. But neither was he capable of deceiving himself. And this lamentable honesty, presenting him with a love that was stronger than death and at the same time a fate that refused him love, drove him to a pitch of self-analysis that was insupportable. His eyes had that strangeness which his mother feared most of all, the look of a man hunted, distracted and absent, desiring flight and incapable of it. He had no cage, yet he had no wings, and this broken-winged lover aroused both in Lady Wyatt and in Margaret an anguish of powerless solicitude. They did not pretend he had lost in a gallant play, or drawn a short straw in a game. They understood he had soared and fallen.

I complain, he puzzled to himself, of the love that pains me, and of the refusal of it. I complain of the heat of it, and of the cold in every vein, both at once. I say it is impossible to be hot and cold at once, or to wish for life by way of death. Yet, by God, love that subdues all things and whose power no life may eschew, hath wrought in me, to my agony, the miracle of the impossible.

This miracle, to which his brain at last forced him to resign, brought no consolation with it.

None, he said to himself, cares whether I sob or sigh. I prolong my pain by struggling. I know right well that to pine brings no redress. To refuse the yoke when it is on your neck is too late. Then what is there to do? His heart cried in answer, only, in full sight of her, that she may know the pain she has caused, to end everything and break forever. But of what avail? To wish, and want, and not obtain; to strive every day and every hour, what good is it? If I stay by the fire yet burn because I do not leave it, what is it but to suffer willingly? Sister and mother may pity and lament my pain, but still I suffer. Anne is the cause of my grief but the thought of it enrages her. My torment does not move her at all. In despair there is no help. Yet to linger on, more dead than alive, what help is that? I am past remedy.

From this miserable defeat, to remorseful anger with Anne, was the next stage in Thomas's wretchedness. How to be heard by her, when there was no ear to hear? She had returned to Court. To pierce her heart was now impossible. The rocks, he said bitterly, do not repulse the waves more continually than she has rejected my love. She may be proud of the spoil she has got, of simple hearts shot down, but vengeance must fall on her. Is she to be the sole woman under the sun to make game of honest pain and go free?

> *May chance thee lie withered and old*
> *In winter nights, that are so cold,*
> *Plaining in vain unto the moon;*

*Thy wishes then dare not be told;*
*Care then who list, for I have done.*
*And then may chance thee to repent*
*The time that thou hast lost and spent*
*To cause thy lovers sigh and swoon.*
*Then shalt thou know beauty but lent,*
*And wish and want as I have done.*
*Now cease, my lute: this is the last*
*Labour that thou and I shall waste*
*And ended is that we begun;*
*Now is this song both sung and past,*
*My lute, be still, for I have done.*

With his clear love at last poisoned by rejection, Thomas entered into the next circle of his hell.

## VIII

YET OUT OF SIGHT was out of mind. Anne was less aware of Thomas. She had returned to Greenwich, just as soon as the deer began to rut and Henry ceased hunting. Wolsey had written from France with leisurely solemnity, "the Pope's consent must be gained, in case the Queen should decline my jurisdiction." On this admission Anne went into action. She confronted her father with it, who in turn solicited the opinion of his chaplain, John Barlow. And she submitted to her lover, who in turn requested the opinion of his secretary, old Dr. Knight. While Barlow and Dr. Knight fermented with this formidable responsibility, Anne bethought herself of outside help, and racked her brain. She induced in her father an interest in the Psalms, making him write to Erasmus about them. She also persuaded Henry to write the great humanist a particularly affable letter. But these were subordinate activities. It was the Pope she aimed at, and she subtly convinced her lover that the Great Matter must now be taken in hand by themselves.

It was awkward. Henry had more than a smattering of theology, and the great matter had bred a little matter, after the fashion of this prolific world. To marry Anne he had to be dispensed from the affinity to Anne which he had contracted by going to bed with her sister Mary. This did not have to be specified in a bull, but without a general dispensation on this score their offspring would not be reckoned legitimate. To ask for the dispensation would not make the best impression on the Pope, yet Henry and Anne agreed that the Pope must clearly be asked to dispense him for the new venture while absolving him from the old.

To take these appeals direct to Rome, keeping the Cardinal still in the dark, no one seemed more reliable than good Dr. Knight. Henry, therefore, gave him instructions which were not to be revealed to the Cardinal, while entrusting him at the same time with another set of instructions for Wolsey's benefit, to be discussed as he passed through France.

By favouring this chicane, Anne had at last accomplished the great object on which she had set her heart. She could not wipe out Wolsey at a stroke, but bit by bit she could detach Henry from him. Until Dr. Knight left England she lived in acute anxiety, but once he had passed safely through France and the deception was a fact, she felt courage to hope for the best. Henry had outwitted the Cardinal. Resolutely bent on pushing through the divorce by her own means, Anne gloried in Henry's compliance. Dr. Knight was not a powerful envoy, but he was the best that they had. Anne was only twenty-four, young in diplomacy.

## IX

"In again?" said Jane Parker to Anne with a smile. "I saw you disappear, dear Nan. You find the Revelling Chamber a calm retreat?"

"Still as a church," said Anne, discarding her cloak.

"To say your prayers in?" Jane teased.

"One might do worse, methinks."

"And a good chaplain, I trow?"

"Right royal," answered Anne crisply. She found her sister-in-law an asp.

"That much is sure," Jane murmured, "but were it wise to trumpet it? You are observed, Nan. You have Mary's house at hand, that served so well."

Anne, so far, had preserved appearances. The Court, that was surcharged with the divorce, never connected her with it. But what Jane chose to voice was the rising suspicion that it was Mary's place, not the Queen's place, that Anne was intended for.

"Mary's house is her own," said Anne quietly.

"Yea, poor thing. She gained little more, for all she hath two children." Jane raised her sharp chin with perfect sweetness of expression. "Once she was all and all."

Anne's brow contracted. To envenom George's wife would be folly, yet to have her name linked with Mary infuriated her.

"You cannot think," she said icily, "that his Grace prevails on me?" She stood over Jane, her face dark with menace.

"What should I think?" Jane cowered. "With George bearing constant messages, with my lady your good mother and yourself withdrawn from the Queen's chamber? What must I think, but that you, Nan, have also lost your heart to him?"

"Lost my heart! Miserable Jane, to belittle me. What do you know of it? That I go in the Banquet House no more. Has George said aught?"

"Not a word."

"Then spare me." Anne, her fists clenched, slowly turned from Jane.

"I must avow," Jane gave a little whimper, "avow you are unkind. I now go to the Queen's chamber."

In the Queen's chamber, within an hour, Lady Willoughby was telling her of her daughter aged seven, to be adopted by the Suffolks, and of her regret that Jane's mother-in-law, Lady Rochford, was now ill. From that they naturally turned to Anne.

Because of her friction with Anne, Jane was wary in the Queen's camp.

"Mistress Anne may still have her chance," smiled Lady Willoughby. "Her old love Percy is to separate from his young wife."

"Anne?" Jane shrugged. "She hath long ceased to think of him, my lady Willoughby."

"Ah?" Lady Willoughby mused. "It is Wyatt, no doubt, and he is also separated. Were divorce a light matter, Anne could readily be contented."

"Were divorce a light matter," said Jane vindictively, "mayhap neither Percy nor Wyatt could content her."

"Oh!" said Lady Willoughby. "Oh!"

And when the Boleyn chaplain soon departed for Rome the whole Court said "Oh!" By that time Mendoza, the ambassador, had written to the Emperor, "If the suit for divorce be successful, the King will marry a daughter of Master Boleyn."

Jane Parker gave Anne a respect that she had never given before. Anne received it graciously, not perhaps as if she were actually on the throne, but as if the throne were certain. By this time Dr. Knight was safely out of France, and the Cardinal returning.

## X

"For my sake, your Grace," said Anne to her lover, "could you not soften your heart?"

Henry laughed loudly. "You find me hard-hearted, sweet. That is severe."

"Not to your slave, but to a poor minion you have banished."

"Who's that?"

"Young Wyatt."

"What, you'd ask me? When already he has confessed he loved you? Anne, is this sage? By my soul, you do astound me." Henry was puzzled, and his arm relaxed.

"Not that, God knows." Anne, who sat on his lap, tied and untied his shirt-string. "Only to show you your trust, stay with Sir Harry Wyatt. And then, when you are there, I'd ask you one thing further."

"Allington is well. What next?"

"Send him to Calais."

"Who? Old Sir Harry?"

"Nay, Thomas Wyatt. How he must mope in Kent. Give him a chare in Calais. Name him marshal, porter, anything. But send him out. Or to the New Found Land. He is too young to fret in Kent, and he's a faithful bedeman."

"As you will, my dearling. Two years in Calais may season the cub."

And it was as good as done, if Henry promised it.

## XI

IT WAS AFTER HIS VISIT to Allington, however, that the King met Cardinal Wolsey in the manor at Richmond.

Until that time Anne had been willing to remain the "foolish girl" whom Wolsey had banished from Court, but now, with a sweep of her eyes, she surveyed the chamber where she and Henry awaited the news of the Cardinal's arrival. Through that door, she said to herself, he'll come to his Master, for whom he has been hot to devise a marriage with Renée of France. It is not Renée of France he'll find here. It is the foolish girl, Anne Boleyn.

Cavendish preceded the Cardinal. He went on his knees to the King. "Where is my lord Cardinal to attend his Grace?" he asked humbly.

Henry had not thought of it. He looked at Anne.

"Where else should the Cardinal come?" said Anne. "Tell him he may come here, where the King is."

The Cardinal's usher bowed himself out.

"Was it the King who spoke?" Wolsey demanded of Cavendish.

"He never opened his mouth," mourned Cavendish, "it was the lady, your Grace."

"Then I was too long absent," scowled the Cardinal. "This is my thanks." He heaved with anger for a moment, grey and purple in the face. Poor Cavendish watched him with distress. Wolsey ran his finger round in his mouth. "I am dry," he muttered. "Give me to drink." When he had drunk he straightened his Cardinal's robe. "Lead on," he said harshly, "to the King's Highness and to his Lady."

He was able, however, to grimace a smile by the time he greeted his Master.

# Chapter 14

THAT, AT ANY rate, was Anne's first direct triumph over Wolsey, and she was whetted by it for a further triumph. She persuaded Henry that he must see the Cardinal and tell him that their marriage had to follow the divorce.

Wolsey had been disconcerted by the presence of so vivid a female. He was prepared for a successor to Mary and to Bess Blount. That, as a celibate who had himself taken a woman, gave him little scruple or discomfort. But when he had arrived as a weighted prime minister, laden with the importance of communicating his immense labours in France, and sure of Henry's response to all he had gone to do and all he had done, since it was the grandiose legend of a collaboration shared by the King, he discovered by Henry's side, publicly accepted, a favourite who behaved as an equal, a hostile yet beautiful woman. All the priest in him had recoiled from her, but, more than that, all the privileged statesman. He had, indeed, striven to be gracious, but he had not been prepared for it, and he had not understood.

Anne had seen him draw away from her as from a sting, and, because he had injured her in the past, she had the unbridled impulse to wreck him. Wolsey felt it at once. Henry himself felt it. And as the interview proceeded Wolsey was increasingly lamed by it. When he had only Henry's mind to meet, he seldom spared his rhetoric, and this time he had been ready to lavish it, but here was a stark will in opposition to his own, an unsparing mind that set its power against his, since she despaired of influencing him. He tried to placate her and failed. He tried to measure her and failed. Anne was resolved he should fail. Only by disputing his hold on Henry, she believed, could she ever become Queen. She set about this with an unmeasured ambition that Wolsey's presence seemed to drive wild.

And Henry was with her. By putting Wolsey at a disadvantage, Anne was enabling her lover to dispute another tutelage, and to shift England's centre from the Cardinal to himself. Yet he was still enough a pupil to be far less unsparing than Anne. Much as he loved her, the Cardinal had always served him and never injured him. He wished, not to destroy him, but to make him include Anne Boleyn.

Anne could feel this tacit reluctance in her lover, and it intensified her. Unless Henry imposed her on Wolsey, their marriage might be hindered. Anne did not believe the Cardinal could be won. He must be conquered. And she did not rest until Henry set out for Hampton Court.

## II

THAT was a friendly male visit, in Anne's absence, and it began with a handsome surprise.

"Prithee be seated," Henry beamed cordially on his host. "Never was Hampton more fair! You'll have the French here?"

"Yea, your Grace, but by then it must be your Grace's own manor, as I have long intended."

This astonished Henry, but the Cardinal had meditated for some time that the increasing opprobrium of his private wealth could only be met by such a gift, and Henry took it so happily that he was proud.

"But," said the King, "we must send the French home content, so feast them here as in your own house. They like good cheer."

"So do they," agreed Wolsey, "and gifts come not amiss. The treaty has reached full time, though there be a lamentable void in it."

"Boulogne? That I lament, my lord."

"Not that," Wolsey leaned from his chair. "Better than Boulogne would be a French bride for yourself, your Grace," and he looked with an ingratiating smile.

"They had devices of their own the last time," said Henry drily.

"But Madame Renée?"

"They'd never consent to it. May they give us the footing in Brittany that they refused my good father? Not so. Clear your mind, my lord. They dare not so."

"We might renounce Brittany."

"Yea, and they England. But let me perish of the Death, and who is Regent, who is heir? You'll have uproar in London, and the Thames on fire. This time, my lord Cardinal, let us be forthright since the case be so plain. Let us clean the slate and start fair again, that our heir, with God's help, will be indisputable. Let us have a bride beyond cavil."

"But she must be French or no one," said Wolsey wearily. "You cannot choose an Imperial lady."

"I'll choose in England."

"Your Grace," Wolsey half smiled, "for choice, yes, and nowhere better. But here you are narrowed to royal blood. Who is there?" His eyes twinkled in their tragic luminousness.

Henry hesitated. The Cardinal's manner, indulgent but incredulous, sapped his faith for a moment, but with the knowledge of his promise and the desperation of his venture he blurted out, "I'll choose Mistress Anne Boleyn."

"To marry her?"

"Yea, to marry her."

"Oh God," groaned the Cardinal, "you have not spoken to her? This is no strict resolve? You have not ventured your word?"

The King wavered. "We have entertained it."

"She knows your mind?" The Cardinal supported himself with his hands on the pommels of his chair.

"That she doth," answered Henry, "and to a certainty!"

With a surge of his whole body, his fur falling from his neck, his head uncovered, the Cardinal flung himself from his chair, at the King's feet.

"Your Grace, your Grace." He seized Henry's hand. "Here on my knees to your Majesty. You cannot take this step. You cannot do it. I beg you, on my knees, recall your word. This can never be. You cannot do it."

Henry saw tears in Wolsey's eyes. He was himself moved to tears.

"How now?" His voice was husky. "You are beside yourself. Is it the lady you inveigh against?"

"Not that," cried Wolsey. "But you have known her sister. Can you be dispensed? And the mother, your Grace?"

"Not the mother, my lord."

"Search your soul, my son."

"Nay, not the mother, that I do protest."

"Leave it so. But her sister Mary, your Grace. That is within the forbidden degrees. Ponder how Rome must see this. To put aside the Emperor's aunt, and then to seek this new dispense. God knows, your Grace is above suspicion, your conscience is clear, but how persuade the Pope? How face your England? Have you considered this? Your Queen set to one side, your daughter born in good faith yet out of wedlock, and then another named who is simple maid-in-waiting— these be blunt words, but think, your Grace, who else dare speak them?"

"Ha! You fear to risk it? You think the hazard too great, my lord Cardinal? You are unsure of Rome?"

"Here, at your feet, my old and cracked body must plead for me. You will always find me a true and obedient servant, delighting in no earthly thing so much as to accomplish all your commandments. There is no earthly good could induce me to endure the labour I hourly sustain except the trust of your gracious love and favour. Of this I would I were assured."

"Arise, my lord." Henry stooped to help him. "You are assured of my love." They faced one another, the King and his servant, each moved to his depths.

"My love of her is such I cannot swerve." Henry's voice softened and pleaded. It was the first time he spoke from his heart.

The Cardinal heard him with immeasurable dismay. To allow Anne Boleyn to become his Queen, and England's Queen, opened ruin in his own path. He almost tottered as he stood. This girl to control the King, with hated Norfolk to head the nobles near the throne, Rochford and George Boleyn to step to higher rank—it was a prospect so derisive that Wolsey bent his head, swallowing his bitter thoughts and writhing with them. The face he lifted to Henry was agonized.

"Was she not sworn to Percy?" he urged.

"Not that I wot of," retorted Henry.

The Cardinal stood dumb, while a great tear rolled slowly down his cheek.

"To this we have come in my absence," he ejaculated, falling into his chair. "Why did I ever go to France!"

His tears overcame him. "Pardon, your Grace." His lips moved, loosely but soundlessly. He was praying.

"Now I have composed myself," he smiled blindly. "Have no fear, your Grace. I'll order myself as you command." His whole face was piteously intense. "We must move with infinite prudence." He then turned quickly on Henry. "You are not living with her?"

"No, by God!" said Henry proudly. "And no one dare say it."

"Ah," sighed the Cardinal. "Then I see daylight. We'll make the Pope do as we will." For the first time, to Henry's joy, he was himself again—his voice almost buoyant.

## III

HENRY had been so impressed for years by the Cardinal's authority that he came away from him in high fettle. His handsome countenance was alight when he stepped into his barge.

"A glorious morning," he smiled on his equerry Norris.

The King had let the morning pass without a word as they were labouring up to Hampton. But Norris read his master. "In faith, the autumn is at its best, sir. The leaves hold out."

They gazed on the faithful leaves. Henry grunted. "He's sore weary, my lord Cardinal."

"So I marked." Norris was sympathetic. "Years seize on him at the last."

Henry grunted again. He longed to lay a genial hand on Norris's thigh and say, "Well, now my brave Norris, who's master now!" Had it been in the old days, with Will Compton, he might have floated into confidence on claret to unload his joyous heart. He smiled at the younger squire, and gave a sigh. Norris sketched a smile in unison.

"The French!" Henry breathed heavily.

Harry Norris pricked his ears. He gave Henry that blue-eyed gaze which a good captain gives his chief.

"This is for you alone," murmured Henry. "They wish me to marry their Princess Renée."

"They look well ahead," said Norris.

"Not so far," said Henry. "Their Bishop brought to mind my late brother Arthur. They deem our marriage to be against nature's law."

Norris was silent. Ordered and circumspect, he made no stir.

"Have you never heard tell," asked the King, "that my late brother did consort with her Grace?"

"In very truth, that I did some time hear."

"You mind who spoke of it?"

"Yea, your Grace, right well. All the gentlemen that time at Ludlow. Their names be known to you, I trow."

"No more of that. But you have heard them speak?"

"Yea, sir, and a dozen times."

"There's no dispensation for that, then. So must we part, though her Grace will ever be good sister to me."

"This is a dire event," said Norris. "A blow from heaven."

"Aye," answered Henry, "and had God blessed us, my sons would have lived."

"So it could be," nodded Norris. "You went pilgrim once for it."

"Barefoot to Walsingham," said Henry. "Ah, I was young. Then had I high hope."

"So now it rests with Rome," murmured Norris. "God pity her Grace, you are her life."

"We near Westminster," said the King. "No word of this."

"Nor of Madame Renée, your Grace."

"Say this, Master Norris, were you to choose, what of a French princess?"

"Were I so bold to speak, sir, might not the Emperor take it amiss?"

"And did I choose at home, what then?"

"One of ourselves?" Norris started visibly. "That were merry, your Grace, the pick of all."

"Well," grunted Henry, "God's will be done." He said this in his brightest, jauntiest air, but added seriously, "You'll keep it dark."

He left him to tell Anne. It remained a surprise to himself that he had mastered the Cardinal as he did, but since he could not live without making Anne his wife, it had given him the power to assert himself.

And he had not lied to Wolsey. No other woman had so resolutely denied him, yet, instead of rousing his self-esteem, Anne's independence increased his thraldom.

By what means a man like himself had passed under her power Henry could not have defined. Her withheld virginity was not enough to bind his whole complicated nature. He loved her with outspoken grossness, as he loved rank pastimes that stirred the fighter in him. He desired her, and this was alive as never before since, with her level look and her quick body, she had given recognition to his violent desire. But, besides this admission of his passion, this common earth they stood on, Anne was yet able to withdraw from him and to defer her capture. There were mornings, hunting mornings, when Henry could feel the cool earth as a virginal presence, and then the bugle could hark to him from the wood, and he could follow it with blood crisp in his veins, as if the world were new and clean. Anne was the first woman he had known who piqued him by such detachment; he made love to her from his inner self, under this compulsion, and with a hawk's eagerness he watched to see whether he had captured her own inner self. Of this he was jealous. He was jealous to absurdity. He was jealous of young Wyatt, whom he had banished. He was jealous of the little page with curling black eyelashes, Francis Weston, about whose adoration Anne had said a few amused and tender words. Henry could not bear to have anyone receive a word in that subtle voice, from that sweet throat, except his own omnivorous self. The opulent youth of Bess Blount he had discarded with relief, and Mary Boleyn had wilted for him like a cut flower. It was not alone Anne's freshness that won him. No other woman— not Anne's own mother, nor any of his many women at Court, least of all the poor Queen—had ever succeeded in evoking in him this inescapable, this ravenous yet discriminating preoccupation. He found in her a complicity that was still as guarded as it was unashamed, an enticement that eluded him. And this she had so related to his inner self that Henry went to her with a rush of eagerness.

She met him as he wished. Hers was that reception which is so like a homecoming. He had touched the coast of love, and torches met him.

## IV

THE CARDINAL could imagine it. Whether he could work with this wench he did not know, but an influence so strong as hers could not be neglected. He had wept at Canterbury over the sorrows and hazards of our mortal life. Here was a new hazard, and perhaps a new sorrow. But, with his heartfelt sigh, he submitted to it, and at once he turned his attention to its details.

Once established at Hampton Court, which the King wished to be re-decorated, he sent for his secretary, Stephen Gardiner.

They took a turn in the park. Wolsey, so old in harness, was accustomed to breaking in the young ones. He had brought Master Gardiner from Cambridge, where he was brisk in Greek and bright in the law, a promising man, and instead of having him wooed by the heretics over small beer at the White Horse Inn he made him into an engine against the heretics in London. Gardiner was sturdy, capable and ambitious. Wolsey put him through his paces: he had a hard mouth, however, and was inclined to pull the lead out of his master's hand.

Still, they promenaded gently, the curt-nosed Gardiner and the Cardinal.

Autumn at Hampton was spendthrift. It had minted more gold than King Francis and King Henry together, and, unlike them, had treasures unspent, a majesty aloft where branches of yellow leaves cut across branches of leaves still green, against a faint high sky, while the redolence of fallen leaves and wood smoke held in the air or drifted to the Thames. Wolsey's eyes kindled. He stood still to inhale it and absorb it: he loved Hampton, he felt renewed.

"Master Stephen," he observed, "you are but thirty years of age?"

"A full thirty, my lord Cardinal."

"And out of East Anglia, like my poor self, though more favoured of fortune. You have had nine years with the doctors, yet abound in energy. You will go far, Master Stephen, you will go far."

Gardiner made a humble noise, though he did not dispute the Cardinal's word.

"The French come to seal our pact, Master Stephen, and I'll be their slave. Study, meanwhile, to learn what bull Dr. Knight looks for at Rome. The Doctor at Rome will be a man in his shirt among the armoured. Seek light on it."

It took Stephen Gardiner very little time to throw light on the secret matter. A first draft of Henry's petition, which had admitted sexual intercourse with a relative or relatives in the first degree, was handed to the Cardinal.

"How now!" he cried out. "What imbecile framed this?"

"Good Dr. Knight, meseems," said cool Gardiner.

"They'll strip him naked," Wolsey said grimly. "They'll learn the lady's name. They'll have all. This, in my absence! I turn my back only to have this dribbler fall in the flames, and I must pluck him out. Hold! My barge, Master Stephen. I must to Greenwich."

At Greenwich, confronted by this document, Henry affected to be ignorant. Wolsey was all the more free to express his mind on it. The imbecility of it, to expose such a motive to such a Curia, to ruin Mistress Anne's reputation, to undermine the elaborate and beautiful fabric of Henry's tender conscience, to house in that Gothic edifice such fornication!

In long words and slow sentences the Cardinal wound through Henry like a river through sullen mud.

Henry saw the error, but he resisted the temptation to take responsibility for it. He let the blame rest on Dr. Knight.

When the Cardinal regained his barge, Henry, his ears red, pondered the damage.

He had, he remembered, been slow to turn against the Cardinal. He was conversant enough with state papers, with theology as well as the rest, to understand what a giant Wolsey was, a giant for work, for versatility and ingenuity. It was Henry's habit to measure himself against other men in sport or play, and when he measured himself against Wolsey in statecraft, as this issue showed, he gained new respect for him. Often he had seen him with the Council, or with parliament or the prelates, had seen him play down Norfolk or play up Suffolk, seen him prepare the aldermen and taste that dish before serving it—Henry was once more driven to admire him. From a simple Dean he had watched him become Cardinal and Legate, even lay hands on the tiara, and, for a man born to privilege, this was an achievement to inspire awe. Instead of resenting him for his sweeping indignation with Dr. Knight, Henry only feared that Knight might further muddle the matter and betray him to the Cardinal. He hurried to consult Anne about it.

The truth was Henry saw no enemy in the Cardinal. Against those who disputed his own existence—his right to the throne, for example, and they included others beside the Duke of Buckingham—Henry struck with all his force, struck to kill. But his instinct was to garner the goodwill of useful servants, even if he had to make scapegoats of unpopular ones, and he prided himself on his reasonableness, his powers of praising the faithful. He bore no grudge now. He was warm in retrospect. This would be embarrassed by Anne's detestation of the Cardinal, and he loved her too well to chide her, but, by St. George, how could he do without him? Where would they be, after all, without the Cardinal?

Anne received Henry with wise tenderness. As a female, she was aware that Wolsey's attitude to herself could count for little. Not until Wolsey collided with Henry, not until he was disloyal and exposed as crossing Henry's purpose and undermining Henry's will, could he be brought into direct danger. Then, and only then, would Henry strike to kill. Anne saw that now, in pursuit of their tortuous purpose, Henry thought the Cardinal necessary to them. She quickly agreed, especially as it touched her virtue. The Cardinal had won.

So, with Anne's help, Henry concocted an inglorious letter of warning to Dr. Knight. "The secret bull is at this hour known perfectly to my lord Cardinal." Dr. Knight was to abandon it. "My pleasure is indeed that you shall make no further labour touching that bull." But not a word, not a whisper, to the Cardinal, that "you were sent, as you be indeed, for things that I would not he should know."

Who was to take this letter?

"Barlow!" exclaimed Anne, "father's chaplain, John Barlow."

It was Hever against Hampton. So the discreet Barlow, picked out of the rut, was sent on the road to Rome.

## V

THE CARDINAL now set out to give popular effect to his labours in France. He spared nothing; neither expense nor toil, nor truth, to force this French alliance to resound. The ambassadors brought with them the order of St. Michael for Henry. "We'll be joined by legs and necks," grinned King Francis to Anne's father who gave him the Garter. By leg and by neck the Cardinal wished to link France and England. He himself said Mass at St. Paul's, with twenty-four mitres about him, and vessels full of perfume burning throughout the foul old cathedral. "Perpetual" peace, this time, amity and friendship as was never heard of in our realm before, as well between the Emperor and us, as between the French King and our sovereign lord.

At Hampton Court the carpenters, the joiners, the masons, the painters and all other artisans had glorified the house. When the Frenchmen came in from hunting, each of the fourteen score was conveyed to his chamber, a great fire and wine was ready for each of them, and they came down (when trumpets warned them of supper) to such order and abundance, with such a pleasant sound of divers instruments, that they were rapt into a heavenly paradise.

Before the second course, my lord Cardinal came in among them, booted and spurred. They would have risen and given place with much joy, but he commanded them to sit still, and straightway calling for a chair, without shifting his riding apparel, he sat down in the midst of the company, laughing and being as merry as ever in his life.

As his guests admired such subtleties as a chess-board in marzipan, covered with gilt, Wolsey made presents of them, and then, from a bowl of gold filled with hippocras, he drank a toast to their Kings, Montmorency returning the pledge and keeping the bowl, worth five hundred marks, as a present. Everyone who pledged the Cardinal kept his golden bowl, so that cups went merrily about till many of the Frenchmen were fain to be led to their beds.

Not until the feast was in a happy haze did Wolsey himself slip out to have a small repast and change his garments.

And at Greenwich there was a genial farce to regale the French, with Martin Luther as a clownish figure, and Martin Luther's wife as another clownish figure. Then was it merry in Greenwich.

## VI

WHAT was one golden bowl or a hundred golden bowls? This was the Cardinal's mightiest gamble, and he was bidding against enemies at home.

He spared no rhetoric to win the people, in spite of corn merchants, wool merchants, Hanse merchants, all the merchants who muttered against French policy and wished for smooth handling with the Emperor's dominions.

Into unfriendly faces the Cardinal blew his fanfare, peace and prosperity, peace, prosperity. He was never so audacious as when he came home to this great matter of the peace.

"I have knit the realms of England and France," he told the noblemen, judges and justices of the peace whom he had assembled, "knit them in such a perfect knot that it shall never fail, for the three Estates of France, which here we call a parliament, have affirmed the same, and therefore now, my lords, be merry. The King shall nevermore charge you with wars in France, nor the Mayor and other merchants shall never be charged farther with expenses, so that with exactions for wars of France you shall no more be charged, for the King shall have no need. He by this league shall be the richest prince in the world, for, as I assure you, he shall have more treasure out of France yearly than all his revenues and customs amount to."

It was Wolsey's hippocras, Wolsey's gilded marzipan, his golden bowl, and behind it was the broad policy he gambled on, France against the Emperor. He had listened to the Cockney mutterings of the wool trade and the corn trade, the Flemish artisans and the Hanse merchants, for a whole political generation, but from Amiens he brought back the mutterings of Europe, the voice of that greater community. The Pope was still the Emperor's prisoner at Sant' Angelo, shamelessly enslaved. In Madrid the two French princes were prisoners, and over their heads hung the sword that would either cut them from France or cut off Burgundy. The Emperor had other triumphs: the first treasure ships were coming from America, Antwerp was wiping out Venice, and the conquest of Italy was a fact. What could stem this? Whatever corn and wool, herrings and sturgeon might have to say, the argument Wolsey believed in was Lautrec's army. Francis I had just sent it into Italy to challenge the Emperor. On this army the Cardinal staked his fortune. Hateful as it was for him to see Anne Boleyn take the place he had intended for a Frenchwoman, he still designed to free England from the Emperor. He had never loved the old nobility, and that ivy would fall when he pulled down Catherine of Aragon.

In the meantime, to inveigle the Mayor and aldermen, he chanted Prosperity, prosperity!

## VII

THOUGH ANNE SANG LOW at Court, throughout these festivities, she had all the confidence that youth gave her, enhanced by her hope of the dispensations and by Henry's unshaken devotion. All through the French visit the Queen sat by Henry's side, morose and stolid. It was hard for Anne not to triumph openly. Lautrec's army, she was told by the French with their charming air of special insight into the workings of the future, was sure to regain Italy. That cheered her. And it cheered her later that the Pope, disguised as a huckster, had escaped from the tower in Rome, to find a perch in Orvieto. There, she believed, he must sign the papers. She left Henry for Hever after Christmas, flushed with expectancy.

Her sanguine attitude was not so unlike Wolsey's in his own sphere. She forgave herself for present delinquencies (such as her treatment of Thomas) because her whole imagination was yielded to the approaching triumph. To be married to the King would excuse and explain everything. She pressed for it, in her own soul, as for an absolution.

Meanwhile Dr. Knight did see the Pope, and the Pope saw Cardinal Pucci. Pucci was a trained canonist for whom the recent grim events had animated certain counsels of perfection. He took a long view. He gave Dr. Knight his dispensations.

Without even waiting to bring them himself, Dr. Knight sent a younger messenger galloping across France. The papers went straight to the King. There they were, permission granted to Henry to marry Anne, and permission granted to Wolsey to nullify the marriage. At first sight of these, Henry could tell how deep his anxiety had been by the immense relief they gave him. Glowing with pride, he summoned Wolsey.

Permission to marry Anne? Yes, the Cardinal scanned it and passed it. Permission to divorce the Queen? With his heavy brows bent on this, Wolsey took full time to digest it while the King fidgeted. He followed the thread of Pucci's canonical mind. He pursed his lips, scowled a little.

"Of no effect or authority," he held up the document with its dangling seal.

"What impairs it?" frowned Henry.

"The Pope holds us by a tether, your Grace. Rome must still ratify the Legate's decision."

"By God's blood! Then Knight has failed us?"

"Not in the secret matter, your Grace. But in the Great Matter he had not acquitted himself."

"What do you propose, my lord Cardinal?"

"By your Grace's leave, we'll choose new instruments. Foxe, your Grace's chaplain, is a right man for this and I have another."

"I know of none," complained Henry.

"My secretary Gardiner."

"Ha! Now you hit the nail! But we must remedy our first request. It be out of no vain affection that we set this cause on foot."

"'Tis a just and sacred cause, your Grace, the scruples of your conscience. That we'll make plain."

"Yet in such fashion, my lord, that Master Stephen may open it to the Lady?"

"Without a fault. We'll send him by way of Hever."


## VIII

A CAT that saw two horsemen come into Hever gave them a searching look, picked up a kitten in her mouth, and disappeared. They were robed in black, two priests, on the first stage of a long journey.

The spokesman of the two, Master Stephen Gardiner, rocked from heels to toes in a nervous impatience. He was waiting for the Lady.

Anne Boleyn paused on entering. Gardiner was a priest, something of a lady's man, and in a single glance, his one of genuine deference and hers distant yet personal, she contrived to create an allegiance. He presented a letter from the King. Her prestige was so evident that, as she began to read it, his gaze stirred a slight vibration in her.

"Darling," began Henry, "this bearer and his fellow be despatched with as many things to compass our matter and bring it to pass as our wits could imagine or devise."

As Anne read she measured Gardiner as an ally.

"Our desired end," Henry spoke of, "which should be more to my heart's ease, and more quietness to my mind, than any other thing in this world." That she believed.

"What," Anne raised her black eyes to the young man from Cambridge, "what do you esteem, Master Gardiner, that be best devised herein?"

Gardiner unrolled a parchment. "You read Latin, Mistress Anne?"

"I wade in it," answered Anne.

"This, then." He handed her a passage.

Anne read, "But as this matrimony is contrary to God's law, the King's conscience is grievously offended."

She looked up. "Is this so novel?"

"It comes next," the priest said. "May I have the honour of reading it? 'On the other side, the approved, excellent virtuous conditions of the said gentlewoman, the purity of her life, her constant virginity, her maidenly and womanly pudicity, her soberness, chasteness, meekness, humility, wisdom, descent of right noble and high through regal blood, education in all good and laudable conditions and manners, apparent aptness to procreation of children, with her other infinite good conditions, more to be regarded and esteemed than the only progeny.'"

"To whom owe I this eulogy?" asked Anne in proud invitation to Gardiner.

"To my lord Cardinal," he humbly admitted.

"How may I duly thank him!" she gasped. "Let me see it for myself." Purity, virginity, modesty, chasteness. Anne found herself decked in snow-white.

"Come, gentlemen," she cried, "lay off those heavy cloaks. Make speed in France, but rest your weary limbs and let us comfort you. Welcome to Hever."

## IX

AT THE SAME TIME Sir Harry Wyatt was saying adieu to the King. In his old hand, which trembled a little, he bore a receipt for all the jewels. His face was flushed as usual, his eyes alert. In every line he was an honest, faithful gentleman.

The King took the list. "All's square," he said at a glance and wrote his initial at the top and bottom. "Now you go home, Sir Harry?" He held out his hand, "My faithful friend."

"A blind old servant," said Sir Harry roundly, "at your Grace's command."

"Ought I can do? Your boy Thomas is on my mind."

"In sooth, to give him employ," replied Wyatt, "would be a kindness."

"Here?" Henry frowned.

"Where youth may best serve your Grace. In the New Found Land, or elsewhere."

"How's Calais? How's Calais for him?"

"Thank your Grace indeed."

"When he is apt, we'll name him marshal. Tell him there's pen and ink at Calais as Lord Berners proved, until the trumpet calls."

With that the King nodded old Wyatt out and carefully put away the list of jewels.

## X

THOMAS heard his father's news: he could escape, he could leave England.

And on the heels of it Francis Bryan rode in. He had private word that Gardiner and Foxe had left for Rome, that the King was now sure to marry Anne Boleyn.

Thomas saw Bryan on his road. Then he plunged into the woods, to try to read his heart, that desolate, unfeeling heart he had so long stabbed down.

It was cold in the deep wood. In the hollowness of it he could hear the bite of a woodman's axe. It struck to his marrow. Newly felled trees were already chopped into firewood: he saw clumps of them in good order by the side of the road, with living moss and fern still clinging to them; and this sign of the inexorable seized on him. He felt, rather than saw, the hewers who moved among the living trees, leaning earthly hands on those they doomed. Their dim forms he caught in the distance, and his separation from them, a breed of men who never spoke or shared their life with him, deepened the wild mood that had invaded him. But he could not remain inside the sheltered wood when the sky was torn outside.

This, then, was it—she had chosen the King. She had been choosing him while he himself was mad for her.

A savage gratitude burst in Thomas's heart. His lips curved with contempt. He broke through the wood, up a hill, and walked against the sunset.

To the south a great murk stood like a wall. Smudges blemished the west. A few long bars stretched on the watery sky; as sunset rolled up, the bars sank into rose and deepened into flame, while the clear sky bathed these reefs in a blue of enchanted childhood, a blue of rapture, innocence and glory.

"Ha, ha, ha!" laughed Thomas. "Ha, ha, ha!"

"I'm free!" he cried. "I'm free." And again he laughed at the blue that deepened from birth to youth, and the rose that flamed into blood.

> *"Ha, ha, ha! Full well is me,*
> *For I am now at liberty."*

The words, the wild surge of them, tore through his mind. For I am now at liberty! For I am now at liberty.

The sunset furled itself. Against the slatey east Thomas went downhill to Allington.

> *"Was never bird tangled in lime*
> *That brake away in better time."*

But there are trapped birds that gnaw through their own legs to free themselves.

> *"Ha! Ha! Ha! Full well is me,*
> *For I am now at liberty."*

He was ready for Calais, years and years of that war-town, hollow as a drum unless war beat on it.

## XI

THE NIGHT THAT THOMAS was to leave Allington had hard frost in it, a change from the storm. It was cold outside, with sharp starlight, and this cold bit into the gatehouse. Only one place in the room was friendly; there a brazier glowed, and the older of the porters crouched near it, his woollen cloak hanging open from his shoulders over his dingy breastplate, and the light or perhaps the stinging heat flushing his graven face. He stank a little, with the earthy richness of rotting leaves, and something of the earth clung to him

Against the dim wall, on a rude bench, the younger porter faced the door, fronting the wicked world with a composed countenance. His features were clear, and he was as still as a wood carving. He sat bundled in his cloak, his cap shading his brown face, and his halberd between his knees.

"Harsh frost," the older man warmed his knobby hand affectionately. "My old bones ache, Steve."

"Old? You be no old man, Master Luke," reproached Steve.

"I'm a mite over sixty, withal."

"What's sixty! You do hear and see as well as young master."

"Aye, young master! He's off this night, and I hate the town of Calais."

"You were there yourself?"

"I'll tell you where I been. Woman for home, they say, and man for war. I left two growing children on the hearth the day I went out to Bosworth Field. That's forty year agone and more. We had no Allington then. Master was in yon London Tower."

"God's mercy he come out of it."

"Aye. Crookback stood over him. 'Cry mercy!' quod he. Master was mum. 'Give him mustard and vinegar,' said Crookback, 'that'll bring it up.' He retched, and no more. Two year he was there, afore Bosworth. So we come here. And, in this young King's time, I was out foreign, to Biscay. And then with Sir Harry, to France, and there I laid eyes on an old turtle, the Emperor that was. Not a sound tooth in his head, the Emperor, and I have all mine still, and God preserve them. And after that time, the Earl of Suffolk took me over sea to fight the Frenchman. But nought since then." With that the old soldier gazed into the bed of living coals, his gnarled hands on his knees, while young Steve, watching him, said in a deep voice, "And all we have out of it be a dearth of corn."

"Trouble all over Christendom, and no lie," said Luke. "Here in Kent, and out in France. Down in Spain and with the Turks and on the sea, and all the way to Rome, nothing but trouble!" He spat into the brazier. It sizzled away, a fried spit, and again he spat into it.

"Rome is at the root of it, they say," Steve ventured.

"Nay, nay," Luke sat up. "Make no mistake. Rome stands."

"They say 'tis coming down."

"Neither to-day nor to-morrow. You might as well try to pluck down the stars as pull down the Church, Steve."

"I was to Cranbrook, to my brother, Master Luke."

"What say they there?"

"There's not a good word for the Church. One says sea water is as good as holy water. Another says if he had the crucifix, and the image of Our Lady in a ship, he'd drown them in the sea. There's no Church of God but a man's conscience, they were telling him. And to set a candle before Our Lady of Grace is to set a candle before the devil. A man need not go on a pilgrimage no more, that's what they say. Men should not kneel to images or set candles before them."

"Aye, aye. Such idle talk! Wait till Sir Harry lay his hands on them." Steve heard him unmoved. "They be good men, withal."

"What manner of men?"

"A shoemaker was one. One was a cutler·and one a labouring man. They had the Evangelists in English."

Luke was troubled. "Good they may be, but no good comes of this. They go against their fathers. Hark!" He listened. "Was that a sound?" They both stood up, and with one accord went to the door.

Thomas was outside, but not alone. He had left the great hall with two pets, a greyhound and a lion cub. These were friends, the fleet Irish hound whom he called Oscar, and the lion cub he called Spot. Just as he was ready to put them in Luke's charge, Spot had suddenly shrunk back from him, his soft flopping body tense, and with a rusty roar, a young yet rasping sound, crouched ready to spring at him.

Before the young lion could spring, Thomas reached to draw his sword. The porters, with their halberds, ran down toward him. Spot, with claws like razors, gathered his limber body, but in the instant that he sprang the greyhound leaped at his throat. Thomas's sword flashed in the starlight. Once again the cub was limp and yielding. Thomas watched him piteously as he died.

"I took him from his nature," he muttered.

Young Steve swung a yellow lantern over him, under the tight windows of the castle. The lion's paws were soft and harmless pads, his body warm. Oscar held his eyes on Thomas.

"That I should have killed him!" said Thomas in surprise. "I who did love him."

Not till they went to the stables, where the warm comforting animal smell rose from the stalls, could he even look at Luke or Steve. His nag turned a sage eye on them, merely shifting a hoof when Thomas laid a hand on him.

Then Thomas's men came to the stables, and preparations for departure began in earnest.

Before daybreak they started for Cornwall. It was from there, later on, he went to Calais.

# Chapter 15

THOMAS REACHED CALAIS, and the moment Anne heard it she longed to be alone.

While he was in England she had been apprehensive. Allington was too near. His passion for her had become so impulsive, so untimely, that she had been angered, and, on the King's account, she wished him away. But, frightened of him as she had been, her heart melted now, to think of his separation from her in Calais. As soon as she could escape from her ladies, she took out the little Venus he had brought from Italy. She gazed at it with her own eyes, and with his; this was the creature she should have been.

Deep in her tissue, that smouldering human tissue which for a million years had been moulded for love, there was a knowledge not learned from hearsay. She was not cold. But she knew that if she gave a sign of surrender, not one but a dozen men would fawn on her, and this was the power that came from her own need to love. Gallantry was the breath of her nostrils because she was provoked by lovable men. Yet, with this, as she dwelt on Thomas's Venus, was the other knowledge of the world she lived in. Under her amorous gaze, in which she saw herself with Thomas's maddened eyes, there was more than the provocative woman. There was the hard woman who, hot as she was, could refuse her lover. She was not to be slain by love, not to be captured, except for a Kingdom. So far as the Court went she knew it without lifting her eyes. Francis Bryan would be on his knees to her at a glance. This she had allowed herself to see. Thomas Cheyney was not without a tenderness for her, and even in Stephen Gardiner she could feel a tremulous note. It ran up and down as she touched them with the lightest intimacy. It was a true power in her, something for which all of the Queen's ladies were, to a certain degree, chosen; but with Anne, since she moved so swiftly, this power was as quick as a sting. And yet, since she was so unwilling to be held, the sting was so faint that no ordinary man, not even a squire like Master Norris, could be sure whether she had given it. She governed it. But the postponements she was now suffering, with their piquancy because of Henry's ache for her, made her inflammable. When casual word of Thomas came suddenly to her she was twisted into his mood.

That night at Hever, naked in his hands, she had trembled with him. His strong body was under her clasp, his sobs shook her, she learned depth beyond depth of his compulsion. Here, at his lips, she drank wine from wild grapes, and crushed the gourd for its sweetness. He took her with him from a little world into a clean and bitter zone where she was no longer unconquered but someone in whose loins there was life, and in whose black hair there would be roses for joy and ashes for grief, a female to give all she had, to be slain in flame and delivered in agony. A thousand women in her blood grappled with Thomas and found fire for him in her womb, clinging to him on that crumbling edge where, in darkness, human beings make each other possible. Thomas's wife meant nothing then, and Anne conceived of enduring all that instinct urged to her, with Hever fading, all of them blanked in the abyss above which she and Thomas had clambered to a ridge, where they could hear and suffer each other and touch stars. It was by simple means they had reached this. They had begun chill and frightened, but warmth they found within themselves, and only dawn could have severed them.

Yet, though she had been driven to him, though she could surrender to the point to which her heart inclined and could be freed, assuaged, submerged and resurrected, yet somewhere in her, striving against him even when she most yearned for him, was the hard woman, she who feared defeat, who goaded and checked her own desires, and persuaded herself to give herself by calculation. She was no longer Thomas's Venus. Even as she looked at it, she lost him. Thomas was unable to speak to her and she put it away.

## II

WHY he could no longer melt her Anne scarcely paused to reckon, but the truth was, at this present moment, when he was gone from the scene, she was preparing for the final struggle as it pressed on her. It was in her nature to be as lively as a tree full of starlings, chattering for dear life, yet within herself she sought self-possession, to master the Court on her own behalf as well as Henry had done, and to do it by whatever means were called for. Love was out of season. Henry she could allure and defer, since he did not possess that trembling self, but until the divorce was secure she had to be clear, bare and hard. It had to be winter inside her. And she, who had been great-eyed, with a steady power of emotion, began to have that edge which is like a prow—to look astonishingly like her mother. So she went about the Great Matter, while Thomas kept watch in Calais and picked out the tracks she had ploughed him with, those wounds that were to be poems.

By her miscalculation with Dr. Knight, Anne had learned more respect for her enemy Wolsey, and, by one of those shifts in circumstance with which politics was to make her familiar, she decided to coquette with the Cardinal. She could not have done it before Gardiner and Foxe sought her at Hever, but that was a recognition of more than a polite kind. She was being consulted as his future Queen. Anne set store by that. She set store by his famous certificate of her virginity. And all of this, following the French alliance and the prospect of French victory, obliged her to see him as a friend.

Henry wished it. He agreed with her that Gardiner was a promising man, compact and forceful enough to batter down the feeble Pope, and at any rate on the right side, even in some ways to substitute for the Cardinal.

She could not say that his energy in making the poor heretics abjure

excited her in his favour. Henry was by nature inclined to the old
Church and Anne wasn't. But while these wretches, pounded into
submission, sometimes with the ominous fagots sewn to their sleeves,
were objects with whom she sympathized, she could not be vocal so
far: Rome, and only Rome, could give her the divorce that Henry,
for the sake of legitimate heirs, had to be sure of. But he could
scarcely convince Anne, who was impatient, that every step had to be
considered. Anne was for becoming Queen with celerity and simplicity. But Henry, however ardent he was, and eager as he was to
believe in Wolsey's prowess with Rome, was much too imbedded in
Kingship to think the change he proposed a light one, or worth
making except in the most workmanlike, most stable manner conceivable. He understood stability. It was his greatest preoccupation.
And his eyes flitted from one consideration to another with increasing
knowledge of the price he might have to pay. But as this disclosed
itself to him, what developed was his confidence. He could multiply
heresy trials, quite simple since Tyndale had printed his New Testament in Antwerp, but to show the Pope who his good friend was, at
this juncture, required the Pope to reciprocate his friendship. And
this long-sighted strategy said so much to Anne, in spite of her natural
verve, that she and her mother took the Cardinal into camp as a first
step in the divorce proceedings.

In Lent, in the middle of the heresy trials, she and her mother
began to crave fish. As a great lady of the Court, and certain to be
Queen, Anne could only flatter the Cardinal by sending to him for a
morsel of tunny, for a carp, or for some shrimps. And as he met her
requests with prompt gratification, it was no longer the butcher's dog
and the foolish girl. She persuaded herself to feel cordial, and her ex-
travagant thanks had such warmth in them that only a very experienced old priest could take them with a smile. Wolsey was not
even surprised when she begged his kindness for Sir Thomas Cheyney
against John Russell—it was merely a request for alliance, and this she
managed to repeat daily.

He complied as he could. She had gone to live in the gallery of the
Banquet House, where she had her own ladies, her own dogs and
servants, her own establishment so that the King could easily come
to her. The Cardinal took it that, to save the day, he must, if not

force Rome to yield, at least force it to shoulder the responsibility for not yielding—and he watched Henry like an anxious physician, to see how he was tolerating it.

## III

CARDINAL WOLSEY'S OWN PLAN, which he had pursued with great vigour, was to go as far as possible in making war on the Emperor. He had begun, before Christmas, with drastic pressure on the public. He had commanded all men not to talk of the King's affairs, or of the Queen. This was so vigilantly supported that every man mistrusted his neighbour. "No man," glowered a Londoner, "durst break his mind to other." And when the Pope, in December, escaped from Sant' Angelo, after seven months' captivity, Wolsey had a Te Deum sung in the King's chapel and a Te Deum sung at St. Paul's. Great bonfires burned in all London. And Wolsey refused to play down the Emperor's part in the Sack of Rome.

"What a cruelty was this," he cried to a picked assembly in the Star Chamber, "to pull down God's Vicar of Rome, and persecute the Holy Father by extreme tyranny, violate the Holy Sacrament and throw the Hosts down on the altar, and like robbers take the Pyx. And, farther, in the Church, they violated virgins, and stupred matrons, and despoiled the holy relics of the city of Rome. And like as the King in hunting time hath slain three hundred deer, and the garbage and paunches be cast round about in every quarter of the 'park,' so every street lay full of the privy members and genitures of the Cardinals and prelates—the whole history were too abominable to tell."

This was atrocity, to enrage England against the Emperor, on whom war was now declared. "The Emperor," he declared, "will encline to no reason. I am sure that I could show you twenty articles of promises, which he hath broken with the King, so that, I assure you, he keepeth no promise with our sovereign lord. Also, *contra jus gentium,* which I am sure the Great Turk would not do, he keepeth prisoner the King's ambassador, the French ambassador, and the ambassador of Venice. And for as much as the Emperor refuseth these offers which amount to eight Kings' ransoms, I trust by this War we shall bridle him, and bring him to peace. And this occasion of war I would all you should declare in your country."

That was easily said, but the Cardinal's select public grumbled. "He lieth," they muttered, as indeed he did. There might be three hundred deer, but there were not so many Cardinals and prelates. And the Emperor himself, who had every reason to keep England out of it, said, "Who would have thought that our Uncle in England would make war on us!" He heard that his ambassador was roughly arrested, taken from St. Swithin's Lane over to Mark Lane, near the Tower. But he feared the French advance into Italy, and he always believed that, to assuage Wolsey, he need only collect a handful of bishoprics and proffer them to him. He, like Henry VIII himself, was marking time.

The English common people suffered a shortage of wheat. The merchants groaned at interference with trade. And the nobles took it as a good chance to embarrass Henry, since he was giving the Cardinal his head.

The Cardinal had carried their fight to them by arresting Norfolk's friend, the Earl of Kildare. Unbridled and stepping high, this saucy nobleman pranced before the Council into a spirited attack on Wolsey. Had his cousin Desmond been conniving with the Emperor? he asked. "Cannot the Earl of Desmond shift," he demanded sharply, "but I must be of counsel? Cannot he hide him except I wink?" Then, with the salty wit of a noble who knew the weakness of any priest among nobles, he broke into a direct comparison of the soldier's lot with the Cardinal's.

"I slumber in a hard cabin," he said truly, "when you sleep on a soft bed of down. I serve under the King's cope of heaven when you are served under a canopy. I drink water out of my skull when you drink wine out of golden cups. My courser is trained to the field when your jennet is taught to amble. When you are be-graced and be-lorded, and crouched and knelt unto, then find I small grace with your Irish boarders except I cut them off by the knees."

The man who thus lashed out was a hardened warrior, but Wolsey rammed him into the Tower, and threatened to have his head cut off. With Kildare a prisoner, he proposed young James Butler for Deputy.

Henry demurred. "Too young for so great a charge," he said. "The noblemen of Ireland would disdain to be led by one who was junior to them all."

Then Wolsey agreed to Sir Piers Butler; but instead of naming him Earl of Ormonde, the King made a new title for him, Earl of Ossory.

So the gouty Sir Piers, less headstrong than a Kildare, dragged himself to Windsor to be invested Earl of Ossory. He was so ill that he had to be lodged in warm and comfortable rooms rather than the Castle, and to be brought to a fire directly after Mass. But the ceremony was royal, and the creation royally feasted, with the King benign to James's father. And when Ossory had paid his deep respects to the Queen, and paid his good crowns to the Court officers, he stopped once more in London to thank the Cardinal.

This creation of an Earl of Ossory saved Henry from arousing too much opposition at Court: instead of naming Anne's father the Duke of Somerset, which would have aggravated Norfolk and Suffolk, he would be able to requite him, in the near future, by calling him Earl of Ormonde and Wiltshire.

Henry grew wary. The Cardinal was too useful about the divorce to be hampered or even rebuked, and however unpopular the so-called war was, however the nobles ached to get rid of him, to get rid of the Papacy, and to seize the abbeys, Henry declined to desert either the Cardinal or the French. He even spoke sternly to an embassy from the Low Countries that asked for a truce.

"Of war I am nothing joyful," he said, "but less am I fearful of it. I thank God I have no cause to feel care, for I have both men and money and all thing ready prepared for war, which things I know the other princes lack, for all their high words. But, ere I make you an answer to that question of truce, some part of my mind I will declare to you. I tell you that although your master be a great Emperor, and a mighty Prince, I cannot nor may not suffer him to bear down and destroy the realm of France, which is our true inheritance and for which our brother and ally the French King payeth us yearly a great pension and tribute, wherefore we of justice and equity must maintain that land, out of which we have so fair a rent and such a profit."

France as a buffer state—it was the Cardinal's argument, and Anne's. Henry gave his clear voice to it. To the French themselves he said, with a shake of his handsome poll, "How to end war with honour and profit, men must needs study." But he added, with his repudiation of Catherine still uppermost, and unshaken, "As touching the defence of the realm of France, I assure you it shall be defended to my power though it be to my loss, and my study is no less to have a peace which might be honourable to your master than to mine own self."

So he stood with the Cardinal.

## IV

BUT FOR ANNE HERSELF, so alive to the prospect before her, so tempted by it, exposed in her pride until she could enjoy it, and still so on the verge of it, the delay in hearing from Gardiner and Foxe was almost unbearable. May arrived, a year after the Sack of Rome, and nearly two years since Henry had pledged himself to her. She could not sleep. Perhaps when Francis I sent on the marvellous bed he had boasted of she would sleep better, but until Master Foxe, the chaplain, arrived from Rome she despaired of a peaceful mind, and it was simpler to get up than to battle in vain.

How sleep plays traitor to the ambitious! The early sun lay a bar of light across Anne's bed, caressing her ankles. Everyone else was asleep. She rose instantly, flung open the window and let freshness into this chambered gallery that viewed north, south and east.

The hour was immaculate. The full light dwelt on the Thames, and through its opal and nacre a barge went ploughing its path. It was a red-sailed barge, squat with a load of brick, its waves thrilling under the surface that held unbroken. Even a feather could have sailed dry on it, keeping its serenity so proudly, brimming with the tide and still receiving the sky with acquiescence. Anne watched it mutely. She cast her glance on the green tilting field and the slope of the hill. In the cool hedge there was a crash of birdsong, and the light on the fields up the hill quivered with a piercing vividness. The shadows lay on the wet grass, where grey dew still bathed each blade and waited for the sun to lick them with its languorous tongue, while the earth under the hedge drank the dew into its soft, fresh fatness. This was a morning when the world lay so tranquil and so rapt that no human being could bear disharmony. Anne had slept naked. She stood in the sun, her black hair against the white flesh, gold glinting in her skin, her breasts rounded like conches, and a pulse in her throat delicately and incessantly throbbing. Tears slowly filled her eyes; an extraordinary expression, intensely full of reflection, gave her a look at once enchanted and melancholy. She stood there alone, the Palace grounds empty beneath her, and gazed out for a long time.

## V

EDWARD FOXE, the chaplain, was hurrying from London later that morning, when the sun had doubled its fist and smitten London.

He and Gardiner had toiled to Orvieto in winter, so hard-pressed by it on the outward journey that one of their best men had died of it. He had rushed back with springtime, to bear tidings to the Royal master, a faithful friend to Gardiner after those arduous months. He had a pinched, fine face, Edward Foxe, but narrow.

A whippet behind him on Three Cranes Wharf was slowly completing a yawn, as if a replica of a young diplomat. He too had been relaxing in the May sunshine, and it was only when a stir went through the little crowd, which with one accord moved forward to the edge of the wharf, that the bright page who had him on a lead was so cruel as to interrupt his yawn in the middle. It was the end of a doggish interlude. The hound had been delicately sniffing at the yellow-heeled Franciscan who was taking two suppliants to Greenwich. With melancholy elegance he had scanned the suppliants until a vegetable man, with a twist of his hand, swung a basket to his padded head. The greyhound deplored the remoteness of that basket, and then, with some misgivings, he ran his eye over a batch of ragged veterans who were coming to Greenwich to trade on their wounds. This was the little crowd who now stirred into motion as they saw the barge approaching.

"Am I late?" A tubby little man bustled to the wharf.

"Nay, good friend," came a quieting voice, "the barge has but put off from London Bridge."

Edward Foxe heard them with a pang of pleasure. London! The late arrival, fanning his big head, gasped for air. Burly as a barrel, his features shone with greasy heat and yet with a soliciting friendliness.

"A mad rush," he blurted. "How to reach the Palace other! By the Cross, I sweat like a bull!"

"It may be warm for May, friend," soothed the companion. He twinkled at Foxe.

"I may catch a rheum," said the fat man. "I cotched one a month since."

"Greenwich is not so far," he was mollified.

"I must not pet," the fat man replied. "My daughter saith, I must not pet. I'll sit in the sun, and no matter!"

So they travelled to Greenwich, whippet and diplomat, suet and sinew. And, as King Henry was not in the Palace, and as George Boleyn was on the watch, Master Foxe was taken to the Banquet House.

"Oh, Master Stephen!" cried Anne. It was an aberration, and the whippet's soft eyes took it without a comment. "Oh, Master Stephen, how I longed for your tidings!" She was palpitant, and yet impersonal. It was a style that grew on her. But Foxe was so full of hope, so laudatory of Master Stephen, so quietly sure of progress, that Anne's heart opened and she beamed on the arriving King.

Foxe had been present at every session of the Cardinals where Stephen Gardiner, his learning spick and span, had harangued the fugitive Pope.

No willow lashed by a storm could have been more responsive than Clement VII. He sat in his bare and beggared Palace at Orvieto with scabrous walls behind him, and his Cardinals on such a bench as might serve a school or a poor tavern. This fidgety Pope, gaunt, with a wisp of a beard, turned his hollow eyes on the vigorous, well-fed Englishman, who, born of prosperous traders, felt ignominy in this dilapidation. Yet, hard as he was hitting this reluctant Pope, and boldly as he pushed his sophistries, not for fifty years had there been so chastened a body as this which sat in a windy palace, with a torn hanging to act as splendour, and crushed lumps of old mortar on the eaten planks. They bent under Gardiner's blows, and Clement twisted and writhed under the necessity of combatting him, yet Gardiner himself saw the forces of which this remnant was the agency, forces of intellectual power to which, however he vociferated, he internally bowed. He nearly convinced them, however. "You have the Keys," he urged plausibly and heartily. "Yea," answered the Pope, "they gave me the Keys, but did not show me how to unlock with them." Yet he could agree to send on a Legate to England, to join with Wolsey in holding a Court.

All this Master Foxe narrated to the King, who had glanced at Gardiner's report, while Anne went into her bedchamber. Henry called her.

"Go over it," he commanded Foxe, "go all over it again. Hear this, dear. Tell Mistress Anne. Repeat everything."

It was marvellous news. Cardinal Campeggio, an old and trusted friend, was to be linked with Wolsey, to try the cause in England. He was to start at once. And the Pope was to give them full power to decide all.

Anne exclaimed with joy when she heard this. She and Henry exchanged ardent glances. Then Henry asked questions. Was the Pope personally friendly? Was Gardiner able for them? Foxe answered glowingly. And he pointed out that, where the Pope had been told that the Lady was with child and a worthless creature, Wolsey's long tribute to her had vindicated her.

It was a great day for Edward Foxe. He was questioned by the lovers until long after dark. Then he took a barge to the Cardinal.

It was 10 p. m. when he came up the Thames. The Cardinal was in bed, not at York Place which was being redecorated but at Durham Place nearby. And he sent Foxe word to come up to his bedchamber. There the old priest, after greeting Gardiner's yoke-fellow, took pains to run over the essential documents by candlelight. With a dry, shrewd glance at young Foxe, who was Eton and Cambridge, he told him to come back in the morning.

This business of carte blanche for himself and Campeggio was anything but sure. Wolsey, however, decided to make the best of it. To himself and Campeggio, perhaps, the Pope might secretly pledge himself. Next day he summoned Anne's father and Henry's theological advisers. These were not bishops. They were new men. The Cardinal gave Gardiner laud and praise. He pointed out that if the Pope committed himself in their favour, the Queen could be granted the right of appeal, and welcome!

Henry saw Foxe again. There were other meetings, not quite so sanguine. The King was resolved, he then said, to do nothing illegal. And the Cardinal, for his part, who had recently been saying he'd rather lose a finger than this, or lose his hand than that, now declared he'd rather suffer his whole body to be torn to pieces than to do anything other than Justice required. Otherwise, of course, he'd make a poor Legate.

This offer of Campeggio to try the case with Wolsey was an excellent one if he were instructed to decide it with Wolsey, and to decide it in Henry's favour. This was a sort of arrangement that could have been counted on ten years, or even five years, before. But the Sack of Rome had done an extraordinary thing, it had brought home to the Papacy that unless it recovered moral authority it would cease to exist, and to preserve moral authority among men there is only one salt: disinterestedness. Among the ruins of Orvieto a new Papacy was struggling for the light. And whatever gloss the good Gardiner put on his story, and however Pope Clement tried to satisfy him, this was the dreadful predicament the Pope found himself in: colleagues who wanted him to be disinterested and an Emperor who had an aunt.

Clement, in his own person, was the political symbol of the late Renaissance. His grandfather was Lorenzo de Medici, but he was a bastard, and his young father had been murdered in the Duomo in Florence. Born in the flush of that golden age, with a shadow of murder across his infancy, he had become his cousin Leo's adviser, while Raphael flourished and there was music. Luther had come, ten years before, and this was Clement's patrimony—schism, uproar, anarchy. Henry's demand came in the hour of calamity. It came with Luther, with the invading Spaniard, with the Turk and with defaulting Sweden. Two Catholic bishops were martyred in Stockholm while Foxe and Gardiner were arguing with Clement.

But for Anne, whose hopes had risen, this was too crushing. And Henry, so obsessed by the rectitude he was able to extract out of argument, made up his mind to write a brief, to put his great thoughts on paper. His book against Luther made him Defender of the Faith. Now, he determined to have a divorce on its merits.

His Confessor had just given him Holy Communion, and he was ready to leave Greenwich for Waltham, to digest his arguments, when

he learned that Anne had symptoms of the Sweat. This settled all
debating for the present. Anne was hurried to Hever. He galloped
to Waltham.

## VI

THE SWEAT was one of those dreadful forms of disease that brought
his limitations home to Henry. It began with a little pain in the
head and in the heart. Suddenly a sweat started. In four hours, sometimes in three or two, the victim died. Ten thousand had died of it in
London a decade before, and this summer of 1528 it began to spread
with frantic rapidity.

Henry was a practical man. There was little danger, he told himself, if good order was observed, if he ate small suppers, and cut his
wine, and once a week took pills of Rasis. But no infection must come
near him, and Waltham was too near London. With one eye on God,
Henry hopped to Hunsdon.

What gave him a strange feeling in the pit of his depleted stomach
was the irruption of the Sweat in his own household. He was still
under control, but he decided to eat alone, or eat with Dr. Chambers
right by his side. He retreated to a tower, and there he kept away
from infection. He decided to make his will. He decided to go frequently to Holy Communion.

He exhibited no heroism, but he exhibited no panic, and he read
his despatches, or at any rate galloped hastily through them. Yet
though he took a turn in the garden and expatiated freely on the
wholesome air, it could not be kept from him that his friends were
dying day by day. None fell ill in his house, but just as he laid down
to rest word came that Will Carey was dead, Mary Boleyn's husband, and this was close. He had nervously sorted letters during
the evening, while his lawyer tried to catch his jerky attention. Now
Henry's attention dangled forcibly over the gulf into which Will
Carey had slipped, into which Francis Poyntz had slipped, into which
hundreds were slipping. He ate small. He received the good Lord,
and "armed toward God and the world." He was in fear and trouble.

Then came word, Mistress Anne has it.

## VII

ANNE HAD LOST HEART before she left Greenwich, and though Henry wrote to her affectionately, wishing she was in his arms so that he could relieve her useless and unreasonable anxieties, the prolongation of the divorce suit crushed her. Will Carey's death was no tragedy for her, but her father was cold and horrid about Mary "in her extreme necessity." Then Thomas Cheyney caught the Sweat, George took it, so did Harry Norris and Francis Bryan. It spread out from London into the country, and William Compton died. The King shut himself up alone, but 40,000 of his subjects had the Sweat in London, half the population, and thousands of them rushed to make their wills. The air was full of "flying tales" and calamity. Henry was prompt to reassure Anne by letter: few women or none had the malady, and he implored her to have no fear at all. He told her not to "let our absence too much vex you, for wheresoever I may be, I am yours."

Anne was isolated at Hever with her father. The King sent over Dr. Butts, for herself and Lord Rochford, while Anne did her best to follow the advice that Henry gave to the Cardinal: "put aside all fears and fantasies, make as merry as you can, put apart all cares for the time, and commit all to God."

It was manly advice, despatched from Henry's new resting-place. He had skipped from Hunsdon to Hartford, and Hartford to Tittenhanger. He committed all to God, but he kept moving.

He kept moving, not only physically but morally. He began almost to develop scruples about chastity—not his own, other people's. In March he had felt called on to denounce his sister Margaret for living in adultery. She had managed, with adroitness, to procure a divorce from Rome. Henry was incensed. He called it "an unlawful divorce from lawful matrimony," and he compelled Wolsey to write her a long harangue about "the shameless sentence sent from Rome." Now, in this fever of righteousness, the only Sweat to which he succumbed, he turned on Anne herself, and on the Cardinal, who had forgotten for the moment the approaching trial and the extreme necessity for giving no scandal.

Anne had asked Wolsey to name Eleanor Carey, the late Will

Carey's sister, as Abbess of Wilton Priory. The Cardinal wished to comply, but Eleanor was not fit to be an abbess. She turned out to have had two children by two sundry priests and to have been kept by another lover. Henry pointed out this with great indignation, as well he might, on the eve of a trial when his own good character had to be asserted. "I would not, for all the gold in the world," he said, "clog your conscience nor mine to make her ruler of a house." Anne instantly submitted. The Cardinal, forgetting Henry's warnings, and apparently upset by the plague, put a woman in charge whose reputation was also damaged. Henry thereupon wrote him a long, stern rebuke, not only for his disobedience, but also for his previous lack of circumspection, and for his meddling with the religious houses. This access of virtue was so close to Campeggio's arrival that it should never have been forced on Henry. So he convinced the Cardinal, who bowed to earth in shame and submission.

Henry dealt him one further reprimand. He thought he was exceeding the law in suppressing religious houses for Cardinal's College. "There is great murmuring of it," he rebuked, "throughout all the realm, both good and bad." But that was the end of it. He had made his criticism, and "there remaineth, at this hour, no spark of displeasure towards you in my heart." So he said with a "fare you well, and be no more perplexed."

His severity with the Cardinal was by no means hidden. Henry wanted it talked about, so he told it to Sir John Russell and the others who were with him. It was part of his rather emotional state, on the eve of Campeggio's arrival, but it was far from chilling his mood toward Anne.

"Seeing my darling is absent," he wrote to her with a sigh, "I can no less do than send her some flesh, which is hart flesh for Harry, prognosticating that hereafter, God willing, you must enjoy some of mine, which, He pleased, I would were now."

It was a simple, amorous wish. Many lovers have entertained it, but few put in words, especially on the eve of a divorce trial.

And all this pother about Eleanor Carey, who loved the priests too well, made absolutely no impression on Anne. If the Cardinal was to judge in the divorce case, she believed in wooing him.

"All the days of my life," she assured him, "I am most bound, of all creatures, next the King's Grace, to love and serve your Grace; of the which, I beseech you never to doubt that ever I shall vary from this thought, as long as any breath is in my body."

This did not exhaust Anne's energy of assurance.

"And as touching your Grace's trouble with the Sweat, I thank our Lord that them that I desired and prayed for are scaped; and that is the King and you; not doubting but that God has preserved you both for great causes known all-only for his high wisdom."

What could these "great causes" be? Campeggio was coming.

But Anne's imagination was worked up for the Cardinal; and when that imagination was aroused, when those black eyes were liquid, when that quick tongue obeyed that facile heart, what a torrent could leap and sparkle over that bed, and become rapids among those pebbles.

"How wretched and unworthy I am in comparing to his Highness! And for you I do not know myself never to have deserved by my deserts that you should take this great pain for me. Yet daily of your goodness I do perceive, by all my friends. And though that I had not knowledge by them, the daily proof of your deeds doth declare your words and writings toward me to be true.

"Now, good my Lord, your discretion may consider as yet how little it is in my power to recompense you, but all-only with my good will; the which, I assure you, that after this Matter is brought to pass, you shall find me (as I am bound in the meantime to owe you my service, and then look what thing in this world I can imagine to do you pleasure in), you shall find me the gladdest woman in the world to do it."

Yes, yes. "Fully determined by God's grace never to change." The doctrine of grace. But the Cardinal was heavy-hearted, in spite of the Night Crow's letter. He could easily promise the King that "your poor Cardinal's conscience shall not be spotted, encumbered or entangled" again. But suppose he and Campeggio could not perform this service, what then? And with the Queen, and the Emperor, to consider, and all those noblemen whose hungry eyes were on the religious houses that only the Cardinal could keep from them?

Neither Anne nor Henry could rest in peace until Campeggio arrived. Henry had even to urge Anne's comformableness to reason and

"the suppressing of your inutile and vain thoughts and fantasies."
"Good sweetheart," he begged her anxiously, "continue the same,
not only in this, but in all your doings hereafter." But this longing
for quietness they both felt—what was it to Wolsey's? That sickness
which had made him merely sweat in summer, it was a plague that
had killed Lautrec, it had destroyed Lautrec's army in front of Naples,
when the Key of Italy was actually in Lautrec's hands. He died before
he could strike the last blow. The Emperor once more was saved.
Once more the Pope had submitted to him. And now, with the common people murmuring, the nobles glowering, Queen Catherine
braced by More and by Fisher, the Cardinal, to retain Henry's love
and Anne's fawning tenderness, had to deliver a divorce.

Could he save himself, he wondered passionately, by Campeggio's aid?

# Chapter 16

No ONE HAD foreseen it, but Campeggio's arrival created a sudden and enormous popular stir.

England woke up to Henry's intention about its Queen. In spite of the usual precautions the people began to collect here and there in London. Whenever Queen Catherine appeared they cheered her, and they could not be kept from the house where Henry had set up Anne Boleyn.

London was a well-watched town, divided into wards that were allotted to strong men in Henry's Court, and given over to summary search and arrest when need be. The fear of sedition never slumbered. Yet this combing process was occasional, the gallows did not deter everyone, and under dark the city was a lair of the untamed, an old warren covering many crimes and many miseries.

Badly lighted, foul, tortuous, congested, the city had drawn to itself Germans, French, and many thousands of Flemish, layers of craftsmen under whom the native apprentices writhed and revolted. Power was shifting, without method or goodwill, violence was frequent, neither Church nor State had full or welcome authority. This swarm of city life, so crowded with riches, so plunged in mud, could descend at times into the horrors and hysteria of the plague, trapped in its filth by inexorable laws, yet out of these defeats and its brutishness it thrust upward with unconquerable vigour and humour, its courage no less marvellous than its festering shame, its love of life refreshed like the silver Thames itself, its faith renewed, its heart replenished, an organism made by man's hideous and glorious impulse, London undying.

Loyal to Henry and the Crown, it still took this change with a stir of instinctive resistance. The rain drove many to their houses, in the wet first week of October when the Legate was expected, but bad weather and long delay could not baulk the people altogether.

Against the monastery wall that faced Anne's house, under branches reddish in a vaporous haze, a small crowd turned its gaze on a mansion whose chandeliers of thick wax candles blazed through tall windows. Across puddles and potholes its shameless brilliance slapped into their faces. They peered unsmiling as halberdiers stood black against it, and horsemen came or went, with pages darting to help. Those London faces had another light in them—staring eyes, spellbound, with shadows graved in their flesh, strong lines to give them striking contours. Pale they seemed, and haggard, in the swamping brilliance, but all of them with experience kneaded into them.

"A goodly lodging, this," said a newcomer. "Who dwells here?"

"Ha ha!" a prig laughed. "You be from the moon, I wot."

"Yea and nay." The man plucked his cloak tight. "Whose be it, good wife?"

"Be this a jape?" The fat fishwife screwed her little eyes at him.

"Nay, 'tis well-intended. Who lives yonder?"

"Who but Nan Bullen!"

"And who's she?"

The youth guffawed again. This ignorance he found monstrous. But a deep voice growled, "The King'll have another wife, friend, and yon's the wench."

"And had a wife this twenty year, God save her."

"Aye, aye!" said several. "Not like her here."

"She is lodged to a King's taste," the stranger said.

"Here he lodges her," a dry old voice crackled, "and lodges in her."

"Stop your prate," the fishwife cried. "You wag your tongue too freely."

"What can a gaffer wag but that?" came shrewdly from behind.

"Hold, hold." The big-voiced man swung about, his leather cap glistening with wet, his long hammer under his palm. "Keep civil tongue."

"What's that to preach?" a fierce voice demanded. "Is there a bill or cross-bow left to use? We have but our tongues."

"Friend, these be evil days. Guard your words."

"Have we uproar here?" asked the stranger quietly.

"Not so, good sir," the blacksmith rumbled. "Here be disbanded monks, men out of patience. Here be poor men whose cattle die of murrain, and soldiers loose-foot from the wars. Yet 'tis spark without tinder, no fire in us."

"By God's bones, that's well put," a craggy, hollow man spoke up. "We had the sweat, and now's the chill. Only misery is constant."

"Thanks to the French," said a sharp voice, "and yon harlot."

"Look nearer home, good folk," the fierce white-faced man turned round. "The poor innocents in their cradles should cry vengeance on the King himself, on my lord Cardinal, and on her uncle Duke of Norfolk, for the wretchedness and poverty we're in."

"You go too far," the blacksmith growled. "I'll fetch the Watch."

"Farther still I'll go. The King, the Cardinal and the Duke set yonder house to blaze. Hear farther, judge if I lie. They are the strongest thieves in England. By craft and subtlety they rob the poor commons of this realm. If a sheep would take it upon him——"

"Seize that villain!"

"Nay, nay. Lay off. He but spoke his troubled mind. Ah ha, see him run for it."

"Oh, laws!" cried a girlish voice. "There's a one-eyed gentle!"

"What? I know him well. That's Master Bryan, her very cousin."

"Well-mounted, be sure."

"And so's she," came from behind, "by day and by night."

"And needs no spur." The rain could not dampen the rough jokes that began about Anne Boleyn. They itched to dwell on it and degrade her.

"Let's leave this," said one. "I'm wet as a top. 'Tis bedtime for us all."

"Hark! Here's the King!"

"Bah, you daw, he never comes this way. He comes by water."

"So does he. Away."

As the crowd began to loosen, the blacksmith turned to the stranger, who stroked the rain from his beard.

"That wretch who harangued us," he mumbled. "He were chaplain to the Duke that was."

"A sharp eye you have," the gentleman said.

"And for others as well, sir," the blacksmith said. "I am a Kentish man. I'd know you in the dark, Master Wyatt."


## II

THOMAS WYATT broke away from the man who knew him, drawing his cloak to his eyes. He had no right to be in London. Just through meeting Francis Bryan in Calais, hearing a word of Anne, the magnet pulled him. By going on board with Campeggio and her cousin he took the excuse to have one glimpse of London. He was to sup with Francis Bryan before he hurried back to Calais.

But the escapade was proving a miserable one. With blinded steps Thomas made his way through gloomy streets. His wound had not healed, and this foolish visit had torn it open again. He had heard the crowd. It longed to spit on her, to lash her, crown her with thorns. Yet, when his love prompted him to turn on the beasts, she herself forbade it. The filth through which he stumbled almost consoled him. He knew the throng that had gone into her house. Henry, then, would crown her. But it was not Henry whom Thomas thought of. It was the divine perfidy that bestowed her secret self on someone else; and this secret self which was denied to him now resumed full power to torture him. An ideal music seemed to steal into him, and from this earth Anne glided from him to another element. She danced from him. He heard the music, yet it took her from him, light, dazzling, serene in triumph, and lost for ever. The ugly words died. He could not revile her, or join the enemy. At first he had had execrable joy in hearing her degraded, but he now felt his inescapable union with her. Those hooks tore through his living flesh. It was impossible to compensate himself by knowing her injured. Nothing could change it. She had entered into his fibre. This power was hers, to reject him yet to hold him.

Thomas found his way to the Three Cranes where Francis Bryan, fresh from Anne, would come to him. Bryan had promised not to say he was in London.

### III

INSIDE THE MANSION on which Thomas had fed his gaze, rude London was far away. Henry had lavished pains to make it a little palace, and there was a glide of gentle music through the hall when Anne and her ladies held court. Only when Francis Bryan entered, home from France, did Anne leave the center of the circle. She gave a cry of delight and led her cousin away with her. In her own room she greeted him again.

"Oh, cousin," she kissed him warmly, "for this I can never thank you enough. I could not bear another hour of it. My lord Campeggio has come?"

"Leg over leg," Bryan pressed his cousin's arm affectionately. "He's with my lord of Suffolk."

"But Suffolk's wife has refused to receive me," Anne clouded. "Could he not have come forward?"

"He's sore vexed with the gout." Bryan hesitated.

"Tell me, Francis. Fear not to tell me. All's not well?"

"Well, cousin Anne, I cannot whoop; Lo, the cuckoo's here, the summer's come, hie to the greenwood! In August I went to meet Campeggio, now's October and I'm no snail."

"Oh, don't play with me, Francis. This delay is torture. Have you learned nothing? Be douce with me."

"You are unstrung, dear Anne. You know I try my best, but this Italian!"

"How old?"

"Over three score and mauled in the Sack of Rome. A shrewd old priest."

"Then why was he chosen? What was Master Stephen thinking of?"

"Patience, Anne. We're in the labyrinth of the law, and he was born to it, the father of five before he took holy orders. But he's Bishop of Salisbury. He is well-inclined."

"I feared this." Anne struck her fists together. "He should have told you what he comes for. Now we are blindfold. I told his Grace we had better marry and defy them all. At least you paid his way?"

Francis Bryan looked at her with his one eye. "We offered him five hundred crowns," he said in a dry, cool voice.

"And then?" demanded Anne.

"Then, my dear, he shook his beard. Mules he accepted, and their meat. No more."

"You think me harsh." Anne's eyes filled with tears. "And you could not speed him?"

"Speed Campeggio! One foot in the grave! To walk forces him to ride, to ride drives him to his litter. If he lies he must sit up, and if he sits he must stand up. He lives in torment."

"So do I," flamed Anne through her tears. "How can I endure it? Quick, before the King come. Have the French a chance? Do they despair of Italy? Must they make peace?"

" 'Twill narrow down to peace if they can scrape up two million for a ransom."

"Yea, and for its quarter they could have won Italy," said Anne sharply. "What can the Pope, when the Emperor holds him by the throat? I saw this long ago. Had we a sword, we had twenty dispensations, but now this priest comes to bemuse us. Not an inch they'll yield. Why attend on him? Why undergo this torture? Why fling our days away?"

"We must outwit him."

"And trust our Cardinal?"

"Hear! The King arrives. Should I depart?"

"Oh, and I have been weeping. Francis, stay by me."

Henry towered over Bryan as he entered, beaming on him graciously. He was himself magnificent from his summer out of doors, over three months of it, and his big perfumed body, his quick sparkle and his abundant presence filled the room. He went straight to Anne. " 'Tis long since I've kissed you," he bent to her. With his arm about her waist, he turned radiantly. "You find her sad?" he touched her cheek. "Is she not comely, withal?"

"Passing fair, your Grace."

"And our cause, Bryan? This trash that the legate is imperial! You have talked to Mistress Anne?"

"A word or two."

"Now," Henry gave Anne a melting glance, "Magellan longed no more for port than I, and now we're here. Farewell, good Bryan."

Henry opened his arms wide. "Now, my sweet." He embraced Anne hugely.

"You'll not forsake me?" Her eyes swam. "I am oppressed with fears."

"I!" Henry shook with laughter. "No power on earth can keep us separate. Nor hold me from your side, or from your bed." He kissed her repeatedly. "To forsake Anne! Oh, you, to think so basely. To have you mine, to learn your flesh, to give you mine! That is what I long for. Soon we'll enjoy it, sweet, and with God's grace. No tears, I beg. Have faith! Dissuade yourself from care. Give me your arms about my neck, or, here, sit with me, and I'll teach you consolation."

The big man lifted her, and swung her to his knees. He took her breast, and fondly kissed it. "Now, you believe?"

Anne looked at her breast, and then at Henry. She swooped down and kissed him, her eyes half-closed. "Yea, I believe."

"Now, God be thanked, our day is nigh. What says our cousin?"

"Let me sit up," Anne pleaded softly. "Our cousin? Where's my head? I'm dizzy with your kisses. What were we saying?"

"Our cousin, Bryan."

"A drink!" said Anne. "My servant must oblige me with a drink. Love gives me thirst."

Henry smiled and fetched her a drink.

"Now," she clapped her hand to her forehead. "What did he say?" Slowly she remembered and repeated everything. They talked in those quiet, melted voices that flow from love.

"He is not imperial," confided Henry. "Of that I'm sure. Whether his commission is in order we can't say. Wolsey must see it." He sat by Anne's side, toying with her girdle. "Now, farewell." He bounced to his feet. "You like your lodging?"

Anne flung her arms about his neck, kissed him, and pushed him out. He stopped to wave to her.

## IV

"Now pray our Heavenly Father," said Francis Bryan ardently, "that we find a grilled lobster and good Rhenish at the Three Cranes. And that saucy wench What's Her Name."

He was cheered that Thomas was on hand. They went in together. The inn was full. Its tap-room, braced by dark beams, had an inglenook ablaze, and a bar to one side. To Thomas, assailed by its fume and warmth after the cool drizzle, it reeked overwhelmingly, and he was dazed by its din, but Francis Bryan scythed a passage through the mob with his single eye. Seafaring men with gold rings in their ears, flouncing damsels to cajole them, hulking watermen who plied the oar, water-rats who gleaned from chance and mischance—they gave way to the two courtiers. Thomas did not swagger like Anne's cousin. He could tell at a glance the green youths from the country, and the old soaks who sponged up beer and London.

An immense fellow met them at the foot of the gallery stairs, Ned Shore the tavern-keeper. "Here, Margery! Cicely!" He took their damp cloaks. "To the kitchen!" Margery, buxom and bright, nodded to the one-eyed guest.

"This will empty like a sluice," said Francis, gazing down from the gallery. "Now, my pretty," he and Margery devised the supper.

"Has Margery unbent to you?" Bryan leaned over.

"She has not honoured me," said Thomas.

"How melancholy! She deigned to pinch me."

As Francis Bryan cast his insolent look on the scene, his mind was really on Thomas. He rather pitied him. A young man with a career, Thomas had given his heart to Anne and Bryan was fresh from Anne, he believed he understood Anne perfectly: she was a woman, another being like himself or inferior to himself; and she was his cousin. Whether the King would marry her in the end Bryan was by no means sure. As her cousin he hoped so. But he was sorry to see a good man caught in the toils. Anne, in his view, was a female who, to gain her ends, would hold out promises she could never fulfil. This was dangerous to any man from the King down, any man susceptible to women and the victim of his imagination. With his own view of life, as a soldier and courtier, he detested woman who played on the imagination for gain as much as he detested priests, and priests he hated like poison. He wished his King would steer clear of them all, all creatures in skirts except war-horses.

"You mitched from Calais for a day! I blame you not, my good Thomas. Drink, my lad." Bryan drank a good half pint. "Rhenish, cool Rhenish, a gallon of it."

"Here's to Luther!" proposed Thomas.

"And his wife!" said Bryan. He finished his pint. "Where's that nipper, where's Margery?" His eye glared up and down.

"Come you my way again?" asked Thomas.

"If this cursed divorce drag on," said Bryan. "They'll send me to that damnable Rome, where all our troubles come from. Why the devil the King of England has to be judged by a Pope of Rome is beyond my poor understanding. What is our Legate for, if he cannot give his Grace a licence. No more Popes for me, Thomas. Let's end this comedy."

"But Campeggio?"

"Campeggio? He's as stealthy as a crab. You know these men of law, who sidle when you look at them, with eyes on stalks, all shell and belly, jaws and tentacles. That's Campeggio. Once he was young, but that's forgotten. Now he's a canonist."

"And Wolsey?"

"A polyp, one-eyed like myself, a polyp with a hundred arms who'll seek to hug Campeggio blind. Those are our Legates."

"And," Thomas's voice quivered slightly, "how doth Anne see it?"

"Anne?" Francis drank again. "She cries loudly for the throne, and apes before a looking-glass."

"Where did she find one tall enough?"

"At Greenwich. And its name is Henry."

This talk, which became more drunken, was Thomas's farewell to England.

## V

IN HIS APPROACH to London, certainly, Campeggio moved stealthily. Not till a lull after his arrival did he leave the Suffolks. Then he was taken by a barge to Bath House, and went to his bed.

It was no wonder he was exhausted, even to begin with. His was a crushing mission. He was the faithful servant of a great Church aspiring to give spiritual order to man's feverish imagination, and this he took seriously. But he was also servant of a papacy whose imagination had been poisoned by power, a papacy lewd in its recent history, unruly and undisciplined. He had never worked for Pope Alexander VI, who had subordinated his office to a murderer who was his son. But he began in the Rota with Pope Julius II, who subordinated his office to a murderer who was his nephew. With Pope Leo X, murder blossomed in the Cardinals' college, a black flower in this renaissance garden. Between that Medici and the bastard Medici who was Campeggio's present master there had been a lucid interval, a northern priest as Pope; but the Roman Cardinals locked him up in disapproval quite as grimly as the Emperor was to lock up Clement VII.

The Legate Campeggio was alive to his priestly office. Under the spur of Luther the Pope was striving to blend his traditions as a Cæsar with the tradition of a Holy Father, and Campeggio was a servant of the Holy Father before all. But sexual laxity was a commonplace in the Church itself. To rule by the sex instinct had not been possible when Popes themselves did not rule the sex instinct, and Campeggio could not parade his principles with any of that overwhelming majesty which comes from an irreproachable history at least within the range of the people's recollection. He had, in a word, no chance to pontificate. He had to negotiate. And his own experiences in Luther's Germany made him tremble before his difficulties.

Behind the curtains of his bed, a mournful old man, he thought of his three principals, Wolsey, the King, the Queen. He had a decree up his sleeve, but this he hid. He counted on the legal art.

He had no policy for the most tenacious of his principals, Anne Boleyn.

## VI

CAREFULLY as Campeggio ignored her existence, Anne rose in front of him to blazon it and to mock his legal method. Handsomely housed at Greenwich as in London, she permitted Henry to caress her openly, and made no secret of his love for her. Her defiance was based on

Henry's loyalty. She was not afraid of the Church, or of the Emperor, or of the public. She urged Henry to build up his case among learned men, jurists and canonists and publicists everywhere. And she drew around her all the Boleyn connection at Court, her father, her uncle, and all of them.

Suffolk was averse, and his wife was hostile. But gradually Norfolk and Suffolk came to see that with peace in prospect between France and the Emperor, an even better chance presented itself for wrecking the Cardinal, whose wealth and whose offices would then be loot. Anne found herself more sought after. She was treated as the future Queen with constant flattery, and at the same time urged to suspect the Cardinal. His failure with Rome, his conspiracies with the Legate, were the lively topics in her company. This was not entirely safe when Henry was present, yet Anne distilled for him the suspicion that her faction secreted.

Wolsey was fully alive to it. Busy as was Cromwell with the suppressed monasteries and the Cardinals' College, his ramifications were already amazing. He had suppliants and confidants everywhere. He was able to let Wolsey hear how the temper of the Steelyard was, the temper of the Flemings now to be deported, the tone in the City and among the nobility. To Wolsey, Anne Boleyn was "the night crow." He had no illusions about her faith in him. Yet contrary to the talk against him, he still kept faith with Henry and herself. He had one single purpose, to bend the Italian Legate to their will. He intended to survive, and the divorce was his sole object.

Lautrec's death and the French collapse whipped Wolsey to an eagerness that Henry, for one, did not for a moment mistake. He knew that Wolsey's eagerness whipped him to Campeggio's bedside, in the dark mansion of Bath Place.

Campeggio moaned to him, but talk of gout, and English damp, and the exhausting journey, left Wolsey entirely cold. With a vehemence that respected neither his own fatigue nor the Italian's, he swept ceremony aside, trampled on the usual polite circumlocutions, and broke open the whole question with a ruthless directness that left the old Italian aghast.

The King, Wolsey set forth, was absolutely resolute. He must have his marriage declared null. On this he had established a case that theological experts could and did support in an impressive array, but it was not to impart this case that Wolsey came so repeatedly, even at break of day, before Campeggio could rise. Wolsey spent three or four hours each time to bring home to the Italian that England was on the brink of following Germany. Should the divorce be granted, England would certainly remain Catholic. Should it be refused, the result must be, not only his own ruin, but the loss of England to the Church.

Wolsey's argument left Anne Boleyn entirely out of it. It was the argument of a priest who had worked to create a national state, and who now declared to Rome the terms on which Rome could survive in it.

"Most reverend lord," he said to the Italian, "Germany is lost to the Faith owing to the harshness and severity of a certain Cardinal. Beware! Beware lest it should be said that another Cardinal did the like to England. Mark my words. If the divorce be not granted, the authority of Rome in this kingdom will be at an end."

With his accustomed energy, with tears, but with unmistakable power and sincerity, Wolsey hammered it home that this was a turning point in English history. It must be the divorce or a schism.

When he had spent all his force on this lesson, the day came when he permitted Henry to be seen.

In pouring rain the two Legates started down the Strand to the Black Friars, Wolsey on his mule, Campeggio in his litter, and everyone drenched to the skin. Into the Black Friars hall they were followed by such a throng that many lost their shoes and had to walk home in their hose. Campeggio's secretary described the Sack of Rome so vividly that all were moved to tears except hardened Imperialists, and Edward Foxe, Gardiner's fellow, was put up to make his eloquent response. But this was formality. Henry's true sense of the Pope's calamities remained to be disclosed when Campeggio would have his first private interview with him.

After dinner the next day they were closeted together for four hours—the Holy Father's Legate and this troubled child of the Church. It was not long before the child was lecturing the father. Henry had not forgotten the book he had been preparing earlier in the year, at the cost of headache; it was fresh in his head, he overwhelmed Campeggio with it.

"I believe," the Italian said afterwards, "that if an angel descended from Heaven, he would not be able to persuade his Majesty."

His Majesty! So Campeggio called him, either that or his Highness. And soon Henry ceased to be his Grace. He became his Highness, and his Majesty. But Campeggio found himself on a narrow ledge, between his Grace and his Highness, the precipice and the rock. There was nothing left for him but to break through the Queen.

## VII

STRAIGHT from consulting Henry, the two Cardinals went to the Queen's chamber.

It was the moment Catherine had most longed for and most dreaded. Wolsey was an immoral man and a bad influence on her husband, but she turned to the papal Legate with the tremulousness of the faithful. Here was Rome itself to safeguard her, if her prayers had been heard.

In spite of Campeggio's effort to remain cool and tranquillizing, he himself was highly agitated.

"As your Highness knows," he apologized, "the Pope cannot refuse justice to anyone who demands it. So the Cardinal and myself are sent to examine this question between his Highness and yourself."

"I know the sincerity of my own conscience," Catherine replied, "and I wish to unburden it to the Pope himself."

"I have been sent by the Pope to hear everything you choose to explain to me, and faithfully to report to him, but in view of all the difficulties, his fatherly office, and out of the love he bears you—rather than pass it to trial, your Highness, he counsels you, of your own free will, to take another course."

These heartfelt words, from a Papal legate, moved Catherine deeply. She was, to the core, a child of the Church. Her plastic years had been spent in the Spain of a holy war; prayer and the sacraments were intense experiences renewed day by day. "I am resolved to die in the Faith," she responded passionately, "and in obedience to God and His

Holy Church. Until counsellors are appointed to me I should say no more, but I hear you wish me to enter a convent."

"That I cannot deny," Campeggio said fervently. "By doing so, of your own free will, you may satisfy God, your conscience, and the glory and honour of your name. Think, your Highness, of the hazard of a sentence. Should judgment go against you, it ruins your reputation, it means grief and trouble, the forfeit of your dowry, and scandal and enmity. But by entering lax religion, you preserve your fortune, you secure your daughter's succession to the throne, you avoid the King's displeasure, and you lose nothing of his person, since that is already lost and cannot be recovered."

These points Campeggio urged from every angle. So did Wolsey. And without mentioning Alexander VI or Cæsar Borgia, who had done the trick for the French King, Campeggio recalled that Jeanne de France had bowed to a similar demand and entered a convent.

"I am a lone woman and a stranger," said the troubled Queen, "without friend or adviser. I must ask his Grace my husband for counsellors, and then I'll give you further audience."

## VIII

SHE WAS ALLOWED to see John Fisher and to reflect. Campeggio believed that she might yield to him, enabling Henry to re-marry under dispensation, and he was happy to receive her early one morning, in order to hear her confession.

But this child of the Church looked to her Mother to safeguard her, not delude her. Henry still made a show of being her husband—ate with her, again shared her bed-chamber, even allowed her to be wifely enough to look after his laundry and mend his shirts. That he was legally her husband John Fisher clearly advised her. Henry, besides, had given Anne fine quarters in the Palace and in London. Catherine saw in her the Jezebel who was driving him to this divorce. To abnegate in Anne's favour, desert as a Spaniard, withdraw as a wife and resign as a Queen—this no longer seemed her duty as a Christian.

Her confession, in effect, was an assertion of her virtue. She had been in bed with Prince Arthur not seven times, she swore to God, and came from him intact as from her mother's womb.

That being her state, Catherine raised her white visage to the Legate and protested that, though torn limb from limb, she would never abandon her lawful marriage. And if, after death, she could return to life, again she would prefer to die for it, rather than change her mind.

"I have been married to him almost twenty years," she declared later to both Cardinals, "and in the mean season never was question made before. Now to say it is detestable and abominable—that is a great marvel! I think in myself that neither of our fathers was so uncircumspect, so unwise, and of so small imagination, but they foresaw what might follow of our marriage. And in especial the King my father sent to the court of Rome and purchased licence and dispensation. That makes me say, and surely believe, that our marriage was both lawful, good and Godly."

Before Wolsey could develop his attack on the dispensation, Catherine turned on him at white heat.

"You, my lord Cardinal," her voice quivered, "for this trouble I have only you to thank. Because I have wondered at your high pride and vain glory, and abhor your voluptuous life and abominable lechery, and little regard your presumptuous power and tyranny, therefore for malice you have kindled this fire, especially for the great malice you bear to my nephew the Emperor, whom I perfectly know you hate worse than a scorpion because he would not satisfy your ambition and make you Pope by force."

Here it was not the countrywoman of Pope Alexander VI who spoke. It was the countrywoman of Torquemada and Ximines.

At each word she uttered, the gouty Campeggio bent over. Oh God! Oh God! Her obstinacy was as incorrigible as Henry's. He saw that desolate, tragic woman, her jaw thrust forward, defying the whole world to take her husband from her. His heart bled. Blind human beings, blind and piteous.

## IX

ONCE QUEEN CATHERINE defied him Wolsey set out by every possible method to break her will.

To Rome he raised his voice with clamour. He proclaimed "ruin, infamy, and the subversion of the whole dignity and honour" of the

Papacy, if this course were persisted in. Prostrate at the feet of his Holiness, he begged him to set aside all delays.

At home, in conjunction with Henry, he began from every side a relentless attack on Queen Catherine, especially as a Spaniard.

Henry aided him. In November he called the Lord Mayor and Aldermen to his palace at the Bridewell, and made a passionate harangue.

"Although it hath pleased Almighty God," he said, "to send us a fair daughter of a noble woman, yet it hath been told us by divers great clerks that neither is she our lawful daughter nor her mother our lawful wife, but that we live together abominably and detestably in open adultery."

Henry's horror at the thought of adultery, when he had recently made his bastard a Duke, was a new thing for his genial self, but his face reddened with eagerness as he continued, "For this one cause, I protest before God, and in the word of a Prince, I have sent for this Legate.

"If it be adjudged by the law of God that she is my lawful wife there was never thing more pleasant nor more acceptable to me in my life, both for the discharge and clearing of my conscience and also for the good qualities and conditions the which I know to be in her. She is a woman of most gentleness, of most humility and buxomness, yea and of all good qualities pertaining to nobility. She is without comparison, as I this twenty year have had the true experiment. If I were to marry again, if the marriage might be good, I would surely choose her above all women."

Having thus perjured himself with manly vigour, Henry spoke of the steps he must take, to secure the succession, and warned his listeners that, were anyone to speak in other terms than he should of his Prince, he'd let him know who was master. "There is never a head so dignified," shouted Henry, "but I will make it fly!"

This melting tribute to Catherine, intended for the City, had not the faintest bearing on his attitude to her, as Anne Boleyn knew so well, and soon he and Wolsey began to beat her down. He would not allow her to have canonists from Spain and Flanders, and those counsellors he gave to her he kept under his thumb. He forced Luis Vives, eminent humanist as he was, to repeat the private talks that he and the Queen had together, until Vives escaped from England, and he forced Catherine to give him her oath that she would write nothing to Spain except as he commanded.

He wished, in short, to cripple her power of defending herself. But this was nothing. Soon he reproached Catherine for behaving too frivolously, for seeking popularity. She did not show such love to him, he said, "neither in nor yet out of bed," as a woman ought to show to her husband. This insult, communicated to her counsellors, came at the time when he was telling the Pope she was too diseased to be slept with. The truth was Anne wearied of his double behaviour, and in the end Henry wrote to Catherine that, as the Council feared it was unsafe for him to share bed and board with herself, he must formally leave her, and, "for like suspicion," the Princess must not come into her company.

Such goadings did not alter Catherine's demand for a public trial. She insisted on it, and a powerful new weapon had been discovered for her in Spain. This was a dispensation by which, whether she had lived with Prince Arthur or not, Pope Julius had licensed her to marry Henry.

To get hold of, to destroy, this fatal dispensation was imperative for Henry and Wolsey. They thereupon instructed Catherine's counsellors how to cajole her to procure it and surrender it. Catherine agreed; but by word of mouth she begged the Emperor to keep back the precious original.

No pressure so far moved Catherine. Wolsey and Henry then began to think of new combinations.

Could Henry go into a monastery, while Catherine went into a convent—and then break his vows with the Pope's consent? Or could Henry be licensed to commit bigamy? These frantic propositions were sent to Rome, while Anne restlessly advocated the search for new devices.

But neither Anne nor Henry could hide the fact that Catherine was unyielding. Six months passed in heartbreaking, futile negotiations.

Behind the scenes the two Cardinals talked it over with relative frankness.

"This concerns matrimony, after all," Campeggio confided to his colleague. "And you know very well the Church must take matrimony seriously. Nothing should be done against justice."

"True," agreed Wolsey; "but, to say the least, the case is doubtful. It would be no great matter to comply."

"But the Emperor, my lord. You forget the Emperor!" said Campeggio.

"Not at all. He has let two of his sisters be turned out of their kingdoms and never lifted a finger. He'll get over it. There are a thousand ways of getting on good terms with him."

"What? Do you really favour this new Queen, a lady the King caresses openly and in public already?"

"Favour!" Wolsey shrugged. "We must satisfy the King's wish one way or the other, and let it go at that. Time mends all things!"

# X

BUT, as Anne saw it, time withers all things. In this third year since Henry fell in love with her, the divorce still pended.

"Your cousin Bryan, sweet heart," Henry came to her. "He fears your anger, but he has failed at Rome. The Pope weeps and wrings his hands but he will not call the brief a forgery. He only wishes the Queen were in her grave."

"A pious wish! What next doth the Cardinal think of?"

"You blame him for this?"

"Well, sir, the King of France, his friend, says, Do not trust him."

"So Bryan told us."

"And my lord of Suffolk will come home with it. And when Master Stephen is home, he'll add his word."

"By Jesu," Henry exclaimed, "I know not what to think. But why so pensive?"

Anne only smiled. She drooped her head.

"Is your servant at fault?" Henry stood over her, his hand on her bare shoulder.

"God knows, not my Master. Sometimes I ask, am I the one—when, as the spaewife says, Fortune is my foe?"

"Forbid your fancy, Anne. Had I never heard of you, or seen you, still was this marriage no marriage, cursed by God, without a son that lived. Remember that."

"Yea." Anne rolled and unrolled a ribbon. "Yet this too doth cloud me. Were no son born of me in like wise, were I so ill-starred, what then of me?" And her black eyes dwelt on her lover.

"Sick fantasy!" He bounded from her. "I move this world to have you. No more I'll say." He stood aggrieved, his mouth drawn small.

Anne watched him closely. "Pray God we have a son," she murmured. "I am unworthy the honour, I only pray to give you this heir, or die."

Henry's ugly look melted. "Nay, Anne, not once, but six times God rebuked me. Six times she was brought to bed and lost a son—a sign from Heaven. Who can deny it? Not all the Popes of Rome can alter that, yet they dispute me and talk of dispensations. Who can dispense a divine law? These canonists! I have read every book——"

"In very truth," spoke Anne rapidly. "But now we must think of these Legates."

"We'll have these Legates meet," said Henry.

"At once?" Anne's face lightened, and she opened her arms with a wild delight. "At once? You'll give my lord the Cardinal the word?"

"So I said."

"Oh, now 'tis merry. Now we may draw a natural breath."

"They may still deceive us, Anne."

"No," Anne cried passionately. She dropped her arms and stood up rigid.

Henry wavered and was about to pacify her when, with a flash of ungoverned feeling Anne cried, "Now it must end. If we fail here, we cannot win at Rome." With a breaking sob she knelt and flung her arms about his knees. "I cannot go on. I cannot bear more."

Henry lifted her and sought to comfort her.


## XI

WHEN THE TRIAL was finally started at Blackfriars, in the first fresh days of June, Henry himself could not know how it would answer his desires. Since, by advice of his Council, he and the Queen had moved to the palace of the Bridewell nearby, he could not consort with Anne

Boleyn, but she was at Durham Place, housed with her father, where every move could be discussed with her.

In this whole affair, as Henry saw it, there was only one independent and uncertain element. That was represented by Campeggio, and Campeggio, so far, had revealed his full mind to no one. Under stress of their anxiety Henry and Wolsey had cornered his secretaries at Windsor Castle and bullied them to gain some inkling of the Legate's mind, but that had proved useless. He was coming to his judgment seat at Wolsey's side, as close and grey and sad as the day Francis Bryan met him. The Queen herself had vainly pleaded with him in recent days. Matrimony, inviolable matrimony, was the matter on which he had to pronounce. It was not a King and a Queen who were at the bar, but two children of the Church, a wife and a husband, and these he now called before him.

He and Wolsey sat on chairs draped with cloth of gold. The table before them was enclosed by rails on which hung carpets and tapestries, and below the railed platform were placed the officers of the court, while the row of bishops faced the Legates. The counsellors were on opposite sides, their benches lengthwise to the bench of bishops.

To Wolsey's right was a throne for the King, under a canopy, and on Campeggio's side was set a rich chair for the Queen.

Outside flowed the Thames, under a gentle sky, with London tense. A crowd of women had cried loudly, "God save you," "God bless you," to the Queen, who came with her usher Griffith. They were the voice of an expectant multitude. Blackfriars was more than a court-room now, it was the vital nerve of England. Here Rome had come, in the person of this sombre Legate, around whose bed fifteen anxious doctors had clustered a few days before. And opposite Rome, on another height, throned Henry. Between them, a mediator whose life was staked on it, Wolsey sat livid with fatigue. This was a duel. The bishops gazed on it in numb submission, old Warham of Canterbury lurched forward with heavy head, while Fisher sat stiff and separate. Henry's nobles, clad for the festival of life, filled the background. All of them, every soul in the hall, was still professedly a Catholic, but as this Roman lawyer judged the cause the Church would stand or fall. Few court-rooms ever waited so breathlessly for the Crier.

"King Henry of England, come into the Court."

"Here, my lords!" Henry's voice was clear.

"Catherine Queen of England, come into the Court."

Without a word, gathering her skirts, Catherine rose up and in a painful silence made her way to Henry's throne, where she knelt in sight of everyone.

Henry stood up and twice he tried in vain to take her hands. Then the kneeling woman lifted her eyes to him.

"Sir, for all the love that hath been between us, and for the love of God, let me have justice and right. Take some pity and compassion on me. I am a poor woman, a stranger born out of your dominion. I have here no assured friend, and even less an impartial counsel. I flee to you, as to the head of justice in this realm.

"Alas, Sir, wherein have I offended you? Have I designed against you? I take God to witness, I have ever been a true, humble and obedient wife, ever comfortable to your will and pleasure. I never said or did anything to the contrary. I was well pleased with all things in which you had any delight or dalliance, little or much. I never grudged in word or countenance, or showed a spark of discontent."

The whole court-room heard Catherine, and thought of Elizabeth Blount and Mary Boleyn.

"I loved all those whom you loved, only for your sake," she said, "whether I had cause or no, and whether they were my friends or my enemies. This twenty years I have been your true wife, and by me you have had divers children, though it pleased God to call them out of this world, which hath been no fault in me. And when you had me at the first, I was a true maid without touch of man, and whether it be true or no, I put it to your conscience."

This was the wife, speaking to the husband. Catherine's voice did not falter. "If there be any just cause," she said, "that you can allege against me, either of dishonesty or any other impediment to banish and put me from you, I am well content to depart to my great shame and dishonour. And if there be none, then here, I must lowly beseech you, let me remain in my former estate, and receive justice at your hands."

With a few words on the full knowledge in which they had married, and her powerlessness to act without trustworthy counsel, Catherine then pronounced her own verdict on the trial. "If you will not extend to me so much impartial favour, *your* pleasure then be fulfilled, and to God I commit my cause."

With that she rose up, making a low curtsey to the King, and so turned from him. But instead of returning to her chair she gave her arm to Master Griffith to lead her out.

"Madame, you be called again," he bent to her.

"On, on!" she said. "It makes no matter. This be no impartial court. I will not tarry. Go on your way."

The doors opened for her, and she was gone.

The feeling in Catherine's favour surged palpably through the court, and Henry was far from combatting it. "As the Queen is gone," he rose, "I will, in her absence, declare unto you all, my lords, she hath been to me as true, as obedient, and as conformable a wife as I could in my fantasy wish or desire." On this he dilated, and then he worked round to his conscience.

"Every good Christian man," he said solemnly, "knows what pain and what unquietness he suffers whatever has grieved his conscience. I assure you, on my honour, this matter has so vexed my mind and troubled my spirits, that I can scantly study anything which should be profitable for my realm and people."

When he began his plea for "the quietness of my mind and conscience only—and for no other cause, as God knoweth," Wolsey put a humble request to him.

"Have I been the chief inventor or first mover of this matter unto your Majesty, for I am greatly suspected of all men herein?"

"My lord Cardinal," Henry answered his judge, "I can well excuse you herein. Marry, ye have been rather against me!"

Henry, troubled in waves of a scrupulous conscience, bowed under the weighty burden of a scrupulous conscience, wounded in his conscience, pricked, vexed and disquieted in his conscience, reviewed the whole cause down to the appeal to his bishops.

"My lord of Canterbury," he said, "I moved you, and so I did all of you, my lord bishops. To which you have all granted me licence under your seals to put this matter in question."

"That is truth, so please your Highness," said Archbishop Warham. "I doubt not but all my brethren here will affirm it."

John Fisher stood up, high and spare. "No, Sir, not I. You have not my consent thereto."

The Archbishop passed the King a document with hanging seals.

"No! Haith! Look here on this," exclaimed Henry. "Is not this your hand and seal?"

"No, forsooth, Sire," answered Fisher. "It is not my hand or seal."

"How say *you?*" Henry demanded of the Archbishop.

"Yea, Sir."

"That is not so," insisted Fisher. "You were in touch with me to have it, but I said to you, I would never consent to it."

"You say truth," replied Warham carefully. "Such words you said unto me. But at last you were fully persuaded, and you let me put on a seal for you myself."

"Under your correction, my lord," retorted Fisher, "there is no thing more untrue."

"Oh, well!" Henry broke in, "it makes no matter. We will not stand here arguing with you. You are but one man!"

With this eruption of another conscience, the court deemed it wiser to adjourn. But at the next session, and from then onward, Queen Catherine's cause was no longer undefended. At the fifth session John Fisher rose again. Were he to lay down his life for it, the old man said, to the amazement of every courtier present, he must assert that this marriage of the King and Queen could not be dissolved by any power, human or divine.

Until this moment, it was Rome against England, Rome against Henry. But here was an English bishop, narrow but pure, austere but disinterested, who staked his life on the issue, the cause of inviolable matrimony.

At this point, to Anne Boleyn's delight, a reinforcement arrived in the person of Master Stephen Gardiner, direct from Rome. To take him into the King's service, away from Wolsey, was quickly negotiated. Gardiner, hard-headed, thick-skinned and forceful, was as New a man as Cromwell himself. And at the next session of the trial he arose to demolish Bishop Fisher. His was a mind that slung not arrows but stones, a crashing instrument. Debate had ceased, and with it Wolsey's mission. The next move was to prove Queen Catherine a liar. The incidents from her bridal bedchamber were now to be recalled from the year she married Prince Arthur—1501. The older nobility, the Marquis of Dorset, the Earl of Shrewsbury, Lord Darcy, Lord Mountjoy, the dowager Duchess of Norfolk, with Sir Harry Guildford and Anne Boleyn's father, were all asked to recollect Prince Arthur's bridegroom words, as he called for a drink early in the morning. "Last night I was in Spain. It is a hot country." So Henry's conscience could be justified.

The trend of the trial was so obviously toward disruption that Henry, hating Lutheranism and radicalism, made a last attempt to save his bond with Rome. He sent for Wolsey.

As Wolsey left him, to take his barge at Blackfriars, the sweat poured from his face.

"Sir," said a bishop to him, "it is a very hot day."

"Yea," said the Cardinal, "if you had been as well chafed as I have been within this hour, you'd say it were hot."

Home at York Place, the Cardinal stripped and went to bed, though it was barely noon. Anne's father arrived in a couple of hours, and came to the Cardinal's bedside. He proposed they see the Queen again for one last effort.

"You and other my-lords of the Council are not a little to blame," groaned Wolsey, "to put any such fantasies into the King's head."

Lord Rochford, kneeling to the Cardinal, bowed under his attack, that finally brought him to tears. But in the end they went to the Queen. Campeggio was sent for.

She came to them out of her privy chamber, with a skein of white thread about her neck.

After a skilful parrying before her own household, in which she humiliated these intruders, she finally took Wolsey by the hand, and led him to an inner room. There she battled with all of them so powerfully, all alone, that she drove them defeated back to Henry.

He had no manœuvre left, except to call fast for a judgment. This he himself listened for, behind the door of a gallery, with Suffolk by his side.

At last Campeggio, silent or evasive for eight months, opened his mouth to declare himself.

"I will give no judgment herein," he said, "until I have made relation to the Pope. The case is too high and notable, known throughout the world. I come not so far to please any man, for fear, meed or favour, be he King or any other potentate. I have no such respect to the persons that I will offend my conscience. I will not for favour or displeasure of any high estate or mighty prince do that thing which should be against the law of God. I am an old man, both sick and failing, looking daily for death. What should it then avail me to put my soul in the danger of God's displeasure, to my utter damnation, for the favour of any prince? My coming, and being here, is only to see justice ministered according to my conscience, as I thought the matter either good or bad. That the truth in this case is very doubtful to be known, and also that the defendant will make no answer, therefore, until I have the opinion of the Pope, and such other of his counsel as hath more experience and learning than I have, I will adjourn this Court."

On these words the gallery door opened. Out stepped the Duke of Suffolk. "It was never merry in England," he called out in ringing tones, "whilst we had cardinals amongst us."

No man made answer.

"By the mass," Suffolk shouted, with a bang on the rails of the gallery, "the old saw is true: never Legate nor Cardinal did good in England."

Wolsey, knowing well for whom he spoke, raised his head to the gallery. "My lord," he said coolly, "of all men within this realm, you have least cause to be offended with cardinals. If I, simple cardinal, had not been, you should have had at this moment no head upon your shoulders."

The whole court-room fell deadly quiet. Wolsey, in even tone, looked over the set faces that gazed on him, the faces of his enemies.

"I and my brother here," he said firmly, "would as gladly accomplish the King's lawful desire as the poorest subject he hath. We be but commissioners for a time and can, nor may not, by virtue of our commission, proceed to judgment without having the consent of the Pope. If any man be offended with us, therefore, he is an unwise man. Wherefore, my lord, hold your peace, and pacify yourself, and frame your tongue like a man of honour and wisdom. Speak not so quickly or reproachfully by your friends, for you know best what friendship you received at my hands—which I never revealed before now, neither to my glory nor to your dishonour."

With these words Suffolk left the gallery to follow Henry, who had vanished, and all the nobles stamped angrily from the hall.

Still in their chairs, the Legates sat looking one on the other, struck dumb by this anger.

# Chapter 17

Wolsey had put it off as long as possible, but the trial was over and he had been driven to play his hand. He rose wearily, kicked the cloth of gold out of his way, and went to Westminster.

Without a parting word to him, Henry had hurried from Blackfriars and was already on his way to Greenwich. Queen Catherine returned in her own barge, and Anne Boleyn followed by herself, in a state of the highest excitement.

In the lucidity that such excitement gives when a terrible strain has snapped, Anne knew that this was the collapse of Papal law in England. Usually so pale, her cheeks were touched with two spots of ardent colour that gave her a dangerous beauty. She moved quickly, thought quickly, spoke quickly. Her mind, in one sense, was in chaos, with plans tumbling madly to reach forward, but one thing was clear: at long last, after years of falsity, by his miserable failure to redeem the Pope's secret pledge, the Cardinal had been delivered to her. Not a whisper or whimper of mercy could penetrate the brutal clamour of her exultation. During seven lean years she had ached for this. She hated Wolsey, and her whole nature cried, Now, now destroy him.

The July day was smouldering down into the river when Henry hurried to her in her gallery.

He embraced her so warmly that, without reflection, she flung her arms round him and said, "Marry me at once, sir. Let us wait no longer."

Involuntarily, he repulsed her.

"I know well," she murmured fiercely, "there is an old prophecy that in this time a queen of England is to be burned, yet I love you so much, I do not fear even death if I can marry you."

"Nay, nay," said Henry bluntly. "For your sake, darling, I make too many enemies as it is." And then, recovering patience and kindness, he explained his fear that if they married before a divorce were granted the Pope might move both the French and the Emperor to smite him.

"The poor people are still deluded," he added. "I was wroth with the Queen, her seeking to win them."

Anne turned her head, to look despairingly at the outflung banners in the sky. Her youth rebelled. Her blood rebelled. Very unexpectedly she slid from him. But she turned back, her face hardened.

"Master Stephen," she said, "could you not make him your secretary?"

Henry slapped his thigh. "By God! And at once."

"And hold him to your side."

"And you as well, my sweet heart. We'll go hunting. We'll have the long summer together."

## II

MASTER GARDINER, now chief secretary, and Master Fox, still chaplain, could not be lodged with the King at Waltham.

"The Sweat," smiled Gardiner. "The very name is too terrible and fearful to his Highness's ears that he dare in no wise approach unto the place where it is noised to have been."

They both chuckled, young, immune, confident.

"Yet," said Fox with a more frugal smile, "not a soul lives of the French embassy but du Bellay himself. All dead!"

"The French disease, man. Ha ha!" He had a brassy laugh, the brass-faced Gardiner.

They were assigned to sleep at a gentleman's house, and to sup with the tutor.

The tutor, ten years older than Gardiner, tucked down his chin as if glancing over spectacles, and then shook hands. He had a well-shaped, capacious head, a reflective face, and that slight air of guilt that afflicts some tutors.

"Why, Master Cranmer," exclaimed Gardiner genially. "Thomas Cranmer as I live."

The younger men, closely attached to the King, brought a breeze of the outer world into Cranmer's still existence. He remembered that these two had been sent to Rome about the divorce, and, as a fellow Cambridge man, he drew them out a little. He listened with that subdued, yet faintly detached, even faintly superior air, which a gentle man exudes when a grossly energetic man bruises against his nerves. Master Cranmer yielded like putty, but when he had heard of Gardiner's triumphs over the Pope and over John Fisher, he allowed himself to express an opinion out of the cool depths of his reserve. So massive was his judgment on the whole affair that both Gardiner and Fox deferred to him. He advocated systematic canvassing of learned opinion all over Europe, opinions of Jews as well as Gentiles, and then advocated Henry's seeking the nullity of his marriage in an ordinary ecclesiastical court in England. An English court, he held, had every right to pronounce on it.

It was the old story: the breezy man had stale ideas, while a quiescent man had fresh ideas. Fox and Gardiner went to their bed deeply impressed by Cranmer's placid approach, by his cogency and conviction. They were young, perhaps a little scared by their new eminence, hence delighted to run into theological reinforcement. From their wrangling at Rome they could tell how sagacious Cranmer was, a cardinal out of place, but Gardiner, nothing like so good a biblical exponent, had ten times the force. He went back to the King next morning with good news bright on his face.

Henry was alert, and so was Anne. Both of them were smarting from the humiliation of the Legates' Court, Henry's mind running on new expedients, Anne's running on Wolsey. And Henry could listen.

"I will speak to him," he rapped out. "This man, I trow, has got the right sow by the ear. Let him be sent for out of hand."

That sow, it was a national church. But Henry's intuition had only leaped to a new trial under his own control. His infidelity to Rome was quite tentative.

Cranmer came obediently. He was a good horseman, as Henry saw with approval when he arrived, a gentleman's son.

Soft and quiet, he was still superbly endowed to think and to express himself. They talked of the divorce. Henry's brisk theology permitted him to judge how broad Cranmer's learning was, how firmly based and finely articulated. All along he had been groping for a man like this, and Gardiner had stumbled on him—an Englishman with a clear head, timid on the earth, but winged in the regions of religious imagination, deprecatory in manner, suave as an Italian in his Cambridge way, a man of taste, of intellect and rhythm. And all he needed, to be connected with this conflict so big for Henry, was to be touched by a fuse! That took Henry two minutes to apply. He spoke to Anne, then he told this don to drop everything else (he was officially a lecturer and tutor), to go to Anne's father in London where he could have a room in Durham Place, and there to prepare a brief, which he must argue, not only before Oxford and Cambridge, but before the Pope at Rome. His income would be provided from benefices.

For a man of forty, whose powers had never been taxed, this was a bewildering transition, but Henry and Anne smiled reassurance to him.

Thus Cranmer entered on fame backwards, bowing low to his King.

Master Stephen could plume himself on this discovery, and now, as chief secretary, he was taught to feel at home with the King and Anne, hunting with them from morn to dark. On one of these expansive days the lovers learned from Gardiner that, in addition to the despatches he bore to Rome on his first visit, Wolsey had entrusted him with a letter to his own agent that proposed English alliance with the Duke of Ferrara. This unsanctioned letter Gardiner produced.

"But, Master Stephen!" Anne was aghast at such duplicity.

"There now," said Master Stephen.

## III

THE CARDINAL had a fine palace at the Moor in Hertfordshire, where he had lovely gardens and fish-ponds. Through his good friend Master

Stephen he had news of the King, and his post, after inspection, was forwarded to him. But calm as Gardiner's tone was, the calm was ominous. The air was heavy and the birds stopped singing.

The shrewder observers began to calculate when the lightning would wither the Cardinal. Master Cromwell picked up a rumour that his master was already out of favour and proceeded, like a shrewd agent, to pounce on his informant. Certain subtle merchants, like Gresham, thought it better to tot up their bills. But nervousness like this was of no account until Henry should give it sanction, and so far he had not done anything to prove that Wolsey had fallen.

"Good God," said Anne's father to his daughter. "If *you* don't know, who does? Why can't you ask him?"

Anne was so pestered by her own people—by the Duke of Norfolk, for one, by her mother, and by George and his wife—that at last, within hearing of her father, she plunged into it at dinner.

"Sir," she asked in her lower voice, that had its own strange throb in Henry's ears, "is it not a marvellous thing to consider what debt and danger the Cardinal hath brought you in with all your subjects?"

Her voice, said Henry, what is it like? Like brown honey? Like a bare arm rubbed against his beard? Her voice grated him agreeably.

"How so, sweetheart?" he answered her.

"Forsooth," she said, "there is not a man within all your realm worth five pounds but he hath indebted you unto him."

"Well, well," laughed Henry, "as for that, there is in him no blame. Methinks I know that matter better than you, or any other." He flicked his white eyelashes at Anne's father when he said this. That old devil was coaching Anne.

"Nay, sir," persisted Anne. "Besides all that, what things hath he wrought within this realm to your great slander and dishonour!"

Henry puffed out his cheeks, as if to say, "Pooh-pooh, darling," while his eyebrows ran up. This angered Anne.

"There's never a nobleman within this realm," she said hotly, "that if he'd done but half so much as he hath done, he were well worthy to lose his head."

Henry smiled.

"Yea," she shook her head vigorously, "if my lord of Norfolk, my lord of Suffolk, my lord my father, or any other noble person within your realm had done much less than he, they should have lost their heads ere this!"

"Why," said Henry quizzically, to tease Anne, "then I perceive ye are not the Cardinal's friend?"

Anne pouted. She knew he was laughing at her in public, but this was no laughing matter. "Forsooth, sir, I have no cause, nor any other that loveth your Grace. No more have your Grace, if you consider well his doings."

Henry took a swift look at Anne's father. There were not such famous pickings for him, or for any of the other attentive noblemen, in this little skirmish of wit.

After this probe one guess was as good as another, but wagers were laid that Henry, when the Cardinal should present himself, would entirely ignore him.

## IV

FOR WOLSEY, who understood his master well, this was no light business. He was gone from power. The parliament that Henry was calling for November was under Norfolk's thumb. It would be used against him. He knew he was beaten, and he trembled for his life.

But Campeggio's leavetaking required him to present himself, so the Legates rode to Grafton Regis two months after the trial at Blackfriars, once more to confront the nobles and their King.

No chamber had been made ready for the Cardinal: this was the first pinprick. But Harry Norris humbly offered him his own chamber, and Wolsey even held a little court there before the King sent for him. Into Henry's presence he passed along a row of the lords of the Council. For each of these he politely uncovered, they returning the gesture, and then entered the little throne room, where he knelt to Henry.

With both arms Henry lifted him (the wagers lost!) and with amiable cheer led him by the hand into a great window. There, however, spied on by everyone, he became serious. He lost no time in taxing Wolsey with his letter to Ferrara. Wolsey's evasiveness made Henry frown. He had not written it!

"How can that be?" Henry searched in his bosom and brought out a letter. "Is not this your own hand?"

The Cardinal hesitated, and then poured out so long an explanation that the King stopped him.

"My lord, go to your dinner, and all my lords here will keep you company. After dinner I'll resort to you again and we'll commune further in this matter."

Henry then joined Anne.

At dinner the Duke of Norfolk crossed swords with Wolsey, but the Cardinal took the greatest pains to be affable and conciliatory.

At dinner, as was his wont, the Cardinal talked freely. He caught a significant word about the negligence of the clergy and the parliament that was summoned. So that was to be the line of attack, before the great lords fell on the Church and plundered it!

"It were well done," he said in his smoothest tone, "if the King would send his chaplains and bishops to their cures and benefices."

"Yea, marry," clanged Norfolk, "and so it were for you too."

"I could be well contented," mollified Wolsey, "if the King favoured it, to go to my see of Winchester."

"Nay," snapped Norfolk, "to your see of York, your greatest charge." York was much farther away, and all the Council cocked their ears, but Wolsey still kept his temper.

"Even as it shall please the King," he blandly answered.

After dinner, when Henry entered the little chamber of presence, all his lords were there to wait on his pleasure. He called Wolsey into the window, began to talk hard, and then led him by hand into his private room. So ably did Wolsey defend himself, and so resourcefully sketch out the next attack on Rome, that once more Henry was persuaded he could use him.

As night came, with this secret conference persisting, Norfolk went to Anne.

"He must not sleep here," scowled the uncle. "And you must take the King off early in the morning. Take him to Hartwell Park. I'll arrange for dinner there. Keep him out all day."

"But this night?" asked Anne.

"The Cardinal does not sup here," Norfolk insisted. "This we have prevented."

When the King emerged he commanded Wolsey to return early in the morning. Meanwhile he was to sleep at a gentleman's nearby.

A great stir went through the courtiers. Many of them, after all, owed their place and preference to the Cardinal, and a quick reversal of mood was evident. They followed him to his departure, and asked for permission to join him. Full of hope himself, Wolsey invited a group of them to supper.

Anne found Master Stephen. "Follow him," she urged. "Find what he intends. This is of import."

At Euston, three miles away, the Cardinal was once more in the centre of a throng, when Gardiner appeared, to pay his respects with deepest deference.

"Master Secretary," beamed his old master. "You be welcome home out of Italy." He paused a moment. "This is the first I have seen of you for ages. Where have you been ever since?"

"Forsooth," said Gardiner, "following the Court's progress."

"Ah! Then you have hunted and had good game and pastime?"

"Forsooth, sir, and so I have, I thank the King's Highness."

"What good greyhounds have you?" Wolsey bent his brows on him.

"I have some, sir," and Gardiner found himself compelled to talk greyhounds.

When he reported this to Anne she gave him a sharp glance and a little laugh. "Never mind," she said, "we'll give him his congé on the doorstep in the morning. That's what he'll have for his pains."

And so, in sight of everyone, the King parted summarily from the Cardinal in the morning, jaunting away with Anne for his day's hunting.

There she set out to undo the effect of Wolsey's visit.

"Go slow, darling," said Henry. "Had my lord the secret decretal, he would yet pronounce for me."

"But Campeggio must have burned it long since."

"There is a chance," said Henry slyly, "that he has hidden it for the Pope's very eyes."

"No great chance, sir," Anne shook her head.

"So may it be. Yet it may be hidden in the Legate's gear."

"Then say he takes gold out of England," cried Anne. "Have him ransacked at Dover."

"Yea," said Henry, "and if 'tis found, we'll have our Legates' Court with our own Legate."

They then sent messengers to have Campeggio searched. Too late at Dover, they overtook him at Calais, where he was ordered to open his baggage.

Those were rude porters who set on the invalid Legate, tore out all his poor belongings, and searched him far in excess of their authority. Over-zealous minor officials, one of the curses of civilization. But when word came back to Windsor that no secret decretal was to be found, Henry's ruddy face turned greyish.

When it came to it, Henry had no real desire either to get rid of Wolsey or break with Rome. He wanted to change wives, but he wanted to do it under ecclesiastical cover, by a series of adroit moves that did not expose his naked desire. This decency was demanded of him not only by opinion in England and Europe, but by something in his nature. The Crown had come to him because his father had slain the rebel, and Henry had not a drop of rebel blood in his veins. To rise against the Pope along with the Lutherans, the Anabaptists and the Turks—that was not in his character. He was a man of equanimity, a man who detested unruly ways yet at the same time one who could use a daring man like Wolsey, and he revolted at the thought of breaking him. But Anne pressed him for it, with her uncle and her father behind her. Fetching a quick sigh, Henry sent for Norfolk and Suffolk.

"Go to my lord Cardinal at Westminster," he commanded them. "Tell him to surrender the Great Seal and deliver it up into your hands."

This was the axe, thrust into his enemies' hands. They itched to use it.

## V

WHEN NORFOLK ARRIVED, with lust of destruction in his yellow face, the Cardinal's first instinct was to fight.

"What commission have you?" he glared.

"Sufficient commission," said Norfolk sharply and haughtily. "The King's commandment, by his mouth."

"Yet not sufficient for me," Wolsey answered superbly, "without further commandment by the King's pleasure. The Great Seal of England was delivered me by the King's own person, to enjoy during my life. I have the King's letters patent to show for it."

The Duke of Norfolk, blackly angry, insisted on his will. Suffolk seconded him. But the Cardinal stood at bay, and they receded.

Next day they returned with a letter from the King. This the Cardinal received with reverence, and yielded up the Seal. He was no longer Chancellor.

Besides the Great Seal, Norfolk conveyed that he must yield up York Place, and everything in it, and retire to the Lodge at Esher, near Hampton Court.

For one who, through his agent Cromwell, had stripped so many abbots, this was a grim recoil of fortune, but Wolsey had not lost his ability to carry out a plan. He brought all his officers together, told them what tables to set out, what silks or plate to heap on them, what lists to compile and how to dispose of the old and shabby stuff. This done, he sent for his treasurer.

"Sir"—the treasurer pulled a long face—"I am sorry for your Grace, I understand you shall go straightway to the Tower."

It was the rumour all through London, but Wolsey was on his mettle to receive it.

"This," he sneered, "is the good comfort you give to your master in adversity! You were always very light of credit, and much lighter in reporting false news." He turned to his officers. "I would all the world knew, I have nothing, riches or honour or dignity, that hath not grown of the King, or by him. So it is my duty to surrender the same to him again as his very own, with all my heart." And once more, with stern gaze, he addressed the treasurer. "Go your ways. Give attention to your charge, that nothing be embezzled."

Down his private steps he took his barge, to go to Putney.

In the river, facing his steps, not less than a thousand boats full of men and women were waffeting up and down the Thames. London had been promised the downfall of its taskmaster, who had bullied them for nearly twenty years. They had come to see Wolsey taken to the Tower.

With irony on his lips, he saw them gaze in astonishment when his oarsmen took him up the river.

At Putney he was lifted to his mule, with his gentlemen and yeomen to accompany him, and as he mounted the hill a horseman came galloping toward him.

"Who should this be?" he asked. His sight was dim.

"Master Harry Norris, my lord, from the King."

Harry Norris stopped at his side and saluted him. "My lord," he said with his steady, honest look, "the King's majesty commends him to you. Be of good cheer, he says, for you are as much in his favour as ever you were, and so shall be." With this he gave a ring to Wolsey, a private token from the King. "He says you shall not lack, your Grace, and though unkindly dealt with, as you suppose, it is for no displeasure that he bear you, but only to satisfy the minds of some who be not your friends. All this he bade me that I show you. Therefore, my lord, take patience. And for my part, I trust to see you in better estate than ever you were."

Such a kind accent went with these warm words, and coming from the manly Norris, it touched Wolsey to the core. He was off his mule like a young man.

"Master Norris," he quivered, "no respect neither to the place or time can keep me from rendering thanks to God my maker, and to the King my sovereign lord, for sending me this comfort in this very place."

With that, he knelt in the mire, and so eager was he to pull off his velvet cap that he rent the knotted laces and knelt bareheaded. Norris himself knelt by him, embracing him in his arms, and spoke soothing words to him.

Then Wolsey staggered to his feet, an old man; he leaned against his mule, too feeble to mount again. With great difficulty they helped him into his saddle.

Soon he recovered his breath. "Gentle Norris," he said, "I have nothing left me but my clothes on my back. But I desire you to take this small reward of my hands." It was a treasured cross, with a piece of the True Cross inside it.

"Though it seem but small in value," the old priest said, "I beseech you to take it in gree, and wear it about your neck for my sake."

"Have me in remembrance to the King," he added, "as often as you shall happen to look on it. I am of no estimation nor of no substance, but only by him and of him, whom I love better than myself, and have justly and truly served, to the best of my gross wit."

They parted with tears, and the Cardinal continued to Esher.

## VI

ANOTHER MAN who wept was Thomas Cromwell. His fortunes were indissolubly linked with the Cardinal's. He had risen with him to Hampton Court. Now he came down with him to Esher, where there was not a cup or plate in the house, or even a bed or a sheet for it. It was cheerless on All Saints' Day, and as Cromwell looked out on the sodden earth, early in the morning, with a prayer-book in his hand, the tears distilled from his eyes and he prayed like a good one. In his bosom, at that very moment, he had an ominous letter from a Lutheran friend. "You are more hated for your master's sake than for anything which I think you have wrongfully done against any man." Yes, hated with his master, dragged under with him, indicted with him, beggared with him.

"Good morrow, Master Cromwell," said Cavendish, the gentle usher.

"Goo',goo' morrow."

"Why, Master Cromwell! What means all this sorrow? Is my lord in any danger, that you lament so? Have you sustained a misadventure?"

"Nay, nay," Cromwell wiped his eyes. " 'Tis my own misadventure."

"How now?" Cavendish was all solicitude.

"I am like to lose all that I have worked for all the days of my life, for doing my master true and diligent service."

"Why, sir," murmured Cavendish, "I trust ye be too wise to have done ought——"

"Well, well," said the round-headed secretary, "I cannot tell. All things I see before my eyes are as they are taken. But this I know right well, I am in disdain for my master's sake, and an ill-name once gotten will not lightly be put away."

"There you speak truth," nodded the modest Cavendish.

By this time Cromwell had closed his prayer-book and dried his tears. Once more he was the man who had kicked out the abbots, and there was a glint in his granite face. "This much I will say to you," he added. "I intend, God willing, this afternoon when my lord hath dined to ride to London and so to Court, where I will either make or mar ere I come again." He lowered his voice. "I'll put myself in their power, to see what any man is able to lay to my charge."

"Well done," said Cavendish. "God be your guide, and good luck to you."

So Cromwell sallied from Esher. He was in real danger, and he knew it. His work in suppressing the monasteries had been done under a papal bull, so that he had a direct share in Wolsey's guilt. This was notorious. He had every reason to be nervous about the little fortune for which he had sweated.

The Court to which he rode on this fateful day was now braced for the opening of parliament. In this parliament the Cardinal was to be heaped with obloquy and indicted under every possible count, and Cromwell was not even a member of it. No one appreciated better than himself the ravenous nobles who bayed after the Cardinal. All of them needing money, and the smell of Wolsey's wealth maddening to them.

Cromwell rattled his brain to discover how he could turn this dissolution of the Cardinal to his advantage.

The see of Winchester was bound to pass from his master's hands, and Stephen Gardiner might be named Bishop of Winchester. To use its revenues for bribes, on the eve of parliament, flashed into Cromwell's mind as a happy thought. He had a money-lender's grim knowledge of the Court, and wheels do not go round without car-grease. He had drily consulted his master. George Boleyn was needy. He was to be given a big annuity, both from Winchester and St. Alban's. Harry Norris was to have a fee. Lord Sandes, the chamberlain, Sir John Russell, and Fitzwilliam as well, were strong enough to be worth placating. Cromwell went fortified, to save his own and his master's skin.

He had to think and act at once. What had moved the King to send Wolsey his ring was not, as Cromwell judged, so much his pity as a fear that if Wolsey should die the whole extent of his effects could not be found. That, too, gave Cromwell something to think about. He knew the Cardinal's effects, none better. There he could be useful.

And what those effects were, as the cupidity of the eye revealed them, Henry had just gone with Anne and her mother to investigate. They did not dare exhibit themselves to London, but they took a barge to York Place.

This, for the prospective bride, was the greatest of wedding presents. The palace itself could become Whitehall—one palace, at any rate, where there could be no room for Catherine. But what caught her eye, what her hands yearned to touch, were the stuffs laid out on long tables in the very gallery where her first love had been disgraced because of a "foolish girl."

The tables sagged under velvet, satin, damask, caffa, taffeta, grosgrain, sarcenet, whole pieces and in every colour. A thousand rolls of fine holland cloth were stacked in order, fresh as the day they left the warehouse.

But what Henry saw was the gilt chamber, off the gallery, and the council chamber, where on trestle tables the plate was set out, incredible in quantity, some plate of pure gold, some set with pearls and precious stones, white plate, parcel gilt, and with it the richest suits of copes that had ever been seen, with cloth of silver, cloth of gold, rich cloth of baldequin.

Those small eyes glistened at the honeycombs stored by the busy Cardinal. Let Anne have silk and satin. Here was gold, clean and compact, the very stuff of power, the meat of it. Henry's little mouth contracted as he gleamed. "You will always find them hard in the matter of money," du Bellay had said not long before. But here, without a pang, was the hoard itself. Henry and Anne revelled in York Place.

"Much better, my darling, than I could have expected."

Into this delicious groove came Thomas Cromwell. He went straight to Norfolk. Norfolk decided that if the King were agreeable he would give Cromwell a seat in parliament—simply by telling the borough of Taunton to call back the man it had elected and take Cromwell instead. So he brought Cromwell to Henry, in great secrecy.

It was not a question of Cromwell changing masters. No one had been more chided for his roughness in milking the White Hind, and he had been in terror of his life as Wolsey's agent. He was still Wolsey's man, but brought to the King by Anne's uncle and Wolsey's enemy.

Henry liked to heft a good tool of this sort. Cromwell had something of Stephen Gardiner about him, a man of great drive, a man who went to the point, not afraid of work, or of dirty work either. It was a common clay that Henry could mould, and a great relief after so many divided men like old Archbishop Warham or Cuthbert Tunstal. But he could not be served by Cromwell in the open. Cromwell must be Wolsey's man. Let him take his place in parliament.

It was now three months since Wolsey had been chalked to be removed, and Henry had not done badly by way of substituting for him. He had Gardiner for the old theology, Cranmer for the new theology, one to balance the other. He had Norfolk and Suffolk for the Council, one to balance the other. And against his new Lord Chancellor he now saw possibilities in Thomas Cromwell.

That Chancellor Henry had chosen in spite of Anne, with an astuteness not unworthy of his father. Norfolk was too untrustworthy and Suffolk too unwelcome to Norfolk. Gardiner was a priest. Rochford was not good enough. He wanted someone who could guide parliament, deal with the Emperor, and save his face at Rome while Cranmer sapped and Cromwell mined. Who was this upright figure? Who but Sir Thomas More.

Earlier, at Hampton Court, Henry had sapped and mined himself. He had dug into More about the divorce, knowing his friendship with John Fisher.

Now, in place of Wolsey, Henry had More, Norfolk, Suffolk, Gardiner, Cranmer and Cromwell. Yet even with these six props he was slow to remove the pillar. The House of Lords was rolling up its accusations against the fallen minister, but Henry wanted no one to force his hand, and least of all the House of Lords.

## VII

ANNE, however, could force his hand. Like most lovers who are not married, their passion grew by what it did not feed on, and Henry, busy as he was, was continually hovering near Anne. Their plan for a theological bombardment of Rome, with all the heavy siege guns from all the universities, was designed to add to the unrest created by

Luther, and to this vast campaign Anne contributed her father and her brother. George was to go to Paris as ambassador, his first important mission. There the Sorbonne, theological Bastille though it was, could be reduced by pressure from Francis I. And Anne's father was to voyage to Bologna, where the Emperor was about to receive the iron crown of the Empire at the hands of the Pope. Anne's father was to urge the Emperor to bow to Henry's theology, and also Anne's father was to read Dr. Cranmer's admirable treatise to him, in spite of the fact that as a Latinist the Emperor was still in a crib.

These were the complications about which the lovers consulted, and in the midst of them Henry found time to create Anne's father the Earl of Ormonde and Wiltshire, and to give George the title of Viscount Rochford. Anne, to the fury of George's wife, wished to be known as Lady Anne Rochford. This was high-handed, but the prospects of the divorce rather intoxicated her, now that Wolsey was gone, or as good as gone, and when Henry gave a banquet for the new Earl and the new Viscount, Anne sat in the Queen's place, and was so tender with Henry, and so fondled by him, that one of her enemies said, "All it needs is a priest to make the lovers exchange rings."

She was, in fact, objectionable. She was taking Catherine's place before the divorce, and she was allowing Henry to pet her in public as he had never petted his légitime. In the realms of precedence, where Anne was suddenly installed at the top, those women who had won high rank by following the appointed course could scarcely forgive her. They found in her all those qualities that upset the nerves of the settled—she was too emphatic, too impulsive, too implacable. They had to defer to her, so long as Henry was her protector, but this was not certain to endure for ever.

Anne tossed her head. Her confidence in her own strength was based not only on Henry's tenderness but on Henry's dependence. He had never before found a woman who was so little frightened in the regions where before he had either been mothered or submitted to, and this gave Anne her arrogance. Whatever she did, she could not placate Catherine's partisans. They hated her with an undying hate. As to winning the others, she was callous. Had she been demure with Henry they would have considered her "sly." Instead of a demure Mary Boleyn, daughter of Sir Thomas, she was Lady Anne, daughter

of the Earl of Wiltshire. By her annoying qualities she had got rid of
the Cardinal, and by the same aggressive qualities she meant to procure a divorce without the help of the Pope. These same qualities
now set her at the head of the table, and in the end everything would
be forgiven if Henry stood by her and she gave him an heir.

This was her mood. She was sure of Henry, and she was defiant.

But those who have studied the henyard say that hens are demons
for precedence, and this was something that it was really dangerous
for Anne to forget.

The "French Queen," for example, was in great need of precedence.
Her whole career was based on the hundred days during which
Louis XII had been propped up to be her husband. That was a short
reign for her, but she was indelibly the "French Queen," and accustomed to rank after Catherine. As the wife of Suffolk she was of no
great importance, even though Henry's sister, and she went in for
gardening, especially knot gardens, as her main interest in life. But
when she came to Court she cherished her precedence. To be put
second to Anne Boleyn was not amusing.

The Duchess of Norfolk resented it even more. It was not so much
that she was married to Norfolk. Her life with him was a horror. She
never ceased to reproach him for his open infidelity with Bess Holland, one of her ladies, but when she became too irritating he contrived, small as he was, to drag her round the room by her hair, and
this lack of amenity at home, about which she poured out her heart,
made her look for amenity at Court. She was entitled to it as the
Duchess of Norfolk, and as the sister of the Duke of Buckingham
that was. To see herself in a lower place than another Bess Holland,
as she deemed Anne Boleyn, was almost unbearable.

As for Suffolk, whose whole life had been spent in advancing himself, he had his own grievance because Anne's uncle had kept him
from being president of the Council, and he knew Henry well enough
to attack Anne at the vulnerable point, which was Henry's confidence
in her.

He found Henry alone. "I owe my life to you, sir, and all I have and
am." He looked at Henry with faithful eyes.

"If 'tis those mules, my lord, I spoke long since to Cromwell
and——"

"Nay, sir, thanks for the gracious remembrance. Would it were
'hat."

"What then?"

"It touches young Wyatt, sir, who comes to Court again."

"Well, what of him?"

"Methinks, if you knew all, you'd prefer his room to his company."

"Why chafe me, my lord? I give you leave to speak."

"To be short, your Grace, as I know you'd wish it, a lady of the
Court came to us privily anon, but swore she would deny what I now
repeat. By the evidence of her own eyes, she says, he and the Lady
were carnally known one to the other."

"You had this your very self?"

"Not me, but the French Queen, your sister. She told me I must
break it to you. By all that's holy, sir, not for a million would I come
willingly, though your fair fame is all to me. Yet were it thus with
Wyatt, as I truly do believe, he should never be no nearer you again
than he finds himself this day at Calais."

"No, by God, enough!" Henry's face flushed angrily. "To protect my
fair fame, this lady goes to your lady and you come to me. You
know that already I have sifted this myself. You were on the green
when I took it up with Wyatt. Should I begin again, this lady hits
what she aims at. There's not a jot of truth in it. Go home, my lord.
Say to your wife, my sister, that she should sort out her friends. And
come when you are sent for."

Suffolk, throwing his whole soul into his eyes, went to his knee with
every submissiveness.

That evening the lovers talked it over.

"But Wyatt is still at Calais, sir?" asked Anne.

"Yea, I made him high marshal with the same number of soldiers
as John Wollop."

"And let him be there," exclaimed Anne. "Until we be married or I
be wholly yours. God knows I could not breathe, if he were here,
with all these eyes that pry and tongues that clack. But to invade you
with it! That is clean malice."

"Who was this, sweetheart?" asked Henry. "Have you a thought?"

"I know well," Anne gave a hard little laugh.

"Who, think you?"

"My brother George's wife. And even now, when you be so good as to send him on embassy."

"Do I know her, darling?"

"Lord Morley's daughter."

"One with a broken nose?"

"Nay. A little bitter wench, with eyes that slant inwards. She ever hated me."

"Now I see her. A face that hath semblance of a cat."

"That is she."

"Then we'll change your name. You cannot share it with this Lady Rochford."

## VIII

But if Anne was the target of petty malice, the Cardinal drew great enmities that had been gathering for twenty years, and not only did Anne share and countenance them but she ceaselessly urged them on Henry, lest this powerful priest climb back into her lover's confidence.

She found herself rich in allies on this one point. Her uncle Norfolk was president of the Council in Wolsey's place. He was no more against Wolsey, however, than Thomas More or John Fisher, than the old nobility, or Catherine's closest friends, or the monks, or the merchants of London. All knew that Wolsey had pleaded guilty to offences under the old Præmunire statute, so as to placate Henry by the surrender of York Place and his other property, but they worked their full fury into the indictment laid before parliament.

Thomas More forgot his lambent humanism when he led the chorus, speaking of "the great wether, which is of late fallen, as you all know," who "so craftily, so scabbedly, yea so untruly juggled with the King." His "scab," in the indictment, was syphilis, which he was accused of coming too near the King with, while other squalid and vindictive articles dragged in his mistress and his children.

Such accusations had no point unless Henry believed him treasonable, but they beat him down with the flat of the sword. He cowered under them. Du Bellay went to see him, and Wolsey could only sob and talk in broken sentences. The Frenchman was painfully moved, and observed that the Cardinal's face had shrunk to half its size. He wrote urgently on his behalf to King Francis, whom Wolsey had succoured after Pavia. But Francis hesitated to intervene. Why help a man who cost a huge pension, when Anne must perforce be anti-Imperial and pro-French? Anne cost him nothing.

Yet, in spite of himself, Francis helped Wolsey. The pension was in arrears, and, since Henry could now collect it for himself, nothing so argued for prolonging Wolsey's life.

But Wolsey's isolation from Henry was effected by Anne's hostility, and the Cardinal fell prostrate under it. Life began to ebb from him.

His Italian physician, Agostini, brought word to the King that the patient was at the point of death.

Henry sent Dr. Butts and three other physicians. Butts came back with word that unless the Cardinal's anxieties were relieved he would die.

This alarmed Henry. Not only did he send him his signet ring but he asked Anne to send a token. Hard as she was, Anne relented. And when the ring and the miniature reached Wolsey they were like an olive branch. He had been swept by the most powerful and wounding emotions. He had written abject letters to Henry. He was a mass of lacerated feelings, his seething imagination at last veering from politics to the values he held to be eternal. Actually penniless at Esher, with bills pouring in on him, and five hundred servitors thrown on the world through his grievous errors, he showed himself, not a dauntless adventurer, but a sufferer, a man who could accuse himself, a sinner who turned to Henry for forgiveness. This spectacle was saved from meanness not only by his lavish sensibility but by the nobility of his anxieties. He was afflicted because he could not help his dependants, because he was powerless to be a father to them; and nothing haunted him so much as his two colleges. For these he pleaded as for two souls.

But Norfolk was implacable. He kept up the pressure on Henry until Wolsey was driven to his archbishopric of York. "If he go not away but shall tarry," the Duke said to Cromwell, "I shall tear him with my teeth." Once driven North, the object was to keep him there, to narrow his resources, to watch every approach to Henry, every approach to the ambassadors, and every approach to Rome.

Henry, however, missed him. Wiltshire, Anne's father, had fumbled his negotiations with the Emperor. George Boleyn and Francis Bryan were not brilliant as ambassadors, and at any moment the Pope might order Henry to send Anne away from Court.

All this time, both at the point of death and after reprieve, Wolsey had only one agent to depend on. Where Gardiner looked stonily away, busy with the King's commissions and bound to Anne, Thomas Cromwell stuck to Wolsey. He was the first to plank down a gift out of his own pocket to save the needy servants, and as time drew on, it was he who incessantly disbursed to save the Cardinal's nerves.

Wolsey leaned on him with that remorseless exactingness of a great master absorbed in his own tragic turmoil, a nature convulsed and torn, labouring day and night in the storm from without and within, magnanimous yet self-deluding and self-glorifying in its exile, and capable of endless and unsparing spasms.

Thomas Cromwell served him, but while he was the only one to meet the indictments in parliament with persistent defence, and the first to lift the quavering master when he tottered, his own need was "to make or to mar." At the time he was responding to Wolsey's insatiable and unreasonable demands, he was measuring the shift in the Cardinal's circumstances, Norfolk's dominance and Anne's strength. He was using his connection with Wolsey to carry him over into the King's service, and, capable above everything, he supported himself on the near bank and on the far. But as the transition became possible he lost patience, and when Wolsey began sending Agostini, his Venetian physician, first to du Bellay and then to Chapuys, the new Imperial ambassador, the danger was too palpable. Cromwell knew Agostini, of course, during his employment with the Cardinal, knew he was needy, and in due time Norfolk was giving Agostini financial resistance.

What Agostini discussed with Chapuys, on Wolsey's behalf, was supposed to be this: that the Pope should drive Anne Boleyn from Henry's presence.

Such a report, on the eve of Wolsey's convocation of all the clergy in the North, was exactly what Norfolk and Anne had been looking for. It touched Anne's honour. "He was a better man than any of you for managing my matters," Henry told Norfolk and the Council.

"Yea, sir," said Anne with white face. "So you believe. Yet before he imperil you again, he should be arrested."

"What say you, imperil me?"

"Yea," flashed Anne's angry eyes. "To drive me from you at the Pope's command. So he hath planned, as my uncle Norfolk holds proof of. But still he deludes us."

"Is there clear proof?" asked Henry dubiously.

"Nay," cried Anne. " 'Twere better I leave you. Then recall him and forget me, and take back the Queen."

"Leave me?" burst out Henry. "You speak of leaving me?"

"As you cling to him, what else will satisfy him?"

"But, sweetheart, you speak of leaving me?"

"Oh," Anne flashed into a storm of tears. "He practises with Rome. He connives with the Queen's Spaniards. All was in vain!"

"If this were true," frowned Henry. He took Anne in his arms.

"My good name gone," moaned Anne, "my good years spent. And for a traitor who ever deceives you. Oh, sir, it is beyond endurance."

"I'll send for my lord of Norfolk. Unsay it, Anne. You cannot leave me. You are my life."

"Leave you I must." Anne broke into uncontrollable sobs. "Leave you I will. He is more to you than I am. You cannot resist him."

It was after this outbreak that Henry at last gave Norfolk a full hearing.

## IX

THE KING'S LIEUTENANT in Yorkshire was a man well known to Anne Boleyn. Six years before the Cardinal had broken him on her account. He was Henry Percy, now Earl of Northumberland.

When word was given to the Cardinal that the Earl was down below in the hall, as could be seen from a loophole in the gallery, the Cardinal went out to welcome this unexpected guest as a father to welcome the prodigal son. He shook hands with the Earl's servants, one by one, while ordering food to be prepared for them and fires to be lighted in their chambers. But as he escorted Northumberland to his bedchamber, he did not forget that his was one of the names signed to his indictment.

As Wolsey stepped inside the bedchamber and went to the window the Earl followed. Laying a trembling hand on the Cardinal's sleeve, "My lord," he said in a very faint voice, "I arrest you of high treason."

Those words, uttered so softly by the youth whom he had broken only six years before, stopped Wolsey's heart-beat. They both stood still, the youth and the old man, and for a long space there were no further words.

"What moveth you?" Wolsey at last recovered his power of speech. "By what authority do you this?"

"My lord," answered the Earl, "I have a commission to warrant me."

"Where is your commission?" demanded his old master, frantic for a legal escape. "Let me see it."

"Nay, sir, that you may not."

"Well, then," he defied, "I will not obey your arrest. Unless I see your authority and commission, I will not obey you."

As Wolsey uttered this, a voice cried, "Go in then, traitor, or I shall make you!" The door under the arch opened, and Agostini tumbled into the room, pursued by a man in a cotton hood. This was Walter Walsh, a squire of the body. He pulled off his hood, and excused himself to Wolsey on his knees. This arrest of Agostini was to hoodwink Wolsey.

Wolsey appealed to him, against the Earl, but when Walsh declared that the King had sent them both, the prisoner gave a sigh. "Well, there is no more to do. I am ready. In God's name, I will obey the King's will and pleasure."

He was then escorted to his own bedchamber, and his servants sworn into the King's service. His removal from Cawood followed in several days. A whole fortnight was spent at the Earl of Shrewsbury's, en route to London, while Agostini was being examined.

Then one day his usher Cavendish came to him, in the leaden light of a November day in midland England. Wolsey, who had been miserably unwell, was seated on a chest in the gallery, with his beads in his hand, leaning on a staff.

"Forsooth, sir," said his gentleman, "the best news that ever came to you, if your Grace can take it well."

Wolsey looked at the gentle Cavendish with one eyelid drooping, his open eye humid and melancholy as if apprehensive of another blow from fortune.

"I pray God it be good news," he said. "What is it?"

"Forsooth, sir, my lord of Shrewsbury, knowing you desire to come before the King's majesty, hath travailed so with his letters that the King hath sent for you by Master Kingston and twenty-four of the guard, to conduct you to his Highness."

Wolsey looked at Cavendish. These were yeomen from the Tower, sent all the way from London. It was to the Tower he himself had sent the Duke of Buckingham. His eyes searched the face of this good, kind and faithful Cavendish who had never deserted him. The Tower! The Tower!

"Master Kingston!" the Cardinal said, "Master Kingston!" With that, he clapped his hand on his thigh, and gave a great sigh. It was the end.

"Content yourself, for God's sake," urged Cavendish. "I assure you, your enemies be more in fear and doubt of you than you of them. That thing they wish—I trust they shall never be able to bring to pass with all their wits, the King being your singular good lord and friend. To prove that he is, see you not how he hath sent gentle Master Kingston for you, with such men as were your old true servants. I humbly beseech your Grace, be of good cheer."

"Master Kingston!" repeated Wolsey. "Well, well, then, I perceive more than you can imagine or do know. Experience of old hath taught me."

That night he was frightfully ill. The next day he took his journey with Master Kingston and the guard. He was then dying. He lodged at Hardwick Hall, in Nottinghamshire, that night. The next night he was very ill at Nottingham. He had to be held up on his mule until he reached Leicester Abbey. There, received by the Abbot, he was helped upstairs by Kingston himself. This was Saturday at night. He died on the Tuesday morning.

When Cavendish reached Hampton Court, to give the King his news, Henry was behind the garden, practising with the bow and arrow. Cavendish did not dare disturb him. He was leaning against a tree and musing so hard that Henry came up suddenly behind him and tapped him on the shoulder before Cavendish woke up and fell on his knee.

"Well, Cavendish," said the bowman, "I'll make an end of my game, and then will I talk with you."

When he gave up his bow to the yeoman of his bows, he went into the Palace with that splay walk of his, saying a word to John Gage but forgetting Cavendish. The garden postern gate closed on him.

But in a minute Harry Norris called Cavendish back, and inside he found Henry in a dressing-gown of russet velvet furred with sables.

"Liever than twenty thousand pounds," said Henry, after an hour's talk, "I wish he had lived. Have you the fifteen hundred pounds that was missing?"

"Sir," said Cavendish, "I think I can tell your Grace partly where it is."

"Yea, can you? Then I pray you tell me, and you'll do us much pleasure, nor it shall not be unrewarded."

When that was threshed out, Henry said, "Keep this gear secret between yourself and me. Three may keep counsel, if two be away, and if I thought my cap knew my counsel, I'd cast it into the fire and burn it."

As he left the King, Master Kingston said, "You are to go straight into the Council, and for God's sake, take good heed what you say. If you tell them the truth what he said, you'll undo yourself."

"Why, sir," said Cavendish, "how have you done yourself?"

"Marry," answered good Kingston, "I have utterly denied that I heard any such words as our yeomen reported."

So, when Norfolk questioned Cavendish as to Wolsey's dying words, Cavendish excused his stupidity. "I was so busy attending to him," he explained, "I could not note and mark every word he spake. And, sir, indeed he spake many idle words, as men in such extremities do. If it please your lordships to call Master Kingston."

"Marry, so we have done."

"Ah, then, my lords, if he heard them not, I could not hear them, for he heard as much as I and I as much as he."

"Lo," said Norfolk to the others, "I told you as much. You are dismissed," he said to Cavendish. And with that the usher left the Council. And next day he received the extra wages the King promised him, and his stuff, and six of the best horses he could choose among all Cardinal Wolsey's cart horses.

# Chapter 18

No BIG NEWS had reached Anne, and yet she had an intent, even a severe look. Her furred gowns had come from the skinner, and lavish as Henry had been for her, and beautiful as they were, she sent them away with scarcely a word. She sat down alone to do her nails. Her head piously bent over, she seemed utterly absorbed in achieving a minor perfection with her despised hand, but what was before her was not her hand. It was a cell in the Tower, the one that had been given to the Duke of Buckingham ten years before. To that cell, Henry had told her, the Cardinal was now to be taken.

Anne's reverie was violently harsh. Her uncle Norfolk had convinced her that the Cardinal was outwitting them. Cromwell had told him so, on the word of Agostini, the Cardinal's physician. This charged her with fury: she abominated Wolsey for this fresh, this final deception.

Ever since his exile, Anne reflected contemptuously, he had been loathsomely obsequious. Messages to her, pleas to her, prayers that she should relent and intervene, words poured out like a perfumed oil, the Cardinal wiping her feet or anyone's feet, Cromwell's or Gardiner's, in the last prone gesture of a broken politician.

Contrite as he pretended to be, Anne never forgot he was sinuous. His audacity was so imprinted on her after the long struggle that she feared him almost physically. By wile he could win the King from her, and then she would be destroyed. This had driven her to storm for his arrest, and she did not regret it.

Anne was fully alive to the dreadful nature of this arrest for treason. It was, in itself, a sentence of death. His execution was certain, and she thought grimly of the Tower—a Cardinal of Rome beheaded. Who was a foolish girl now? But it was not that, it was his work against the divorce that had made her resolute to have him brought down as a traitor.

"Come in."

Her mother came in alone. That ravaged face was peculiarly unsmiling.

"The Cardinal, Anne. He is dead. He fell ill at Leicester."

"Bless us!" exclaimed Anne, dropping her little scissors. "Then Master Kingston never reached him."

"Yea. He was under arrest."

Anne stood up, seizing both her mother's hands. "But, Mamma! No trial, no delay. This is unbelievable fortune!"

"It is not the end of all," Lady Wiltshire said flatly.

"Mamma! When we have such joyous tidings."

Lady Wiltshire looked at her daughter, whose parted black hair and deep black eyes made her so piquantly vivid. "Sometimes, methinks, the devil is in it. We now go to Greenwich for Christmas, and the Queen, my old mistress, is still there. It is displeasant, and it is the third or fourth year of it."

"Yea," flashed Anne, "you do not plumb this marvellous news. You do not see the end."

"You are proud of your work?" the mother said coldly.

"I am," retorted Anne vehemently. "He was a cur. He caused the divorce to revert to Rome, when the Pope was pledged to leave it here, and uncle Norfolk knows that he was selling himself to the Queen, to have me excommunicated and driven from Court. I should have waited to have him do this? I'd have killed him with my two hands. Or so would uncle likewise. Now thank God my way is clear."

"You frighten me, Anne. They whip you on."

"I am as I am."

"Well, you do not know your men. You are no match for them."

## II

ANNE WENT REJOICING to the Christmas at Greenwich, and when she met renewed animosity she was quick to combat it. Her enemies sneered that she was now as brave as a lion, and so she felt herself. She had no fear of the future.

She did not hope to win the faithful ones who clung to the Queen. She shrugged her shoulders when she met them. But hard light blazed in her eyes when those who stood by his Grace on the divorce still tried to treat her as the schemer who caused it all. To be regarded as a mean interloper, without loyalty of nature or nobility of purpose, drove Anne almost insanely angry. Was the King right to seek a divorce? She considered he was. Was she then in any measure to blame? Was she at fault to marry him? She did not forgive a single member of the Council or a single person at the Court who attempted to frown on her. She had not overlooked Sir John Russell when he sided with the Cardinal and she had forced the King to send him away. She would not be slighted or affronted at a Court where the King, who was their master and their patron, freely chose her to be Queen. To these Christmas festivities of 1530, following so closely on the Cardinal's death, she brought a clarity of spirit that made everyone apprehensive, including Henry.

Henry disliked the brightness that Anne shed on this entanglement. He twittered around, with herself in one apartment and the Queen in another, wishing he could soften both. He had promised Anne not to exchange New Year's gifts with Catherine, and he had given her a large sum for her own New Year's gifts. His bounteousness, in fact, was continuous. He gave her a handful of groats and a handful of silver for her gaming, and at the same time he was expending about 10,000 crowns on jewels exquisitely wrought. These things pleased and touched her and increased the amiability between them. That old jewel of hers that she had pledged to her sister Mary for £20, he redeemed it; and since they were beginning to talk of a quiet rendezvous with the French King, he had bought her cousin's great horse and sent it to Francis. Henry loved to please her. He was rebuilding York Place into Whitehall, and making St. James's Park for her. She exclaimed with delight over the eleven new clocks, but he promised her a clock that would be worthy of her. And yet, warm, even tender, as it often was, it always came back to the other woman. They were both under the same roof and each chafed against the other.

Henry thought it annoying. For besides Anne's sharpness he had to endure Catherine's steady recrimination. She took cruel advantage of this season to trap him alone, and knowing that it did not suit him to break with the Pope, in spite of threatened censure and rebuff, she felt encouraged to press on him his obedience as a true Catholic and to reproach him for the unhappiness he was causing her.

Catherine's tone was worse than wifely, it was maternal, and even now, though an avowedly incestuous man who was torn with scruples, Henry could not help wilting when she began to scold him.

"You give great scandal," Catherine soberly admonished him, "by having her with you the whole time, especially here. What can anyone conclude but that you are living in sin? It is scarcely a marvel that the Holy Father has publicly reproved you."

Henry flushed but controlled himself. "You have no right to say this," he retorted. "You are entirely mistaken."

"Then why is she never out of your sight?" asked the aggrieved Queen.

"Because I keep her with me to study her, to learn her character."

"What for?" demanded Catherine.

"Because I intend to marry her."

"But the Pope——"

"The Pope! You cannot talk to me of the Pope, who broke his word to me. He is the slave of your nephew."

"But he says——"

"Do I care?" Henry was purple. "Whatever he say, I intend to marry the Lady."

By this attack Catherine spoiled her Christmas, yet with her stiff simplicity she held to the belief that, since she was the voice of his better self, Henry must come to obey her.

The pressure she put on him, her good and loyal women put on Anne Boleyn as well. But Anne was openly defiant. As Lady Anne

Rochford she had had new liveries made for her servants, and these badges announced that no grumbling could stay the inevitable divorce. "Ainsi sera, groigne qui groigne."

"Lo!" said one of Catherine's matrons with that thin smile which is ice on the milk of kindness, "how unfortunate for the Lady. She has chosen the old Burgundy device, 'Groigne qui groigne, et vive Bourgogne.'"

When Anne learned this, all she could do was order the badge to be ripped off the new liveries.

"I wish the Spaniards were all at the bottom of the sea," she flared.

"You forget, Madame," said Lady Willoughby, "that our Queen was born in Spain."

"I do not forget," retorted Anne. "And she is not my Queen, since she be not married to the King."

"Yet my Lady of Norfolk has thought well to come with these tokens," and a maid glanced at a present of game and an early ripe orange.

"Yea," smiled Anne, "Mistress Holland hath stung her again. This is to make my uncle fume."

"But the Duke's good mother as well," murmured Lady Willoughby, "pays respects to a mistress of right royal descent."

"Not *my* mistress, and be hanged to her."

If these skirmishes upset Henry, Anne was unmoved. His were those lordly regions where he could choose when to subdue and when to show resentment. He had kingly power and the habit of it. Anne had no power. Seeing Thomas More as lord Chancellor, with Bishop Fisher circulating a book in the Empire in favour of Catherine, while placards defamed her in Flanders and her excommunication was urged on the Pope, her blood raged for action. She could have no rest or security until she was married.

So, with the Cardinal gone, she devised a Te Deum. It was the Christian custom to impale a traitor's head on London Bridge and to jab up the dissevered remnants here and there. As Wolsey's worn-out body had found hasty burial in the same graveyard as King Richard III, this could not be done. But Anne and her family had a play performed in which the great scene was Wolsey's arrival in Hell. It filled them with merriment, and Norfolk had it printed.

The French ambassador was asked to enjoy it with them. His master had said to Francis Bryan, "I knew that one sprung from so vile a stock would in the end show forth his base nature." But this was statesmanlike malevolence while Anne's was personal. and the ambassador was shocked. Anne was too human.

Henry also found her too human. She derided his asking the Pope to give Wolsey's Cardinalate to Ghinucci, an English agent.

"By God," Henry pouted to Norfolk, "she says things I never thought to hear. Not in her whole life has the Queen behaved like this, or spoken such ill words to me."

"That I can well believe, your Grace," said Anne's uncle, and he meant it.

## III

But for anne it was a deadly struggle, the one for which she had at first favoured Gardiner, then Cranmer, and now Cromwell. Nervous as Henry was about his coast defences and about Catherine's possible connivance with the Emperor, Anne thought nothing about the dangers of a war or the thunders of the Pope. She knew that her father and her uncle evaded and hesitated, she discovered reluctance in Henry, but she, and she alone, kept on her way relentlessly.

The public was hostile, but beneath her. The Pope was against her but contemptible. The Emperor was no less against her than Pope and people. Yet Anne was not deterred. Her mind revolved about her difficulties, with no one to lean on, and a certain stridency came into her thinking. Henry's equity and justice, they were now boasting in parliament, were mixed with mercy and pity. Anne's excluded mercy and pity. She had turned her back on those gentlenesses that are born of love. She had renounced Thomas for good reasons, but to be refused the crown that Henry's love had promised her was so unthinkable that she nerved herself as never before to speed the divorce and come to the end that would justify her.

Henry had been in love with her five years, and he was still in love with her. Anne knew this better than anyone. Her unbending pride and her quick temper often led her to fling herself on opponents that he would have spared, but though he gave tongue at times, and at times heaved a despairing sigh, his course was in no sense the variable one that the ambassadors and the courtiers daily whispered. They watched him through peepholes that narrow the view as well as sharpen it. And no peephole could tell enough to explain the balance that kept shifting between the erotic and the politic Henry.

Anne's life was tense, not in the coquetry that held him or the amorous moments that engaged them, but in shaping this balance so that her fate would not be sacrificed. Henry's objects were complicated. He refused to break with Rome until he had matured his own Church, just as he refused to part with Catherine until he had gained every advantage from huddling behind her. But this astuteness drove Anne to tip the balance by any means she could reach on. She had destroyed the Cardinal in spite of him, and she now meant to get rid of Catherine and Catherine's advisers.

Her uncle Norfolk was no great aid to Anne. Now nearing sixty, worn by years of ungrateful toil, he shouldered her campaign like any other, but it went against the grain. She was too Boleyn for him. In a world where his younger brother was rotting in poverty, where the King wanted to force an inferior marriage on his only son and then make him playmate to the bastard, where his Welsh brother-in-law was about to be beheaded, and Suffolk was Earl Marshal, and his wife rebellious and the King eternally wary, Norfolk was not exactly tractable. He watched Anne with a squint and a sneer, unable to imagine her. His emplacement as a duke was rigid, giving him power at the cost of mobility, few men so fixed in their ideas, or so devastating. By refusing to adapt himself, Norfolk browbeat many into submission, but Anne was rebel to his notions and she could hope for nothing more from him than his fears and interests exacted.

But there was Cromwell. He was just as mobile as Norfolk was rigid. Ever since the first day by the fountain Anne had made note of Cromwell. Now he was coming up in the world, and she studied him when she went to her uncle's and every time that Henry spoke of him. Thomas Wyatt, besides, had long ago convinced her that somewhere there was a good Lutheran concealed in Cromwell.

He had, of course, been the Cardinal's man, to begin with, but that did not trouble Anne. She saw him climb up out of the Cardinal's wreckage without a scratch, and she understood the adroitness of that. At the darkest hour, having purloined the royal licence on which

Wolsey had been emboldened to break the statute of Præmunire, Cromwell could bargain: by surrendering it he put the King in his debt at the same time that he put himself at the King's mercy. After that he could safely go on serving Wolsey. He had Wolsey's confidence, he never ceased to exchange letters with him, or to save him trouble. He never took his eyes off him. Long after he was hand in glove with the enemy, he kept enveloping his old master with that constant, that deeply serviceable and lulling attention for which he had such untold resources of craft and energy, the propulsion of poverty behind him. He watched and anticipated Wolsey, nursed him, only beginning to show his teeth when Wolsey wearied of being an outcast and resumed asserting himself.

That transfer of allegiance, so deft and so gradual, was rather drastic at the end. When Wolsey began to be haughty with the ambassadors, Cromwell naturally saw how dangerous and reprehensible it was. He had known Agostini, Ghinucci's nephew and the Cardinal's physician. He was aware how needy this Italian was. And, before long, the needy Italian came to be locked up and well-cared for under Norfolk's roof, where, as one of the ambassadors drily said, he sang the tune as they wished him.

Cromwell lost nothing in Anne's eyes because he had facilitated the Cardinal's downfall. But Cromwell would not have done this had he not previously made certain of his footing with the King.

At first Henry had fought shy of him. He was also of a vile stock and had a base nature. But soon, Anne discovered, the fellow glittered into Henry's consciousness as she wished. Though his brutality in breaking up the monasteries had made him notorious, and though Henry shrank from contaminating himself with a knave who had earned such unpopularity, Anne put in her word for him whenever possible. He was not a noble, or a clerk, or a courtier; but this was a new era and he was a New Man.

Had Cromwell been less well grounded in Church affairs or the parliament, he could not have won a place in the privy council within a few months. He was the last person to be brought close to a prince, with that strong bulldog jaw and that bulldog eye, a sturdy dog who smiled with grim teeth, and yet could wag and look fidelity. But this dog was powerful. For all his respectfulness, for all his utility (and

his breed was the most useful in her world), Anne saw the glint in
him that Henry did, the metal of intellect, a toughness in it that was
redoubtable. He might not be as meek as Cranmer. He could not
slide around with George Boleyn's refreshing flippancy. He was a
usurer by habit. He knew the Court from the reverse side and Henry's
instinct was to keep him out of view. But the great place that the
Cardinal had left required to be filled by a man with a policy. Henry
had marked Gardiner to be a bishop, while Cromwell, his keenest
rival, could emancipate Henry from all bishops, and had the courage
to say so in spite of his humble air.

"I know myself to be very ignorant," he confessed to Henry, "but
if your Highness will excuse me daring to offer an opinion——"

"Go on, Cromwell."

"It is only because my loyalty to your Highness does not permit me
to be silent when there is the least chance of my being able to serve
my sovereign lord."

"Yes, yes. Go on."

"Someone must do so," rejoined Cromwell firmly. "All these wise
and learned men favour the divorce. The only thing that lacks is the
Papal sanction. But should your Highness hesitate if it cannot be ob-
tained?"

"No, by God! But what course do you propose?"

"With the voice of your clergy and of your parliament, let your
Highness declare yourself Supreme Head of the Church in England."

"The clergy?"

"Your Highness, you have them. They were all as guilty as the
Cardinal. They have all obeyed papal jurisdiction. You can fine them a
million crowns, and then refuse pardon until they acknowledge you
Supreme Head. Who is to resist your Highness?"

"Bishop Fisher?" asked Henry drily.

"He'll either bend or break, if your Highness wish it. And, if your
Highness permit it, I can make you the richest King that ever was
in England."

After Wolsey's voluminous imaginings, so superb in colour but so
yielding in substance, this concise proposal cut into Henry's mind. He
felt one of those responses which a whole life prepares a man to give,
a response creative, in the real sense catastrophic. Out of this response

to Thomas Cromwell, who could work parliament from the inside and knew the Church in every diseased fibre, a whole ancient religious order was to be subverted, and a new order born.

But while Henry was prepared to spend endless time and mental effort on this policy, going forward with a steady protestation that he was a true son of the Church, Anne could not linger for him. Thomas More and Bishop Fisher were too formidable for her. Fisher had just cried in the House of Lords, "For God's sake, see what a realm the Kingdom of Bohemia was, and when the Church went down, then fell the glory of the Kingdom. Now with the Commons is nothing but, Down with the Church, and all this meseemeth is for lack of faith only."

"What, Master Cromwell!" exclaimed Anne. "Is this old man to practise thus?"

"He is not long for this life, my lady," shrugged Cromwell with a smirk. "May we not show patience?"

"Patience," she scoffed. "I am no more urgent than his Grace, I trow, but know this, good Master Cromwell, I am urgent, urgent."

He could understand it, though he climbed to the top of Norfolk's ducal house with that hard face of his impenetrably closed.

Cromwell stood for a second on the top landing, musing on the houses beneath him and inadvertently picking his nose. He was very different from the man who had wept at Esher. There was nothing anxious about him now, he was firm, brisk, dangerously alert and come into his own. Seldom at ease with a young lady, he commended Anne for that good, clear mind she had, and her grasp of her own plight. He sympathized with her. He thought she was right to speed the King. The parliament was a slow poke. Nominally, of course, it was free. Cromwell grinned to himself at Henry's letter to the Pope. "The discussions in the English parliament are free and unrestricted; the Crown has not power to limit their debates or to control the votes of the members. They determine everything for themselves, as the interests of the Commonwealth require." That was good stuff, concocted by Cromwell himself, and when he thought that the most part of the Commons were the King's servants, when he thought that every night he disclosed the secrets of the Commons to the King himself who often sat for hours to watch his servants in action, Cromwell chuckled so that his belly shook. Free! At times they did shy at something, just as a horse, no matter how well driven, will shy at a piece of paper. Only when it directly touched their pockets did they chaw on the bit. And free as they might feel, he could always play the sort of joke on them as he did on the good man who was free to decide about the King's fisheries. When that innocent gave it against the King, he woke up the next morning to find that his beautiful row of elms had been cut down. That was a rare joke! The man nearly had a stroke. Cromwell took off his cap and scratched his poll. At times, he thought, he could undo his doughtiest opponent. He could toss them around and crash them down with a dexterity that honestly amused him. But Thomas More and Bishop Fisher? His smile died then. More was at least his equal. To defeat him would take all his dexterity. And, with this grim knowledge descending on him, he turned abruptly around, produced an enormous key, opened a lock and shoved in a door.

## IV

"WELL, well, Agostini," he said as he locked the door. "The book is near the end?"

"Ah, my friend," the young physician danced to his feet. "Be seated."

"That cannot have been a very pleasant jaunt of yours from Leicester?"

"They played the whole comedy with me," said the Italian.

"But all's well now?"

"Yes," shrugged Agostini, pouting his red lips and making round black eyes.

"And when the book's finished, you can go home."

"Not back to Italy," he shook his head vigorously, his black hat rapidly rotating. "No, no."

"Why? You should be quite at home in Italy."

"No, no."

Cromwell gave the least snarl. "What prevents it?"

"The Church is doomed here. My uncle won't see me now. I can't go home."

"We'll make you an Englishman, then, give you papers as a denizen. Doesn't that help?"

"Naturally," Agostini nodded, "but——" he shrugged again.

"Come, what is your mind?"

"What have I, Master Cromwell?"

"How about a hundred pounds, to begin with, if my lord of Norfolk agree. Would that be of any use?"

"Naturally," he brightened. "That would much help. But I wish to—— Between ourselves, it can only help at first. Can you not send me to Germany to be with my old master Campeggio? I can be useful, you know."

"You are being useful. But, one thing, you gave proof of your skill as a physician so long that the poor Cardinal's end was very sudden. That white powder?"

"I was not there, Master Cromwell," Agostini shook his head.

"But you prescribed it. It can do you no harm, my friend. Tell me how it happened."

"I left one for the Earl of Shrewsbury's apothecary to give to him. The English understand nothing about medicines, everyone knows that. So I left it for him."

"After you were arrested at Cawood, Agostini?"

"Yes. Cavendish took it for me."

"And that did not save him?"

"He had time to confess and make his soul. He knew the exact hour he'd die."

"And these white powders of yours, are they tasteless?"

"Absolutely tasteless in a pottage. A little bitter licked off the palm."

"They dissolve?"

"Like salt."

"A marvel! Has your gear come to you?"

"Oh, that is another thing. It was carted to the Tower. How well you thought of it."

"You'll have it. I should like some of that white powder. Could you spare me some?"

"Enough for five or six," smiled Agostini. "Are you sure you can risk it?"

"I'll risk it," said Cromwell briefly. "I'm your friend, Agostini, and as I see you, they'll see you here in England."

"I know that," Agostini smiled sharply. "You are the only Englishman I know who might be an Italian. But when you talk to the Duke, could you not suggest two hundred? Is that too much? Well, a hundred to begin with."

He bowed Cromwell out, this black-robed Venetian, with quick, lizard-like movements, and his facile smile.

## V

IT WAS NOT A GREAT SUCCESS, Agostini's powder. Bishop Fisher failed to eat his pottage as expected. It did kill two people in his household, the gentleman Curwen and a poor widow—two unintended, unimportant people. But the cook was found guilty of high treason.

"Are you stout enough to come with me?" George said to his sister Anne. "To see London at the crack of dawn?"

Anne sighed. "I am stout enough for anything except delays. His Grace is wroth with me, George. Am I to blame because this delaying frets me?"

"No one I love is ever to blame."

"Your wife?"

"No one I love, I said. Come to the side door like a pale seamer or a poor flower girl. Nothing rich."

Anne nodded.

"And what a pity you cannot see the Standard at the Cheap. Two of your friends are there all day, John Tyndale and Thomas Patmore, faced to their horses' tails and their cloaks weighted down with heavy books."

"What books, brother?"

"The New Testament."

"No!" gasped Anne. "For that they shame them?"

"For that, my dear, they'll burn them."

Anne frowned. Then she pressed him away. "At five of the clock."

They crossed London on foot in the hush of the morning, from Whitehall to Smithfield. It was a strange feeling for Anne to walk at her brother's side, just as if she were one of the people, an inferior person. But soon she forgot herself. On that same morning at Smithfield cattle market an immense throng was gathering. They had been coming from before daybreak, in the damp and acid cold, with an occasional peevish child's voice or a berating woman's, while an odd shout or brutal laugh told that many had left their taverns to clamber to whatever ledge or vantage point that offered, inside or outside the walls. Some youths found places for themselves by clinging to chimneys. Others perched in trees, sat on walls, or one even on the ridge of a roof. They were humbly clad for the most part, black-capped and pinched as the morning painted them drab, but it was not a market crowd come to the market place. It was a motley of London, packed into this open theatre with a rude eagerness to mould themselves around a vacant space which was protected from them by stout men with pikes who wore breastplates and helmets. A wooden barrier alone enabled these guardians to hold back the mob.

In the centre of the vacant patch were a couple of workmen. One of them opened a sort of furnace that stood on the ground, its red eye glaring as he swung back the metal door to poke the fire, which thereupon shot up a flame. The flame fanned out and licked the bottom of a huge cauldron or kettle, from which there steamed up vapour that thinned and vanished in the air.

While one of these dingy figures rammed his fire into a blaze, the other stood and gave him fuel, or craned his neck to see did anyone approach. He and his comrade went over their simple operations repeatedly. One of them, the helper, mounted a platform almost on a level with the top of the cauldron, peered down into it, and nodded to his mate. Then he came down and stood from one foot to the other. Only once did he take a sheepish look at the innumerable crowd.

This spectacle, so far, had no variety in it, but soon there came a little group, at whose approach the whole mob quivered and bristled like a beast that beholds an enemy.

The group consisted of halberdiers with a single slight figure in grey. He was the quarry. "Rowse!" "Rowse!" "The cook!" "Ho, Richard!" These cries burst out, while, rolling his eyes, the tiny figure moved like a mannikin, barely able to stand on his feet. His limpness, the grey of his flesh, the black cavity of his eyes, conveyed little impression that he was sentient, but something in the figure was alive. His hands had moved. He had brought them into the gesture of prayer.

No priest was near him, only the sheriff and some burly men who now came to the steps of the platform.

As the sheriff said a word, the crowd broke into a dreadful roar, half yelp, half shout, wholly animal, deafening and continuous.

The insignificant being on whom all this attention was centred, a being without a friend or an attachment visible, a being so utterly cast out that the earth shook with these voices roaring against him—this rejected man was half-pushed, half-pulled, up the few wooden steps to the platform.

At the top of it he was pinioned, while the crowd roared. Anne found herself trembling as she watched him. Then he was blindfolded. His head moved back and forth, even after he was blindfolded, but suddenly a yelp rose to frenzy as a piece of sacking was pulled over the entire figure.

The bundle was then sewn by a man who had pack-thread and a big needle. When he had finished, three or four lifted the bundle and slowly and laboriously steered it into the cauldron of boiling water.

Anne then looked away, while wave on wave of dreadful sounds surged from the mob.

Rowse was now boiling alive, as by the 9th of the 22nd of Henry VIII, which called to his royal Majesty's blessed remembrance "the making of good and wholesome laws."

"But," said George as they hastened away, "poisoning is to be discouraged. No person can live in surety otherwise."

Anne moved her grey lips to answer, but no sound came. So she just smiled.

## VI

THE MEMORY of this execution would not leave her mind. She tried to drive it away, but it came back for weeks with the fidelity of a cur. The victim was so lonely that Anne could not cease thinking of him, and his end gripped and twisted her imagination. She was one of those unfortunate people who cannot help being more moved by a visual experience than by a spiritual one. Thomas Wyatt lonely in

Calais left her tranquil, though she herself had caused it, but the fate of this cook who had been induced to shake a powder into the pottage as a hocus-pocus was so infinitely more terrible that it inhabited her. And yet she wished John Fisher had been poisoned.

Agostini had gone out of England, leaving his bond behind him, and there could be no possible connection between Agostini and this cook, or between Cromwell and Agostini. Yet Anne thought of this cool ruffian so close to Henry, and instead of repulsion she had a queer fascinated horror. Her anxieties, disappointments, checks, the long journeys and false alarms and new tangles and dejections—oh, how they had been a hell for her, with Henry so loath to be hurried and so angry when she became impatient. What she longed for was to find someone a law unto himself. Cromwell could dare to act. Even though Bishop Fisher had escaped and Sir Thomas More had succeeded for the time being in upholding the clergy, Anne's courage was reinforced by the boldness that enabled Cromwell to shift the struggle from Rome to England. Where Henry remained aware of the Church as a European power, Cromwell was outside it. He had the terrifying immunity of the innovator, a conqueror with deadly weapons among hordes who wilfully and stubbornly limited themselves. Anne's defiance outstripped Henry's. She despised old Warham. She thought Fisher a miserable superstitious fanatic. Around Catherine she saw sallow monks and lugubrious friars who droned so unendingly to edify her, and throughout devotions Anne thought of the scandals, all the lasciviousness and greed of which Cromwell had crushing knowledge, this rottenness now protected by the mantle of loyalty that Thomas More flung over the Church. Instead of being impressed by More and Fisher, she took them to be enemies. When they burned the New Testament that Tyndale translated, she believed they were afraid of the Word. Anne's opposition to them increased as she saw their long faces and prudish glances. They called her the Concubine. They called her the Whore. Her heart hardened and her body became taut when their hatred struck into her. From the very first their partisanship to the Queen had induced them to cover her with filth, to whip up the mob to pursue and insult her, and to carry this enmity into the heart of Greenwich. Spies everywhere. Eavesdroppers everywhere. Tale-bearers everywhere. But if they imagined that anything could weaken her or make her draw back, they did not know her. Anne, when she was alone, paced her chamber with clenched fists and a straight furrow in her forehead, the figure of a Bellona. She trembled at the memory of what she had seen. It froze her blood. Yet curse them and damn them, she was alone, just as alone as Catherine when it came to it, and she would not give in. She would drive Henry forward. She would drive Catherine from Court and defy the Papacy. She would beat them.

This recklessness did not make Henry hate Anne, but on the Fisher affair he was stubborn. He refused to take these short cuts or to lead the way into anarchy. He was willing to be slid into supremacy of the Church, and Cromwell was so shrewd, so attentive to detail, so legal in his method, that Henry gave him more countenance. He let him hit the bishops one body blow after another by inflicting crushing fines for small offences, and Tunstal and Fisher were simply not summoned to the House of Lords, though admitted if they came. To inflame the public with every sin of the clergy, to point to every shilling that was charged by the ecclesiastical courts, every penny that was exacted in death duties and every intrusion and insolence of the proctors—this Henry favoured. The air was thick with accusations, black with atrocities, until the clergy staggered from bewilderment to chagrin before Cromwell and the rest of the King's servants crumpled them up. Cromwell built up a horde of followers. He raked in gifts that varied from venison and capons to pewter and geldings, cash and grants of land. Henry allowed him to inflict terror when the victims were weak, and to promote Audley and Riche, or whatever other New Man would carry out his policy, but parliament was the tool he insisted on. His method was not to break the law but to make it, and he no more smothered speech in the Commons than he forbade outspokenness in his own chapel at Greenwich. At a certain point, however, he slammed open the window of his oratory and shouted red-faced to the preacher, "Get on! Don't tell falsehoods!" The opponents he squared with, in a genial give-and-take, as he squared with Stephen Gardiner, were well advised not to presume on this geniality. Henry "loved a man," but to cross him was a ticklish business, and Cromwell soon discovered it when he tried to recall William Tyndale to England.

"One King," Tyndale had said, and Henry loved him. "One King, one law in the realm; no class of man exempt from the temporal sword; no law except the law of the land." Anne and Cromwell felt they could use Tyndale against Papal law and against Thomas More. So Cromwell sent his agent to Antwerp to persuade the exile to return.

Tyndale was indeed a tragic exile. He felt bitterly his absence from his friends, the danger in which he lived, his hunger, his thirst, his cold, his eternal hard and sharp fighting, and his appearance of disloyalty to the King of England.

"As I now am," he confessed to Vaughan, Cromwell's emissary, when they met in a bare field outside Antwerp, "very death were more pleasant to me than life, considering man's nature to be such as can bear no truth." But he longed to obey the summons and return to England.

Before this news reached Henry, however, the good Tyndale published a pamphlet in which he touched on the divorce. He believed that Wolsey had thought of it as a political move, which was true enough, and he denounced it as immoral.

The pamphlet came under Henry's hot eyes, and when he received Vaughan's glowing letter about Tyndale on top of it he turned savagely on Cromwell, tearing the letter in two. "Your Vaughan," he shouted. "He bears affection to Tyndale! He'd bring him into my realm to sow sedition here!"

"But this pamphlet, your Highness——"

"A venomous book, by Jesu! Packed with lies. A damnable, pestiferous book." He glared dangerously at Cromwell. "I am very joyous," he shook, "to have this realm destitute of such a person."

"Malicious, perverse, lewd, ignorant, erroneous, detestable." When Henry began, he had a rich vocabulary. Cromwell simply hung his head.

"Why," said Anne to Cromwell, "when his Grace was so benignly minded to him, must Tyndale touch on the divorce?"

"Yea, my lady," deplored Cromwell. "If only Master Tyndale were able to reconcile himself to his Highness's opinions, then we might save the New Testament."

Anne shook her head. "Not now. Not if his Grace spoke of sedition."

"He said that, and more." Cromwell's mouth gave a peculiar

twitch. "He spoke of his sowing evil seed, digressing from the laws of Almighty God and wholesome doctrines of holy fathers."

"Lo!" said Anne prudently; "then indeed we may desist."

Yet Henry's violence about Tyndale did not impair his geniality for more than a day. That night he had up the sergeant of the cellar to play cards. That week he had Anne's desk garnished with laten and gold. He bought a farm for her. He lost a lot of money gambling with George, and when a woman begged from him as he and Anne's brother walked out together, saying "for the love of St. George!" Henry gave a hearty laugh and tossed her a crown. He was kind to the blind harper and to the dumb fisherman. He was robust and profuse and genial. He bought a house for George. He paid for Davy's funeral—Davy who had picked him out of the ditch and actually saved his life. And he spent fifty thousand pounds, in our money, to replenish his cellars with wines.

## VII

HIS EQUANIMITY, however, was not proof against the Pope when he was summoned to appear at Rome. The days of Canossa were gone by, and his Council shared the indignation that this summons provoked in him. On the strength of it, he asked them to join the bishops and go in a body to Catherine, to persuade her to another, a nearer, tribunal.

It was a warm June evening, between eight and nine, as they trooped to her, with Cromwell in the rear. Young Northumberland was of the company, old Shrewsbury, many grim new figures and many depressed older ones. They found Catherine by herself. In her cordial manner, so simple and well-bred, she bade them rise from their knees and they crowded into the dusky, candle-lit audience chamber, thirty of them facing her as she seated herself. The room fell very still when Norfolk, clearing his throat after an audible sigh, began in his somewhat grating tones to set forth the King's grief and displeasure that, owing to her, he was cited to Rome.

Every point that he raised, Catherine answered temperately with clarity and frankness. She made no harangue. As for Supreme Head, she said, in his own realm she would obey and serve her lord the

King, but in the spiritual realm the Pope was the only true Vicar of God.

One of Cromwell's men, Dr. Lee, broke in on this point of sovereignty by saying in a blunt voice that the Queen had been known to Prince Arthur, and on that account her marriage to Henry was detestable and abominable. Catherine said quietly that she was not carnally known to Prince Arthur, but that Dr. Lee would find other than women to argue with at Rome.

Dr. Sampson, more respectful, accused her of being precipitate.

"Dean," she answered, "if you had experienced part of the bitter days and nights I have endured, you would not say I was precipitate."

All the prelates took turns at harrying her in this fashion, including Gardiner. What proof was there that Prince Arthur had not known her? Catherine still parried in good temper. Henry, she said, was loved by her as much as any woman could love her husband, but she never could have wished, or did wish, to live with him contrary to her conscience.

The discussion astonished her, she said. So many grand personages could appal the world, coming to surprise her when alone and without counsel.

"But your Grace has counsel," said Norfolk.

"Yea," said Catherine, "fine counsellors! Bishop Tunstal says he dare not advise me, he is the King's subject and vassal. The Archbishop of Canterbury says, The wrath of the Prince is sure death. And Bishop Fisher says, Keep up your courage!"

When Suffolk heard this he gave Harry Guildford a nudge. No one felt particularly happy, and as the men of the long robe went silent, Anne's father together with Norfolk tried a few feeble excuses. Cromwell kept his mouth shut.

"The best deed in the world," exploded Guildford as they came away, "would be to tie all these doctors in a cart, and send them to Rome to fight it out among themselves, since it was they who started it all."

Henry was waiting anxiously to know how Catherine had met them. "I was afraid it would be like this," he said gloomily, "considering her courage and fantasy. Well, we'll have to provide other remedies," and he continued to frown.

"The Queen," Suffolk ventured to interrupt his brooding, "is ready to obey your Grace in all things but two."

"You mean the Pope and the Emperor?" said Henry quickly.

"No, sir. God is the first, and her conscience the other, and these she won't disobey for anyone."

Henry ignored this, but Anne was furious with Sir Harry Guildford for the remark that Cromwell reported.

"You had no right to say that!" she assailed him the next day.

Guildford, corpulent and imperturbable, gave Anne a pitying look that stung her to the quick.

"When I am Queen," she burst out, "I'll see whether you'll remain Controller."

"When that time comes," he said, "you won't have the trouble, for I'll give up the office myself." He turned on his heel and went to the King's chamber. There he told Henry what had happened and surrendered his wand.

"I cannot have it." Henry handed it back to him. "Why do you pay attention to what a woman says!"

Guildford shook his head. He refused the wand. "No, sir," he said, his face yellow-grey, "I must decline."

"You are a sensible fellow. You know what women are like, Master Controller. Come, now."

But the faithful Guildford shook his head decisively, and left Greenwich for ever.

To Anne this was a godsend. And Catherine's obstinacy had so exasperated Henry that his courtiers soon concealed their flutter of sympathy for her. In a few days Anne started on progress with him, with only George and a couple of others to accompany him.

There was one last link that Catherine had counted on. Mary, their daughter, was just fifteen. She was a solemn child, studious and myopic, very loyal to her mother. The strain of her parents' dispute had borne down on her, especially as her own legitimacy was in question, and she was now in a difficult period, unable to eat, very lonely, ill and hysterical.

When Henry learned of this he was instantly stirred. But when Catherine presumed on it to ask that she come to Court, Henry turned on her sharply. If she wished to see Mary, he said, she could go to her and stay with her.

This was still in his mind when Catherine proposed, as usual, to join him on progress. He said no. He ordered her to remain behind him at Windsor.

Catherine, from her own windows, could see the little cavalcade that was to go off with Henry and Anne. It had been one of the happy interludes in their royal life, the summer progress that was filled with hunting lore, and changing scene, new people, easy modes, late suppers and pleasant talk. The young woman was now at Henry's side, and Catherine could hear a light laugh, a few words, and then the horses' hoofs. She saw them ride out together. Henry pulled up to let Anne go on before him, and that was the last time that Catherine ever saw him.

When Anne returned to Windsor, in August of 1531, there was no other woman to dispute Henry with her. There only remained that awkward formality, the divorce.

# *Chapter 19*

FOR ANNE IT was a heavenly relief, to return to Windsor and find that Queen Catherine had obeyed Henry and removed from it. Anne looked out on the tranquil view with a sense of touching it for the first time. She had enjoyed Amboise, but here was a site beyond all others for a royal castle, and as her eye travelled over the forest, with Eton in the distance, the immensity, the sumptuousness, of her new conquest laid its quieting finger on her and stilled her into awe. Henry had been nervous and captious. Her mood had been roughened by him. But nothing had been worse than the Queen's presence. To have her gone was a promise that the new era could come—and then no sour faces, no guarded looks, but friends, and a merry England.

Yet Catherine's withdrawal, delicious as it was, had not taken place quite soon enough to give perfect relief. Anne's comfort of soul was not complete. The Queen's tenacity, her stolid, passive face, her sustained and level note of protest had endured for a thousand days and more, so that, while she had lost Henry and the crown, it still had contaminated Anne's ease of mind. Had she been alone, it could scarcely have hurt Anne. Once she had been beaten out, she would have disappeared. But gone though she was from Windsor, and from

378

every royal haunt, certainly though she was banished, Anne still knew she was there. Henry laughed at her for this, but Anne was in no strong position to be laughed at.

"Had the Emperor money!" she said to Henry.

"Pooh!"

"I do not trust Chapuys," said Anne. "Sir Harry Guildford is dead now, thanks to God, but he was imperial. I could name you twenty in this very castle."

This directness with Henry made him uncomfortable. When he came down to it, Catherine had exhausted his sympathy for her by her faculty for disagreeing with him. "When I am gone," Catherine had assured him, "there is no one who can, or who dare, contradict you." That was just it. He loved a pretty woman, but he loved a pretty woman to soothe and concur and charm him. Life for Henry was not a bed of roses. He knew from Cromwell, and from others that Anne had no inkling of, how many and how strong the imperials were. He had his eyes on them. But he could not bear to have his sense of himself unduly ruffled, and while he loved Anne for the vivacity and sparkle of her mind, her glad nature, there were times when she forgot that he had his eyes open.

"My lord of Suffolk," he said, "hath come back again to young Wyatt."

Anne heard this too clearly. She could no longer see those wooing distances, where hills raced over hills like waves running. A thunderous anger came into her face, and in her eyes there was lightning. That lisping Suffolk, lazy and stupid, who lounged from woman to woman, and cared only for the King because in that way he cared for himself. Anne remembered hearing a few chuckling words that Henry had once spoken of his boon companion.

"Yea," she said, "my lord of Suffolk—he is the right sort to say this manner of thing." Her bosom heaved.

"Why, darling, he never speaks a harsh word, good Suffolk."

"He never respected or was faithful to a single woman, not even your Grace's sister—a man who is accused of having had to do with his own daughter."

Henry stopped smiling, but he could not say anything. He had told it to Anne himself.

This dampened the ardour of returning to a vacated Windsor. Suffolk belittled Anne because she and her crew isolated him from his adored Henry. And Henry could never blame him for that. He had a soft spot in his heart, and in his character, for Suffolk.

He and Anne, however, did not deepen the ruts that their predicament made. Henry found a chance to reprehend Suffolk, and to console Anne for this irritation he was causing. He and she had gone too far toward their marriage to harass themselves with Suffolk.

## II

IT WAS IN PARLIAMENT, not in the whispering galleries, that Catherine's friends were to rally. Archbishop Warham was plucking up courage at last. He came to help John Fisher and Thomas More.

Henry could not, as yet, see his way clear to their marriage, but by Thomas Cromwell's masterly handling of parliament the independence of the clergy was being crushed and the connection with Rome broken. Henry had gone about it smoothly enough. When Thomas More came back from Cambrai, at the time the Emperor and the French had patched up their peace, Henry had told him to talk over the divorce with young Foxe and one of his bishops. Still the honest More had avoided committing himself. Henry was not angry with him. He loved More so much that when he gave him the Great Seal he had said, "I promise you freedom of conscience on this Great Matter. First look unto God, and after God unto me." More refused it. "I am unmeet for it," he pleaded. But his master's request was reinforced by such urgent and even imperative words that a good servant could only bow to them and take the Seal out of its white leather bag. So, on his knees, he became Lord Chancellor.

But More remained cruelly aware of the dangers that beset him. He smelled conspiracy in the Fleming, Chapuys, whom the Emperor had sent as ambassador. Chapuys had a letter from the Emperor he wished to give him; More refused to see it. And for the honour of God, he said, do not come to me. He could only speak freely to Henry if he were beyond reproach. But when Cromwell demanded reform of Church law, and the King's supremacy over canon law and legislation, the fight was over, and Thomas More resigned.

The victor went to see the vanquished. More, weary and unwell, gazed on the powerful Cromwell whose gifts for discharging his labours no one could better value. Each had it in him to be a truly admirable servant. But More faced a new type of servant, one who served the State as an end in itself, and he shook his head sorrowfully.

"Master Cromwell," he said, "you are now entered into the service of a most noble, wise and liberal prince."

The gleam in Cromwell's ironic eyes brought a darker, deeper gleam into his own. "If you follow my poor advice," he said, "you shall ever tell him what he ought to do, but never what he is able to do. For if a lion knew his own strength, hard were it for any man to rule him."

Cromwell's mouth twitched, but he said nothing. On his way home he chuckled. What ought he to do? He asked himself, and he answered quickly, "What he is able to do, that's what he ought to do." He did not wish to rule his lion. He wished his lion to be a lion, to seek whom he might devour, to be a very lion, proud and beyond fear and terrible.

And Thomas More, relieved from office, set about that work which he had long ached to perform—to serve his other Master, to combat heresy.

With a pen ceaselessly active, he wrote headlong against Tyndale, raging in his denunciation of the Reformers. And Henry was willing to see it: heresy and sedition he held to be allies.

## III

MORE'S RESIGNATION gave Anne a happy day, and the French bishop, Jean du Bellay, urged her that they should marry at once. Anne listened to him eagerly, but Henry hesitated. Much as he longed to end the dreadful strain, he preferred to ask his Council to make this as a request to him.

The Council was far too divided to meet his wishes. Anne's uncle and her father had done everything they could to browbeat the old Archbishop of Canterbury, and, failing there, to persuade the Lords to send the divorce to an ordinary lay tribunal. But these efforts were taken without sympathy, and the Council was so unfavourable to marriage before a divorce that even the Earl of Wiltshire pouted out his submission and admitted the folly of it. The country was too unfriendly.

So tepid were her supporters, when it came to braving the Queen's friends, that Anne scorned them with her whole heart, and she was correspondingly grateful to Jean du Bellay.

He approved of her marriage. Of course he did. The Spanish bride that his King had encumbered himself with, Charles's sister, had been hung on a peg, like an old coat, and forgotten. Du Bellay wished to see Catherine of Aragon discarded for the same reason, and the more umbrage it gave to the Emperor the more helplessly allied to France the English must become. So whenever Anne consulted this keen, smiling bishop, he said, "Marry at once!" He hinted he was something of a Lutheran, and he suggested France might go into schism. Marry at once, and shame the Pope! Nothing could put more pressure on the Pope. He might lose two countries, France and England.

Anne could have hugged du Bellay for his aid, and he went further by completing the arrangements for an interview with Francis I, at which she was to be received as the future Queen of England.

This interview excited Henry as much as Anne, and du Bellay found himself treated like a member of the family. Anne kept him by her side. She had his measure taken for a green hunting outfit, and he joined her, to her extreme delight, with a horn slung over his episcopal shoulder and a greyhound at his heels. Henry played up to them. He drove the deer to them so that they could use their crossbows at short range and be sure of killing him. The deer shied from the fate that awaited them. They turned their twittering tails. But the inexorable Henry sent them forward; they gathered themselves and bounded madly to pass the trees where Anne and her bishop whanged the arrows at them. Some darted by, with a burst of speed which dazzled those in ambush, their throats high like little pillars, their breasts distended, their hoofs as clean as flame. But some of them, aggrieved by the sudden thrust, threw up their black muzzles and fell over. Either Anne or the bishop had scored. And yet it was only pastime, they had come to debate the interview at Calais, with a sortie to Boulogne. But Francis's Spanish wife—she was to be kept out of it.

Henry said he hated anything Spanish like the devil, "And no mockers or jesters!" he begged. He wanted no rough jokes about his intended bride.

This open French support gave Henry courage to talk definitely of his marriage for the first time. He called his Council to him.

"The Pope has no power over me," he told them in a loud voice. He repeated this. He often repeated things two or three times, and with an oath. "I am resolved," he added, "to celebrate our marriage in the most solemn manner possible."

He had spoken. But where? And when? The members of the Council stood nose to nose. The master had not told them where and when. They now felt he really meant it. "He'll do it in France!" one of them said. And another said, "Watch him. He'll do it within Calais." But they were in the dark.

His unequivocal words were elixir for Anne, after these years of concealment. Her heart swelled with happiness. She had feared he meant to wait until the Archbishop of Canterbury died.

"If he die?" she asked him.

"I think of Cranmer," said Henry.

"But would Rome ever agree?"

"Why not?" said Henry coolly. "They'll have no annates otherwise."

This was one of Cromwell's legal dodges and Henry delighted in it. Besides, Cranmer had been at Rome and had come away with a small sinecure from the Pope. Cranmer was so meek, even the Emperor had taken to him. He would be a most valuable Archbishop of Canterbury.

The imminence of the marriage was at last upon them. For Anne, after six years of concealed uncertainty and driving will, Henry's words were elixir. But she wanted the marriage in England. She could never feel herself Queen unless she went from the Tower to be crowned in the Abbey. That too, all of it, trumpets and all. It must be hers. She had waited for it and she would have it.

"Lord!" she cried to Henry, her eyes dancing, "look what George has sent."

Two nightingales in a cage.

"We must hear them sing to-night," cried Henry gaily.

They sat under the trees in the warm evening with the caged nightingales at their feet. No one was near them. Anne had her lute.

"Pray sing," she said to her lover. "And then may the nightingales sing."

Henry and she would sometimes sing together. They did it prettily. He looked at her with ample indulgence. She was his torment, headstrong, wilful, ready to defy the world, with such singular winning ways in spite of fieriness, and so special.

As the holly groweth green,
And never changeth hue,
So I am, ever hath been
Unto my lady true,
    Unto my lady true.
As the holly groweth green
With ivy all alone,
When flowers cannot be seen
And green wood leaves be gone,
    And green wood leaves be gone.

Now unto my lady
Promise to her I make,
From all other only
To her I me betake
    To her I me betake,
Adieu, mine own lady,
Adieu, my special,
Who hath my heart truly,
Be sure, and ever shall,
    Be sure, and ever shall!

It was his own little song. They lilted it together at the end, Anne with the lute and Henry giving himself to it with that lightness of heart which comes when a hard adventure nears its end.

The nightingales listened from their airy cage. Anne and Henry let silence fall on them. There was a single note, but nothing further.

"Not from the cage," said Anne.

## IV

NEXT MORNING at Ampthill her uncle of Norfolk stopped her in a window. He looked rather sour. "I have here a letter," he fumbled, "which it is my duty to submit unto you." He dug it out.

His manner was ominous enough, and Anne opened it warily. It was from her old friend Percy's wife, addressed to her father, the Earl of Shrewsbury. Ah, thought Anne, Catherine's good friends. She read it with a stony face. The Countess told her father that the reason Northumberland gave for deserting her was his not being her husband, since he had been solemnly betrothed to Anne Boleyn, which in the sight of God was a marriage.

Norfolk watched Anne down his nose as she pondered the letter. This would give her somewhat to think about.

"I perceive!" Anne looked straight at her uncle. "Come, my lord. Let us to his Grace. This touches him as well as me."

"You mean to show it to him?" Norfolk was startled.

"At once," Anne answered shortly.

"Then Northumberland is mistaken?" he asked as they moved.

"Or his lady, who writes it," Anne said icily. "But if I call it a falsehood, whom do I convince? Let my lord of Northumberland speak for himself. Let the King examine him. Let the Council examine him. Let him take oath."

"If you care to risk it." Norfolk stroked his nose. "I was obliged to show you this."

"For a duty such as this," Anne replied, "I may always count on you."

Henry sent orders for the Earl of Northumberland to come to him at once. The cloud grew each day until he appeared, but he arrived so pale, so distracted, so effaced, that not Anne's bitterest enemy could believe he would make a case against her. There was no case, he told Henry. He went before the Council to deny the story his wife had vindictively circulated, and he went to the Archbishop of Canterbury to swear to its falsehood.

Anne Boleyn welcomed this. "Were I dead and gone," she flashed to Henry, "every word that Mary Talbot says would be believed. But I am here to meet it. Now what will they say next!"

"Sweetheart," said her lover, "they may say what they will, I laugh at them."

And shortly after this Archbishop Warham died. From his palace at Knole, from his palace at Lambeth, he had watched the growing might of the State. "They call me an old fool," he once had said to Wolsey, but he paid no attention to them. On his death-bed, however, he beckoned to his notary. All these new laws, Cromwell's laws, "We neither will, nor intend, nor with clear conscience are able to consent to the same, but by these writings we do dissent from, refuse, and contradict them." It was a debt he owed, and now he paid it, to his honour.

## V

THOMAS CROMWELL had the King's ear before Warham died, during his attack on the clergy.

For several months the opposition had, indeed, shown fight. One or two members of the Commons were rash enough to urge Henry to return to his wife. Bishop Gardiner, secure in his see of Winchester, resisted a policy that was threatening all bishops. And even Norfolk, who heard open attacks on the Pope from the pulpit, was wroth. "Were it not for my lord of Wiltshire and another person," he snarled, "I'd have these Lutherans burnt alive."

Cromwell allowed none of this to go unnoticed. Henry called the Commons to heel, rebuking them at a private audience. Norfolk was so received that he left the Court in indignation. Stephen Gardiner was too good to be broken, but he was sent on embassy out of England. And whenever the mob jeered at Anne, as they did on Henry's progress through the midlands, there was arrest and stiff punishment. Cromwell was ready to use torture and the gibbet for anything that bordered on insubordination, and where Wolsey had blustered, he moved secretly and panther-like. He could fell the opponent since many magistrates were under obligation to him, and he had learned the ins and outs of many a county. Imperfect as yet, his control was sufficiently sketched to give Henry proofs that he could meet public resistance beforehand.

But Warham's death was so welcome to him that he had to go to Henry with it.

Henry permitted Cromwell to see him alone. He was back at Greenwich, to guide the details of the French visit.

"How about Gardiner, Cromwell?" Henry suggested the new archbishop. He could always count on Cromwell's attacking Gardiner.

Cromwell fell into the trap, yet he was so convincing that Henry weakened.

"Then," he said decisively, "Cranmer is our man."

"In truth, your Highness," responded Cromwell warmly, "no man in your service hath better parts. The Pope will confirm him. Then may he take his oath to you as Supreme Head, and the divorce and your marriage may follow."

Henry heard this, his blue eyes fixed and dark. No one could be more easy than he to take a view that fitted his private feelings. This particular view was full of complexity. His connection with Rome was already a masterpiece of intricacy. "The Pope," he had said publicly, "is a worthy fellow enough, but I give not a fig, not a fig, for excommunication!" Yet, while he made open defiance, he had not broken the connection with Rome. He was nursing it. He intended to nurse it. And still he was only nursing it to have someone of his own made Archbishop who, under the laws and statutes of England, would acknowledge him Supreme Head of the Church. He must keep his connection to acquire the tool by which to be able to sever the connection. And while doing this, even as he talked to the base Cromwell and arranged it, he never lost his bright spontaneous quality. His voice could go high and squeak, but he had the air of a well-fed general, with a robust manner that was at times hearty and familiar, at times haughty and choleric. That he could have moved so sinuously, with so many reservations, keeping a mask so ingenuous, was one of those oddities to which a public manner gives no clue. And he even warmed a little in his contact with the low Cromwell, who so well perceived the chance provided by Warham's death and how to use it to advantage.

But there were aspects of it that Cromwell knew and felt little about. An immense difference between himself and Henry was the part that women played in their lives. Cromwell was still at self-preservation while Henry had gone on to reproduction. Cromwell's wife had been a dull woman. His boy was a dull boy. He was now providing for his clan, buying furniture, being excited about inlaid chests and mappae mundi, where Henry was giving him sketches for the jewels he wished to appear in, and wished Anne to appear in, when they came under the gaze of King Francis. And Warham's death, that capped a new Church for Cromwell, was for Henry a private assurance that marriage must follow divorce. And its joy could not be full and deep until he shared it with Anne. She had the swift nature, the liveliness and sparkle, which made it a double pleasure to share things with her. But this time it was more than a promise to her. It was the final barrier removed, and she had often said that when marriage was certain, they would have no reason to wait.

He was rather a stout-hearted man, at the age of forty-one, but the approaching moment a little upset him.

They had suffered so many cruel disappointments, he reflected alone. He still loved her, but love with him was still tentative, for all his bluff exterior. It was not exactly an overflow to bless a woman who had created in him a flood of self-esteem, but to maintain his love did require a steady warmth in his woman, without which it might languish.

Being a good twelve years younger than himself, Anne was rather high-handed with him at times. As she saw it, he grumbled and fumed, and then she smote him. She was less timid, certainly, than Catherine had been. Having seen her mother cow Thomas Boleyn for so many years, she had at times treated Henry with something of the same cold insolence when he seemed thoroughly unreasonable. So far he had submitted to her. Her references to Queen Catherine were often so pointed that he winced. She held up Catherine in all her narrowness, all her exigence and obstinacy. It had been the only way, she felt, to keep him from becoming unbearably retrospective. But this discipline that her nerves forced her to employ, this adroitness in stinging him, had made tender the desire to be her servant which had first led him to kneel to her. Catherine, indeed, had kept none of Henry's heart. She had been too harsh with him in these trying years. But she had been faithful to him. Though he had thrown off that fidelity with the most resolute and vigorous efforts of which a wearied husband is capable, trampling on it and spurning it, he still had moments of revery, after supper, when he said, "No one, by God, could say she was not faithful." In a woman it is a matchless quality. Henry clung to it, just as he clung to bows and arrows, to a certain ritual with his barber, to the Emperor in spite of every war and every wrangle, and to the Seven Sacraments. He clung, in short, to his habits. He even missed the Cardinal at times. And in Anne, piquant as she was, there was a restlessness that ruffled that sense of himself which was to his balm and contentment.

Her vivacity disturbed him, and yet for her vivacity he loved her. With a queer, brisk toss of his head, he went to see her.

Anne was cool. All his strategy she praised, but when he brought it home to her that the last barrier was gone, that they were virtually man and wife, Anne became restless. She did not trust the Pope, that was it. This touched him like a little cold breath from a forgotten window. It diluted the warmth in which he had hoped to find her consoling.

But her coldness did not create indifference in him. It made him hate her and love her. She was at his mercy, when it was seen in cold blood, but his blood was not cold, and, good strategist as he was, he was yet unable to conceal his desire to capture this approval that receded from him.

He had never possessed her fully, much as it was believed he had, but now she put him off. Why? He could not fathom her. He decided to tempt her.

He talked of the Queen's jewels.

"It is offensive and insulting to me," Catherine had said, "and would weigh on my conscience, if I were led to give up my jewels for such a base purpose as that of decking out a person who is a reproach to Christendom, and is bringing scandal and disgrace on the King, through his taking her to such a meeting as this in France."

Henry did not tell Anne this. He meant to have the jewels, however, and said so.

"Yea," pouted Anne, "but you do not make her send them, sir." She said it coolly, not harshly, but, since he had wished her to dilate on his approaching victory over Rome, this was petty.

No, Anne did not find it petty. He was taking her to France and his Queen, and yet he was allowing the Princess Dowager to keep the jewels. Her eyes, mournful and large, conveyed to him the gap between his big words and his deeds.

"I will have them." He could not do more than say, "I will make Catherine send them. I will have them for you, sweetheart."

"It comes true, then." She slid to him, convinced by his manner. "We may make the list of my ladies. I care nothing for those who do not wish to be asked. My own friends are many."

They made a list, and Henry approved. "And now," he melted, "I have somewhat to tell you.

"You may fear the Pope, but how if I name you the lady marquis of Pembroke, with its revenues, to see you into France with becoming dignity, and for the heirs of your body, should ought hap, which God forbid."

"A Tudor marquisate!" cried Anne. Her father was an Earl. "May God protect you, you speak lightly of mishap. It makes me shiver."

"Not I! Now you smile again. Come, be merry with me. I have had your lodgings fresh garnished in the Tower. They are for you to see, well repaired."

"Where I am to lodge?" Anne sparkled. It was the coronation she thought of.

"Yea, to crown you from it, as you wish it."

"Ah," she threw her arms around him, "you devise all! And now, I crave a favour, since you do so pamper me."

Henry smiled.

" 'Tis poor Wyatt. You purged Northumberland of all offence, in spite of slander. Wyatt was nothing so much to me as wretched Percy. Give him your favour, now we are in surety."

"You are all mine?"

"Your minion, and for ever."

"Let him come to Court. He may come with us into Calais."

"Ah," exclaimed Anne, as tears rushed to her eyes, "this will solace the wretch who so longs to serve you near. I could wish for mercy in the world. May God give us a son, and end those deep cares you suffered, and light us to happiness." She then kissed him with her whole heart, murmuring tenderly.

Henry's eyes softened. He looked at Anne, and read consent in hers. It was the night for which he had lived so long.

It was then Anne discovered that Henry was not as powerful as she had supposed. This frightened her, but she was tender with him, and in the end it seemed to be as it should be.

## VI

ANNE could see Thomas again. She had heard Cromwell say that Thomas was in England again. Cromwell, now treasurer of the jewels, had cast his eyes over the list of jewels that should be in the jewel house and then over the actual valuables that were under his hand. The gaping holes in the existing regiment of crown jewels gave him goose flesh. Amidas was dead. His widow was so enraged at the suggestion that anything was out of order that she began, with some inconsequence, to talk of Henry's early amour with Lady Boleyn. Master Cromwell soon clapped her mouth shut, but what these honest gentlemen, Sir Harry Wyatt and Thomas Wyatt, had been doing with the jewels was hard for him to know. Had they been dishonest, Cromwell could have understood it, but he could not suppose. But where were the jewels? With all his hard positiveness, his driving accuracy, he set down, for the first time, every single item that should be under key. Jewels do not melt away, walk away, or rot. He had been trained in a sphere where the concrete fact is in itself an imperishable jewel. He hated the untidy and the casual. To manage anything, he felt, there must be a rule, and the same impulse that made him want to begin registering births, deaths and marriages in England, that made him desire to break the Earl of Kildare's neck for disturbing Ireland—that impulse, revolted by disorder, made him send to Calais for Thomas Wyatt and ask for a word with him.

Thomas would have drawn his sword had the new treasurer been suspicious, but Cromwell met him with a smile, put the jewels and the lists before him, explained that Amidas was the latest responsible one, and asked for help. And then, out of Thomas's memory, came troops of amiable but unrecorded facts. That plate had been borrowed by the Queen's lady, and he could find a receipt for it. He found a box of receipts. All sorts of valuables had been lent into the Court, or melted, or exchanged, or made over. The gaps began to be filled. Cromwell shook his black head and laughed. Such a method,

in a royal office that should move clocklike, filled him with wonder.
Yet, at the end of it, he turned to Thomas.

"A friend and follower of William Tyndale is in trouble," he said.
Thomas's face showed his concern.

"John Frith," murmured Cromwell. "His book on the Sacrament
hath aroused the late Chancellor. They have trapped him at Milton's
Shore, by Southend."

"In Essex?"

"Yes. Could you go there, Master Wyatt, to keep an eye on it?"

Thomas was glad to go, to make sure that Frith was not mishandled.
And he was in Essex when summoned to join the royal host at Dover.

He had been four years out of England, living a soldier's life. In its
intervals, slotted between thick walls, he had sat at a table in a high
window, white paper before him, and while at times he had glanced
vaguely over a flat and inexpressive land, his mind had only followed
emotion, or the memory of it, within.

Thomas had lost her, but what had sunk into him was the heart-
lessness of the woman he had loved. He had not sought a dream. He
had sought a true woman. His wife had gone to another man, and
he could not blame himself for that, but Anne he had loved and sued
out of a whole heart. He had craved her as the one thing on earth that
was of worth to him. Never once did he need to search his heart to ask
whether he had loved her. He was undivided, and how he had burned,
pleaded, and suffered, was graven into him for ever. He was now
nearing thirty, but the deception that Anne had wrought, when she
had given him cause to believe in her, made him older than his years,
incapable of that stable confidence in years to come which is possible
to a man heartwhole and unwounded.

The chamber at Calais was not unlike a prison cell, though the window perch was free, and the window wide. Thomas came and went in
the changing moods of his mess. Some days there was the clamour
bred by a sortie—scraping feet, quick voices, laughter, jokes, and
bracing danger. He had his part in that. When sodden winter ceased,
and the French sky became clear, tender and infinitely innocent, his
heart yearned for a moment of the old happiness, for an hour in which
her eyes could still melt and his hands take her breasts, and their lips

meet. The promise of life had been contained in that woman, not for his desire of her but for all that she brought with it, the sanction of his being.

I was determined, he said to himself, to have loved. I found her. I thought never to see her like.

> *To trace this dance, I put myself in press,*
> *Vain hope did lead, and bade I should not cease*
> *To serve, to suffer, and still to hold my peace,*
> > *In eternum.*

Never would he have given her over. He had stood through many long evenings, the least glimpse of her a sustenance. The rest of the world could fling itself into its headlong spin of amorous play. George Boleyn could look at him over the shoulder of a woman whose immobile face never said she was ensnared. Francis Bryan could romp with six of them and make his jest. The whole Court had an interplay which Thomas once had sight of. It was part of himself, yet meaningless for him. Whether Madge Shelton loved one or the other, he cared not. Will Brereton and the rest—he heard them for months and to himself he said, "In eternum, in eternum." His mind affirmed his heart. The picture of it, Anne's sudden signal and their moment snatched, a hot palm, a word and their tortured parting—he could look out beyond these walls to see nothing and of Anne he could see everything. They had embraced like eagles, and it had been his pride.

Now his pride forced him to say it: she had never loved him.

> *It was not long ere I by proof had found,*
> *That feeble building is on feeble ground;*
> *For in her heart this word did never sound,*
> > *In eternum.*

What he had embraced was not that flesh, sweet as she was to him. He had surrendered himself to a fidelity. Not without her pledge could he have done it, but it was the only fidelity that beckoned him. Religion had lost itself in dust. His King asked nothing from him. Thomas had only this loveliness to make his own, his powers drawn from those regions where man is his own deity. Yet Anne had not loved him.

> *In eternum then from my heart I cast*
> *That I had first determined for the best;*
> *Now in the place another thought doth rest*
> *In eternum.*

This was his mood when he was called from Calais, and it was still the same when he was summoned to meet Henry and Anne at Dover.

## VII

THE EMBARKATION at Dover came in the middle of October. The crowd that watched it was not warm. It was possessed, indeed, by inordinate eagerness to see a lady for whom Henry had discarded his wife, and, by the mere awe that the preparations had instilled, with thousands to accompany the King, and by the surveillance that Henry had ordered, respect dwelled in the scene.

Henry had ordained it all. The costumes of the ladies had been chosen by Anne and himself, and at royal expense. By summoning the Norfolk connections, some of the oldest and noblest families in England had sent their younger women to attend on Anne, and they, along with Jane Rochford and Mary Boleyn, went before their mistress with every grace a queen could wish for. The mood was royal. Ships had not been easy to collect at short notice, since so many had left for the fishing grounds off Iceland and Newfoundland, but Harry Guildford's brother had scurried to find the enormous number needed, and the *Minion* had come round from Gravesend, with its gala flags to welcome them, Henry and Anne having ridden on dry roads from Sir Thomas Cheyney's, with October still benign.

This was an audacity on Henry's part, the visit to France with a young woman by his side who was not yet his wife.

"She's his hoore," sneered a bystander who had come from Winchester, "and he's put off a good woman for her."

"Aye," said another, "and a goggle-eyed hoore."

But the ladies-in-waiting saw no hostility in these faces that watched them. They were so finely nurtured, with such acute nerves for their own performance, and so little touch with the low people, that they came to the strand to regard tall ships as nearer witnesses than the lowering, glum multitude held back from them.

And if these light-limbed, shapely women, the novitiates of charm, were undisturbed by such hostility, Henry was still more removed from it. He was armoured in himself. His eye took in his ships, the direction of the wind, and the course of the waves. There was a pounce in them, but no rudeness. This promised well for the crossing, which, even in a big boat like the *Minion,* could be so merciless and brusque that none except a hero could take it calmly, while ordinary mortals, male and female, were soon stripped of pride, and knelt in bilge to pledge the Virgin candles, or gifts, or pilgrimages, if She would only save them. The blue waves that tumbled on the beach had a sharp whiteness in them, but Henry judged them harmless. He and Anne breathed a spanking air, and admired the *Minion.*

Henry was unfailing as a King—portly and gorgeous, with a glance that ran along the people like a scythe, so that they fell to their knees. Dover was a sight to see, with his Cinque Ports to raise a lion's paw and clamp down on an enemy, to save a coast that thrust its white breast against the world. He believed in defiances, should any dispute the law with him. But his visit to France, in the Marchioness of Pembroke's company, would do more for his equanimity than a million crowns. He was content to woo the French. He had seldom been so happy.

Anne, by his side, was almost frail. Suave in movement, with an innate fineness of limb and a new clarity every time she turned her head, she was alive in glance. Nature, as one partner in this artifice of a lovely woman, had not withheld a soul, and as Thomas saw her come to the shore, regally bedecked, he believed she was the same as he had known: the viol in him trembled, and she ran the bow across him as if to draw music from him. It was six years since he had become hers, and for a moment he was sundered, one part of him unknown to the other. He had been so in accord with that loving Anne, existence a reverberation from her and within her, that no pain had daunted him or no hardship impaired him. He had known this resonance, with harmony in it, the universe established in its meaning by a touch, proved from depths within and yet beyond him. He had never believed he could lose it. She approached, at another man's side, and Thomas saw them, attentive to himself.

Henry was thicker than on the bowling green, coarser, with a more brutal glance, yet still his King, royally poised.

Anne's face had changed. It was set and hard. The brilliance of the day, with the sea tossing and flinging light from its quick surface, made it difficult for Thomas to look into her. And, for himself, it was as painful as looking at a sharp fire. He dared not. He could not tell her anything, and a glance would tell her all. He dropped his eyes. But the loyalty she had starved, the prison he had outlived, told him she meant nothing to him any longer. His faith in her was gone, and it was faith that had worked his wild felicity.

They now embarked, to row out to the *Minion*. The multitudes of courtiers followed. When he knelt to them on board Anne was all grace and Henry grunted affectionately. So they stood on the broad deck, while the crew caught a little wind, took up anchor, and then forged grandly forward.

## VIII

BRILLIANT as it all was, Anne was angry with her reception.

"But the Queen of Navarre is unwell, sweetheart. They told us so," Henry apologized.

"She was ever my friend," answered Anne. "She is the King's sister, and he must have commanded her not to come."

"But he sent you gems you were pleased with. They welcome you. He comes to see you."

Anne sighed. Henry himself was to leave her, to visit Boulogne. She and her ladies had to remain in Calais.

"Let you amuse yourselves." Henry kissed her. "To leave you for an hour is pain to me." He was loath to go. Then she smiled.

"You may hear that the Pope forbids us to marry, and will excommunicate you."

"Then France, as well as ourselves, will break with him."

"Yea," said Anne ironically, "when King Francis had the estrapade built for heretics, to roast them like beef, down to the fire and up again."

This distressed Henry. She so often said these awkward things. A lady does not say such things.

"He is ready to stand by me."

"So do I hope," pleaded Anne against her lord's disfavour. "But I beg you, sir, ask if he intended to give his son to the Pope's niece, Catherine de Medici."

"Pooh!" said Henry. "He is too proud! He wishes the boy to marry us. He could not stoop to a Medici."

"They stooped before," said Anne drily. She knew King Francis to the bone. But since her lover wished to remain friends with Rome until the Pope made Cranmer his Archbishop, Anne could not press him.

Her own mind was troubled by the French tepidity. They never failed to urge Henry to marry her, and yet they treated her as his *amie*. Anne had no power to change this, but nothing could hide from her the jealous pride of the caste which had met at Blois and Amboise. She was herself a marchioness, and her state was in effect queenly, with maids-of-honour to stand round her when she dined, and dozens to serve, and her household constantly increasing. But her eyes were wide open to the French reception, and she said to her mother, "Methinks they deceive us about the Medici marriage."

"Of what import is it?" Lady Wiltshire asked wearily. Henry was so in love with Anne that she could not understand Anne's impatience.

"It will bind France to the Pope. What friends have we then?"

"But the Medici are princes."

"The Medici!" said Anne. "Cosimo was no more than great-grandfather Geoffrey Boleyn! He was but a burgess in Florence. And yet they choose them before us."

"You are here now," soothed her mother, "and King Francis is to be here for Sunday."

Anne's spirits quickly revived when the magnificent supper was served. She and her ladies were masked in gold and crimson, with veils of cloth and silver. And Anne danced with King Francis. He saw her unveiled by Henry, and then they sat and conversed in French.

No one was so light and charming as Francis. He gave Anne his sister's regrets with the most convincing words of her illness. He was touched by Anne's condolence for the loss of his mother. He could barely speak of it. Then, with a break in the cloud, he suddenly smiled and asked, "You are still quick with the needle, Mademoiselle?"

Anne smiled, somewhat bewildered.

"Poor Saint-Même," Francis said, "who was a lion at Pavia, he told me you were a needlewoman."

Anne and he had much to talk about. He had a husky throat and was rather worn, but with great verve and emphasis he assured her that he would put every pressure on the Pope. He knew exactly from Jean du Bellay what Anne desired to hear, and he urged her to go forward with absolute confidence. His face glowed as he said this, so that she utterly believed him.

Francis was no liar. Or, rather, the dishonesty of every word that he said about his son's approaching marriage to a Medici, was combined with an honest desire to serve Henry with the Pope. But he could not conceive that Henry would break with the Pope, or that England would become schismatic. He was, in other words, glad to encourage Henry to embroil himself with both Pope and Emperor by marrying Anne Boleyn. He himself could not imagine marrying her. He did not understand his royal brother. But he applauded the foible by which Henry was handing him one end of a rope and then putting a matrimonial noose around his neck. Once that noose was tightened by an actual ceremony, as Jean du Bellay convinced his master, Henry could never be friends with the Emperor. He must trot after the French.

So they danced to it. Henry petted Francis's children. He gave away enormous presents in jewellery. And, through it all, Anne and he kept hearing wedding bells.

# Chapter 20

**T**HE WEATHER WAS so bad at Calais, after Francis's departure, that Henry could not think of taking Anne to sea. It blew great guns, with tempest and thunder. Calais was badly crowded, though it had thousands of beds, but the King was not disappointed to have plenty of time to inspect its walls, its towers, its bulwarks and its bastions. Thomas Wyatt was one of the small group that went around with him, and, wild and cold as it was, with sheets of rain that slapped into them and deluged them, he could not deny his King a mighty tenacity of will. But when the inspections were over—and Henry smiled to recall the first night, in the Terouenne campaign twenty years before, when he had cheered his soldiers at three by time of day—then he changed to his handsomest surcoat and his finest shirts, to sit by Anne, to talk with her before the others, to dice and play cards with his favourites, or play indoor games with arrows or balls. Thomas was again one of the old circle, but not the most tortured husband could have seen in his face the least alarming gleam. He was too impersonal to amuse Anne. She looked at him, bit her lip and averted herself from him. Henry, in any case, could only leave her to exercise his body or scheme out plans for a Calais that one day could forge an English link with Boulogne.

But both he and Anne retained a happy impression of their late host.

The pride of man, indeed, has uncertainties in it. Anne had remembered Francis from before the Camp du Drap d'Or. No one had ever had more pride of life than he when she first saw him, a gleam in him as if he were a blade, with a tossing head and a plumed front, so that Europe might bow to him. Now she had seen an older Francis, still gracious and a king in port and glance, but with such bitten features, the grimness of Pavia and Madrid like scars in him— blemishes for which his pride had no philosophy. These he carried with him, tall man as he was, and the blade that once bent and sprang had lost its temper. Henry, by his side, was a two-handed sword. Yet even Henry and she had to become friends with disability.

"He looks fifty," Anne observed drily, "and he is younger than you, sir. His skin so flushed and angry-looking!"

"He told me how exceeding lovely he thought you," said Henry quietly.

"Lovely, forsooth? What were his words, in very truth?"

Henry wrinkled his forehead, and then repeated them. This cheered Anne, and both consoled themselves that, once the two French Cardinals reached Rome and spoke their lesson to the Pope, all these briefs commanding Henry to appear at Rome might be forgotten.

"Hath not Campeggio a say in it?" asked Anne earnestly. "You treated him well."

"Yea," said Henry, "and he'll have several thousand ducats to boot if he forward this matter of the new Archbishop."

For a year Henry had been trying to make gifts to the Papal Nuncio, Clement's ambassador in London. He liked to facilitate opinion.

Toward the middle of November the sea calmed. A thinness in the air, a tranquillity that went with a high light, made the passage promising, but then there came a mist. Since Henry had shipped his bedding, he could not linger. It cleared at midnight and by torches they took ship. Thomas wondered, as the dawn gave the sea the colours of a dove, how so terrible a power could lie so meek, and for an hour he steeped his gaze in its pale gravity.

Anne, meanwhile, pondered her state, and during the passage murmured to her lover that it might be wise to marry secretly at Dover.

"Wait, sweetheart," said Henry. "Let us not spoil the ship for a happorth of tar. Once we have word from Rome, then we'll marry at Greenwich."

Anne nodded. But would that be by December or January?

The middle of January, Henry surmised, to be safe. He loved her, and he then and there made up his mind that if all in the world went wrong, if the Pope showed firmness and the Emperor fury and the French timidity such as all might be possible, and if he were thus compelled to take back Queen Catherine, still he would keep Anne as his mistress. She was loving in these days, and Henry longed for Rome to comfort him.

## II

CROMWELL had the right priest for him, a monk named George Brown. Toward the middle of January a good word came from Henry's ambassadors in Rome. The French visit had frightened Pope Clement, and Cranmer would be confirmed.

Such good news entranced the King. He had the daybed removed from his armoury. Under the cover of those courtly entertainments that always followed on Christmas, he made a few preparations which could enlighten no one and arouse no curiosity. George Brown could flap into the Palace at any hour without being noticed. Lady Wiltshire lived there. And Cranmer was at hand to report of his embassy as a matter of course. No one else, except George Boleyn, was strictly necessary. Records could be signed that could at once be hidden, and perhaps destroyed. All that was essential were a few witnesses, a consecrated priest, a bridegroom and a bride.

Anne arose without paying any attention to the dawn. She let her ladies help her to dress as usual, with no great fuss, and she went to mass. Leaving to visit her mother for breakfast, the two ladies walked down the gallery and were no longer in sight. Her father and George followed, and then Madge Shelton came with George's wife. Their disappearance was of no particular import. And Henry, at that hour, often left his squires for the body.

A wedding takes ten or fifteen minutes, if the clergyman can resist making a sermon. George Brown stood in front of Anne, the

Marchioness of Pembroke, and King Henry, making the usual challenges about any just impediment, to which there was the usual silence. So he pronounced them man and wife.

The absence of the daybed from the armoury had removed one dumb and yet important witness. No one had remembered, under the Supreme Head of the Church who was now being married, to obtain a dispensation for him in view of his incest with Mary. But for a wedding which preceded a divorce that would have been pedantic. Neither Henry nor Anne cared for anything but the presence of the future Archbishop of Canterbury. Once his attentive eyes had dwelt on their clasp of hands, and once he had heard their answers, the seal of authority was set on an act which otherwise was less than a parish church would give to a hind and a milkmaid.

They were now married, with Greenwich utterly ignorant. One by one the little company broke up.

"Sweetheart," said Henry, "I'd give my life for you. I'd beg from door to door for you. Now I begin to live." And Anne buried herself in his protecting arms.

### III

HAD HENRY, in fact, been an able-bodied tramp, a big vagabond who begged from door to door, sleeping in the hedges, scratching himself for lice, his beard blown in the saucy wind and Anne at his heels, to be skelped at his pleasure and to be grappled for love, perhaps this exchange of rings might have brought them days and nights of joy. Then he could have stolen chickens and dodged gamekeepers with a humbler art. This picture he had of himself, a stedfast lover, was complicated by Kingship. Anne had not married him or wished to marry him; she had married a Throne. And a Throne is a slave-owner. Only by enslavement could she hope to keep both husband and monarch, and a slave like herself must possess that control over the species which produces a baby when wanted, and a baby of the right sex. The lover in Henry could forgive her for failing him, but the monarch in Henry was a creature of circumstance. This both of them chose to forget.

Busy as Thomas Cromwell was with the opening of parliament, this secret of the marriage, for which he had found George Brown, gave him more sense of mastery than he had ever before experienced. The King's was a magic name to him, and he knew himself an agent in the decisive act that the little armoury had hidden. Other men might revel in another kind of rendezvous, but Cromwell hugged this one as a proof he had come to power. The King trusted him, depended on him and looked to him. He went about his other work with this secret seething and bubbling inside him. Not Norfolk or Suffolk or Gardiner had contrived it, but his own stout self, with Cranmer tripping in his footsteps. Against such a marriage, the gates of Rome could not prevail. He had done something that two legates could not do, or the College of Cardinals.

But the secret, perfectly as it had been kept, had consequences not to be hidden, and within a few weeks neither Henry nor Anne could hold it any longer.

Her uncle, returned to Court, gave her a dig such as an old soldier permits himself. "Not married yet, my dear niece?"

"I am now as sure of my marriage," she retorted, "as I am of my own death."

That was enough. But when she gave Henry a banquet in her own chamber, richly hung with royal tapestries and the sideboard spangled with gold plate, the entire Court was on tiptoe. Suffolk had to come to it. Cromwell's Chancellor, Audley, was present, and a host of guests. Henry was unusually loud at table. He laughed a great deal, his wit smothered in his mirth. Anne, on his right, forced him to give some attention to her grandmother, the old Duchess of Norfolk, a matron who prodded through this new generation on a stick. Henry complied.

"You admire the gold plate, ma'am?" Henry blurted to the grandmother.

"Yes, yes, sir, very cold," said the duchess. "I feel it in my feet."

"I said the *plate*," shouted Henry, laughing, "the Cardinal's plate."

"Yes, methought the Cardinal's a lovely place. Such good water, sir. No lime in it. Water, I love water, even to drink it."

"She can't hear me, poor old lady," said Henry. "You try, sweetheart."

Anne tried.

"Oh, the *plate!* Dazzling! I have feasted my eyes on it the evening long."

"Has not the Marchioness got a grand dot?" laughed Henry.

"A grand what?"

"A grand dot," said Anne, very slowly.

"Is this plate part of her dot?" the Duchess demanded. "All this?" She looked so keen that her nose and her chin nearly met. The Norfolks were poor.

"All that we see," waved Henry grandly, down and across the loaded table, "and the rest of the plate"—he waved to the mounting shelves—"all hers. Is not that a rich marriage?"

"Porridge?" said the Duchess. She shook her head, laughing. "Much too good for porridge."

By this time the whole table, all the ushers, the sewers and waiters, the servants, and everyone behind the scene, knew more about the plate than the Duchess of Norfolk. It was part of the Lady's marriage portion. They saw Henry tipped up like a cornucopia, and spilling superb and massive gold.

"All belongs to the Lady," grieved one of the sergeants at arms. "Those were his whoreson words."

They had eaten and drunk so well that joviality had taken possession of Henry, and communicated itself to Anne. The banquet had gone glowingly; Queen Catherine had been orderd to vacate her old residence and to go farther away, and some undercurrent of celebration, of secret festivity, intoxicated the King. He was unusually exuberant and boastful.

Thomas Wyatt watched him with sombre eyes. He observed Anne's company with some detachment, and the malicious, the resentful and the treacherous seemed to him in high proportion.

Suddenly she made her way over to him. "Thomas!" she called.

It was a command, and in it there was more than that—there was an assertion of unforgotten intimacy.

He came to her as a courtier should. Her body was beautifully alive, her breasts bare almost, and her shoulders nervously naked, without the least fullness to take away their look of youth.

"Thomas," she gazed at him, "for three days I have craved apples. Never in all the days of my life have I craved them before." She watched him and gave a laugh, he was so solemn. "And know you what his Grace saith?" She gave a quick look at him, and pealed out laughing. "He says I am in the family way." Then she threw back her head and laughed wildly. "I say," she stopped, "'tis nothing of the sort." And then, with another sharp, hard laugh, she picked up her skirt and left the hall.

Before she was out of it, everyone ceased talking. What she had said to Thomas was heard far and wide.

He turned aside and himself left the hall as early as he could.

Now that it had come it made little difference. She was the King's. But this harshness in her was worse than his exile. No Greek had ever seen a broken temple with more pain. He could not blame her for anything, except that she was no longer there. Yet without her was a ruin.

When he reappeared Henry took him by the hand. "Come, Wyatt, you must join the dance."

Thomas held back, but Henry drew him on. "You are too sad. You must learn to play the fool at night."

"Yea," said Thomas; "but if I'd be thought wise in the daytime, sir?"

Then they laughed, and Thomas went to dance.

## IV

IT WAS USELESS to keep up the mystery any longer, for Anne was really going to have a child. The next day the King sent for her brother, and told him to prepare for France.

"This marriage of his boy to Catherine de Medici," frowned Henry. "You must show him the low extraction of the lady."

"And so will I, sir," said George.

Henry gave him a look. "Say that, according to his advice, and anxious for male issue to establish our Kingdom, we have—ah, we have proceeded effectually to the—the accomplishment of our marriage."

George bent his head to make a note.

"And now must he do his part, by God's blood. Say that to him. Say that as a true friend and brother he must maintain me against the Pope, as I would do for him. To our great dishonour the Pope names a day for me to appear before him! Ought a Prince to submit to the arrogance and ambition of an earthly creature whom God has made his subject? Ought a King to humble himself, and pay obedience to him over whom God has given him the superiority?"

Henry stopped in his stride to glare at George, who solemnly nodded repeated agreement. For a moment the King boiled, then, in a quieter tone, he said to George, "This would pervert the order God has ordained, and be as bad for him as me." Then lifting his voice again, he said, "I'd be glad if he'd despatch an agent to the Pope, and thus instruct him." Here he paused, and then enumerated various definite points on which King Francis was to follow out instructions.

George watched his master somewhat quizzically. After the banquet and the dance the King, his brother-in-law, was highly irritable, so George merely wondered how he could soften his commands for Henry's friend and brother, who also had his bad mornings.

"If I be now the King's brother," he said to himself as he hurried to the treasurer, "and if King Francis be also the King's brother, then must King Francis and I be also brothers. That is a sacred thought."

Before he reached Cromwell he encountered Thomas Wyatt. "I go to Cromwell for a thousand pounds," he grinned.

"What ho!" said Thomas. "And whither away?"

"To quiz my good brother Francis, to plaster the chinks in our loving friendship, to bemoan the low-born Medici, and to mock the Great Devil."

## V

GEORGE'S MOOD was never in key with the seriousness around him, but Anne made up for it. Once her marriage was known, Catherine's pretensions to be Henry's wife became intolerable as never before, and she insisted that Catherine must yield to her the sole title of Queen of England.

"But," said Chapuys, who was never afraid of Henry, "begging you to take this in good part, since your Highness despises what men say, have you no fear of God?"

"I have, I have," said Henry. "God and my conscience are on very good terms."

"It is a strange case," sighed Chapuys, "after five and twenty years of marriage."

"Not as long as that," Henry rapped back. It was actually twenty-four years. "And if the world find this divorce a marvel, as you say, still more should it marvel at a Pope dispensing without the power to do so."

"But you have a daughter, sir, endowed with all imaginable virtue and goodness. Nature points to her as your heiress!" And Chapuys, first under the rule of Margaret of Austria, and now under the rule of Mary of Hungary, knew that a woman could rule as well as a man.

"I know better than my daughter," retorted Henry. "They put her up to this. I wish to have children."

"Wish!" said Chapuys quietly. "But can you be sure of having them?"

Henry turned white with anger. "Am I not a man like other men? Am I not a man like other men? Am I not a man like other men?" His brow was pearled with sweat, and he glared at Chapuys so wildly that the ambassador quickly said, "I have no reason to say the opposite. I am not privy to your secrets."

Henry grunted, and collected himself. "You'll soon have proof to the contrary, then," he muttered.

"But," said Chapuys, "you cannot divorce the Queen because of your late brother. You yourself have told me that she was a virgin when she came to you."

"Ph!" exploded Henry. "I only said that in fun. When a man is dining well and jesting, he says a good many things that are not true. Now, have I squared you? Now are you paid off? What more do you want?"

Seeing his humour restored, Chapuys did not pursue him further. He was as much a gentleman of the old school as was Sir John Hackett, the Irishman who was his vis-à-vis at the Court in the Low Countries. He had reverence in him, was keen and deep and scholarly, with a high sense of Queen Catherine's dignity, with compassion for Princess Mary and an implacable contempt for the Concubine. He could scarcely keep his temper until he reached his barge, and temper was bad for him because he was somewhat heavy and gouty. He only wished the Emperor would declare war on England, to bring Henry to his senses. His heart bled for Queen Catherine, and for Princess Mary, now a bastard.

The Duke of Norfolk, observing his distress, managed to halt him.

"It is all true?" Chapuys asked him. "They mean to strip her Grace of her title and honour?"

"So I fear," Norfolk said.

"And the good Princess?"

"The Lady says she'll make her eat humble pie. She'll make her one of her maids and marry her to a varlet."

"What!" Chapuys darkened. "Wait till his Majesty the Emperor learns this."

"It may mean war?" Norfolk started, his bloodshot eyes fixed on Chapuys.

"The insult to his House cries for it," Chapuys roundly declared. "I cannot answer for it."

Norfolk looked after him, then entered the Palace and went to Henry.

"Yea," said Henry with brutal alacrity, "I desired to see you. You and my lord of Suffolk must go to Ampthill. Tell the Queen not to trouble any more about me. Tell her I have taken another wife. You mark my words. Another wife. Her property is her own, but she must give up a title that was never hers. She is to be called Duchess, or Princess of Wales. This you must do now."

Neither Norfolk nor Suffolk relished this duty. And when they had greeted Queen Catherine they simply told her that Henry had been married secretly for some time, from which they went to other topics, and left it to her chamberlain, Lord Mountjoy, to break the news about her title.

"As long as I live," Catherine answered, "I'll call myself Queen."

"After Easter his Highness cannot pay your expenses here."

"If he grudges me that," she answered, "I'll go wherever he wish. And if he deny me that, and I lack for food, I'll go and beg for the love of God."

"That," said the chamberlain, "is not his wish."

"No," said Catherine, "he is not ill-natured. It is this Anne who has put him into his perverse and wicked humour. She'll never cease until she has seen the end of me, as she saw the end of the Cardinal."

Lord Mountjoy did no more, since Holy Week was approaching, and with it so much that Norfolk and Suffolk had warned him of.

## VI

ANNE'S FEVERISH DESIRE to break Catherine's will was far from personal. Around Catherine, so long as she remained staunch, gathered not only such ardent advocates as Bishop Fisher and the old nobility but everyone who favoured the imperial connection, and the Emperor himself. The rival to the child in her womb was Princess Mary, and except for her own immediate family, for a few courtiers like Francis Bryan, for the Archbishop elect and the bishops who obeyed Henry, and for such members of the household as Will Brereton, Harry Norris, Francis Weston and some others, the vast majority of the common people and the great majority of the Council were against her. Thomas Cromwell had quietly and adroitly placed reliable men in strategic positions, hard and smooth men who could operate the turntable. But had Anne Boleyn not been as brave as a lion, and had Henry not been baited by the supremacy of the Church and the sure prospect of an heir, the constant assaults by Chapuys, speaking with the might of the Emperor behind him, would have halted this astonishing marriage on which they had set their obstinate hearts.

Like an insignificant hill on which two armies clash, this marriage brought out every resource of the Papacy in England, in Flanders, in Spain, in France and Italy. Every assault they launched shocked Anne Boleyn, but neither she nor Henry attempted to retreat. Day by day, hour by hour, they rallied to the last assault which was to pierce the air with proclamation. Had Anne not been sure to become a mother, Henry might even now have forsaken her. He passed through many a flurry that gave her a pang. But the heir to the Throne was granted, and all the King's men and all the King's horses were harnessed for triumph. She could be crowned as soon as Cranmer, named archbishop, obeyed Henry's orders for the divorce.

On Easter Saturday Anne went to mass in royal state, loaded with jewels and clothed in cloth of gold frieze. Trumpeters went before her. Her train was borne by young Margaret Howard, whom Thomas Wyatt was so fond of, the maid who was to marry Henry's boy the

Duke of Richmond. Sixty young ladies had been assembled for a suite, and they heard solemn prayers for Queen Anne. Henry stood by, after church, watching faces more closely than on a New Year's Day, when gifts were offered in person.

"Go speak to her," he told Lord Derby. "Say a word to the Queen," he ordered Lord Rutland. Under his eyes, they knelt to Anne, and in every face she read the reluctant or the bewildered soul. Behind her, in her own mind, were Cranmer and Cromwell. Behind her was the King. What they said in Lancashire or Lincoln, she was not afraid of. She'd tell Percy to join the conspirators, if needs be, to learn the worst they planned against her. Her prowess was in the unborn son.

The coronation was the next stage, once Cranmer was installed, and that made an anxious month of May. One thing she desired bitterly, to have Thomas at her side.

"Poor Sir Harry is too feeble to be ewerer," she said to the King.

"Then let Thomas act for him," said Henry. "He'll be well as ewer-bearer."

This command she transmitted to Thomas. A hundred commands went out, so that London rippled with them. But instead of acquiescence, more grumbling came than in the Cardinal's time. A congregation stumped out of Austin Friar's when George Brown prayed publicly for Queen Anne. The people cheered Queen Catherine. A huge mob of women, with men among them dressed as women, tried to waylay Anne when she ventured to take dinner at a villa up the river. The Steelyard promised that, if there was a coronation, London would see surprises.

But all this had its element of bluster. Henry did not send troops to the city. He had few. But he told Cromwell what to do. The haberdasher who was Mayor assembled the trades at their various guildhalls, and commanded them, on pain of the King's indignation, not to murmur at his marriage, to prevent their apprentices from so doing, and to stifle their wives. Meanwhile the trades received big orders for the great day, were told by the King to prepare pageants, and Cromwell greased the wheels. The city submitted and went to work.

"God loves this marriage," said one Londoner, "the Queen is so soon with child."

"Nay, not so," said another. "The Pope will curse all Englishmen, the Emperor will invade the realm."

But the imperials were also dealt with. Bishop Fisher was taken in custody to Bishop Gardiner's house. Tunstal and Clark and Gardiner presented themselves to Thomas More at Chelsea, to give him a large sum to buy a robe for the coronation. The money he took with a smile, and then told them of a martyred virgin. With him, he said, it would be just the same. "They may devour me, but God being my good Lord, I will provide that they shall never deflower me."

The bishops who heard him went thoughtfully on their way. By letting Henry get rid of Catherine, they were letting him get rid of Rome.

And the first riddance was now a matter of days. Gardiner and Clark were to go with two other bishops to a little place called Dunstable, to open a divorce court with Cranmer, and Henry had finally pressed his will into the new Archbishop like a seal into warm wax. Here was no Cardinal Wolsey, with another order of thinking than that of the national state, another political orientation and another heritage. Cranmer strove, in his first dealings as Archbishop, to assert the Church's will against the King's. Henry soon dictated an attitude to him that left no doubt who was the master. "We being your King and Sovereign, do recognize no superior on earth but only God, and not being subject to the laws of any earthly creature, yet because ye be under us, by God's calling and ours," so he did not refuse Cranmer's "humble request" to end the Great Matter, but "inclined to his humble petition."

Francis Bryan headed the trio who summoned the lady Catherine to come over to Dunstable. She spurned them. So her marriage, after the hearing of evidence, was in a few days declared null.

## VII

THE NEXT TEN DAYS were lived by Anne in a fever. The divorce came on May 23. The ceremonies were to begin on May 29, a Thursday, at one in the afternoon, and to go on until the end of the banquet on Sunday. The ceremony was to be as gorgeous, as traditional, as detailed

and impressive as Church and State could make it. Anne had arrived
at the state of emotion where the procession of events is itself so
dramatically ordained that merely to keep pace with it is an exaltation.
All the officers of the State had submerged their judgment on the
divorce. They were now nobles who had inherited certain functions,
and to discharge them was nothing personal, it was laden with a sublimity that lifted them from their own lives to a share in a greater
span than the individual's, a span of centuries which, like the rim of a
rainbow, spreads luminosity against the black and bridges the horizon.
The Duke of Norfolk claimed to be Earl Marshal, the Earl of Oxford
to be chamberlain, Lord Lisle to be panter, the Earl of Arundel to be
butler, Sir Harry Wyatt to be ewerer, and the Duke of Suffolk, for
the time being, to be constable. These were friends and enemies, but
it was not Anne Boleyn whom they served; it was a woman whom the
King had chosen. Much as they disputed the actual woman, who had
no mystery about her, who was a girl about the Court, one of the
Boleyns and one of themselves, they still yielded to the overpowering
sentiment of office, and began kicking their legs into new hose, patting
themselves into new doublets, cursing the tailors, and worrying about
the order at dinner. Palfreys, canopies, the mace, the litter, the white
lace on the left sleeve of a Knight of the Bath—all this became of
primary importance. And Anne had to think about her hair.

In some amazing way, with Cromwell to coach Sir Stephen Peacock,
the haberdasher, with Cranmer and the other bishops to put their
heads together—Cranmer had rhythm worthy of Westminster Abbey
—with Henry's choristers to rise to their purest flight, and with all
craftsmen to turn their hand to this glorious ritual, something could
come of it to which Cambridge as well as Oxford, St. Paul's as well as
the Tower, the guilds and the bargees, the Flemish and French and
Italians in London, the armoured knights, the trumpeters, the cooks
and the artists in marzipan, could one and all contribute. This was
not Anne Boleyn's coronation. It was England crowning Anne Boleyn.
Since May and June were both to see it, to waft this ceremony from
Greenwich to the Tower, and march it from the Tower to Westminster, only malice could mar it. It was destined to be ideal.

Somewhere, under Anne's febrile energy of preparation, there was
a throbbing sense of triumph. Life had taught her to trust nothing

completely. She had little faith. But since Henry loved her so much as to offer to marry her, her pride demanded this assurance. It demanded a crown on her head. Within that head there was little conceit and no great vanity, but there was an astounding, undiminished pride, and to have come to the Throne, to have England at her feet, flooded her with a passionate exultation. Banners and music, sunshine and bells—she went from her chamber to the water-gate at Greenwich half-way between tears and laughter, to have this dream come true. There were nearly two hundred boats in the river, and several hundred smaller boats. Barge nosed after barge with streamers flying from them, shawms and trumpets, dragons casting fire, terrible monsters making hideous noises, and pennons wavering in the wind.

From Greenwich, in half an hour, she arrived at the Tower, with Henry to kiss her at the postern by the waterside, while she turned back again to thank the Mayor and the citizens with many goodly words.

Two nights in the Tower, in the chambers she had inspected with Henry, prepared Anne for the great procession through London, and then, on the final day, for the coronation itself. Her pride had been injured so deeply in the six long years the divorce had taken that she was sensitive to the humiliations that might be offered to her, and ready to resent them. She was still childish enough to feel it unjust that she should not be accepted, since the King accepted her, and even one covered head or a long stony stare could hurt her. Her nature was so impetuous, in this respect, that she treasured the injury like a naughty child. And yet she, who had inflicted on Catherine this tragic injury of the coronation, rode forward, buoyed by excitement, against the barriers of welcome that had been raised for her, barriers that fell as she approached. It was the first of June, late in the afternoon. The sun shone on her litter of white cloth of gold. Two white palfreys, covered in white damask, led it slowly forward, and four knights bore a white canopy over her. She was clad in white tissue, furred with ermine, and her black hair hung down, with a coif on her head rich with jewels.

That night, having secretly escaped to Henry by barge from York Place, he and she talked it over. And in every tavern in London on that Saturday night, in every home, the crowds also talked it over.

"What thought you?" one Spaniard asked another.

"The city itself was well enough, but I saw many caps on heads and heard but few tongues."

"I heard them call the French ambassador, 'whoreson knave, French dog.'"

"And her fool cried out, 'You have all scurvy heads and dare not uncover.'"

These were the grumbles that came from Catherine's friends, though Henry had exempted the Spaniards in London from a special coronation tax. But on the morrow, at Westminster Abbey, Anne was crowned by the new Archbishop with every grace and every splendour imaginable to priest or knighthood. Catherine's friends said she had a wart, and that the crown did not fit her. But by that time, having been anointed, Anne longed only to find a resting-place, and, being five months with child, she was glassy-eyed with fatigue.

There was a moment, at the banquet, when Thomas poured rose-water for her, that his grave glance recalled her to another life, a life where she had been young. But by this time she was no more fit to think or feel than a soldier who has marched in broiling heat. Thomas's heart was touched by her. She was fit only to lie down.


## VIII

THE IMMENSE and squandering stupidity of life had begun to torture Thomas Wyatt. He and Anne were the same age, thirty, but he recognized the forces against her, and he saw that no matter what she did, she must suffer. He was good enough, inside, to suffer with her, but how terrible these forces were, and how beyond control, he was only about to learn.

Word was brought to him by an usher that Thomas Cromwell would like to see him in a field beyond the garden.

"Are you free on the morrow?" asked Cromwell, eyeing him hard.

"Free as a lark."

"You mind John Frith?"

"None better. I saw him taken to the Tower."

"Well, he goes to another place. I want you to go with him."

"I, Master Cromwell?"

"At the new Archbishop's behest. And hear my instructions." He gave Thomas minute instructions. "You will do this for me?"

"That I will," said Thomas grimly.

Cromwell held out his hand. "Well said, and fare you well."

On the morrow, with his own servant at his heel, Stephen Simmons from Allington, Thomas rode to the Tower of London, where his own father had been imprisoned. He presented at letter to Sir William Kingston, with the King's name to it, and the young man John Frith was brought out and delivered to him.

A small boat took them up the river, and on the way up Thomas told Frith who he was and that he had known William Tyndale.

"Master Cromwell much favours you," he said. "You are a learned man, and now towards the felicity of your life, young in years, old in knowledge, and of great forwardness."

Frith hung his head, with his eyes on the bottom of the boat. He looked very faintly ironic.

"You are like," continued Thomas, "to be a most worthy member of this realm."

"But not for long, mayhap." Frith's glance met Thomas's stedfastly.

"That depends on yourself, Master Frith. Neither Cromwell nor my Lord of Canterbury will ever permit you to suffer any shame if you will somewhat be advised by their counsel——"

One of Frith's hands moved impatiently, but he dropped it from the wrist.

"Otherwise, if you stand stiff, it is not possible to save your life."

"I know that."

"You cannot know how good friends you have," Thomas rejoined earnestly. "But for as like as you have good friends, so you have mortal foes and enemies."

Frith nodded. "That I believe, friend. I thank you kindly. But on the presence of the body of Christ in the sacrament I cannot hide my opinion, not even were it to expose me to death."

They stopped at Lambeth.

"We must walk to Croydon," said Thomas, "so let us have meat, and then on."

As they went forward, Thomas fell to walking with Stephen Simmons.

"Steve," he said, "you understand all this?"

"In faith, right well, Master Thomas."

"Then we'll tell him to take to these woods on the left, and so into Kent, while we'll give the alarm and start the man hunt to the right."

"God's word," said Steve, " 'tis well devised."

Thomas strode ahead and joined his prisoner. He explained what they had agreed on.

John Frith lost power of speech for a while. He was one of those candid, lean, clear men whose dark eyes are wells of faith. He worshipped God's word, and he worshipped William Tyndale. A short time before he had married in Antwerp, and his life was there. He knew Greek, could recite the Iliad, and had great work ahead of him.

His face was impassive. Only his Adam's apple moved. Then he turned to Thomas. "Before, I tried to escape," he said, "to go on with my Greek, and to enjoy my liberty, according to St. Paul's counsel. But now, if I should now start aside, and run away, I should run from my God, and from the testimony of His Holy Word—worthy, then, of a thousand hells."

"But these bishops!" said Thomas. They all three stood in the road, with woods on both sides of them.

"I most heartily thank you both," said Frith, "but I beseech you, bring me to the place appointed, else I will go thither all alone."

Thomas had failed. At Croydon Cranmer examined him, and later Gardiner and two others. And just as the Spaniards had been favoured during coronation, so the heresy-hunters were favoured after coronation. On July 4, Frith and another young man were lashed back to back and burnt to death at Smithfield.

"Fear not threatening," wrote the ardent Tyndale to him. "Neither be overcome of sweet words. Let Bilney be a warning to you. Let not their vizor beguile your eyes. Let not your body faint. He that endureth to the end shall be saved. If the pain be above your strength, remember, 'Whatsoever ye shall ask in My name, I will give it you.' And pray to your Father in that name, and He will cease your pain, or shorten it."

Lutheran beasts, Thomas More called Tyndale and his friends. But Frith had died without a word, before Tyndale's exhortations came to England.

## IX

PASSIONS so strong as this, moving both orthodox and heretic, could hardly be kept under the surface. The old guard was fighting to keep England loyal to the Pope, within the law, and not a day went past without fervid assurances to Chapuys from the old nobility that they hated the Concubine, and stood by Queen Catherine, and were ready to do anything or almost anything to go back to the old faithful ways.

Against these combinations, which in so small a society came easily to the surface, Henry and Cromwell had employed the weapons of the law. The Commons and the Lords had been bent to their will. Whatever use was made of torture, the fires at Smithfield, fines, imprisonment or browbeating, no explosion had taken place of any consequence. Cromwell had been so sharp and so assiduous that the ugly possibilities had all been foreseen, and England so skilfully manipulated that the anchor, so to speak, had been lifted before the ship had given the least quiver of disturbing motion. Cranmer had gone on aboard, silent and meek, the ideal pilot, and even now Henry held a rope to connect him with Rome. Meanwhile, when Chapuys came to remonstrate, Henry was blustering. Furious as he pretended to be with the Pope for the thunder that had followed the coronation, he renewed the pressure on Catherine, and prayed fervently for a male heir, the sign of God's approval.

There was no nonsense about the pressure put on Catherine. In every parish church in England a notice was hung up to say she was no longer Queen but the Lady Catherine of Spain, to be called Princess Dowager (Arthur's dowager), and this had to be brought home to her. Days of wrangling brought forth her old defiance. She strongly disavowed, and with horror, any desire or intention of bringing war to England, but she stuck to her ground as Henry's wife.

She had to receive the Council while she lay down, unwell and lame, but when she saw "Princess Dowager" on their document she vehemently drew a pen through it. One of them suggested she could not bear a lesser title.

"I would rather be a poor beggar's wife," she answered, "and be sure of Heaven, than Queen of all the world, and stand in doubt thereof by reason of my own consent. I stick not so for vainglory, but because I know myself the King's true wife."

"You are his subject," objected Gardiner, "and must obey his law."

"You call me the King's subject! I was his subject while he took me for his wife. But if he take me not for his wife, I came not into this realm as merchandise, nor to be married to any merchant. Nor do I continue in the place but as his lawful wife, and not as his subject to live under his dominion otherwise."

They all knew she could not escape. She was Henry's prisoner.

"Were your ladyship to depart, it would stir strife and cause danger to the realm."

"I have always demeaned myself well and truly toward the King," she said. "And if it can be proved that either in writing to the Pope, or any other, I have either stirred or procured anything against his Grace, I am content to suffer for it. I have done England little good, and I should be sorry to do it any harm."

"But to agree now would prevent much harm, my lady."

"If I should agree, I should slander myself, and confess to have been the King's harlot for twenty-four years."

"That has been determined at Dunstable."

"By what subtle means, I cannot tell—here, within the King's realm, before a man of his own making, the Bishop of Canterbury, no person impartial, I think. And for the place, I think the place had been more impartial had it been judged in Hell. No truth can be suffered here! Whereas the devils themselves, I suppose, do tremble to see the truth in this cause so sore oppressed."

The delegation left Ampthill in the same overwhelmed spirit as it had done some years earlier. Catherine neither flinched nor raged. She was as lofty as she was simple.

Cromwell walked away, a strange look in those hard eyes. Then he glanced at Gardiner, and his whole face was a sheet of wonder. "Nature injured her in not making her a man," he said. "She would have surpassed in fame all the heroes of history."

Then, at Greenwich, he advised Henry to cut her revenue into two portions, the larger to be administered by the Crown. This would allow even closer surveillance.

## X

So EAGER for a male child was Henry that he consulted the astrologers. They gave him the good word. So did a witch who made her way to him. Quite a few odd people had inner knowledge of nature's working, and Henry, half-shamefaced and highly credulous, looked down on them smiling and gave them a coin.

A rich and most triumphant bed, once given in ransom by the Duke of Alençon, was set up for Anne to labour in. Henry was very restless, made big plans for jousts and rejoicings, and kept his physicians on their toes.

She began to have pains on September 6. The Duke of Norfolk was out of England, gone to France on embassy, but the old Duchess was at Greenwich, and all the family.

Henry was so nervous, and Anne so nervous, that they hurt each other without meaning to. She complained that he was away from her so much.

"You are after another woman already," she said, half-bitterly and half-jokingly.

Henry's white eyelashes flitted up and down. "What if I were? What if I were? You ought to shut your eyes, and take it as others of higher station have taken it. I could humble you again more quickly than I exalted you, but you seem to forget it."

This outburst convinced Anne she was right. She buried her head in the pillows, and shook with sobs.

With the redoubling of her pains, however, on September 7, they all crowded into her bedchamber, until it was as full as a barge. All five physicians were on hand, with Anne's French maid, and her own ladies, Mother Butts as midwife inside the curtains of the bed, and her own mother, her father, the Duchess, and Henry, while Anne, her eyes dazzlingly bright, her skin rosy, strove madly to endure it. A sickening sweetness came from perfumes and the flowers that were trampled into the rushes. Hippocras and comfits and wafers stood on a table for the noble visitors. Various religious relics had been brought to Anne during the morning. And until the end everyone in the chamber begged and prayed it would be a boy.

At the very moment she was delivered, Dorset and Exeter, of the blood royal, were inside the curtain to make sure that this was the child of her flesh, and then Mother Butts, severing the cord, took the baby on her ample knees, wrapping her in a towel.

So strong had been the Boleyns' desire, and Henry's desire, to have this a male heir, that disappointment was not to be concealed. Henry looked at Mother Butts, who was solely occupied with the mite on her lap. Hers was such a good, competent and honest face, that to hurt the King was not in her power, but she opened the towel and looked at him with large pity.

Henry wrinkled his forehead, and winced. But his pride enabled him to mutter a word to everyone who murmured his joy.

Anne's own pride sustained her. She had failed him, and her enemies would gloat. But as the tidings overtook all the preparations for bonfires and the rest, and quietened the rejoicing to female dimensions, Henry came behind the curtain of the great bed. She was pale and small by this, and at the dolour in her face, the helplessness, his heart opened. He leaned to her with tenderness, while tears came to his eyes. "I would rather beg from door to door than forsake you."

# Chapter 21

THREE DAYS AFTER the birth Anne surrendered her baby for the christening. She was to be called Elizabeth, after Henry's mother and Anne's mother, and the ceremony was to be at Greenwich.

It was a cool September day, but ritual was no less buoying to the Court than when Anne had been crowned. They knew their parts, these gentle and subtle folk who were not so much themselves as the living kernel of their class. Anne had not captured them, far from it, and Henry resented this with a violence which they, since he himself barely suspected it, could hardly grasp, but for appearance sake, and for the sake of the realm, they filled their roles. They set forward from the hall, through the walled passage to the Friary, with arras on the walls and fresh green rushes under their feet.

It was a striking procession of gaudy costumes and proud personages. First, two by two, came the aldermen in crimson and the lesser notables. Then Lord Exeter, Henry's familiar since childhood, bore a taper of virgin wax. The Marquis of Dorset bore the salt. The chrisom robe, white for innocence, was in the hands of Lady Mary Howard, and the oils were borne by the Earl of Essex. So they trooped from the hall. The old Duchess carried her great-grandchild in a mantle of purple velvet, with George and two of Norfolk's brothers and Lord Hussey holding the canopy, with Norfolk and Suffolk to either side, while Anne's father and the Earl of Derby and Countess of Kent held up the Duchess's long train.

This nameless baby, three days old, was still vaguely blinking at the great change of scene she was encountering. But she was in firm hands. Cranmer was to be her godfather, the old Duchess and the old Marchioness of Dorset her godmothers, and Anne could ask for none better.

The child was halted at the door and then taken to a little enclosure in the body of the church, made to protect her from draught, with a pan of fire in it, and there she was unwrapped for the ceremony. The silver font was raised on three steps, with a rail around it, a square red satin canopy over it, and Anne's ladies with aprons and towels to wipe away every speck of dust.

The baby was soon christened. Her confirmation followed at the altar. Then, in a ringing voice, Garter King of Arms cried out, "God, of His infinite goodness, send prosperous life and long, to the high and mighty Princess of England, Elizabeth!" The trumpets blew. And five hundred torches were lighted to attend Elizabeth into the Palace.

The mayor and aldermen had come to Greenwich for it. Norfolk and Suffolk thanked them for attending, they toasted their new Princess in the cellar, and then went to their barge.

## II

SUCH was Anne's achievement, a drawn battle in the first campaign, but she was barely thirty and Henry, busy as he was, showered her with devotion.

He had run into a shocking assault on his nerves within the year. Before he took Anne to Calais, a firm young nun had so demanded audience at Greenwich that she had succeeded in reaching him.

"An angel sends me," she declaimed. "If you marry this woman, the vengeance of God will fall upon you. Amend your life! Take back your Queen! Destroy these folks of new opinion, the works of the new learning! Take none of the Pope's right!"

Henry had given her ear, and when she came a second time, "I am commissioned by God," she cried with lustrous eyes, actually clutching Henry's arm. "It is revealed to me that within a month after your new marriage, you will be destroyed!"

Her name was Elizabeth Barton, a nun from Kent, who had formerly been a servant. She had been hearing voices. She had had visions. Angels came to her in her trances.

Who had put her up to it? Cromwell sniffed treason. He now found that Sir Thomas More had seen her, with Bishop Fisher and several monks. Lady Exeter was also brought into it.

So soon after the christening, where her husband had borne the taper of virgin wax, this was overwhelming. Henry himself confronted her.

"I am a woman," she pleaded, "fragile and brittle, easily seduced and brought to abusion and light belief."

It was the very nature of woman, but Henry forgave her. Sir Thomas More, having sternly warned the nun in writing against touching prince's affairs, was not to be tripped by Cromwell. But two monks, and the nun, and feeble Bishop Fisher were at once brought to prison.

While Cromwell spread his net to catch the imperials, he had no hesitation about intriguing with Chapuys.

"Come to me at Waltham," he muttered to Chapuys, "when we are hawking to-morrow."

They had something in common, this wily Fleming and the Englishman who had been a wool stapler in Middelburg.

"Why don't you make your master take the Queen back?" demanded Chapuys coolly. "Most of the Council wish it."

"It's a little soon," smiled Cromwell. "A fortnight after the christening."

"But many Kings have done it."

"Who, for instance?"

"Oh, Lothair, Philip I, Philip III."

"Wait," said Cromwell. He always had paper with him. "I'll note them." He began, but Chapuys stopped him.

"I have the histories, I'll send them."

"Good," said Cromwell, "that may be useful. And the second wives?"

"Adulteresses. That speaks for itself."

"Ah, very good," Cromwell laughed. "That would be neat. But deeply grateful as I am to you, and glad as I am you trust me, it is much too difficult at present."

"Why is that?" asked Chapuys.

"The marriage is too fresh. He is too much in love with her."

"But later on?"

"Ah," said Cromwell, "the time may come. For my part, Master Ambassador, since it would be so easy for the Emperor to make war on this kingdom, and even to destroy it, I am simply watching for the occasion to set things right. But, we can ruin everything. We must go slow. We must be careful and take time."

"But you?"

"Of course. But time, time!"

That was toward the end of September. Henry was extremely busy since Norfolk's return from France, and scarcely able to leave Greenwich. He was able to go hawking at Waltham for a few days, but that was just a chance, in the fine weather. On October 6, since he wished Anne to amuse herself, he sent her to Whitehall attended by Harry Norris.

"Take the dear little spaniel," he said. It was Lord Lisle's spaniel, which had fallen in love with Anne. Harry Norris carried it.

"You must tell my lord of Lisle that I would be bold on him," said Henry, "but I do like it so well!"

"Yea," said his squire, "and it shall please him mightily to give it to your Highness."

Cromwell saw them leave, Anne's first outing, with her ladies and her gentlemen.

"There they go," he noted, "to Westminster." Before they had settled into the barge, he heard Anne cry, "Send for Mistress Madge!"

"Nay," Norris bowed, "not when you be ready."

"Lord," said Anne, "you are not so very faithful," and she gave a little laugh. She had sparkled prettily with the adventure of going up the river again.

Cromwell watched them with as cool a smile as ever a gambler gave horses led to the starting-place.

"Give that one a chance," he thought. He heard music from the departing barge. "What the devil!" he listened. "Music and that wasp-waist with the spaniel! Every penny he had from the Cardinal he owes to me, and he treats me like dirt!"

## III

HENRY DELIGHTED IN THE BABY, and Anne was in high favour. But Gardiner's first despatch from Marseilles, where King Francis and the Pope were conferring, completely shattered his mood. He took the despatch, crumpled it with an oath, burst into a stream of denunciation. "I am betrayed!" he shouted, livid with anger. All the tension that had slumbered since Elizabeth's birth now burst into his veins like a poison.

Pope Clement, whose memories of Bishop Gardiner were not happy, had been in a very different mood at Marseilles in warm October from his shivering and cowering sessions in icy Orvieto. He was at Marseilles to marry his niece to Francis's son. Anne de Montmorency, Francis's constable, was a bulwark. And here was a bumptious little priest called Bonner, Francis Bryan in a state of ribald cynicism, and Gardiner who had been one of the bishops at Dunstable. The Pope did not fulminate. He did not want a schism. But the time had gone when he could be hectored. Sentence against Henry in the divorce suit had already been pronounced adversely, and Cranmer's appointment had been annulled. The French, desperately anxious to keep Henry a Catholic, proposed to have the suit re-opened at Avignon, but Gardiner and Bonner were rough.

"A General Council!" said the Pope. "O good Lord!" He heard Henry's arguments, rolling and unrolling his handkerchief. He groaned, moaned and stirred uneasily. He could barely keep his temper.

King Francis himself flared out. "If my brother," he said to Gardiner, "wish to have the Pope for him, as he told me himself he did, how can the Pope be made such a fool as to hold his peace at a sentence given by the Archbishop of Canterbury, therein confessing himself to be no Pope?"

Francis tackled Gardiner with a heat straight from the Midi.

"We told you of all this," said Gardiner.

"Ye told me of it," said Francis, "but I understood not so far as I do

now. Ye require a Council, and that the Emperor desires. I go to bring
the Emperor from the Pope, and ye to drive him to him! Can my
brother call a Council alone?" He flashed a knifing look into Gardiner.
"Ye have clearly marred all." He threw out his hands. "Why did I
ever meddle with it? I would not for all the gold in France be caught
in this."

Here was the impasse. The French said, "Be allied to France through
the Holy See," and then the Emperor could do them no harm. But
Henry, so long as Elizabeth was not called illegitimate, cared nothing
for the Holy See. And now he saw little chance of getting the Pope to
admit that his children by Anne could be deemed legitimate.

He did not really enjoy Christmas.


## IV

ANNE TOOK EVERY CHANCE, just the same, to sharpen Henry's mind on
the dangers from the Papists in England.

"That lady," said Chapuys to Lord Exeter, "may not nurse her own
baby, but she is the wet-nurse of heresy."

Henry went out to see the baby at Hatfield, and Anne took great
pains to keep him from any contact with Princess Mary. Her establishment had been broken up. Beaulieu had been given to George,
Anne's brother, and Mrs. Shelton, Anne's aunt, had charge of Mary at
Hatfield. She was the stern heiress of an injustice, seventeen years old,
and just as brave as Anne herself. As her father was leaving Hatfield,
Mary left her spinet and came to the balcony. Henry and all his squires
saluted her; and his eyes filled with tears, several days later, when he
mentioned her to the French ambassador. Still, he agreed with Anne
that she was wilful and obstinate, she called herself princess, and he
had no patience with her. Anne herself, visiting the baby a little later,
vainly coaxed Mary to leave her suite and salute the Queen.

"I know no Queen but my mother," she sent back word. And Anne's
temper made her wish to beat her.

But it consoled her, in the midst of Papist irritations, to find that
Henry liked Thomas Wyatt's company. And, with her gravest and
most queenly manner, she made him join them in the Queen's chamber before the blazing fire, when they had a chance to talk naturally.

"What think you, Wyatt," began Henry. "Were we to take over these naughty religious houses? Would it stir up tumult?"

"Among the people, sir?"

"Not stringers and weavers, but gentlemen, the men of your own stripe?"

"Times are hard with them. What if the rook's nest were buttered, sir?"

"So Cromwell says," Henry grunted. "I could cuff that rascal, yet often he confounds me. He is at one with you at many a point. You even renounce the sacrament of penance, Wyatt?" Henry had heard it from Anne. He glanced at her, but she kept watching Thomas.

"Heavens," exclaimed Thomas, "that a man cannot repent him of his sins without the Pope's leave!"

"Nay, nay, you make too light of it," frowned Henry. "By God's blood, I forgo not repentance."

"Nor I, sir," said Thomas. "I jest not, by your leave. If the Athenians would not show a farce on the scene where Euripides showed tragedy, much less may I make play of things religious."

"Ha!" said Henry, "you be no Vicar of Hell, then. Come, we'll match wits at shuffleboard."

So Anne saw them desert her. She was now no maiden to taunt Thomas. "The Queen hath a goodly belly," was the current observation in April, and to Thomas she was as remote as the cupola on a temple. He was grave, and in a degree melancholy. Frith was still in the Tower, but already the nun of Kent and eight men who had taken her trances in good faith had been hanged, drawn and quartered at Tyburn. "I was a poor wench," the epileptic said, "they bear me in hand that it was the Holy Ghost and not I that did them. I pray God to have mercy on me, and on all them that here suffer with me." It looked black for Bishop Fisher. Henry and Cromwell had parliament behind them, and Thomas More's arrest was now a matter of weeks, since parliament named Anne's child the heir to the throne.

For Thomas this was a sign of the widening fissure in England, and the dreadful danger from without. This act of succession was a battle cry.

Du Bellay had come post haste from Rome, and Anne was so relieved to see a friendly Frenchman that she had held him and kissed him on the cheek. But his news was bad. Her uncle Norfolk had collapsed and nearly fainted, a year before, when he learned that the Pope had given the divorce against Henry. Now the dying Pope declared England in schism. Henry was white with apprehension. He despatched Anne's brother and Fitzwilliam to France. That alliance was his anchor. He fidgeted and fumed, ready to brag at one minute and desperate at the next, telling Anne he must himself cross to see Francis, and yet not daring to risk leaving England.

This tension created a subtle misery in Thomas's veins that he could not conquer. He hated the Emperor's might, but there it was: he was formidable in the Low Countries, solid in Spain, triumphant in Italy, and now at last promising to take Tunis and control the Mediterranean. Henry was now conniving with Marcus Meyer, and with the Protestant princes in Germany. But this was the most complicated of intrigues. Another May had come, Thomas's unlucky month. He was restless. It was a relief when the King gave him a message to the young Duke of Richmond.

## V

IT WAS A SMALL MATTER that took Thomas to Windsor, the wrong discharge of one of the young Duke's staff. But when he reached there, both Richmond and his companion, the Earl of Surrey, were so eager to see him that it was like a light from another world.

Norfolk's heir, who had been in France with Henry's boy, was just as swift as young Henry was sweet and placid. He wore his hair in a low straight fringe across his forehead. He had a long, pointed face, with eyes wide apart, and in those eyes Thomas saw the most touching look of young devotion, of starry wonder and of blissful absorption. Surrey had a rather short, thick nose, as obst.nate as could be, but for the rest his quality was neither male nor female, but rarefied and eager, and when he felt himself in Thomas's presence, the presence of another poet, he ceased to think of himself, he lost all that dreadful shyness which is the fear of pain, and gazed in worship on his Wyatt. Poems that Thomas had written had come into his hands. Thomas's name had been remembered in France. And now, while he himself was barely seventeen but already quick with rhyme, this benign, tall, older poet was smiling on him.

They went to the parapet together, the wild forest beneath them, so astounded with spring that every green was flaming. They talked of the chase, and in the boy's limbs there was the nervous joy of the chase, the hope of speed, the dread of long delays. Already he was man enough to revel in it, the hounds crying, the horns merry, his horse swift breathing. Thomas forgot the agony of his own life. Here was a fresh unblotted page, and Surrey, his courage still as untouched as the stamen in a flower just opened, drew him to the gravelled tilt-yard, where, with swords and friendly hearts, he and Richmond ran their courses.

The large green courts were below the tower. There they played tennis with their open palms instead of racquets. "And we often miss," laughed Surrey, "if our ladies are on the leads and we catch sight of them."

Thomas parted from the boys, Richmond so quiet and gentle, Surrey so gallant, with an extraordinary lift of the heart. Here, if life favoured him, could be a poet for all time in England's diadem.

And the boy, seeing Thomas depart, felt in his veins that magic which the pure disciple feels.

"So stern and mild," he groped, "with that piercing look, that courtesy, that gentle, distant smile!"

And then they went to tennis.

## VI

YES, that gentle, distant smile. Thomas returned to Westminster, and could thank himself for his pains. The King was at Richmond.

At St. James's he had stopped for a moment. A man with a hammer and chisel was carving H and A in the stone. Thomas stopped to look at him, his heart tightening with each hammer stroke. A sudden blind fury took him, before he went on. He was still disturbed when he reached Francis Bryan.

"Oh ho," said Bryan, "you'll sup with me. A wench, a wench, my Kingdom for a wench."

"Marseilles is a hell-hole," he told Thomas. "I wrote old Lisle that

dead men there were more plenty than quick capons. The wines were
evil, and the beds wanton. I told him to have a hard bed ready for me
at Calais, rather than a soft harlot. Now let's drink to the Great Devil
and make a night of it."

"Was the Pope——"

"A bawd. But we had a cur with us, by name of Bonner, who
snapped at his heels. The Emperor kissed his foot, we heard. Happy
it was no other place. I told old Lisle I had absolution from his Holiness, and to have a band of courtesans at Calais to furnish and accomplish my desires. Come yourself, I said to him, and be here absolved,
though neither Pope's niece nor her gentlewomen will seem as fair to
you as Lucresse."

So he kept it up. "Good wine Greek," he wanted, "wine amiable
and coarse," and women to match it. No three-halfpenny beer, but
wine for his dry gullet, and ten dishes for his first course. He had
little good to say of anyone in Anne's family. George, who was
favoured for all embassies, he described with that merciless asperity
which began with Cain and Abel. He was equally brotherly about
Anne herself, though Thomas diverted it. Yet through this warp of
malice there ran wild, gleaming threads the other way, and under it
all a sort of unwilling respect, mingled with superciliousness, for
Thomas.

They drank well, with the Three Cranes full of that savour they
loved so much. It had the sea smell, and Francis Bryan was at heart
a seaman. They talked of embassy, of France, of Calais, and of the
Court. They talked of Bryan's debts.

"Why do you wear your body to the bones?" asked Thomas. "For
ever on the trot, from realm to realm, when you might sleep at home
in your bed of down, and drink good nappy ale?"

"I serve my Prince," said Bryan, "my lord and yours. Let the others
stuff their paunches, so I may have enough to feed me and mine."

"By God, well said!" replied Thomas. "But why not keep a ward for
your son, like Suffolk, and then hobble her yourself?"

Bryan laughed sardonically, and, except for the Queen, they had an
unsparing talk that wiped out many scores and solaced scratches. For
all Bryan's tongue, he neglected all, to go on ill-paid missions, while
the plums went to lighter men.

"What's this from Calais?" asked Bryan. "You may not break a stave on a porter's head without a process? Where's this to end?"

While they held forth a quarrel had started below, and when they went down, the door was barred.

"You durst not leave," said Shore, the hulking innkeeper. "The watch!"

"Make way!" cried Bryan. "This be nought to us."

"Prithee, sir."

"Out of the way"—he drew his sword—"unbolt your door."

Shore lifted the oak bar. It was dark outside, but in the doorway stood a band of London's watch. Thomas, who was behind Bryan, saw the tall halberds gleam from the light within; glints on the breast-plates, and half a dozen faces, stout, lusty men whose visages were red with authority. They filled the entrance with their bulk, and several halberds thrust at Bryan as he stepped forward.

"Up with them!" he commanded, and clenched his sword. Thomas drew his own.

"What is this brawl?" asked a voice.

"I know not," said Bryan, "make place"; and he struck up the halberds.

Tall before, and bristling against the dark, Thomas saw the halberds lowered, and as Bryan rushed to clear a way he followed him. A sudden thrust forced him to parry. He heard a cry. His sword was knocked from his hand. And then, before his eyes, like a sack going limp, he saw one of the watch, who had worn no breastplate, sink very slowly to the ground. His face turned the colour of pale cheese, a few bubbles frothed his lips, and then his eyes rolled open.

Hands laid hold of Thomas. He stood there, outside the closed inn, and while, with clumsy hands, they bore the inert body to the wall, it reached him that, in folly, he had killed a man. He had heard the scraping noise with which the door was closed. He heard the sign of the Bush creak over him in lonely soliloquy. Clean and free from the lower reaches of the Thames, the wind caressed his burning face, his hot wrists, his eyes. This could not ease him. He had killed a man.

## VII

WHILE THOMAS WAS IN PRISON, with his elderly parents and his sister Margaret thrown into frantic concern for him, the summer invaded London, and drove Anne and Henry to the open country.

It was a glorious summer. God shone on the new marriage. And since Anne was bearing his child with a buoyancy that encouraged him, Henry went hunting in good spirits. She spoke to him of Thomas. Displeased as Henry was with lawless violence, the penalty was certain to be made light. Cromwell noted it, and Anne apprehended no difficulties. So long as Anne was with child, nothing was too good for her. Her high hand with Catherine and Mary, who contemptuously defied the act of succession, in no way angered Henry.

Chapuys had for so long desired to see Catherine that, gathering sixty of the Spanish colony in London, he started to her on a pretended pilgrimage to Our Lady of Walsingham. The merchants and his household were nearly a hundred horse. All along the summer road they went merrily, with their minstrels and trumpeters, hoping to bring joy to Catherine's heart. But Cromwell was before-hand. He despatched Stephen Vaughan to Kimbolton. Catherine was allowed to send out game and wine and venison to the pilgrims, and while some of the bolder ones got as far as the moat, their gay pranks showing how little they were afraid of Catherine's keepers, Chapuys himself had to keep a civil distance and at length turned back. Their pilgrimage had miscarried.

His secret encouragement to Mary, however, had the greatest effect in making her resist Henry's authority. He wrote out the words she was to utter, and when she went out with little Elizabeth, she pushed forward, on Chapuys's instructions, to the most honourable place in the barge. She even slowed it to salute him, as she passed up the Thames, waving and waving until he was out of sight.

Anne's fury at these pinpricks was ungoverned, but before the time came for her return to Greenwich she lost the baby she had hoped to bear. For her it was a wild disappointment, but the depth of it could not be fathomed until she saw how Henry took it. Then her eyes opened.

He was in a salient, so to speak. By naming himself Supreme Head of the Church, on top of naming Elizabeth his heir, all the Catholic forces, on one side, and all the Catherine forces, on the other, massed against him with their veiled yet threatening power. He had a good grip on the clergy and the bishops, and, as Supreme Head, he could dissolve the wealthy abbeys. But the passionate sincerity of the Carthusian monks, of John Fisher and Thomas More, compelled him to harass them by every means, and they stood out against him invincibly. This, on the Catholic side, taxed Cromwell, though he was coolly preparing to send them to the scaffold and the stake. But on the Queen's side, Chapuys was inciting and intriguing with the nobles. The Earl of Kildare had just died, leaving his bones in the Tower, and his son, Silken Thomas, had burst into widespread rebellion in Ireland. Norfolk and Cromwell had broken into a wrangle about it in Council, Norfolk saying he would go to Ireland to quell this trouble if the King would have a bridge built for him by which to come home. This could be coped with, but while Henry's allies in Lubeck had cut across the French plots, those Lutheran plots had failed. All attempt to divide and conquer Germany had gone up in smoke.

The autumn began ominously for Anne. The serene months that had followed Elizabeth's birth, promising happiness and triumph, were now, with the fall of the leaf, threatening Anne with renewed anxieties. And when she turned for help to her intimate circle, her own people, they merely heaped trouble on her.

"Your sister Mary," rapped Henry.

"What is this?"

"She is going to have a baby."

"But she is not married."

"No."

In the accession of the Boleyns, Mary had had no share. Anne had taken her to Calais, but from then she was left in the cold. The usher with whom she had fallen in love was a Stafford, but he had no fortune. Anne was brutally hard. She drove Mary from Court with merciless speed.

"I saw that all the world did set so little by me," pleaded Mary to Cromwell, "and he so much, that I thought that I could take no better way but to take him and forsake all other ways and to live a poor honest life with him."

Cromwell glanced down. After all, Mistress Carey had two sons who might make their way.

"Write me a letter, ma'am," he said curtly. "Put it all down. I'll say a word for you."

But Mary's frailty, which gave Anne her cutting edge, was soon forgotten in this miserable autumn.

Anne had not yet recovered from her miscarriage when Jane Rochford lingered by her bedside. Beaulieu had been given to herself and George, so she could purr to Anne. She had it in her power to convey, not affection but a direct animal rapport that was singularly difficult to resist. In the timbre of her calculated voice, her hands, her little licking glances, and a kind of dark clairvoyance, Jane Rochford could enforce her personality.

"Methinks," she said to Anne, "we have a new favourite."

"But of all the trash!" exploded Anne contemptuously. "His Highness is above it. You may not permit yourself these hints, sister."

"Were you at his side," said Jane calmly, "it would be otherwise. But if you bid me to be silent, I obey." She arranged Anne's counterpane with gentle perfection.

"Who could it be?" ventured Anne. "I believe no word of it."

"You will be wroth again," said Jane meekly. "I shall hold my peace."

"You'll tell me," said Anne fiercely. "Now you have roiled me."

" 'Tis but a small thing." Jane stood by the head of the bed, twiddling her pearls as she spoke, with her eyes contracted. "But I have seen it. I know the signs." Her eyes dilated, as if George had taught her the ways of hell. "But I'll make more certain first."

"Who is it?" Anne ground her teeth. "You stand there twiddling. Who is she?"

The cat-faced sister-in-law engaged her with a long look, at once apprehensive and full of resistance. "Nicholas Carew leads him on," she purred.

"Then," said Anne, "it would be the Guildford girl."

Jane started. Anne had guessed her. Anne sat up. "If you catch her," she said, "let me hear of it."

Jane nodded, and it was as if her claws retracted and crooked out again. She wished to catch her. With a certain warmth she said, "Lie down, sister. And depend on me, for 'tis shameful when you lie here."

"It is nothing"—Anne lay down—"but when I am weak!" She did not cry, but she lay hard and tense, her disfigured hand pulling a gold fringe.

Joan Guildford was fresh at Court, a dark thing with laughing white teeth, adroit and beautiful, who could easily amuse Henry. That warm resistance he found enticing.

Anne taxed him with it, at the first proof of his growing tenderness. "So," she said, "you amuse yourself when I lie unwell."

"You have little cause to chafe me," he retorted.

"But when you made me Queen," flared Anne. "That Guildford child is but a lure to catch you. When we have so suffered, sir, to do this to me, you who have done all to make me Queen!"

"You have good reason to be content, all I have done for you," he said.

"But send her away, sir. No more do I ask."

"If it were to begin all over again," continued Henry bitterly, "I would not do it."

"Nay," pleaded Anne. "Unsay this." She was white.

"But you began it," puffed her husband.

And a fortnight later he came to her. This time, Pope Clement VII, the Great Devil as Cromwell called him, having just died, Henry was defiant.

"It is that catamountain," he said, "my lady Rochford, who is haunting me. You shall send her away."

"But the other?"

"Send my lady Rochford hence. I'll not have her."

"As you will, sir," murmured Anne. She conveyed the news to her sister-in-law, who took it with a sneering smile. "Such are my thanks, God wot!" And curtseyed to her mistress.

But in a few days, when Anne found Henry in better mood, she complained that Mistress Guildford was bold and discourteous to her. This Henry resented. Not only did he avoid her, but when Francis Bryan thought it opportune to disparage Anne's brother, Henry publicly snubbed him. Their troubles were not in themselves, if Anne could help it; but on their horizon mounted tall clouds compact with storm.

## VIII

WHEN King Francis's slight companion, Chabot de Brion, arrived on embassy in November, his former gallant tone to Anne was greatly chilled. He took little interest in the dances. He did not trouble to watch Henry playing tennis.

"Would you not like to see the Queen?" Henry suggested.

"If it please your Highness," said Chabot languidly. He was polite to Anne, but made no effort to please her.

With Chapuys, on the contrary, he was open and affable.

"You have visited the Tower," said the smooth Fleming, "and seen the ordnance, but you have not seen the gem of the Kingdom, Princess Mary."

"Ah," exclaimed Chabot, "I am as vexed as possible, to have to leave without that pleasure." After a polite word about Mary, he lowered his voice. "Let us bring our masters to accord," he urged Charles's ambassador, "and all the rest will go well."

"But when you give countenance to this shameful divorce, Monsieur."

"Ma foi," shrugged Chabot, "is it for my master to trouble about this King's conscience?"

They gave a State ball for Chabot before he left, and as he sat on the dais next to Anne, Henry went to fetch Gontier, another of the ambassadors, whom he thought would amuse Anne.

While Chabot was telling her about this Palamede Gontier, Anne ceased to listen to him. Henry, pausing to chat with young Joan Guildford, had forgotten Gontier. He was gay with the girl. Anne suddenly began to laugh.

"What, Madame!" flared Chabot, "you laugh at me."

"He went for Gontier," cried Anne, "and he forgot—he forgot——" she could not finish.

Chabot, a counterpart of Francis Bryan, could only look at her with cold irritation.

But he exposed it for good reasons of his own. King Francis's intrigues with the Lutherans had so failed, and their placards inside his own palace had been so flagrant, and the Sorbonne had so definitely overcome his attempts to broaden the Church, that, with the advent of the new Pope, Paul III, he had decided to change his note and trumpet his orthodoxy to the world. Marguerite, thinking to help Anne, had warned Norfolk that the Papal party, under de Montmorency, was growing dangerous. Chabot de Brion now knew that Norfolk wished to play de Montmorency's role. He was openly civil to him. This was so clear to Anne that she resolved to meet it by a test of force.

"Anne is a ribald," burst out the Court fool, "the child is a bastard." All the courtiers who had prompted it were convulsed. "Anne is a ribald, Anne is a ribald."

Anne was so incensed that she attacked her uncle before her ladies. She had learned that the late Pope urged him to marry Surrey to Princess Mary. She poured such wrath on him, and threatened him so violently, that he left the Court beside himself with anger. "The big whore!" he snarled to Cromwell. And with her he linked her new Archbishop.

It became worse for Anne in January. King Francis had a holocaust in front of Notre Dame. The True Cross, the Crown of Thorns, the lance point, the sponge and the purple robe were all solemnly borne in procession. Six heretics were burned to death, in front of these emblems of crucifixion, and Francis, bareheaded, made a pious discourse.

The alarm that this bred in Anne was deepened by Henry's brittle humour and his attentions to the Guildford girl. She did not fear it in itself, but she feared the group that might promote it. Old allies like Nicholas Carew had gone over to Catherine and Princess Mary. The nobles were more than hostile, they were positively threatening. The Court atmosphere was charged with scorn and malice.

With Mary and Jane Rochford gone, her father glum and her mother grim, Anne was haggard and worn. Henry, at her demand, set out to arrange with the French a royal marriage for Elizabeth, but they decided to use this to heighten every claim they could think of, to shove Henry from one point to another, and put his back to the wall. Chabot de Brion's indifference to Henry's tennis had been quite cold-blooded. No conceivable Boleyn joke could have made him smile. And

Gontier returned with the jewel of French friendship still more expensive to redeem, considering Henry's troubles at home and with the Emperor. Henry was now asked to remit all debts. He was asked to give up all his old claims to French territory. And, in return, the new Pope might possibly soften his papal strictures. But a marriage with Elizabeth, was it not, after all, a very dubious honour for a French prince? Henry, in addition, was asked by King Francis as a personal favour to name Nicholas Carew a Knight of the Garter, instead of George Boleyn. And various other little items were thought of.

Henry leaned against the sideboard as Gontier expounded this to him. But he controlled his panic. He argued point by point with cool tenacity. He kept it up for hours and hours.

## IX

"COME HERE," he said to Fitzwilliam, the meat-headed, solid Fitzwilliam.

"You were at this dinner that Morette has now given?"

Fitzwilliam was. It was a Catholic celebration. They had heard all about the holocaust at it, Suffolk and Norfolk and the rest. Many of Catherine's best friends were there.

"Well," said Henry, his eyes flitting, "it all hangs on my recent marriage. Were I to divorce the new Queen, what then? The Archbishop would consent."

"But then, sir, you would still be married to Queen Catherine."

"Good God!" exclaimed Henry, "not that."

"These French," ventured Fitzwilliam, who was an old hand by this, "when they are aloft, sir, they are the highest men in the world and the soonest to forget their benefactors. But when they are a little under foot they are the humblest."

"True, true, by God," said Henry.

"Now they are in some hope," continued Fitzwilliam, "to accommodate themselves with the Emperor."

"That leaps to the eye. Go on."

"Therefore they crow so high."

"I told him so," muttered Henry.

"But, in the end, the Emperor would rather have our amity than theirs."

"Yea, but the divorce! She is his aunt."

"Even so," said Fitzwilliam firmly. "Let us use all gentleness with the French. I would not break with them until we hear more from the Emperor."

Henry nodded. "Myself," he said, "I heard my brother call his two boys at Boulogne, and in my presence say to them, 'You must never forget the Emperor's inhuman treatment to me and to yourselves.'"

"Yea," said Fitzwilliam, "but I like not their fashion."

Henry gave him a quick slap on the shoulder, a friendly nod, set his jaw and went to Cromwell.

## X

HE SOON WENT to Cromwell again, and this time under cover to Cromwell's own house.

Anne believed that with Catherine and Mary to give her enemies a rallying point, she could have no rest.

George tried to restrain her, but her demolition of Wolsey, her triumph over Catherine, Norfolk's sour submission to her, and her fear of Henry's backsliding, made her take a desperate tone. Her black eyes now had in them the fiercest light that George had seen.

"If I were to burn for it," she said of Mary, "she must be starved or done to death."

"You are out of your senses," George chided her.

But Anne's breast heaved. "I was never so sane. She is my death and I am hers," she said. "And I will take care that she shall not laugh at me after my death."

George kept Cromwell at a distance. "That is the ruffian," he said to his uncle, "who is responsible for all this."

Norfolk gave a quick, angry shake of his head. He was back at the King's heel.

But Cromwell's private talk with Henry followed a great piece of news. The Emperor was setting out to conquer Tunis and beat the Turk. England was saved. All Henry's magnification of the fortresses at Calais and the defences at Dover, which he had brandished at

Gontier, was now quite unnecessary. France and the Emperor could
not, at the moment, combine.

Cromwell had sounded Henry on his present wife, his obdurate
Catherine, his obstinate Mary. He advised him to pay Percy's debts,
since Percy had given Chapuys a symbolic sword. And he took
Chapuys into the fields.

"What evil or danger," he asked Chapuys pointblank, "would arise
from the death of the Princess?"

Since Lord Sandes had been telling Chapuys how easy it would be
for the Emperor to conquer England, Cromwell's threat was not
without its effect.

"She is at the root of all the King's perplexities," renewed Cromwell. "She has not been so well, and, please God——"

His dark look said the rest. Cromwell's spies told him that even
Sir William Kingston was ready to house Mary and Catherine in
the Tower with their restoration in view, and as each of these rumours
came to Anne she raised her voice. "Rebels and traitors!" she called
them.

Only Cromwell's vigilance prevented Mary's being smuggled to the
Low Countries. Several monks had already escaped, to carry news
to the Emperor. Cromwell put on such pressure that Norfolk took his
part in bullying Mary. Were it otherwise Cromwell could expect to
be carved out of office. And in the meantime, with the dissolution of
the monasteries so certain to enrich Henry, with Skeffington to crush
the Irish, and his various policies assured, Cromwell took his bit in his
teeth. The Emperor was out of the way.

The temper on both sides hardened. In May the Carthusian monks
were condemned to the most painful of deaths, and Henry showed his
entire sanction of it by sending Norfolk, his own boy Richmond,
Anne's father, and Anne's brother to see them disembowelled, with
Harry Norris and a troop of horse. This had been only less flagrant
than the struggle between Cromwell and Henry, on one side, and
Thomas More and John Fisher, on the other. It had condensed into a
conflict on the succession of the Bastard, but in reality it went back
to that duel between Church and State on which Thomas More had
come so early to his despairing insight.

All through those fetid weeks—and he had been months on months in the Tower—More had battled with his adversaries until there was no longer a shadow of obscurity on the principles at stake. Catherine might be retired to a damp and lonely house. Spies might report every word she said, and her daughter might still brave Anne's anger and arouse her fury. But Thomas More was the author of Utopia, a European figure, a lifelong humanist, a friend of Erasmus, a patron of Holbein, and as high in Henry's service as his ambassadorships and his chancellorships could make him. John Fisher, by his side, was of equal sanctity, and of such courage that for ten years he had never flinched, even when alone, in the assertion of Queen Catherine's rights as a married woman. Each in his own way, with a bravery painfully born from natures so finely wrought, bore witness to their truth through every complexity of the law and every twist of their examiners' sophistry. They held by truths that Henry himself had professed for years. Now, in the changes that the separation from Catherine had led to, they stood closer to Rome than to his convenience, and they were to be beheaded.

Sir William Kingston, still constable of the Tower, with tears running down his cheeks, bade More farewell.

"Good Master Kingston," said More, "trouble not yourself, be of good cheer. I will pray for you, and my good Lady your wife, that we may meet in Heaven together, where we shall be merry for ever and ever."

# Chapter 22

Aɴɴᴇ ᴀɴᴅ ʜᴇɴʀʏ took these executions without a quiver.

In the middle of them, she and Henry went hawking. Out beyond Waltham Forest there was to be a mummery on St. John's Eve. Henry decided to see it, the night after John Fisher's beheading, since everyone was burning bonfires and singing and making gay. Taking a two-handed sword, the big stalwart man splayed ten miles to the show, and there, in the house where it was staged, the King was taken off in mummery as hacking off the heads o' the clergy. This made him so stifle with laughter that, in order to be at his ease, he finally allowed himself to break into laughter, letting the people recognize him.

To Henry, as well as to Anne, the issue was high treason. She was vehement enough to believe that one signal punishment would frighten all the religious houses, and she was right. She only wished that Catherine and Mary could be sent the same way as More and Fisher.

Cromwell was inclined to be with her. He had failed in all his diplomatic efforts to win success with the Lutherans, but he meant to try again. He and Henry forced Norfolk to take a hand in condemning Thomas More. He himself had handled the Carthusian monks. In his house at Stepney, where Henry had been closeted with him, he had privately tried to browbeat them. But theirs was not so comic an end as Henry had found it. For seventeen days the monks had been so chained in the Tower, with iron collars linked to a post and fetters bolted to their legs, that they could not find ease and must of necessity befoul themselves. This had not broken them. The King at last gave them over to be partially hanged, then cut open, disembowelled and castrated. From these horrors Anne induced Henry to distract himself. She had contrived to divert him from Joan Guildford to her charming cousin Mary Shelton, and this was one of his most lively distractions in the early summer. Anne tolerated it. She agreed with Henry in calling the Countess of Salisbury a fool, Princess Mary's former guardian, and it was Reginald Pole, Lady Salisbury's son, who made the Pope send John Fisher the Cardinal's hat.

"I'll send the head to Rome for it," Henry laughed.

And both of them took the good news of the beheading from William Kingston, who came with it out to Waltham Forest. They had gone to the greenwood for a long summer, as in old times, and Anne was sanguine.

"Her Grace," Kingston told his wife, "hath as fair a belly as I have ever seen."

"Much good may it do her," said Lady Kingston.

Henry, at any rate, rejoiced in it. His unbending will to be Supreme Head of the Church had not been shaken. He still looked to Anne for his heir. The rebellion in Ireland was being quelled. His own defences were in order. Constant tricklings from the conspirators around Catherine told on his nerves. So did the news of the Emperor's triumphs. But Henry was so encouraged by his immense accretion of power from this prostrate Church that no danger from outside seemed quite real.

## II

BUT THE LITTLE RESERVOIR of goodwill that Europe could count on was being depleted everywhere. William Tyndale, the translator of the New Testament, was betrayed by an English agent, one of Catherine's side, and John Poyntz was moving heaven and earth to free him. Cromwell, obeying Henry, was ready to weed out the seditious Anabaptists who had come to England. Calvin had been driven from France, following the use of the estrapade all over the country, and the Inquisition in Spain was extinguishing Erasmianism.

And as Europe began to show what little universality it had by its consternation at Thomas More's beheading, and as the French proved difficult and the Emperor's triumphs became more certain, Anne grew less happy.

Her child miscarried.

This, after Catherine's many miscarriages, blackened Henry's looks. It made him wonder whether, after all, Anne was not ill-fated.

Anne was soon at his side again. The French sent a new embassy, in view of the Emperor's triumph, but where Gontier had a bright eye and a red lip and a Celtic sparkle, Dinteville was a Bishop with an implacable clarity of brain and will. That flat façade had no balcony for Anne to attach to. His brain could not conceive of her. A war to regain Milan was the programme, but in that case the English must foot a third of the bills, out of one-eighth of French resources. Francis even remonstrated about Thomas More, and Henry, with sharp rejoinder, ordered Stephen Gardiner to go to France for him.

Anne began to have fears. Cromwell still had hopes of the Lutherans. Edward Foxe, who had been high almoner with a right to all the goods of foolish suicides, was now to have the goods of a suicide Church by becoming Bishop of Hereford, and he (whose heart was with Catherine and Mary) was to go to Germany to fish for Lutheran help. But all this gave Anne no solid comfort. She sent for a young gentleman in Dinteville's suite.

"Will Luther send Melancthon to France?"

"No, Madame."

"Thank you, I thought not." She brooded, and then, with haggard face, she said, "Tell the Queen of Navarre that two things I desire on earth—to have a son, and once more to meet her."

The Frenchman knelt and promised.

Against the imperials, against du Montmorency, this was her hope. The vision of Marguerite's benignant, gentle countenance brought her to tears. But they were both in the hands of Kings.

## III

FROM JUNE TO OCTOBER they kept in the country. They wanted to hear and see England.

"Those lovely unicorn heads," exclaimed Anne at Winchester Cathedral.

"We must have those," said Henry promptly. "And that very fine silver cross."

They kept going, their eyes and ears open.

Henry had greatly liked the Seymours at Wolfhall, where they stayed for some days. And he was promptly enamoured of the gentle daughter of that huge family, Jane Seymour.

This time Anne laughed. She was beginning to be used to his mid-summer lightning. Of all the maids-in-waiting who came from Queen Catherine, Jane Seymour was perhaps the least incisive. Where Anne was herself so quick to declare herself, so brilliantly present and hence stimulating, with a climate where the breeze is brisk, the sun lost but re-found, the day at once an affront and an adventure, with quick caresses to follow on black scowls, this mildly visible, sweetly diffused, and equally attentive Mistress Seymour was at a clear disadvantage. Yet, during the days at Wolfhall, where this family's noble discretion wore so well, Henry became pleasantly attuned to Jane Seymour, and Jane became aware of it.

He was corpulent, forty-four, and an autocrat. So is the sun, autocrat and corpulent. Jane privately discovered how warm was this regal rotundity.

She was a gentlewoman, and Henry's benignity drew her to him and meant much to her. Under her surface, and she was now twenty-five, she had a knowledge of the world that was less spirited than Anne's but in its way more sagacious. It went with an amorousness that had much patience in it. Henry was swift to discern this. He gave little grunts of satisfaction in Sir John Seymour's fine Wiltshire home. It soothed him. He rather supposed that it still rested on the laurels that the Black Prince had bestowed on one of them. It was a relief after George Boleyn.

The defences that Henry saw on the coast gave him cheer. He was satisfied with the state of the navy, into which he could now put a few abbeys and convents. But Anne's newest miscarriage dogged her, and not that alone.

## IV

"YOUR SISTER," said Henry furiously, "this Lady Rochford."

"What hath she done?" asked Anne.

"She and Lady William Howard cheered and waved to my daughter Mary."

"When? Where, sir?"

"On her passage to Eltham."

"And was no one there to stop such unseemliness? I never heard the like."

"A great troop of citizens' wives went crying and weeping, but those I name to you were seen, and now lie in the Tower."

"Good riddance!" cried Anne. "And when I see Master Secretary I'll beg him to keep it in mind."

But Cromwell had too much to keep in mind. The weather had been so bad the whole summer that not half the corn was saved. All the people were marvellously discontented, and cursed Anne for it. New Acts went through parliament to widen the net for treasonable folk, but these were so many, and speaking so improperly of Anne, and so well of Catherine, that it began to look critical. If war takes place, the French judged, the people will rebel. Trade in cloth, in blankets, in hides and tin and lead, would all be crippled if the Emperor struck, and the Emperor was saying that it was impossible with honour and a good conscience to treat with Henry.

"The French now insult you," said Anne to Henry, "by asking for the Lady Mary's hand."

"While I live, she shall not marry."

"If we have war, 'twill be she that caused it."

Henry was driven to agree. "Your tears and wry faces," he said to the councillors who pleaded for her against her keeper, Mistress Shelton, "they are of no avail. She must bow to the law. Even if I lose my crown," and his glare convinced them, "I'll not forbear."

Cromwell stood behind him. He was weary of their importunities, with the Emperor's return from Africa the return of a conqueror.

"I'll no longer remain in this trouble, fear and suspicion," declared Henry roundly. "I have endured enough. By God's passion, I'll wait no longer."

Not one of Henry's councillors dared to face him as Chapuys faced the lot of them. They had seen Thomas More's head set up on London Bridge.

"Where is Lady Mary to receive her New Year's gifts?" asked Lord Exeter meekly.

"I'll contrive that soon she'll want no New Year's gifts," he broke out. "She'll be an example to show the whole world that nobody is to disobey the law." Then, with a loud voice and not a trace of his humour, or his good fellowship, "I'll prove the truth that was told in a prophecy, that I'd come in as gentle as a lamb and end more fierce than a lion."

Cromwell heard him. He passed his hands over his twitching lips with an odd gesture. He had trained this lion.

## V

"Gi' up, you bitch!"

He was a young carter with a ruddy, rollicking face. He was out on the winter road, bringing home a load of wood, and he was speaking to his mare.

His mare knew that loving voice. Her hind quarters moved with that round placidity which made her beloved, and he watched her, pleased to think how well he cared for her, how wet the road was, how good the Christmas ale had been, how good life was.

"Gi' up, you bitch."

"Holloa! Holloa!"

He pulled up his rude, boat-like cart.

There by the roadside was a lady. Not a county lady, but a stranger, clad in black but clad in black with fur.

" 'Twas my mare, lady. I never laid eyes on you. I take the best of care of her. Never mind those words. Many a rough word is kind, and many a kind word is cutting." While he rambled, he got down.

"Oh," she said, in a strange accent, "you are kind. But, I beg you for the Lord's sweet sake, give me your help, my man."

"What help?"

"Take me on that mare of yours to Kimbolton Castle."

"You on my mare?"

"Behind you."

"As God sees us this day, I'll do it for a lady."

He drew his cart aside, unyoked his mare, and helped the lady up.

"Not for that kape who calls herself the Queen," said the tow-haired lad, "but for God's Queen, the blessed lady, her Castle I'd take you to."

So they jogged to Kimbolton.

"Gi' up, you!" He jounced his mare on. And so the porter at Kimbolton saw them.

"I met with an accident," the fainting lady said, limping to the gate. "For God's sake, a place near the fire."

In this way Maria de Salinas, who had heard that her old mistress was dying, passed through the King's portals into Kimbolton.

It was a glass of Welsh beer that had made her so ill, and now she was dying.

At the end Cromwell made no difficulty for Chapuys, though he had refused Lady Willoughby.

They were all at Greenwich for the jousting, Thomas Wyatt, Thomas Cheyney and all of them. And Cheyney was at the water-gate to wait on Chapuys.

"His Highness awaits you," he smiled.

"Ah, my friend." Henry put his arm around Chapuys's neck as he used to embrace Thomas More. "You wish to visit Madame?" He nodded. "As you wish. She cannot live long." He then turned to the approaching war between France and the Emperor. "I am a man who says what he believes. I am an Englishman. I never say one thing and mean another, or stir up jealousy for my own profit.

"If Madame dies," he added, "the Emperor will have no cause to trouble himself about this realm. But I believe it is the Pope who stirs him up, and starts the absurdity about the Emperor conquering this realm for France."

"The death of the Princess Dowager," said Chapuys with tight lips, "can do no possible good." And he looked straight at Henry as he said it. He was certain Catherine had been given a white powder in that beer.

## VI

QUEEN CATHERINE'S DEATH followed in a few days, and whatever doubts the world had about either Henry or Anne were dispelled on the following Sunday. Anne appeared in a full yellow gown, to display both her grief and her pregnancy. Henry wore yellow from top to toe. He was in the best spirits, and after dinner, when everybody was dancing, he sailed into the dancing chamber, with a white feather gay in his yellow bonnet.

"God be praised," he said quite loud to Anthony Browne, who was a good courtier and already had his eye on Battle Abbey, "God be praised, Browne, we are now free from all fear of war."

They chatted for a while, and then Henry called Nan Cobham. "Fetch the Princess, my dear."

"Whither away?" asked Lady Worcester, Anthony Browne's daughter.

"To fetch the Little Bastard," whispered Lady Cobham.

Henry crowed merrily to Elizabeth, who hardly knew him. She watched him, as if waiting to be introduced.

"See them dancing," he cried.

Elizabeth, whose teeth hurt her, said, "See them dancing," half taking her finger out of her mouth. Pretty ladies, pretty ladies dancing. And then Mark, a pretty man dancing. She englobed her world on her eyes' evidence, and the evidence of her teeth. Her attention was at once frenzied and fixed, as if to hold flight by stabbing it with a look.

Henry enjoyed her, and then packed her off to Francis Bryan's mother. She was the old mother-hen who really understood a clutch, and took Elizabeth under her wing. There the grave and fearless child was at home and, already at two, as developed as a child of four, thanks to Mother Bryan.

Anne and Henry made no disguise of their feelings; the Queen's death rejoiced them. But where Anne was glad that Catherine could no longer hurt her pride by impunging her as wife and Queen, Henry was glad for more practical reasons. He sent for Francis Phillips.

"Phillips," he said, "you must give up what you have belonging to the Princess."

"Sir, if it please your Majesty," the hard-headed Spaniard made wilful answer, "I have nothing belonging to the Princess."

"I do not mean that"—Henry grew red—"but what you have belonging to your late mistress."

"May it please your Majesty, all that I have belonging to the Queen, my mistress, who is in glory, I will give up. But look, your Majesty, I served her for thirty years and never received any wages."

Henry was so angry that he glared at him and marched away. Cromwell then dealt with Phillips, who gave up everything.

Catherine had left him a legacy of forty pounds. Henry simply cancelled it. Queen! Princess! The words were actually treasonable by law.

But when the first flush of relief was over, Catherine's death emerged as a convenience for Henry and Cromwell. For Anne it was a disaster.


## VII

WITHOUT REALIZING IT, Anne had been sheltering from the enemy behind this encroachment on her pride. She had torn it down, with Cromwell's help, and then the enemy had her.

Even at the very beginning, Henry turned on her.

"Thank God," said Anne, "her death was hastened at the end."

"Who hastened it?" demanded Henry savagely. "I know nothing of that."

"But Master Secretary . . ."

"What say you? By God, you'll unsay it. You'll write to my daughter Mary. Tell Mistress Shelton you'll have no more to do with her. Keep clear of this. I have Pope and Emperor to threaten me."

Henry, so gay in yellow, began to combat the suspicions he had aroused. Plans to kidnap Princess Mary, to save her from being poisoned, had at once been elaborated, and a Flemish vessel stood off Gravesend for the moment she might come by land or water. Henry's attacks on Anne were renewed with savage hostility. She had never seen him like this before. With her old vigour she hit back, but he bristled with such ferocity her nerve suddenly and absolutely snapped. She broke down under him.

"I'll be like another mother to her, if she'll let me," she wept.

"You will!" retorted Henry. "You'll poison her. You'll practice witchcraft on her, as you did on me."

"I swear," Anne renewed, "oh, I swear, sir. She need never carry my train at Court. Nay, if she lay her obstinacy aside, her obstinacy toward you, sir, I'll be her best friend in the world."

"Come. Call your ladies. We go to dinner. Your eyes are red."

Cromwell saw that Henry was no longer even civil. He was brusque, frequently absent, either playing cards or out in the tiltyard.

"Why should the Emperor profess grief for his aunt?" Cromwell smiled fixedly on one of Chapuys's young men. "It is very convenient and advantageous to have her gone, for the preservation of friendship between my master and his Highness."

"Yea," said the imperial, "but, as the Pope sees it, his Highness is now a widower."

"All the better," smirked Cromwell, "we can arrange a marriage for him."

"But while this Queen live, you'll have herself and her crew to hinder you."

"That depends on the Emperor. She may not live for ever." Knowing that his words would reach Chapuys, Cromwell had no more to say.

## VIII

ANNE had her unborn child in her favour. The new panes in her yellow gown had been inserted with glee by Madge Shelton.

As Anne was lying at ease in bed, happy in this pledge of fortune, Henry, stout as he was, had gone back to jousting. Then the door of her chamber was thrust brutally open and Norfolk, looking very old, came grimly in.

"His Grace!" he said. His teeth showed.

Anne rose on an elbow. "Is he dead?" she cried.

"Not so. But a bad fall at the tilt. His great horse on top of him. Right in front of me."

"God save him! How dire! Madge, ask Brereton to go. Ask Norris. Send someone."

Then fresh word was brought. He had been badly stunned, but no injury to be found. The physicians were with him.

Norfolk brusquely took leave of them. Anne, with a terrible cry, said, "Quick! Mother Butts."

Soon the physicians had two patients. Anne's ladies began to weep. For the third time this had happened.

"Never mind!" said the pale creature, "this is not the end of all."

Henry's fall kept him from her side for several days. At last he entered her bedchamber. He asked how she was, looking at her with resentment. "Three and a half months, and then this!"

And when he had hastened out, Madge Shelton gazed soberly after him. "You will not think me bold, your Grace, for I do pity you, but his Highness . . ."

"Not Mary; not your sister?"

"This time he cumbers Jane Seymour with his love."

"The fraud! Great presents?"

"A purse, which she sent back, and his letter still sealed. Were her own seal unbroken, all were well."

"And this when all the Court was emptied for the funeral."

"Yea, my lady of Worcester gone forth, and Bray and Oxford and Willoughby—all tall candles bright for christenings and funerals."


## IX

ANNE PROFESSED not to be disheartened. The next child, she smiled, would be both conceived and born after Catherine's death, and then no one could cry "Bastard."

After his first visit, Henry had given her a moment.

"When you are *remise*," he said meaningfully, and curtly left her.

To mend, then, was her salvation. But she had ample time at Greenwich while he was in London.

George had been cut out of embassy by Gardiner's going to France, and he had no more to do with his wife. Anne passionately besought him for an hour at Christmas to make what headway he could with France. He had no hope. They demanded too much. And the incredible ingratitude and wickedness of the French was now the eternal cry. Had Anne known it, Cromwell was in conclave with Chapuys in London to tell his very story. They met after mass, amid the bricks and mortar of Cromwell's new residence.

Henry's pursuit of Jane Seymour was no longer to be concealed. And now, for the first time in her life, Anne saw herself in the role of the forsaken lover, another person utterly preferred to her.

"I loved him too well," she first cried out to Madge. With this thought in her mind she became so dejected that she began steadily to weep. But Madge rallied her.

"Anne," she murmured, dropping her title, "in very truth, is it for sure love of him you grieve?"

The question, from this honest friend, went deep.

"You have a heart," continued Madge, "but was it for him you kept it?"

Anne, still in her triumphant bed, with her ladies at her beck, a queen in every measurable thing, at last looked into the silver mirror Madge held up to her. She began to pull her hair back from her head.

"My neck is a cabbage stalk," she said. "My face is pointed like a shoe." She was shown a new coif and then chose another.

"Madge," she murmured, "though I have been his Grace's, and so faithful to him, I say it now, I could not love him." She lay back, and motioned ladies away. "Let me confess myself. I chose to lie in this marriage bed with him, but love! Have you ever seen Cromwell when he's afraid of the King?"

"Nay," said Madge.

"He looks—Chapuys said it for ever—he looks as if he were giving a halfpenny to an elephant." Anne burst out laughing. "Who could love an elephant?" All her melancholy left her. A gleeful, malicious light came in the dull plum-black eyes. "Were I again to marry, who knows, though I could never sink so low as Mary, I might willingly be no more than Anne, the English Queen, like Mary, the French Queen, and so hold light my precedence."

"St!" said Madge. "Old Mistress Wingfield!"

"Ah!" said Anne, "Greenwich is a honeycomb. When poor Percy, now dying on his feet, first craved to marry me, and came within an inch of it, our every step was smelt out by Lark, the Cardinal's hound. He was the make of this Frenchman Dinteville, displeasant and severe, a terrier at a burrow."

It did Anne good to talk, to talk recklessly, with her black hair down her back, the mirror flat against her counterpane, and Madge's honest eyes scanning her so calmly and so largely.

But while she was planning her *remise,* when her lord and master would again have use for her, he was forming other intentions.

In London, by the first of April, Cromwell was in ecstasy at letters from the Emperor's niece, and Lord Montagu was saying to Chapuys, "Cromwell is on bad terms with your friend the Concubine. A new marriage is in the air."

The same word was over all London. Elyot, the needy gentleman who wrote, that had begun with Anne but swopped his horses, now turned a hungry loving face to the Seymours, and the story of the purse full of sovereigns and the unopened letter was doing service in big houses on the Thames.

"No greater riches in the world have I than my honour," Jane Seymour told Henry, "that I would not injure for a thousand deaths. And if your Majesty wish to make me some present in money, I beg it might be when God enables me to make some honourable match."

"Most virtuously she behaved," Henry confided to Cromwell. "I showed her I only loved her honourably. Henceforth I do intend to speak to her only in the presence of her kin."

"Most wise and gentle of your Highness."

"But remove from that little secret chamber of yours in York Place, I wish that I may go to her unperceived."

Thomas Cromwell hastened to comply. "If my idiot of a son," he said to himself, "now take that widow sister of this Seymour, then the Cromwells will not be out of it." He took an increased interest in Jane Seymour, who had nine brothers and sisters. And Sir Edward, also to be housed at York Place, began to pay his debts.

## X

THE POPE was still the *bête noire*. To keep the jaws of France and the Emperor apart was Henry's anxiety, while the Pope urged Francis and Charles to clench so they might devour.

Henry kept a grip on himself. By the very intensity with which the Emperor was warming to him, he understood that the Emperor's need of him was growing. It was morally impossible for Francis not to renew attack on Milan, since it had lost its duke and since Francis had built up his strong militia.

So this went back and forth. Cromwell built his great mansion to entertain ambassadors and the King still more sumptuously, and direct the taking over of the abbeys in a lordly style. Many abominations Henry and he were uncovering. He made long lists of naughty nuns, of bad monks and choir boys.

But until the Emperor had spoken at Rome, which he was entering as the Emperor from his African conquests, Francis's challenges to him could not be defied, or Cromwell and Henry clear how to behave.

On Easter Eve, however, April 15, a courier arrived for Chapuys. George, Anne's brother, hovered about in Greenwich, trying to overhear what Norfolk and the French ambassador were saying. Anne was once more on her feet, ready for Easter. She was now aware that Jane Seymour had been come upon, sitting in the lap of the Supreme Head, and this, with his long absence, brought fire into her being. To see Henry alone was impossible. Great man though he was, he had a power of slipping lightly away from her.

Anne's father, in an emergency like this, had no substance left. He had become bone-weary of the opposition to his daughter. Her mother was unwell. There was only George. Francis Bryan turned the wrong eye to her.

But Anne had kept out of the great whirl since January. During those three months she had, in a certain manner, gone back to Hever. Luther and Melancthon she had talked of with George, and Bishop Foxe's attempts to win them. Poems had passed from hand to hand, jokes had been repeated, but the beautiful bindings, the exquisite

gowns, the jewels and the fine gear that had come to adorn her life—
these she paraded, while Mark danced, and Norris brought her the
red and the white spaniel he had commanded from France, and
Brereton and Weston treated her as royalty.

She found one difference, however, since Queen Catherine died
and Jane Seymour came into favour—her ladies had divided into a
loyal few and the many who had been hostile. Nan Cobham and her
friend young Lady Worcester made no effort to please her. All the
Guildford and Carew connection had grudges to satisfy. Spite in-
flamed the Palace, and Henry was not there to frighten them.

Yet Anne was gay again.

"You are back?" she teased Norris, "and I have somewhat to show
you."

"Yea, your Grace?"

"Others we wot of may be ungentle, but you, Norris, know you what
the goodman said of you?"

"No good, I trow."

"He said, 'Master Norris, he's not like the others. He's a one-
manner man.'"

They then could laugh.

"You are not married yet," she said, "and gone from us a month?"

"I'll tarry a time," the bachelor said. Anne had known him as a
bachelor, and Henry's equerry, since the Field of the Cloth of Gold.
That was seventeen years.

"I know you," she said, "you look for dead men's shoes. If aught
came to the King but good, you'd look to have me."

"If I had any such thought, ma'am," he answered shrewdly, "my
head would come off."

"Then you are in my power," she said, "and you must marry
Madge."

But Francis Weston, who heard her, said afterwards, "'Tis more for
you, your Grace, than for Madge, that he come unto your chamber."

"Then it is you, you naughty husband, who love Madge more than
you do your wife."

"Mayhap," said Weston, who had been her page and who floundered
in debt in spite of Anne's bounty, "mayhap I love one better in your
house than either of them."

"And who is that?"

"Mayhap 'tis yourself." He gave her his eyes.

"Thus you must not speak to me, Weston," she rebuked him. "You know that every ear is cocked, and you cannot wish to harm me."

Anne was angry with him. But badinage, love poems, forfeits, and gossip were their habit. Then they could dance, these fine ones who diced and gamed, and talk of hounds and horses.

But once more, after this trivial interlude where Greenwich had gone back to Hever, the great play began again, and Anne thought no more about Harry Norris than about a clothes-horse. This was not hand-holding amorousness, such as Suffolk had practised under Henry's eyes with Margaret of Austria, the stealing of rings, the wantoning glance, with sighs and strong oaths and deep good-byes. Harry Norris was a one-manner man who had just been away to see the abbey lands that Henry was giving him.

But the real game, the game of Henry's place in the European war that was about to recommence, with France to be invaded from the South this time—that was the great game. Anne came into the thick of it on Easter Saturday.

And here, trained by Wolsey for twenty years, the King ran rings round Cromwell as a diplomat. Where Cromwell had let it out to Chapuys that Henry held the French army as broken, Henry's whole tone with Chapuys was utterly independent. Cromwell sweated with anxiety. All the merchant in him palpitated. He thought Henry was about to lose the big customer. Henry, on the contrary, was sanguine as he had never been since the Cardinal died. King Francis was already in Turin. War was inevitable, a real war that would exhaust both combatants, and while he thus could escape from the French who had sent Morette to scowl at him and Dinteville to nip him, he did not propose to concede anything to the Emperor until all the black marks against him as Supreme Head of the Church were wiped from the board.

He talked so angrily, so reproachfully, and so loftily to Chapuys, that Cromwell sweated with terror. He had to leave them, to sit on a chest, and ask for something to drink. But Henry knew his men. Chapuys answered him with extreme gentleness and patience.

George Rochford did his best to carry it off. Anne was gracious to Chapuys. The surfaces gave a little crack or two, but held. And Henry dined with Anne and the household, while George took Chapuys to dine in the presence chamber.

"Why is Chapuys not with us?" Anne asked Henry.

"Not without good reason," grunted her lord.

"Is it not a great shame," said Anne, "for the French King to treat his uncle of Savoy thus? He must be weary of that disease of his, and wish to end his days by war."

That was the wrong tune. Henry grunted again, and said nothing. Women!

The whole Council, even, behaved like women, begging Henry, on their knees, for the honour of God, not to lose so good an opportunity to establish the imperial friendship, so necessary and advantageous.

Henry felt like a lion. All on their knees to him, everyone. He understood this coming war. They didn't. They asked him to sell himself to the Emperor, who must in reality bid high for him, and knuckle under to the Supreme Head of the Church. Henry's sense of his own superior power had been steadily growing. He was well aware that the Emperor had tried to make the French take over the duty of punishing him, in accord with the Pope's cries to Heaven. The Emperor could not see himself cut off from Flanders by sea, or have trade crippled, or have Henry driven for ever into Lutheranism. To regain him as a Catholic, on any terms, was Charles's fervent wish. It was the basis of his policy. And Henry, cold, practical, just as divorced from Rome as he was from Catherine and about as sorry for it, played on the Emperor's pious response to Reginald Pole, the Montagus, the Exeters, the Nevills, the Dorsets—all the old guard, who meant precisely as much to Henry as Buckingham had done, or as Bishop Fisher had done. It was his son and heir against theirs, his Tudor stock against their Plantagenetcy. He meant to have a boy, to knock them out. He meant to have the Church wealth, to knock them under. And this had given him a gleam of courage, an audacity and a breathtaking arrogance which Cromwell, Machiavellian though he was, had not the insanity to share.

Cromwell said to Chapuys, "Dine with me. I must see you."

## XI

"She, she is the stumbling block," said Chapuys in Dutch. "That she-devil of a concubine."

"But Cranmer will give him a divorce," said Cromwell, "that's nothing."

"Divorce! And have her live, have her build up a party!"

"Who is there to help her?" sneered Cromwell. "She has no one but me."

"You are mad," Chapuys told him. "I'll show you how this goes. For ten years, ever since the King threw out his Queen and made his daughter a bastard, this devil has made him give land and fortune to all these men in the Household. They carried messages back and forth. They saw it all. They watched the King when he was unguarded. A clean sweep of them! Confiscate their goods! You wiped out the Observants, my good friend. Wipe out these observants. Everyone of them."

"But how? But how?"

"How?" Chapuys's thin lips curled. "Rochford's wife was in the Tower, and he never went to her. Lady William Howard, whom the King made love to, was put into the Tower. Nan Cobham, they call her, good lord Bray's daughter, and Master Browne's daughter, and Fitzwilliam's niece—see, my friend! You have a thousand, ten thousand things, to go on. Who is that squire? Norris. He and her brother are the most dangerous."

"But evidence."

"Evidence, Master Secretary? Do you pause to find Ganymedes in these monasteries? You load nuns with babies they have buried. You take friars by the cartload to the Tower. You catch Thomas More writing with chalk and coal. Then you speak to me of evidence. Evidence!"

"But a Queen of England?"

"No Queen, sir. The Queen of England died like a saint, God save her. This is a harlot, the King's harlot. The whole country will breathe relief when she is under earth. I care nothing for the new one. Your

King cannot keep his hands off women. But let us begin afresh. Wipe them out. Leave no roots. Destroy them, root and branch. Have no pity. Spare none of them."

Cromwell heard Chapuys's tirades. "You think of Princess Mary as the heir?"

"I do."

"And to name the little one a bastard?"

"So I do."

"And a Spanish marriage, perhaps?"

"That too. But no crew to fight for the Little Bastard. No one to live who can tell tales. Get rid of the tale-bearers. And George, her brother. He is Lutheran. He is the worst of all."

"But to drag him in? What act of treason?"

"Treason! You can find treason in him, and improve on it, or I do not know you."

Cromwell had read Machiavelli. He had never met him. He had, before this, hinted murders to Chapuys and found him unflinching. But this had a deeper root, a wider branching.

"I must think," he said. "Leave it to me. I'll stay at home and say I am unwell."

## XII

THESE THINGS cannot happen. Anne heard of the Emperor at Rome, who denounced Francis in a merciless oration before the Pope, and it no longer reached her. She was thinking of her husband, and walked to the round window.

Mark Smeaton stood in it. He was the lad who loved lavender. She smiled at him. He had played the spinet for her at Winchester, when they had taken such a fancy to the unicorn heads and the big jewelled cross. Henry had roomed below her, as she was recovering from her second mishap.

"Why so sad?" she said to the youth, who gazed into the garden. Her tone was kind, but scarcely personal, and yet his dancer's hollow cheeks, those nimble feet, gave her a thrill of beauty that, in these beating days, were like a soft touch to her.

" 'Tis no matter, madame," he answered.

Of course it was no matter. "You may not look to have me speak to you as I should to a nobleman," she explained in a kind voice, "because you are an inferior person."

"No, no, madame," Mark Smeaton made a low bow to her, "a look sufficeth me, and thus fare you well."

Was it impertinence? She thought not. She had given him dancing shoes and gifts. He moved away with a limber, rhythmic gait that showed every play of muscle, his doublet short and his light haunches gloved in his hose.

Anne left her presence chamber, and thought no more about it. She had something more to engage her than dancing men.

## XIII

THE FIRST OF MAY, when the dew on the grass will take away your wrinkles, dawned pleasantly for Anne. George was to joust. Thomas Wyatt had come up for it.

Anne sat in her gallery at the tiltyard. It was like old times, but instead of Suffolk and Henry, here was Henry at her side, and George and Harry Norris come to salute her. She smiled at them, her handkerchief dropping. Norris restored it to her, and they smiled again. Very soon, with a sudden jerk, Henry rose.

"Tell Norris I want him," he sent a page.

Then, with Norris withdrawn, Henry and he rode in to London.

Henry did not come home. But next day, a Tuesday, the privy council met, and Anne got word to come before it.

This alarmed her. Will Brereton had disappeared five days before, Mark Smeaton on the Sunday, Harry Norris the day previous. She and Madge Shelton and Margaret Lee, Thomas's sister, had felt shivers of apprehension. Greenwich was tense. But until she sailed into the council chamber, to face her uncle and the rest of them, she had no clue to what was happening.

The moment Norfolk began questioning her, she rose in her dignity. All the tattle of the presence chamber was before him. But when she swept it aside, "Tut, tut," said her uncle. "Answer this." His tone was the tone of a court-martial, arbitrary, rough.

"You are cruel!" she protested. She was indignant.

"Tut, tut," he said again. "You spoke but a few days since to this dancer you favour, in the round window. It is idle to deny this. You allowed these familiarities. Very well. Let us hear them from your own lips. What led you to speak to an inferior person? You are the Queen. Let us hear from you."

Before Anne could well collect her wits, a barge was at the water-gate. She saw halberdiers come, beefeaters so-called, and, almost breathless with amazement, found herself on the barge, taken to the Tower. She had no one to advise or defend her. She was under armed escort, and accused of conspiring at the King's death, and all manner of things.

Sir William Kingston was on the steps.

"Am I to go to a dungeon?" she gasped. What had happened to the Carthusian monks was well known to her.

"Nay, your Grace," said Kingston, "but to have your own lodgings in which you lay at your coronation."

"It is too good for me!" she burst out in relief. "Jesu, have mercy on me." She had begun, even on the barge, to fancy that the end was already here, but these lodgings were human. She fell on her knees, with a wild laugh, and then broke into tears.

"If I could have the sacrament," she said, when she was lodged, "in the closet by my chamber. I'll pray for mercy."

Ladies were summoned, four matrons selected by Henry, two aunts who had never liked her and two others. Mistress Cousins was to be put there to catch every word uttered, and pass it on to Henry and Cromwell.

"I am free of the company of man, as for sin! I was so cruelly handled at Greenwich."

She addressed Kingston. She wanted George to help her.

"I pray you," she said, "tell me where my lord Rochford is."

"I saw him afore dinner in the Court," said Kingston, who had come from Henry at Whitehall.

"Oh, where is my sweet brother!" Anne said frantically. She turned to Kingston. "I hear say that I should be accused with three men, and I can say no more but Nay, without I should open my body." She opened her gown wide. "Oh, Norris!" she exclaimed, "have you ac-cused me?" Her face showed her incredulity. "You are in the Tower with me, and you and I shall die together!" She opened her eyes.

"And, Mark, you are here too!" It was too much to believe. "Oh! O my mother," she burst out, "you will die for sorrow." So moved was Anne that she began to sob.

"And Lady Worcester!" she turned to the Constable's wife. "Her child doth not stir in her body."

"What should be the cause?" asked Lady Kingston, who did not know that Cromwell had wrung Lady Worcester dry in his first examination at Stepney.

"For the sorrow she took for me," said Anne.

The ladies whom the King had deputed to attend on her, and to spy on her then filed into the apartments allotted to Anne. At the sight of them she turned with despairing face to the solemn Constable, "Shall I die without justice?"

This was the cry that Wolsey might have uttered to him, or John Fisher, or young John Frith. The Constable looked at her with impassive face. "The poorest subject the King has, hath justice."

At this rejoinder Anne tilted her head back and broke into wild laughter. Incapable of understanding this, her jailer and his wife withdrew and bolted the door.

## XIV

AT WHITEHALL Henry was waiting restlessly for this definite news, and Cromwell was bearing it to him. He had watched Anne from the Council chamber to the Tower. He could now report to his Master that she was safely in Kingston's hands, as Will Brereton had been for six days, the boy Smeaton for four days, and Norris and Weston overnight.

From the Tower to Whitehall gave Cromwell long enough to review his story. He had begun with the women whom Fitzwilliam's niece had obligingly named. Lady Worcester had wavered when Cromwell's manner had changed from suavity to grimness, and this had ended in her breakdown. Lady Cobham was the next to be probed. She had been an early friend of Thomas Wyatt's wife. She had hated Anne from the beginning, and as her own large family grew up about her she had the more judged Anne to be the light manner of woman to whom men instinctively flock. Jane Rochford had come forward with sharper eye and keener tongue. Cromwell understood from her that old Lady Wingfield could also add to the story of the bedchamber. Another witness was Thomas Percy, Northumberland's younger brother, who had seen himself beggared by Northumberland bequeathing his entire inheritance to the King. He told Cromwell to look into Mark Smeaton's behaviour toward Anne.

Gradually Cromwell had composed his two detailed lists of infidelities, one for the grand jury in Middlesex, the other for the grand jury in Kent. He spread these infidelities from 1533 to 1536, the whole period of Anne's married life from the birth of Elizabeth onwards; Norris in October 1533, Brereton in December 1533, on Christmas Day, at the height of the festivities; Mark Smeaton in April 1534, Francis Weston in May 1534, and George Boleyn, her brother, in November 1535, when she was already known to be pregnant. These offences were all placed at Westminster, except the one on Christmas Day at Hampton Court. Such were the incidents Cromwell allotted to Middlesex. For Kent the list was similar, some of the supposed episodes coming in the months when Anne had a "fair belly." All of them were distributed among her admirers with an odd regard to symmetry. And it was to look into these accusations that Henry had appointed a joint commission of his councillors and judges as early as April 24.

Brereton was the first man arrested, but as he proved stubborn and would confess to nothing, Cromwell asked young Smeaton to his isolated house at Stepney, and there, following his procedure with the Carthusians, he had ordered two stout young henchmen of his to stand behind Smeaton's chair. They had a stick and a knotted rope. To crown Smeaton with the knotted rope, and twist the stick in it, was to be the means of inducing confession.

"I have wanted to speak to you for some days," said Cromwell, "but I have had no chance till now." He then asked him how he had come to be spending so much money. "And I give you notice now," he said sternly, with a tight-lipped glance at his yeomen, "you will have to tell me the truth before you leave here, either by force or of your good will."

Smeaton threw a horrified glance at the silent men. He had wide open eyes, a curling mouth, the pointed face of a peculiarly graceful and impressionable youth to whom life had never before shown this visage. The son of a poor carpenter, he could hardly deny that all his money had come from a rich source but rather than hurt his benefactress he held his silence.

Cromwell nodded to his men. One of them slipped the rope around the boy's head. "I am sorry you will not tell what you know with a good grace."

A few twists of the rope made him cry, "Master Secretary, no more! I will tell the truth." Then, with the rope removed, "The Queen gave me the money."

"You have nothing to fear, if you tell the truth," said Cromwell curtly. "You will be pardoned all. But if you do not tell it, by the life of the King I swear I will torture you till you do. Why did the Queen give you so much money? Why? Why?"

The torment of the cord, twisted more and more severely by the two men, at last made Smeaton cry out. "No more! I will tell you everything that has happened."

When he then declared that Anne had been in love with him and had made him lie with her several times, he was again threatened with torture unless he revealed what he knew of other men. By this time he was sobbing. He named Norris and Brereton as her lovers as well.

No sooner had he made these statements and, in the tremor of his broken will, signed a confession, than he was removed to the Tower and put in irons. The prospect of a terrible death was then exposed to him, while Cromwell, triumphant with this document, reached Henry with it just before the tilting on May Day. Henry stayed in the tiltyard until Norris left to disarm. He then sent word for the captain of the halberdiers to fetch Norris, and as they rode side by side in the intimate fashion of master and squire (they had been companions for seventeen years and more), Henry asked Norris to inculpate Anne, on the promise of a pardon. Norris admitted nothing. At London Bridge they parted for the last time, and Norris was delivered to the Tower.

How much more was to happen Cromwell did not know. Young Page had been named, and perhaps Henry would order his arrest. Now, at least, he could assure his Master that the she-devil, escorted by a hundred halberdiers, had been taken in the great barge to the

Tower. That she had been plotting with Norris and the others to have the King poisoned was, he thought, even more telling than the list of her abominations.

## XV

By night there was no one else to arrest, except Francis Bryan.

By the time Cromwell arrived, George Boleyn had already been seized. He was taken before his uncle Norfolk and Audley, the Chancellor.

"You often went to her chamber at night," said the Chancellor, "and thereupon told the ladies to leave you. 'Twas a bold thing to do, and calls for great punishment."

"But, look you," George answered him coolly, "even did I go to her when she was unwell, surely that is no proof that I was so wicked as to do great crime and treason to the King."

"Hold your peace," said Norfolk. "The King's will must be done."

When put to the torture, old Lady Wingfield had been asked about Thomas Wyatt. She had never seen him speak to Anne privately, but always openly, so Cromwell had left Thomas's name out of the statements. Suffolk, however, could not see Anne's following come to such a pass without remembering Thomas Wyatt.

"I told the King," he declared to Norfolk and the others, "that Master Wyatt here was one of the very first to meddle with her, and had his Grace then listened to me, this all were voided."

With his hand on his sword, Thomas's eyes flashed murderously. "You have never forgot, my lord, two thousand pounds of debt you were enforced to pay me. Now you lie, as well as know it, since this lady be fair game."

"Arrest him!" shouted Norfolk.

Thomas was ready to be sent to the Tower by the time Cromwell reached Whitehall. This he had not planned. He told Audley sharply that it would be as absurd as to involve Francis Bryan as to hold Wyatt unless better evidence could be found.

"Cut down those others," scowled Cromwell, "and no one will befriend them. Cut Bryan down or Master Wyatt, and you give her voices for ever."

He then knelt to Henry, and in a parched tone he dwelt on the conspiracy to murder him, with Harry Norris to step into dead men's shoes.

That night, when the Duke of Richmond came to ask his father's blessing before he went to bed, "My boy," wept Henry, "you and your sister ought to thank God for having escaped the hands of this woman, who had devised to poison you."

Those in the bedchamber who heard the King took little time to spread the word.

## XVI

THE FEVERISH WOMAN in the vicinity of death had no illusion about this last struggle with Henry. So long as du Bellay had come to England, or anyone from France who leaned to the Lutherans, Anne had another nation behind her. But once the French lost ground in Lutheran Germany, once de Montmorency became Francis's chief general and the Sorbonne dictated burnings and torturings, she was as much without a friend as Wolsey himself had been, and her own feeble efforts, and George's feeble efforts, to placate Chapuys on Easter Sunday were the last wavings of a white flag. All those bedchamber talks with George before Christmas had been desperately prolonged to find some way of circumventing Gardiner, an implacable ambassador who walled George away from France. But they could find no way. And once a fright had led to her mishap, her last rights were gone. Catherine's death then saved the Emperor's face. With the French by the side of the Pope, Henry was driven to the Emperor. Anne had admitted this by softening her tone to Mary. That white-faced tragic girl with a man's voice was Elizabeth's arch enemy, yet Anne had given her an armistice, at Henry's savage command.

Beneath all this, as Anne now recognized with waves of horror, was Henry's insatiable self. Her own hatred of the Cardinal, as well as her pursuit of Queen Catherine and Queen Catherine's Catholic supporters, had been to clear her path as Queen of England, but she had not adopted high moral grounds or asked for moral sanction. Henry's whole case, on the contrary, had been to assert a conscience that had to be vindicated. Anne had seen this conscience grow to a monstrosity under which his self-esteem had equally swollen. In her last quarrels with him he had frightened her. For the first time in their married life he had been alien. He was no longer the Henry who had courted her. He was a Prince who had no superior but God.

Day by day in the Tower, from May 2 to May 15, when she was to go on trial, Anne went deep into herself. Northumberland, Butler, Thomas and Henry—she thought back to every moment.

"My pride," she said to herself, "my sin was my great pride."

Young as she was, and at three and thirty the pulse of life beat against time in her body, she escaped long enough from her entangling self to know what disastrous motive had ruled her, while, with a sharp intuition that nothing could deceive, she saw Henry's evil destiny, to make the whole world, the Pope, the Emperor, the Church, support this tyrant ego in him that his astuteness served.

On Easter Sunday, George had seen him drum his fingers on his knee and say, "I am not a child, first to be slapped and then caressed and invited back again and called sweet names." He pouted like a child as he said this. "The Emperor must write me a letter," he grunted, "asking me to forget and forgive the past. No more need be said thereafter, but such a letter I must and will have." And later, as all his councillors knelt to him to plead for the imperial alliance, "I would sooner lose my crown," he told them, "than admit I have given the Emperor cause to complain."

So Anne had come to know him. "And before I die," she said fiercely to herself, "I'll speak out the truth, even from the scaffold."

The scaffold! Then, just as a bird with frantic wings beats against the window pane, the spaces free beyond and yet the window impassable, as clear and hard as sudden death, so Anne, reminded she must die, broke into wild abruptnesses of laughter, and snatches of talk, and thrusts of her spirit against the immovable. But under it, "Fortune was my foe," she saw again how, with Fortune to beckon her, she had spent all for pride.

But had she and Henry been in the right to dispossess Queen Catherine? Here was Anne's bitter struggle. At last she spoke to Lady Shelton, her aunt whom she had dismissed for kindness to Princess Mary.

"God pardon me," she said, "I was cruel to Mary. For that I may never be forgiven."

In these toils of remorse, but with Henry's accusations scorned, Anne waited for the men's trial, which came before her own. To this their gallantry had brought them, and when she thought of it she welcomed death.

"I could not live," she burst out crying. "Poor Norris!" Even Mark, the boy who had accused her, she pitied for his weakness. But what torture Cromwell employed, and Henry assented to, none knew better than herself.

Her macabre humour was so close to these storms of weeping that Kingston was bewildered. He had never had prisoner like her.

But, in spite of her unstable nerves, Anne gave not an inch to the King. She despised his dishonesty of nature. His plans for re-marriage had been already made in February. The Emperor had written in March to base reconciliation on them. By that time Henry had assured himself he could have a baby by Jane Seymour, and for this he was marrying her. With re-marriage so imminent, the case that Cromwell had prepared fitted into his political needs and his instincts much too perfectly to have left Anne a loophole. Empson and Dudley, Warwick, Buckingham, Ap Rice—all these had had to go. And he had no chivalry for a female who had never, not from the beginning, been sufficiently his creature. The populace had called her a whore at the start. Henry was now ready to gratify the populace.

"She seduced me by witchcraft," he said to Cromwell.

"Hundreds of men have enjoyed her," he told Suffolk.

And all of this, the black guilt that his outraged self demanded of her, made Anne, throughout these days in the Tower, see how completely she was encircled. He wrote to her, inviting her to be "honest and open" with him. She answered by telling him she was innocent. But once her thoughts did veer to her Archbishop, to Thomas Cranmer.

## XVII

CRANMER WAS AWAY from Lambeth when he learned of Anne's arrest. He hurried back to his Palace, on a command from the King, and stayed there, by the same order. He wrote to Henry, at the first shock of the news, to beg him to accept adversity and bow to God's will. If reports be true, he said, Anne's honour is clean disparaged, "and I am in such perplexity, that my mind is clean amazed, for I never had better opinion in woman than I had in her, which maketh me to think that she should not be culpable. And, again, I think your Highness would not have gone so far, except she had surely been culpable." So he balanced "not culpable" against "surely culpable," and "perplexed" against "amazed," until Cromwell told him to present himself at the Star Chamber, where Audley and several other Councillors spread out the record for him.

Cranmer had not yet sent his letter, and here his eyes were opened. "I am exceeding sorry," he lamented, "that such faults can be proved by the Queen, as I heard of their relation." That was her friend Cranmer's postscript, on May 4. Anne could not know it, but he deemed her false to the Gospel on what the four councillors had informed him. "As I loved her not a little for the love which I judged her to bear towards God and His gospel, so if she proved culpable, there is not one that loveth God and His gospel that will ever favour her, but must hate her above all other, and the more they favour the gospel the more they will hate her, for there never was creature in our time that so much slandered the gospel, and God hath sent her this punishment for that she feignedly hath professed His gospel in her mouth, and not in heart and deed."

He returned to Lambeth from the Star Chamber, bowing his sorrowful head. He had no need to hear Anne's defence against these charges. No, no. He desired the offence to be punished without mercy, "to the example of all other." And Cranmer prayed for his Grace, whom he likened to Job.


## XVIII

THE BEST WAY for Henry to tell the populace how he felt was to be merry. He ordered the royal barge prepared for festivity, and then, with the Seymours and their friends, to the sound of music, he spent the May evenings going up and down the Thames.

The sound of this music, carried to the Tower, told Anne that the Court was as gay now as when Catherine had died.

Her mood became desperate as she realized how strongly she was beset, and then she was resolved to die.

"But the next hour," Kingston told Cromwell, "the contrary of that."

"If I die," she said wildly, "they'll see the greatest punishment for me that ever came to England, and then I shall be a saint in Heaven, for I have done many good deeds in my days. But I think it much unkindness in the King to put such about me as I never loved."

Her demand for a trial before her peers was not to be refused, and two days after Norris, Brereton, Weston and Smeaton were condemned at Westminster, Anne was herself brought to trial on May 15, within the Tower. The trial was public, with several thousand present, and the judges were twenty-seven of her temporal peers, with her father excused and her uncle Norfolk to preside, as his own father had presided at Buckingham's trial.

Anne had so prepared herself for this ordeal that even the sight of her uncle and of Northumberland among her judges could not unnerve her. Northumberland, however, collapsed and had to leave the hall. She saw this without weakening. In clear tones, with command of herself, with moderation and patience, she defended herself until even Norfolk was in tears. She was accused of having poisoned Catherine, and of intending to poison Mary, of having committed incest with her brother and adultery with the other four, and of leaguing with Norris against the King. She was also charged with having ridiculed Henry and shown she did not love him. She was firm in her denials, and in her answer to other charges, but her firmness could not prevail against the Master at Whitehall. Every peer from the youngest back to Exeter and Suffolk, adjudged her "guilty," and she was taken away by halberdiers, to be brought to the Green and "there burned or beheaded, as shall please the King."

Her brother's trial followed as soon as Anne was removed. He was asked to answer "yes" or "no" to a secret question on a piece of paper. He read out the question, which referred to Henry's impotence. This, and the ridiculousness of Henry's codpiece, were so proclaimed by this last fling of George Boleyn that all prospect of acquittal, which had become conceivable with his vigorous defence, was instantly cancelled.

## XIX

"THE WOMAN sat unmoved as a stone," Steve Simmons said to Luke Wakeman at Allington, "and carried herself as if she was receiving some honour."

"Go to God!" exclaimed old Luke.

"Aye," said Steve, "they let her have a chair, and she bowed to the lords as she took her place. She said few words, but her face spoke more than words, and no one to look on her would have thought her guilty."

"Could that be so?" Luke wondered. "Mistress Anne, with her mother broken-hearted at Hever, and Master Thomas in the Tower along of her. Oh, God save the boy, God save Master Tom. The old Master and the Mistress are well-nigh demented, and Mistress Margaret hath gone to the Tower to her, with an order from that Cromwell."

"I heard every word," resumed Steve, "though two thousand itself was in the Great Hall. 'I dispute not the judgment,' she said at the end of all, 'but I appeal to God.' Old Norfolk cried as she did say it, though he be black as doom, to look upon him."

"I have seen bloodhounds with that same visage," said Luke, "though they be gentle hounds. And how of this dancing man who confessed to her shame?" asked Luke. "Mistress Margaret said no word to you?"

"'Did he not acquit me of the infamy he hath laid upon me?' That the Queen asked. And, when she was shown he was to die without clearing her, for fear of being hanged and quartered, then said she, 'Alack, I fear his soul will suffer for it.'"

"Say what they will," said Luke, "Mistress Anne be stout of heart. But to bring Master Tom into this pass! 'Twill do for poor Master."

Steve Simmons gazed at Luke without a sign of having heard him. "I go to London for it," he suddenly declared.

The older man shook his head. "To see her brent?" His mouth opened. "To see Mistress Anne brent at yon stake?"

"She'll not be brent, Luke."

"Seventy year old I be." He stood up without a sign of feebleness.

He walked with great deliberation to the door of his gate lodge, and back again. "Let the one keep t'other company, Steve." He stirred about, moved almost beyond control. "We'll go to yon Tower, to be nigh Mistress Anne at the end."

## XX

THEY WERE THERE from the night before. Luke's old face was set in its lines by all he had lived since Richard III had murdered the children in the Tower. He could scarce credit that Master Thomas was a prisoner there, in a chamber over the gate, but Cromwell had sent secret word there was no danger for him, nor for Master Bryan, and it was the old Tower where Sir Harry had been tortured which loomed through the night for Luke rather than the present one where Mistress Anne Boleyn was spending her last night on earth, in the room from which she had gone to be crowned.

Luke was still a good Catholic, loyalty to the faith struggling with loyalty to Kent over this misfortune that had overtaken Hever. He remembered her as a girl, running after Tartar, a hound she had, running breathless and headlong, in her leather hose without a skirt to hamper her, and then leaping into the brake as she caught sight of him. He had laughed that day, the pretty damsel in her hose. A long way she had come since then. He heard the bell ring. That was six o'clock and sun up. He said his prayers, with hundreds of quiet men and women about him. The crowd was patient. Luke wondered, with a simple wonder, how many hundreds and hundreds that were there.

Steve, who was now Lutheran under cover of Thomas's approval, took it with a sober melancholy that showed in every modelling of his grave face. He had looked to the Queen as the Gospel's hope, and this morning was steeped in sadness such as the day John Frith was burned. The King was still so unassailable that even to bear a thought against him was unnatural, yet Steve said to himself, "This is no man. He be a base and wicked monster." And this swelled in him so terribly that his breath came in brief gasps and his fists clenched. There are infamies which go deep by the very heights from which they are designed. To Steve Simmons this was one of them. He allowed himself to feel it, though it went through him as unbearable.

The holocausts of Notre Dame had thus pained him, and the killing of Anabaptists. To him, for all the talk of the Queen's guilt, this was a deed that had its roots in a wicked heart, from whose wickedness a tree was springing with fruit that would drop tears of blood. All through that May night, the Tower a dark bulk against the sky, Steve thought how she would never be asleeping, but praying and talking the night through, attending her own wake, every spark in her burnished in the wind, the last quickness of a spirit in a blaze. In those light frenzies, when the human tide breaks sudden against fate, he believed her faith in God must be much daunted, and yet he stood in this packed multitude, praying for her in new-minted words of Gospel, yearning for a creature proud, hard and wilful, now come to dye this green with blood. He had no subtle way to save himself from this sharpness. He was one of ten thousand blue-eyed, silent English folk who coped with life in secret simplicity, incapable of denying its passionate price, the ancestors of Puritan and Pilgrim. And he knew that, over the prison gate, Master Thomas would be on his knees at the same moment, dying in heart with Mistress Anne, his wings as broken as her own. Whatever she might be, or might have done, this was an end beyond the compass of his imagination, or his dumb and suffering heart.

Thomas, indeed, was praying. She had been no longer his when once she married Henry, yet however proud she was, however reckless of these men who had gone out in white shirts the day before to be beheaded by the axe, he could no more save himself from Anne than from the sky above him. She inhabited him for ever, though she had broken the mould of his nature, and he would not live five years after her, under this Master who gave her death.

Anne, as he thought of her, had sent for Kingston.

"As I receive the good Lord," she said, "I wish to show you that my innocency were always clear."

"Master Kingston," she said after Communion, "I hear say I shall not die afore noon, and I am very sorry therefor, for I thought to be dead by this time, and past my pain."

Her face was haggard, but Kingston was gentle. "There should be no pain, ma'am, it is so subtle."

"I heard say the executioner be very good, and I have a little neck." With that she put her hands about it, and laughed a little wildly.

Kingston saw her, with her eyes bigger than ever before. "This lady," he thought, "hath much joy and pleasure in death."

Not until nine o'clock did Cromwell and Suffolk and the young Duke of Richmond come, by the King's orders, to the high form raised on the green. They, and the other councillors stood to one side, while the great crowd watched for Sir William Kingston, who was to lead her out.

Anne was dressed in dark red damask, with an ermine cloak. As she crossed the green, to reach the scaffold, she turned to look back to Margaret Wyatt and the three other ladies who followed her. On these she seemed to depend. Kingston helped her up the steps, and the ladies followed. She stood when she reached the railing.

"Mistress Margaret!" cried Luke. But Steve waited only for Anne's voice. At last he heard her, unnaturally faint.

"Christian people," the little voice floated over the great crowd, as gulls flew in from the river, "Christian people, I come to die—but think not, good people, that I am sorry to die, or that I have done anything to deserve this death. My fault has been my great pride, and the great crime I committed was in getting the King to leave my mistress Queen Catherine for my sake, and I pray God to pardon me for it. I say to you all that everything they have accused me of is false, and the principal reason I am to die is Jane Seymour, as I was the cause of the ill that befell my mistress."

Here Cromwell stopped her, and she halted.

"Where is the headsman?" she asked.

"He will be here presently," said Fitzwilliam, "but 'twere better for you, ma'am, to confess the truth, and not to be so obstinate, for you can hope for no pardon."

"I know I shall have no pardon," Anne answered, her black eyes blazing, "but they shall know no more from me."

Then, from this group on the scaffold, a Frenchman, costumed as any gentleman, stepped forward and knelt to her.

"Madame," he said, "I crave your Majesty's pardon, for I am ordered to do this duty, and I beg you to kneel and say your prayers."

Anne knelt at the block, but so grimly did the moment haunt her that she kept her eyes on him.

"Madame," he said gently in French, "do not fear. I will wait till you tell me."

"You will have to take this coif off," she explained in French, with her hand on the coif.

With that, the Frenchman went to the steps. "Bring me the sword," he called.

Her hand still on her coif, Anne kept watching the steps. Stepping quietly to the other side of her, the Frenchman signalled to his helper, who drew the long sword from under the straw. Then, as Anne still waited for it to come, with a swift flash he struck off her head.

From the trunk poured out a wealth of blood, while her hands clutched convulsively and her body writhed. Her features, at the same time, shuddered with agony as the severed head lay on the straw.

Margaret Wyatt covered the head with a white handkerchief, while the other ladies lifted the body into a coffin.

" 'Tis no coffin," exclaimed Luke, " 'tis but an old arrow-case."

And so it was. They bore the arrow-case down the steps into the chapel. And there, in the choir, Anne was buried.

As the crowd broke up, Steve and Luke lingered, but the cannon had already told London that Anne Boleyn was dead, and the halberdiers cleared the Tower.

## XXI

THOMAS was released in June, through Cromwell's friendship. And within a few days, since Jane Seymour had not yet taken Princess Mary and Princess Elizabeth under her wing, Beth Darrell and Thomas went to Mother Bryan's to see the child.

"Thomas," said Beth, "whose child is she?"

"The King's," Thomas answered. "He can count nine months as well as anyone."

"Poor creature," murmured Beth, "three years old, and in truth an orphan. What future hath she!"

"Who knows?" Thomas gazed long on Anne's daughter. The little girl stood with both hands open, eager to pounce on a bird. She might have been my child, he thought, and he wondered what fate had in store for her.

Beth watched him.

"Fortune was her foe," she said softly.

Thomas looked at Beth. "You do not hate her?"

"Yea, do I," said Beth. "She made you suffer."

"Let us look at the child," said Thomas. "She's a bright one."

"Yea, the 'Little Bastard'! And what is to become of her?"

The infant saw them. She watched them gravely, and then her black eyes opened wide and she gave the man a lightning glance, and smiled.

"Who knows!" Thomas repeated, painfully moved. "One day she may be Queen Elizabeth."

# History in This Novel

For those of my readers who are not familiar with the Tudor period, and especially with the history of Anne Boleyn, I should like to explain the main details with which I have amplified the historic record.

To suggest Anne's character in the formative period, I have invented her mother, about whom next to nothing is known.

The childhood at Hever, the visit to the Field of the Cloth of Gold, the contact with Marguerite d'Angoulême, and some of the later episodes such as Anne's witnessing the execution of Rouse, have all been imagined. So has her relationship with Cromwell. Rouse was, in fact, boiled alive, though we have no description of it. Anne was, as a young person, resident at the Court of France. But so much is still unknown about her—the date of her birth, for example, the date of her going to France, even the date of her marriage—that it has seemed legitimate in a novel to choose those dates which, in the excellent phrase of my friend Professor Gregor Paulsson of Upsala, would make the whole story more "plastic." The bear-baiting at Hever is an invention, and it is only a guess that there were woods around Hever. But it is certain that she was there as a child.

The latter part of Anne's career is naturally the better documented. Her trial, however, has had to be patched together from odd scraps and rumours. The report of it is not to be found among state documents.

Lord James Butler did come from Ireland to court Anne, and he may have stayed at an inn in London. What he was like, however, is mere guesswork. I have tried to guess it by looking at his tomb in Kilkenny, but who knows whether the tombstone resembles him? We can luckily turn from the brass of Sir Thomas Boleyn, which is meek and mild, to the portrait by Holbein, the portrait of a weak, sleek courtier, in no way prettified. Holbein gives us documents that are honest "sources" of history, not the touched-up "sources" of such adroit reporters as the Venetian ambassadors, so often quoted as if their slick portraits were straight from the life. It is strange how the professional historians rely on such documents, where they would smile at, let us say, an account of Mussolini sent home by an envoy of Japan.

The Darrells are mere names in history. So is Thomas Wyatt's wife. Allington, Cobham and Hever, however, do exist as places, though Hever was little more than a manor house. It was bought by Anne's great-grandfather, Sir Geoffrey Bullen, perhaps forty years before she was born.

Thomas Wyatt is no figment. He is known to us from his poems, a few letters and despatches, contemporary and post-mortem allusions, and from Holbein's portraits of him. His mother, and his talk with the family friend Bishop Fisher, have been imagined. He did go to Cambridge and he knew the Poyntz family well, but his encounters with Tyndale and with Frith cannot be substantiated. His meeting with Surrey is an invention, though they were friends, and his visits to France and Italy have been much amplified. His return from Calais to watch Anne's house could have happened, but while the talk of the crowd has been concocted from state documents, his chat with Francis Bryan is surmised. Piecing his poems together, in relation to the known events of his life, my version of his intimacy with Anne follows the hints that to me are irresistible, though little can be asserted as a matter of fact. The way in which I suppose Anne to have deserted him is inferred from his passionate and agonized poems— poems which a scholar a few years ago described as "cold." Both Tillyard and Foxwell have to be carefully studied if one seeks to get hold of Wyatt, but the story is not all on the surface.

Thomas Cromwell has been well studied by Merriman. He is not officially credited with the known attempt to poison Bishop Fisher, but Agostini, the Venetian physician, was in fact his associate when Wolsey employed both of them, and he did become a secret agent. His talk with Cromwell is an invention. So is Cromwell's visit to Antwerp and his link with a Dr. Salmon. Cromwell, however, was actually in the wool trade in the Low Countries and did have a hard fight to rise in the world. He was a tough citizen.

Enough has been said, I think, to show the kind of liberties I have taken with known history. I have given my fancy full play in order to build on the existing foundations. In John Donne's words, "study and play made this hermaphrodite." Just as authentic dialogue has been supplemented time after time, so events have been simulated, to carry out an illusion of reality.

But the study of the period has given me an Anne Boleyn, I beg leave to say, which does not follow the tradition. If my readers accept her as convincing, it will not be because they have always known her to be like this. It will be because the present age, which enables me to see her in a new light, enables them to share this light, and to find her familiar. It was quite different, I can assure them, in the last generation, and my object is to shatter the version of the last generation, which is surrounded by so-called scholarship, just as certain public statues are surrounded by spiked rails.

In order to reach this Victorian statue, I have had to get over the rails. From 1924 to 1939 I have occupied myself with the first half of the sixteenth century, except for writing a few articles and one novel. A biography of Queen Anne Boleyn might perhaps have been the outcome of the last three years, but I have ventured to cast the material into the form of a novel for definite reasons, as follows:

1.  Historical research taps that enormous impulse which makes children gather sea-shells, leads them to stamp-collecting, and carries them to the crossword puzzle. I nearly ruined myself by studying Francis I too closely. I became researchful. It is a tendency I decided to fight against.

2.  There seems to be a doctrine of "ancient lights" in English professional history. Professor Pollard commands outlook on the Tudor period. Professor Bryant overlooks the Restoration. Professor Neale has the Elizabeth allotment. Professor Williams has staked out Henry

VII. It is all very pleasant and cosy. But when an outsider comes on the scene, unaware of these vested interests, the uproar is unseemly. Disciples arise in every periodical. They come not single spies but in battalions. All one can do is either to butt in or butt out, especially since literary editors have to rely on specialists, and the specialists are all in the union.

3. This union, moreover, is seldom international. It is usually national, and bitterly national, except in the most eminent of practitioners, or in periods when nationalism is not stirred up. So, while setting down nothing without reference to a "source," filling in no detail without some sort of evidence, and arranging the whole to relate to previous studies and connect with subsequent ones, the regular historian, moving from humility to asperity in his footnotes, sticks to state annals as much as possible. Within this political framework, in my opinion, one is forced to pervert the story. To arrive at Anne Boleyn without a close study of state papers is of course impossible, but to know her by an exclusive or even preponderant study of state papers is also impossible. There are few state papers on children, for example, and none on children who are not "in the spot," yet the child is mother to the woman. Besides, significant as every official or semi-official word may be, the acoustics of these utterances ought to be devised so that it is not the State speaking of political beings that we have, with State-necessity in mind, but it is the all-round narrator speaking, with human beings and human necessities in mind.

For these three reasons, in spite of my building on professional research, to which I owe so much, I had to choose between a biography at which dead cats would be thrown because it was "novelized," or a historical novel based on long and close study. I chose the novel. It deprives me of all claim to "authority," since it does not "satisfy modern requirements of matter-of-fact accuracy," to use Leslie Stephen's phrase. But if the reader is convinced, in spite of this, I am fully rewarded.

And before I leave "authority" to the professional historians, allow me to add a word of warning.

When I began this novel three years ago, I cast my eye over the versions of Anne Boleyn to be found in the leading authorities.

The most obvious of these, if a reader has the impulse to check up my account of her, might be the Encyclopedia Britannica, at least in England and America. That is where one usually learns the correct or received opinion.

There, at any rate, the probable pronunciation of Anne's name is at once suggested by its calling her "Boleyn (or Bullen)." Bullen, I take it, to rhyme with woollen, though some might rhyme it with sullen. Anyway, it is not Bullion, Bo-leen, Bo-line, Boylan, but plain Bullen, nothing high-sounding.

This article on Anne, signed by P. C. Yorke, M. A., had several phrases in it that struck me as familiar. It says, "she appealed to the king's less refined instincts." Now, how many years of research lay behind that? I got out my Pollard, and there was the plum, "she appealed to the less refined part of Henry's nature." I presume from the date that Pollard said it first.

I thought this rather naughty of the Encyclopedia, but there was more to come. "It is not credible," says Professor Pollard in a guarded sentence, "that the juries should have found her accomplices (!) guilty, that twenty-six peers, including her uncle, should have condemned Anne herself, without some colorable justification." The Encyclopedia, writing in almost the same words, says, "It is almost incredible that two grand juries, a petty jury, and a tribunal consisting of nearly all the lay peers in England, should have passed a sentence of guilty contrary to the facts and their convictions, and that such a sentence should have been supported by Anne's own father and uncle."

What is "incredible" or "not credible" in a state trial ordered by Henry VIII is certainly a matter of opinion, not a matter-of-fact. My own opinion is that the juries were packed, and the peers were just as scared as if they were Russians in 1938. They had reason to be, since Henry killed half a dozen of them later on. But do not rely on the Encyclopedia when it tells you that the sentence was supported by Anne's own father. And disregard the glaring misstatement about the number of her children which immediately follows.

But there is Professor Pollard to turn to? Alas, we must be wary of this usually so careful authority on the subject of Anne Boleyn, too.

"The Boleyns were wealthy merchants of London," he says on

page 187 of his *Henry VIII,* "of which one of them had been Lord Mayor, but Anne's mother was of noble blood, being daughter and co-heir of the Earl of Ormonde . . ."

Now Anne's mother, of course, was Elizabeth Howard, daughter of a peer who became Duke of Norfolk. It was on the Boleyn side that Anne was of Ormonde blood. Professor Pollard has misapprehended her status as an aristocrat. It is true that her great-grandfather was a Mayor, not a Lord Mayor as it seems, but he married a member of a noble family, according to old Sharon Turner, his son married a Butler, and Anne's father, who married a Howard, was a courtier all his life, and what we should now call a professional diplomat. Professor Pollard is at pains to argue that Henry (whose own great-grandfather was a clerk of the wardrobe) "lost caste" by marrying Anne. While the Boleyns were certainly of merchant origin, like the Poles who were Henry's strongest rivals to the throne, it was surely Anne who gained caste rather than Henry who lost it. I confess I was myself seriously misled by Professor Pollard's positive statements in this connection until I looked into the matter for myself.

His estimate of Anne Boleyn, on page 189, is still more questionable. "Her place in English history," he pronounces, "is due solely to the circumstance that she appealed to the less refined part of Henry's nature; she was pre-eminent neither in beauty nor in intellect, and her virtue was not of a character to command or deserve the respect of her own or subsequent ages."

Sweeping!

But granted that there was a less refined part of Henry's nature, many women appealed to it, and they have no place in English history. They are unsung. Why is Anne the exception? The answer is unavoidable: her place in English history is by no means due to this sole circumstance on which Professor Pollard lays mighty stress. It is due to three indisputable circumstances, as any cool person will agree: Henry married her; he gave her a child who became Queen Elizabeth; and in the end he beheaded her.

But if there is a quibble that unless she had seduced him by a low appeal she would never have been heard of, a rebuttal of that smug accusation is called for.

Judge Anne's looks as you will, with one authentic portrait to go by

and two or three descriptions by the most heated of religious con-
troversialists, guess at her intelligence as you like, and damn her
character as you have a mind to, there are other facts that must fit
into your formula. During the years from 1526 to 1533 that Henry
held to Anne before they married she appealed to the more as well
as the less refined part of his nature, if we are to use terms so elegant.
She appealed to the versifier in him, to the lover of dance and music,
to the sportsman in him, to the reader of Erasmus, the theologian,
the lover of objets d'art, the intellectual and the politician. Her sister
Mary knew him in bed. Anne knew him everywhere, and dealt with
him on many scores beside the erotic. This is all a matter of record,
and Professor Pollard's formula, if I may say so, has its origins in an
overwhelming impatience with a painful passage in history, complicated with what Lawrence of Arabia calls "infuriating male con-
descension toward inglorious woman."

It shows a strange indifference to the complexity of human nature
that Anne Boleyn should be seen according to one set of State con-
ventions whereas her daughter, Queen Elizabeth, so like her in so
many ways, should have been Gloriana to them all. But these are the
oddities of power-history. Read the power-historians on the Czarist
court, if you wish a concrete illustration, up to the time that it
crashed, and then read later accounts, when Rasputin could be
talked about, even by the same historians. The increase in candour is
startling when the façade need no longer be upheld. As the Imperial
Policy Group says in its earnest and mournful circular, "The striking
lesson which the Committee has learnt is that there is an extraordinary difference between the realities and the picture presented by all
too many organs of propaganda and publicity." Where there is ro-
mantic nationalism, there are always elements of propaganda and
publicity, and no amount of footnotes can make science of them.

And when the state papers are meagre, one must not be too limp.
There is nothing in the shop-window about Henry's "divorce," for
example, till the Bishop of Tarbes came into the open in 1527. But
let us remember that there was no mention of Mrs. Simpson in England for eight or nine months after she was news elsewhere. It is my
belief that Cardinal Wolsey planned the "divorce" of Catherine of
Aragon soon after Pavia, and that Henry sought Marguerite d'Angou-

lême's hand in 1526. Politics, not conscience, set the great game afoot, and he did not turn seriously to Anne Boleyn until Francis I had rejected him. The negotiations for Marguerite were secret, but we have hints of them. It is regrettable that in Friedmann's *Anne Boleyn,* the best book on the subject, this point has not been pursued. It is one of the conjectures at any rate that is at home in a novel.

And such conjectures are necessary if one is to define the proud Anne as she was. "A young and lively woman," says Professor Brewer, "who possessed none of the higher qualities which could inspire nobler feelings." "Lively and attractive as she might be, she had not the qualities to inspire awe." They talk of this hard, powerful and dangerous female as if she had not met her match in Henry VIII, a great egoist who killed one close associate after another, who had to be flattered, who could not be trusted, who bribed, who assassinated, who robbed, who played the game of his State with incessant wile, and who in addition had a "conscience." We in 1939 can better imagine his statecraft than the Victorians could. And we are not so tempted to demand that Anne Boleyn should have been an understudy of Queen Victoria.

In writing this novel I sought the aid of my friend Miss Joan Curzon, who is trained in research. She consulted authorities and examined records, took photographs and copied some documents. As I did not work systematically, however, or call on her through the whole period, my errors and superficialities cannot be laid at her door. I must also express gratefulness to the Royal Library of Copenhagen for letting me have the Letters and Papers at home. In conclusion there are certain friends and acquaintances who animated and I hope mellowed this narrative—the Wyatts, the Seymours, Lady Ottoline Morrell who was a Cavendish, Lord Eustace Percy, and the Wingfields. When I met Lord James Butler's direct descendant on a race course in Ireland, I wished I had the power to make the first Earl of Ossory as pungent as the latest. For, whatever cut-and-dry historians may think they were all most human.

Hornbaek, Denmark
August 9, 1939